Secrets of a Baron's Daughter

(Merry Men of Eton Book 1)

Teah Kemp Weight

Contents

Dad. I wasn't ready to let you go, but, truthfully, I don't think I ever would have been. I hope this book makes you proud.

Chapter One

A loud banging thundered from somewhere in the house, arousing Emma from a world full of dreams. Her startled movement sent the book in her lap flying to the floor. Looking around, she tried to orient herself. The small family library was dim, indicating the waning sun of the cool April day.

The loud pounding came again. Emma wiped errant strands of golden curls from her face, straightening her position in the upholstered wingback chair. She could hear her butler Gibbons's steady, measured footfalls as he made his way to the front of the house.

Someone was at the front door, and from the sound of the knocker, they were quite insistent. It had been months since someone had knocked on the front door without first sending word. Her chest tightened and a whooshing sound filled her ears. Dread arose from somewhere deep within at the prospect of unexpected visitors.

Her first thought was to have someone run for Mr. Clayton, but Gibbons would have the door answered long before anyone could get word to the vicarage. She waited tensely for several minutes praying Gibbons would quickly turn whomever it was away.

The creak of the library door as it opened, and the light that came with it caused Emma to stiffen. Surely her servants knew better than to lead someone to her so hastily.

"Miss Hensworth," her housekeeper called out. Emma relaxed when she saw the woman standing completely alone.

"Yes. I am here, Mrs. Gibbons. Who has come?"

"There's been an accident, miss. A young man is terribly hurt. I hope you don't mind, but I had 'im taken up to one of the guest rooms until the doctor can be sent for."

They were not here to see her in particular. Relief flooded her limbs, and her fear subsided, allowing her to jump into action.

"Very good, Mrs. Gibbons. Please have the doctor sent for immediately. Also, please send word round to the vicarage. Tell my uncle we are in need of his presence at Engalworth Court."

"Yes, Miss. Would you also like me to summon Smith for you?"

Emma nodded. It would be best to have her lady's maid with her if there were unknown men about the house.

"Which room have you put him in?"

"The Oak Room, Miss."

"Have Smith join me there. I would like to assess the situation myself."

Mrs. Gibbons's eyes widened at her pronouncement. "Beggin' your pardon, Miss Hensworth, but there was a fair amount of blood on the young man when his friend brought him in. Are you sure you want to subject yourself to that?"

Emma was not sure she did, but with her father gone, there was no one else. She was mistress of the house for now. She needed to do her duty, and she could not do so if she stayed hidden in the library.

"I shall be fine." Emma straightened to her full height, which, admittedly, was not very tall. Mrs. Gibbons still stood a full head taller. However, her petite size had never stood in her way before, and she was determined it would not do so now. Her father's oft-spoken words echoed in her mind. "Do not trouble yourself, half-pint. Small you may be, but a half-pint of your spirit is enough to knock a man flat on his back." She smiled at the memory. Time to show the strength of that spirit.

Mrs. Gibbons stood for a moment, questions still evident in her eyes. Then finally she nodded once and excused herself to fulfill Emma's requests.

Emma made her way to the divided staircase that led to the second level of the house. Engalworth Court had been built around a main center with five wide steps leading to the main doors before they separated, turning to the left and right. The stairs to the left of the front door led to guest rooms while the stairs to the right led to the family rooms. All rooms opened to hallways from which one could view the entryway and open court of the house below.

She climbed the left staircase carefully, questions swirling in her head. Who would she find in the Oak Room? How had the man been injured? More to the point, how badly was he injured? What if he died in her home?

As she reached the second level, voices could be heard coming out of the Oak Room down the hall. She was glad the housekeeper had thought to put the man in there. It had more space about the bed than any of the other guest chambers, especially the Elm Room. The Elm Room was certainly the closest to the stairs, but would not provide ample space for people to move about tending to the injured man.

Emma heard quick steps behind her. Looking over her shoulder, she saw Smith scurrying forward to join her. She acknowledged her presence before entering the bustling room. A man lay upon the big four-poster bed moaning and mumbling. Another man stood by his side, begging the injured man to lie still. A footman rushed in with a big basin of water in his hands while Gibbons was in the process of removing the injured man's boots.

As the second boot was removed, the injured man screamed out in pain, then suddenly all was still. Emma's nerves stretched tight at the sudden silence as she tried to ignore the prone form in the bed. As shocked as she had been at his cry, his silence worried her more. Gibbons murmured something to the standing man.

"Yes, I believe you are correct. He seems to have passed out again from the pain, which is probably for the best," the tall, dark-haired man responded.

Gibbons turned, and seeing her at the door, stilled his movement. His rigid posture seemed to catch the dark-haired man's attention. A strained smile crossed the man's face before he nodded his head in acknowledgement. He turned a questioning expression to the butler. Emma realized the awkward position they found themselves in, for there was no one to make introductions. Were social niceties really necessary in a situation such as this?

Gibbons cleared his throat, and took the task upon himself. "Mr. Fairchild, might I introduce Miss Hensworth, of Engalworth Court. Miss Hensworth, Mr. Fairchild."

It would seem that was all the introduction they would get as it was clear Gibbons knew no more information about the gentleman than she did. Perhaps it was for the best. Stepping out from between Mr. Fairchild and herself, Gibbons busied himself, giving instructions to the footman to bring more heated water.

"Miss Hensworth, it is nice to make your acquaintance," Mr. Fairchild said with the same strained smile. "However, I wish it were under different circumstances."

Emma nodded to Mr. Fairchild, believing a curtsy would be awkward in such a situation. "I understand the sentiment. Who is your friend here?" She gestured with her hand to the unconscious man in the bed. Wrapping her courage about herself, she stepped closer to examine him. His light brown curls were matted with blood on one side of his head. Someone had laid a towel upon the pillow and it was now stained with red.

"This is Lord Hamdon, viscount to the earldom at Lincolnhurst."

Emma nodded again, feeling out of place as the unconscious man could not possibly respond. These introductions seemed trite in light of the grave situation these men found themselves in.

Looking back at Mr. Fairchild, she said, "I have sent for the doctor. You are in luck. He lives not five miles from here, and unless he has already been called out, should be here within the hour."

Mr. Fairchild nodded gratefully. "Very good. I thank you." The man's eyes drifted back to his unconscious friend, a look of strain crossing his face.

Emma chanced another glance at Lord Hamdon, her eyes traveling down his person. He was a young man, probably near the age of her brother. His form proved to be athletic in build, but not overly bulky. He was not an incredibly tall man, but he was not short either. His friend, on the other hand, was quite the tall gentleman. Mr. Fairchild must stand a whole head taller than her father.

Blood rushed from her face and bile rose in her throat as her eyes landed upon the injured man's right leg. Was that bone she saw protruding from his shin?

A gentle hand steadied her from behind. Glancing to her side, she saw Mrs. Gibbons supporting her. A wave of lightheaded swept over her.

"I have called for Mr. Clayton. Would you like to wait for him in the sitting room?" her housekeeper asked, brows furrowed in concern.

Bless Mrs. Gibbons for giving her a good excuse to remove herself from the sick room, and for lending support without making her look weak in front of company.

Turning back to Mr. Fairchild, she said, "I will have tea brought up immediately and make sure Dr. Jones has everything you all will need."

"Thank you, Miss Hensworth. Tea would be greatly appreciated," Mr. Fairchild said, "When will Mr. Hensworth be available?"

Emma stiffened at the question. "My father, Lord Gladsby, is away on business and will not be home for quite some time, but I have asked Mr. Clayton, the vicar, who is my uncle by marriage, to come aid you in any way you might need."

"Lord Gladsby?" he asked, eyes flicking to the ceiling as if he was trying to recall something. Fear gripped her heart. Did this man know her father?

"Yes, Baron Gladsby. Proprietor of Engalworth Court," she clarified reluctantly, indicating the room around them.

To her relief, he did not show any signs of recognition. "And your uncle is a vicar, you say?" Was that fear she saw in the man's eyes?

Realization dawned, and she rushed to say, "I called him here for my own comfort, not because I worry his services will be needed." Dipping her head to indicate the severely injured man in front of her, she accidentally glanced at the leg again, and her stomach lurched.

In desperation, she quickly bid Mr. Fairchild a good evening, exiting the room as dignified as she could manage, Smith following in her wake. Taking a deep breath as she stepped into the hall, Emma felt her equilibrium returning. She had tried not to look at the man again, but the grotesque nature of the injury had drawn her eyes back without her permission.

It was not as if she had not seen blood before, but the protruding bone was so repulsive she could feel her empty stomach ready to heave again in protest. It would have been terribly embarrassing to swoon or cast up her accounts in the stranger's presence after she had tried so hard to portray strength and composure.

Walking down the hall to the stairs, she let out a sigh of relief when the front door opened and closed, admitting Mr. Clayton. He caught sight of her as she descended the stairs. Seeing her pale face he opened his arms so she might step into them.

Oh, how she needed her uncle's comfort just now. Emma took the last steps quickly, flinging herself into the safety of the older man's arms.

"Emma, dear, are you all right? Owen said there was an accident," he said, referring to the stable boy.

"Two men," she stammered. "Strangers."

"Thank goodness for that."

Emma could not agree more, as she tried to remind herself that she was not alone. Nervous tension and fear of discovery expressed itself with several shuddering breaths. Mr. Clayton's aged hand made a soft circle on her back as he held her.

I am not alone she repeated in her mind, grateful for this sweet man who held her secrets so tightly.

Chapter Two

Emma sat at the dining table eating brown bread and stew with Mr. Clayton. The food calmed her racing thoughts, the heartiness of the meal providing comfort to her beleaguered soul.

"Dr. Jones says Lord Hamdon took quite the knock to his head when his mount threw him."

"Yes, it looked as such," Emma said, trying not to think of all the blood upon the pillow.

"But it is the leg he believes to be the more serious injury."

The reminder of the man's leg made her stomach turn, and she put down her spoon, unsure if she could take another bite of food without casting up her accounts.

"I am sorry, Emma. I suppose this is not good dinner conversation." Her uncle looked at her discarded spoon.

She sent the older man a tight smile. "How long did the doctor say it would take for the leg to heal?"

"As long as infection does not set in, it will be six to eight weeks at least, possibly longer as the break was quite severe."

Emma tried to push away the memory of Lord Hamdon's scream of pain when the leg had been set. It had echoed throughout the entire house, making the hair on her arms stand on end. Her heart ached for the poor injured man.

"You realize, Emma, that he will not be able to be moved for at least a month? Even then, it would not be wise for him to travel any distance as a strong jolt to the leg could re-break the mending bones."

She had realized as much. It was the very thing she had concluded when she first laid eyes upon the man, but how was she, a single woman, supposed to entertain two gentlemen respectably in her home for that long of a duration?

Emma lifted the napkin from her lap to dab at her mouth. Placing the cloth back upon the gray silk of her gown, she voiced her thoughts. "Until now everyone has left me well enough alone, assuming I have adopted a longer than usual mourning of my brother's passing. But with the admittance of these two gentlemen, questions will surface. Especially those about the propriety of their presence in the house."

"Yes. I realized that as well. I can stay with you for a time, but you must write your Aunt Marshall to come stay, Emma. I can only be away from my duties so long before my parishioners will suffer."

"If only Aunt Clara were still with us," she lamented, "I would much rather have had her presence than Aunt Marshall's."

"As would I," Mr. Clayton said, his expression somber.

Aunt Clara's passing four years ago had left a huge hole in both their hearts. Having never been blessed with children, Aunt Clara had doted on Emma and her brother, as had Mr. Clayton. When her mother had passed, Aunt Clara had stepped into the role of mother almost seamlessly.

Now, at nineteen, Emma could not help but think how unlucky she must be for those who had held parenting roles in her life. What did that mean for Mr. Clayton?

"I worry that Aunt Marshall will ask too many questions," she said, studying her uncle's well-worn face as he took another bite of stew. "She is far too intelligent and even more nosy." She wrinkled her nose. It was not that she disliked her aunt; she just did not get on as well with her as she had with Aunt Clara. Aunt Clara had been quiet, comforting, and kind, while Aunt Marshall was a gossip, incessantly chattering about this and that, happy to be the center of attention. Emma could have overlooked her aunt's faults if she was not always so critical of everything Emma did.

"What if she finds out?" Emma asked, her eyes pinched, her brow furrowed in concern.

"We must make sure she does not, my dear," Mr. Clayton said with meditative look. "We can trust Mr. And Mrs. Gibbons to keep their peace, and Smith is as quiet as they come. I know I will not let on, so it is up to you to find a way to distract her from her questions."

"That is easier said than done," she said with a frown. "I hate telling falsehoods. Unfortunately, I seem to be getting better at it with every passing day."

"What does that say about me as a vicar?" he asked with a wry smile. "Remember, I am the one encouraging you in this path."

"Supporting, Uncle. I believe the word is supporting. You know I would have chosen this course on my own even without your help."

"Either way, I am still a full participant, but I have great hope the Almighty will forgive us both for our deception. It is my belief He is more understanding than many believe. At least I hope so, for if not, I am sure I will not be inhabiting a place with the angels next to my dear Clara."

"Let us both hope for that, as well as for a good many years to repent." Emma quirked a smile as she lifted her spoon. Her stomach had finally settled enough to allow more food.

The dining room door opened, drawing both their attention as Mrs. Gibbons entered. "Pardon me, Miss, but should I send up some dinner for Mr. Fairchild and the doctor?"

"Oh, yes, Mrs. Gibbons," Emma said, realizing the men would probably appreciate some good food. The bonesetter had already left, but Dr. Jones would be spending the night watching over Lord Hamdon and would need food to keep up his strength. Mr. Fairchild had also voiced his intention to stay by his friend's side. Mr. Clayton had offered the use of the Maple or Ash Rooms that flanked the Oak Room, but Mr. Fairchild said he intended to stay where he was, at least until morning.

Emma was impressed with the man's dedication to his friend. It was rare a person came across such levels of devotion among the nobility. She should know. As the daughter of a baron, she had yet to find friends who did not see her as anything other than a stepping stone to a better life.

As a little girl, her lack of female companionship had never bothered her. Her mother and aunt had doted on her so much that she had not even noticed anything was missing in her life. She was content running after her older brother and cousins. But the last few years without aunt Clara had been daunting, especially the year her father had ventured out to give her a season. It had been quite the disaster.

Emma had sworn never to return to the likes of London. The cattiness of the women there was more than her tender heart could handle. Thankfully, her father had cared more about her than money or standing, and never asked her to subject herself to a season again.

It was lonely without her mother and aunt. For three years it had just been Emma and her father. And, of course, Mr. Clayton's occasional presence. She glanced at her uncle while he ate. Perhaps if Alan had not been so impetuous and run off to play soldier, life would not seem so lonely. But he had, and look where that had gotten them all.

Mr. Clayton cleared his throat. "I do hope that dark look was not for me, my dear," he said, smiling. "You look as though you were ready to embark upon a campaign against Bonaparte himself."

"If only woman were allowed such a privilege," she said darkly. "Perhaps then I could make the man feel all the pain he has caused this family these last three years."

"I do not believe it is exactly his fault your brother was so careless."

"No, he may not be responsible for Alan's thoughtlessness, but if we had not been at war, then Alan would not have succumbed to the temptation to run off to defend king and country."

"That is true. What is done is done, however, and we must follow our course until it is finished. No matter what the outcome." He said firmly.

"Do you still believe what my father said? Even after all these months?"

"How can I not? It is the only hope we have to hold to."

Emma nodded decisively. "I believe the same. I cannot bear to think otherwise."

"Well, my dear," Mr. Clayton said, dabbing at his mouth and placing the napkin next to his plate as he rose. "It is getting late. I believe we should turn in for the evening."

Emma bobbed her head in agreement. As her uncle pulled out her chair, Thatcher, the footman, stepped in to clear away the dishes. Mr. Clayton asked the footman after his things—the stable boy having been sent to the vicarage to obtain the clothing he would need for a short stay. Thatcher confirmed their arrival.

Holding onto her uncle's arm, she followed him into the main area of the house. The usual stillness of the house pervaded. She could almost pretend that nothing of significance had happened that day, but Mr. Clayton's next words brought her back to reality.

"You will write your Aunt Marshall in the morning, I hope?"

Emma let out a deep sigh. "I had hoped you had forgotten," she said with an impish smile.

He chuckled at her melodramatics. "Come now, Emma, it cannot be all that bad. It will be good for you to have female companionship again. You have scarcely let any of the neighborhood ladies past that door in four months."

She acknowledged the truthfulness of his statement. "But does it have to be that female in particular?"

"Emma," he scolded, but the effect was lost due to the twinkle in his eye.

"All right, Uncle. I shall write her first thing in the morning."

Chapter Three

It had been five days. Five days of listening to the moans and irrational words echoing from the second-floor room. Five days of people coming and going with cool rags in basins of water. Five days of tense dinners with her uncle and occasionally Mr. Fairchild. Five days of worrying that any minute the doctor would bring bad news.

On the sixth day, Emma woke to find the house completely silent. No one was bustling around. No moans came from the upstairs room. Mr. Fairchild was nowhere to be seen at the breakfast table. She feared the worst.

She sat tensely looking at her meal when Mr. Clayton entered holding a few letters in his hand, a smile upon his face. Crossing to where she sat at the table, he bent and gave her a quick peck upon the cheek. "Good morning, dear Emma. I have some correspondence for you," he said, setting the letters in front of her. "Gibbons gave them to me on his way to check on our patient. It seems Lord Hamdon's fever broke sometime during the night, and he is finally sleeping peacefully."

Emma sighed in relief. "That is good to hear. I must admit I was concerned when the house was so quiet this morning."

"Yes, I understand. I believe Dr. Jones and Mr. Fairchild are getting some much-needed rest. Thatcher, as well. Poor men. I am sure they are all spent with the long vigil they have kept."

"Indeed," she said, feeling compassion for all three men. She looked down at the letters Mr. Clayton had left on the table. On the top of the stack, she recognized her Aunt Marshall's elegant, loopy handwriting. Picking up the letter and holding it so her uncle could see, she said "It seems Aunt Marshall was very prompt in her response."

"Yes, I noticed. I thought I should bring them to you right away instead of waiting until Gibbons could get them to you."

"Do you mind?" she asked, indicating the letter.

"By all means. I shall just dish myself up a spot of breakfast."

"Please do." She broke the seal on the envelope. Scanning the letter, she let out an exasperated sigh. It would seem Aunt Marshall not only sent her acceptance in the invitation, but a reprimand for not enumerating upon her situation sooner. This letter was exactly why she had not. Her aunt's overbearing nature set her on edge, as though the woman still thought her a child of ten rather than a woman who would soon be celebrating her twentieth year.

"Is it all that bad?" Mr. Clayton asked.

"Some of the same. She has already begun chastising me for not calling upon her sooner, impressing how inappropriate it is for a young, unmarried woman to stay in a home with only her maid as chaperone."

"But you have never been wholly alone. The vicarage is a scant ten minute walk. I am never far away."

"Indeed, but I do not think she takes that into account. She seems to think I have been flitting about Society these past four months like a butterfly on the wind."

"Well, pay her no mind, my dear. I shall set her straight. When does she intend to arrive?"

Emma looked at the date written in the corner of the letter. "She says she will set out in three days' time. The letter was written two days ago so we should expect her tomorrow evening, perhaps Sunday at the latest."

"Let us hope for tomorrow. I have my duties to perform on Sunday and will need to be away from the house the rest of the day."

Emma understood her uncle's wishes, but for her part, she hoped to delay her aunt's arrival for as long as possible.

Anthony felt the dryness of his mouth and the scratchiness of his throat before he was even able to pry his eyes open. It was as if he had been traveling in the desert without water for weeks. Lifting his heavy eyelids, he was nearly blinded by the light. However, he desperately needed water.

He tried to shield his eyes with his left hand, but was surprised to find it difficult to move. He was weak, but not so weak he could not lift his own arm. Why did it feel like it was glued to the side of the bed?

Cracking his eyes open again, he allowed the slightest bit of light in. When he was used to that small amount, he allowed more. To his surprise, the day was actually quite overcast. Turning his head ever so slightly, he looked down at his hand upon the bed. The sight confused him.

His left and right wrist were bound to the bed, as was his torso and legs. His right leg was wrapped in some sort of splint. An acrid smell of ammonia hung in the air. To his chagrin, the bed beneath him was quite wet.

An older woman with brown hair streaked with grey bustled into the room and began rummaging in the bureau drawers. Her simple, dark blue dress and the chatelaine attached to her waist denoted that she was probably the housekeeper. Anthony tried to call out to her, but his dry tongue seemed stuck in place. The only sound that escaped his mouth was more like a groan than a word.

The woman whirled around, clasping her hands over her heart. Seeing his open eyes, she said, "Ah! 'Tis good to see you awake, my lord. I'll fetch the doctor immediately."

Before Anthony could protest, she was already out the door. He really just needed a drink of water. Turning his head slowly to each side he inspect his surroundings. He could see a pitcher and glass sitting upon a small oak table to

the side of the bed, but with his body bound, there was no way he could obtain i
t.

A middle-aged bespectacled gentleman entered the room, a small smile curving his lips. "So, you are finally awake!" he said with enthusiasm. "You, my lord, gave us quite the scare." He stopped at the side of the bed.

Anthony tried again to speak, but only got out a quiet "Wa." The man understand immediately and stepped to the pitcher of water and poured a glass.

Slipping one hand behind Anthony's head, the man gently lifted it until he touched the cup to Anthony's lips. Anthony took a few sips before the man pulled the cup back. Worried the man would take the water away, he leaned himself forward trying to reach the cup just in front of him. He was relieved when the cup was again pressed to his lips. This time he took several big gulps in case the man took away the cup for good.

"Easy, Lord Hamdon. We do not know how your body will take to that much water yet." Placing the half empty cup upon the table, the man said, "Now, how are you feeling today? Are you in much pain?"

He had a throb in his leg and an ache behind his eyes, but what was it to this man and why did he have him bound?

"Who are you?" he managed to squeak out. The other man looked confused.

"I am Dr. Jones. I have been caring for you since you were brought here six days ago. Do you not remember?"

Anthony reviewed his last memories but only found fuzzy thoughts and scary dreams. At least they must have been dreams, for none of them really made any sense. The last clear thought he remembered was laughing with Nicholas as they rode toward Blackwell Manor.

Suddenly the doctor's words registered. Six days! He was supposed to be at Blackwell Manor four days ago to attend his mother's birthday celebration. While ridiculous for someone of her age, it was the only reason he had left the season so early. Well, that and to pay a visit to his friend Bradley.

"What? Why?" He tried to move his hands.

"Ah, yes. One moment," Dr. Jones said and bent down to free him from his bindings. "You were thrashing around something awful, so we were forced to bind you to the bed to keep you from causing more damage to your leg. I am afraid if you do not recall me, you may not recall that you have broken your right leg quite badly."

Anthony rubbed at both wrists after they had been loosed, moving his stiff fingers about. The doctor removed the binding about his waist and must have caught a whiff of the smell. "We shall get you cleaned up as soon as possible. I will call in the footman and butler to help you. Perhaps even your friend Mr. Fairchild."

At the mention of Nicholas, Anthony asked in a slightly more even tone, "Where is Fairchild?"

"Abed, I hope. The man sat like a guard dog by your bedside these last five days, taking little rest, and eating far too little. When your fever broke, I insisted he get some rest in a proper bed."

Anthony smiled. When he, Nicholas, Bradley, and Fredrick had met at Eton all those years ago, he never would have guessed their odd little group would grow as close as they had. If he could have anyone be there when he was ill or injured, it would be one of them. They really were the only people in his life who truly cared for him as a person. That Nicholas had been so devoted to his care did not surprise him in the least. Anthony knew that they each would go to the ends of the earth to help the other. He would have done the same had the roles been reversed.

"What happened?" Anthony asked as the doctor fussed with the dressing on his head.

"According to your friend, your horse spooked at some loose bedclothes that blew across the road from a nearby cottage. He began bucking and threw you into a stone hedge. I suspect that is where the blow to the side of your head came from. However, that was not the only damage. In one of the animal's frantic jumps, one or both hooves came down upon your lower right leg, creating a fracture that broke through the skin. You developed an infection that I feared would be your end, but the housekeeper here insisted she bathe the wound in hot garlic water every day. Odd remedy that it was, I did not feel it would hurt since I had lost hope around day three of your fever."

Dr. Jones went silent a moment, and Anthony felt a tug as the doctor pulled a strip of bloodied cloth away from his head. After a while the doctor said, "I believe your head wound is healing well, and we no longer need to keep it wrapped. We will clean the remaining blood off when we wash the rest of you." Then, looking back at Anthony's face, he said, "I am glad the garlic water worked for your sake, my lord, for you are far too young to be stepping into the grave."

Anthony made a mental note to thank the housekeeper for saving his life. He, too, felt he was too young to 'step into the grave' as the doctor had put it. At five and twenty, he had a whole life ahead of him. One that, for some reason, felt a little more worthwhile at the thought of having it almost taken from him.

Chapter Four

Word spread throughout the house that Lord Hamdon had awakened. Emma insisted upon seeing the gentleman, but the housekeeper advised her to wait. She opened her mouth to resist until she saw their only footman carrying pitchers of hot water up the stairs. Realization dawned that the gentleman was probably in no state to be seen, so she held her peace.

When he awakened again several hours later, Gibbons sent word that they might come up. As Emma entered the room upon her uncle's arm, she was shocked by how much thinner and paler Lord Hamdon was from the day he arrived. His curly brown hair, though a touch messy, was now clean. Lips that had been pink were now brilliant red, cracks and dry skin dotting their surface. Dark circles hung around his deep blue eyes, but they were alert as he took in their entrance with curiosity.

Even with the changes, she was surprised to realize how handsome he was. Not in a sharp angular way like Mr. Fairchild, but he possessed a softness to his features that lent an air of approachableness and comfort. His adorable curls gave him a sweet boyish quality.

Mr. Fairchild greeted them, a much more relaxed expression on his face than Emma had seen these last six days. The man truly cared about his friend which was so refreshing. Most people in nobility barely tolerated each other, let alone cared enough to give up a bed for five nights.

Turning to his friend, Mr. Fairchild said, "Lord Hamdon, may I introduce Miss Hensworth, daughter of the Baron Gladsby, whose home we have had the privilege of residing, and for whose care we are greatly indebted."

Emma let go of her uncle's arm and curtsied to him. He gave a slight dip of his head, but to her surprise, when his head came back up, he was glaring at her. The change was so drastic that she sucked in her breath with astonishment. What had she done to displease him so?

"And this, Lord Hamdon, is Mr. Clayton, vicar of the Worthin parish and uncle by marriage to Miss Hensworth."

Again, he dipped his head, the expression upon his face becoming even more severe than the last. Why, she wondered, had she thought him approachable? At the moment, he looked quite the opposite.

Finally, Lord Hamdon opened his mouth and said coolly, "Thank you for your hospitality. I am sorry my care was thrust upon you in such a manner."

Emma stepped forward, straightening her spine. "We are happy to help. Other than the laundress's cottage near the road, we are the closest home on the route you were traveling. There is no other home for at least another mile."

His expression lightened slightly at her explanation, and he nodded. Suddenly that dark look crossed his face again, and annoyance built in Emma's chest. What right did this Lord Hamdon have to glare at her so? She had done nothing but offer care and shelter to him, but it seemed he felt something lacking in either her, or perhaps in his care.

Her father's holdings may not be as grand as that of an earldom, but surely he could not find anything wanting in his accommodations. The bed was fine. The food was plentiful. And the doctor was one of the best England had to offer.

That only left her. Emma had done all in her power to provide care and comfort to the gentleman, if she could still call him that. She had been polite and respectful, what else could he find amiss? Perhaps he took umbrage with her actual person.

She knew she was not completely what the ton found fashionable these days; she was far too small and thin. However, blonde tresses had been all the rage two years ago, as well as blue eyes. Surely, they had not gone out of fashion so quickly.

No, he could not find fault in her looks to the extent he would scorch her with such an unkind glare. He was just a disagreeable lout. That was all. There was nothing more to it.

Anthony stared at the little pixie in front of him. The girl could not be more than sixteen, he thought, but her cultured voice and mode of address indicated otherwise. She was not in any way silly or flighty as he might expect of a girl barely out of the schoolroom. She was composed and intelligent if his senses did not deceive him. Perhaps seventeen, entering her first season.

But she was so very small. She probably stood no taller than his upper arm, perhaps his shoulder, if one counted the mass of golden curls piled atop her head. She certainly was a pretty little thing. At least she would be if she would stop scowling at him.

His head ached terribly and every time he dipped it forward to acknowledge another person it set to pounding again. If that was not bad enough, his movements pulled on his leg in a way that shot pain all the way up the injured appendage. The doctor's earlier offer of laudanum was now exceedingly tempting.

Mr. Clayton stepped forward. "You are welcome to stay at Engalworth Court as long as you need, Lord Hamdon."

"I hate to be an imposition," Anthony responded, knowing he had already spent nearly a week being just that.

The vicar looked to his niece who stood silently, having schooled her features to a cool, unconcerned look. An uncomfortable silence filled the room as Mr. Clayton waited for her to answer. When she did not, he put himself forth.

"It is no imposition at all. We are happy to have you," he said, casting a confused look at Miss Hensworth.

Dr. Jones spoke up from his place in the corner. "You will need to be in bed another three weeks or so, my lord, then you might move about in a bath chair or upon crutches, but absolutely no traveling, especially by horseback, until your limb is sufficiently healed."

"And how long might that take?"

"The break in your leg was quite severe and will need ample time to mend back together. I would give six to eight weeks at least, but first we must focus on the initial mending and work from there."

Nearly two months in bed! Anthony barely did well for two days. How was he to stay so long in one place? He looked to Nicholas, panic exploding inside him. Nicholas would never be able to stay that long. He had a mother and sisters to care for and would be needed back at Fairfield Manor long before his healing was complete.

Nicholas seemed to read his thoughts. "I can stay one more week, Hamdon, but then I must return to my family. I had not planned on being away this long already, and my mother will need my help."

One week! That was all. Then what?

Perhaps Lord Gladsby could be prevailed upon to... to... to what? The doctor had said he could not be moved. It was not as if the man could decree otherwise. Suddenly, Anthony wondered why he had not been greeted by Lord Gladsby, as well.

"When will I meet Lord Gladsby?" Too late, he realized how terse the question sounded as he blurted it out. A strange look crossed the Ice Fairy's face. Anthony smiled at the name he had hit upon. Ice Fairy? Yes, it fit her quite well with that pale skin and those icy blue eyes that now seemed to be glaring daggers at him.

"My father is away on business. I am unsure when he shall return," she said coldly, almost as if she was reading a script.

"I will be at hand, however, to provide supervision," Mr. Clayton interjected. "That is, until Miss Hensworth's aunt arrives."

"When do you expect your wife's return?" Anthony asked.

"No, you mistake me, your lordship. It is a different aunt. Unfortunately, my wife passed four years ago."

"I do apologize. I meant no affront."

"It is no matter."

The room grew eerily silent until the Ice Fairy spoke up. "Well, we shall leave you to get some rest. I will have Thatcher bring your dinner in an hour." Turning to Nicholas, her expression morphed into a beautiful smile. "You are welcome to join us in the dining room, as usual, Mr. Fairchild. Unless, of course, you want to take your meals here with your friend." The change was so drastic that Anthony was taken aback.

Nicholas smiled back in response. "Actually, I believe a change of scenery would do me good. I would love to join you both for dinner."

"Excellent! Then we shall see you in an hour." And with that, the tiny woman swept out of the room without so much as a backward glance. Her uncle watched her go, the same confused look still upon his face.

"Well," he finally said, a little unsure, "I should probably let you rest. You have had a rough week. Might I suggest willow bark tea or even laudanum for that headache?"

Anthony was surprised at the man's intuitiveness. He opened his mouth to ask, but the vicar simply said, "It is my job, Lord Hamdon, to assess people's needs, physical and spiritual. Many people come to me for both. While I cannot heal the physical, I can often find nourishment for it. As for spiritual, if you find yourself in need, I always have a ready ear. Good evening, your lordship." Then turning to Nicholas, "I will see you at dinner, Mr. Fairchild." After a brief bow, the astonishing man left the room.

When Anthony was sure both the vicar and his niece were far enough away that he would not be overheard, he turned to Nicholas. "That was an interesting interaction."

"Yes, I was surprised at the vicar's remarks."

"I was not speaking of Mr. Clayton, although his perception did surprise me. I was speaking of Miss Hensworth. Is she always so cold?"

"Cold?" Nicholas said with dismay. "She is a warm and sweet lady who, might I add, has gone to great lengths to make sure you were cared for. It is you who is the problem. Why did you glare at her so?"

"Glare at her? I did no such thing. I may have grimaced a time or two, but that is because my head feels as though it might pound right off my shoulders."

"You could have fooled me. I thought you were insufferably rude to her with your dour expression. Perhaps next time you should voice your discomfort, for you looked as though you intended on giving the poor woman a thorough scolding."

"And lead her to believe I am no better than a sniveling child complaining of my pain? I think not. A man has his pride, you know."

"So you would rather she think you a boorish brute than one who feels pain after a horrific accident? Well, suit yourself, but I would rather not start off a two-month stay on such terms. It would make for a most uncomfortable situation."

Anthony supposed he was right, but why could she not have shown a little more compassion like her uncle? It was not as if he had glared at her on purpose. He knew her capable of kindness, for she had managed a pretty smile for Nicholas. Why could she not have been at least civil with him?

Chapter Five

Emma was determined not to see Lord Hamdon the next day. She did not need to expose herself to his sour expressions. Mr. Fairchild, on the other hand, had been a most amiable gentleman. At dinner the evening before, he had not only expressed his extreme gratitude for her hospitality, but added invigorating conversation to an otherwise dull evening. Now that was how a gentleman should behave.

If Lord Hamdon could be more like his friend, perhaps the next several weeks would not seem so daunting. As it stood, Emma was dreading the next two months. With her Aunt Marshall in tow, she did not need a crotchety invalid to make matters worse. Of course, if it were not for the crotchety invalid, Aunt Marshall would not be rushing to rescue her reputation.

Trying to turn her mind to more pleasant thoughts, she focused upon this evening's dinner. She looked forward to the meal and the prospect of having the handsome Mr. Fairchild's witty conversation at the table.

The sound of the knocker on the front door brought her head up from where she focused on embroidering roses into the edge of a square of linen. It seemed she would not be afforded one more day before her aunt's arrival, if the noises from the front entryway were to be understood. Apparently, her aunt had come in all her splendor.

Deciding it was better to get their greetings over with, she exited the east sitting room and approached the front entry. Thatcher was accepting trunks from the liveryman, taking each one up the stairs as Aunt Marshall waved her plump arms, giving directions to her maid and any other servant who happened into her line of vision.

"There you are, child!" Aunt Marshall's boisterously cheery voice called out. Her cheeks were red and her light brown coiffeur was slightly askew, most likely from the long journey and all her animated gesturing.

Emma tried to summon a pleased smile but was worried the expression did not quite reach her eyes. Walking the few wide marble steps up to the front landing, she was engulfed in the matronly woman's arms.

"It has been an age," she said stepping back and holding Emma at arm's length. "Well, let me look at you. My, how you have grown!"

Grown? Since last summer? She had not gained a single inch since she was fifteen. Something she greatly lamented, but she did not contradict her slightly taller aunt, deciding it best to just smile and get through the greeting as quickly as possible.

"How was your journey, Aunt Marshall?"

"Oh, dismal as always. You know how I hate long carriage rides. I suppose it could have been worse. But I tell you, sixty miles of good road is about all this old woman can take. All the shaking, bumping, and jarring is enough to rattle a person's teeth loose."

"You are not that old," Emma protested, hoping it would please her aunt enough to forgo her usual corrections and criticisms, which she knew were not far behind the friendly greeting. However, there was some truth in her words. Ten years her father's junior, Aunt Marshall was the youngest of the three Hensworth siblings, having just celebrated her forty-eighth birthday. Compared to Mr. Clayton, who was nearing sixty, she was quite young, indeed.

A voice from the top of the stairs caught both their attention when Mr. Fairchild fairly bounded down the stairs. "Mrs. Marshall! Is that truly you?"

"Nicholas, my boy, what are you doing here?"

"Anthony was thrown from his horse on our return to Blackwell Manor, and this was the nearest home where we could find shelter."

"Lord Hamdon is the invalid you spoke of in your letter?" Aunt Marshall asked, accusation in her tone as she turned to Emma. There was the bite she had expected.

"Yes. You are acquainted with these gentlemen?" she countered, trying not to let her aunt's tone rattle her.

"Of course!" she said, as if Emma should have known better. "Nicholas and Anthony are some of my Fredrick's dearest friends from school. I know them almost as well as I know my own boys."

"Wait! Lord Glad's – Be!" Nicholas exclaimed as he looked directly at Emma. His hand came up to rest on the side of his head. "I am unsure why I did not put it together sooner; you are Fredrick's baby cousin. I should have remembered your father's distinct title. As boys, we always used to say he had the happiest title in all of England," he said with a grin. Apparently, Emma was not the only one who had forgotten details from her childhood.

"Ah, but I would not expect you to remember everything, my boy. It has been, what? Seven, eight years since my Fredrick left for the Navy? And you have had very little time with him since."

"Very true," Mr. Fairchild said solemnly. "By the by, when does he have his next shore leave?"

"I am unsure. What with the war with Napoleon, I never really know when he will be back in England until he arrives at my door."

"Well, I should love to see him when he is returned."

"I shall dash off a letter the moment he arrives," Aunt Marshall said, patting Mr. Fairchild's cheeks as if he was a little boy. "Now, take me up to see dear Anthony. Emma's letter said he was in a bad way, something of a head injury."

"Yes, and a broken leg," Mr. Fairchild added as he walked with the woman up the stairs.

She hesitated for a moment, not really inclined to see Lord Hamdon nor spend more time with her aunt's disapproving looks. Suddenly, Aunt Marshall looked over her shoulder and said, "Well, come along, Emma. Don't dawdle."

Emma's cheeks suffused with color. Why did her aunt have to treat her like she was still a little girl? Then again, Aunt Marshall had done the same to Mr. Fairchild who was at least four or five years Emma's senior, and he did not seem to mind.

Following meekly behind, she listened as Mr. Fairchild detailed some of the early moments of his and Lord Hamdon's arrival at Engalworth. When they reached the Oak Room, her aunt rushed in ahead of them. Her quick movements reminded Emma of a mother hen—wings spread out, providing balance as she bustled forward to the injured man in the bed.

Lord Hamdon was propped up by a mound of pillows looking toward the door. At the sight of her aunt bustling toward him, a huge smile spread across his face reminding Emma of how she had first thought him inviting and approachable. Aunt Marshall scooped up the man's hand, and while patting it, started tutting over him.

"You poor boy. What a trial you have been through."

"I thought I must be dreaming again when I heard your voice in the hall. How are you, Mrs. Marshall? It has been far too long."

"It has, it has. I have missed seeing you boys running about the place. Now enough about me, I have come to take good care of all of you. I am glad you happened to be near my brother's place when such a horrid accident occurred. Dr. Jones is one of the best doctors in the country. If I thought we could hire the man away from here, I would have had Mr. Marshall do so years ago."

Emma stared on in confusion. The man looked as pleased as punch to see her aunt; not one cross word or look at her coddling. If she was not mistaken, he was excited at the prospect of having the plump woman fussing over him.

She felt completely out of place in the happy conversation that began to flow around her as Mr. Fairfield, Lord Hamdon, and Aunt Marshall began reminiscing. Looking to the window, she noticed a light drizzle had started. Fitting, she thought, her previously sunny day, like the weather, had turned quite dismal.

Pulling her eyes away from the window, her gaze collided with Lord Hamdon's. He was looking at her with that stern expression again. She tried to school her features into nonchalance, but worried she was failing. Why did he always have to look so severe at her? Did her appearance displease him in some way? She had not said a single word since entering the room, so she could not have expressed anything to have incited his ire.

"That was a splendid summer," Aunt Marshall said. "Well, I have had a long journey and must get some rest before dinner, but I shall be back up to check on you, Anthony, before I retire for the night. You will be joining us for dinner, won't you, Nicholas?"

"Of course, Mrs. Marshall."

"Oh, do drop this ridiculous Mrs. Marshalling and call me Aunt Vie as you did when you were boys."

Aunt Vie? Emma had never been permitted so much familiarity. Who were these men that commanded so much affection from her aunt? It was an affection she had never seemed to achieve.

She looked to the door wondering if she might slip out without anyone noticing, but glancing back, she saw that Lord Hamdon's eyes were again upon her. He was not glaring this time, but his eyes remained on her for so long that she was she there must be something wrong with her person. Glancing down at her favorite grey dress, she could not see anything out of place.

Emma ran her hand down the skirt loving the way the silk wavered between grey and silver. She had already dressed for dinner even though the meal was still several hours away. These last several months, she found it did not matter much when she dressed for dinner. So, she dressed whenever she wished, sometimes skipping the practice entirely. At this moment, however, she realized how odd it must look to her visitors. Perhaps that was what upset Lord Hamdon enough to stare unforgivably long at her.

When she looked up again, his eyes were focused on her aunt as she recounted yet another story. Had the woman not just said she intended to retire? But she just prattled on while both gentlemen smiled, nodded, and occasionally chuckled at their own childhood misadventures.

Emma realized belatedly she had not really been listening to the tales when Mr. Fairchild took note of her. "Come now, Miss Hensworth, you must have a diverting childhood story to tell as well."

For the first time in almost a quarter hour the room went silent, the occupants turning their attention to her. After being forgotten for so long, it was disconcerting to have everyone's eyes on her, but eventually she found her voice. "I do not recall any, at present, that could be deemed as diverting. Mine was a rather quiet childhood."

The statement was not quite true, but she did not want to expose herself in front of these people. Emma dearly loved to laugh, but did not like to be laughed at, and with the present company, she feared that was exactly what would happen. Seeing their disappointed faces, she decided to take her leave before Aunt Marshall started telling stories she would rather keep to herself.

"If you will excuse me, I must meet with Cook to inform her of your arrival, Aunt Marshall." Dropping a quick curtsy, she made a hasty exit, breathing deeply the moment she was out of the room. The next few weeks seemed to stretch insufferably long in front of her. How was she ever to stand the company of her effusive, yet disapproving aunt, as well as the handsome, ill-tempered Lord Hamdon?

Her thoughts caused her to pause halfway down the stairs. Handsome? Had that word truly crossed her mind in connection with the sour man? No, she could not possibly find someone as prickly as Lord Hamdon handsome. However, just because she did not think him handsome did not negate his good looks. She supposed a man could still be handsome even if she did not care for him.

Shaking her head in an effort to clear his image, she again began to descend the stairs. At least one person would be truly relieved at Aunt Marshall's arrival. Mr. Clayton could now return to his duties as a vicar with an assurance that she was well-chaperoned. She dearly wished he could remain to give her support. Things did not seem quite so dire with his cheery presence about the house.

Chapter Six

Four blasted days in this miserable bed. Technically, from the time of his arrival at Engalworth Court, it had been nine days. Anthony had never stayed so long abed in his entire life.

Of course, he had never grown so weak in his life either. The days of fever had sapped a great deal of his strength, and he found he slept more than usual. However, while his body yet recovered, his mind grew increasingly impatient with the healing process.

Nicholas, bless him, tried to provide entertainment through conversation and reading during Anthony's waking hours, but as the initial pain from his injuries subsided, Anthony spent much of his time just staring at the same four walls.

The room, tastefully decorated in navy and white, was not terrible to look at. Indeed, the polished wood of his bed was particularly admirable. The craftmanship was more intricate than anything Anthony had ever seen, with ivy vines climbing the bed posts and small ladybugs interspersed throughout. Even so, it was still just a bed and could only be studied for only so long.

"When must you leave?" Too late he realized he had interrupted Nicholas while he read aloud.

"That desperate to get rid of me?" Nicholas asked with a good-natured smile.

"Quite the opposite. I fear once you have gone, I will be left to rot in this bed."

"That is unfair to our hostess. She has provided excellent care for you in the time you have been here."

"The same hostess who has not shown her face in my room since Aunt Vie arrived three days ago?"

"Antsy to get another glimpse of her, I see. She is strikingly beautiful with all those golden curls framing such a delicate face, and I do not think I have ever seen someone with eyes of such light blue." Anthony could tell by the raise of Nicholas's left eyebrow that he was goading him.

"Hardly. However, it sounds like you might be," Anthony retorted. "No, if Aunt Vie was not here, I should think the Ice Fairy would leave me to starve *or* freeze me out."

"Ice Fairy?" Nicholas said with a laugh. "That's quite the moniker. I do not understand why you have taken such a great dislike to Miss Hensworth. She is such a delightful young woman. I have not met many women who are so easy to converse with. She has been exceedingly gracious to us both."

"Perhaps we are not talking of the same Miss Hensworth. The one I speak of is cold and inattentive, leaves injured men to fend for themselves, even though they might die of very real boredom. Does she perhaps have a sister? You might be confusing them."

"Nothing of the sort." Nicholas chuckled. "You have not been the most amiable companion of late, you know. However, I am used to your grousing. You never could be laid up for too long. I remember how irritable you were four years ago when you had that terrible bout of influenza. I thought you would combust from inactivity after being confined to your room for nearly a week."

"So I am the one to blame for Miss Hensworth's icy disposition? I did my best to control my expression, which you thought so dour, when last she graced us with her presence."

"Yes, but you also did not speak to her either."

"So, you *are* saying I am the one to blame."

"No, not precisely. Only that the two of you may have misjudged each other. I have noticed she seems to avoid conversing about you as much as she avoids conversing *with* you. Of course, it could be something else entirely. Perhaps it is only the thought of a sick room that makes her shy away."

"You think she is squeamish?"

"Not exactly, but she did almost swoon the day you were brought in." Looking off to his left, Nicholas half muttered, "Then again, the sight of your shin bone protruding from your leg was hard for me to stomach as well, as ashamed as I am to admit it." He returned his gaze to Anthony. "However, I still think your cool reception of her is the actual cause of her caution."

"I told you I was not being cold; I was in pain."

"Yes, but *she* does not know that," he said emphatically.

A tiny knock sounded at the door. "Enter," Anthony called, a bit of irritation seeping into his tone at Nicholas's assertion.

The only people who usually knocked were the servants, so he was not surprised when a maid of some sort opened the door. However, when Miss Hensworth stepped through in front of the woman, he was taken aback.

"Speak of the devil," he murmured under his breath, but apparently not quiet enough.

"Pardon?" she asked, raising her eyebrows.

"I said, how do you do?" Anthony lied. To his side, Nicholas coughed into his hand trying unsuccessfully to cover a laugh.

Miss Hensworth looked suspiciously at Nicholas before she turned back to him. After smoothing her expression into something proper and unemotional, she said, "I am come to inquire after your health, Lord Hamdon."

The inquiry did not sound congenial in the least. In fact, she acted as though the question was being forced from her by a sense of duty rather than kindness. Why was it so hard for her to show at least a little cordiality?

"I am as well as can be expected," he answered slowly, matching her emotionless tone.

"Is there anything I might get for your comfort or entertainment?"

"Fairchild is reading to me at present, and that has been sufficient." In truth, it was not. The books Nicholas chose were exceedingly dry. While he enjoyed learning about world politics, the topics were not often stimulating enough to keep his attention. Perhaps he should suggest his friend choose something less proper.

He could really go for a Minerva Press novel about now. A nice gothic would be in good keeping with Miss Hensworth and her icy disapproval. She was as good a villain as any he had read. A picture of Miss Hensworth formed in his mind, her form depicted on the cover of a gothic novel, frozen dress, frosted curls, icy scepter and all. The mental picture was quite entertaining.

Something changed in Miss Hensworth's expression. He could not put his finger on it, but her eyes, usually cold, now blazed with something akin to blue fire. Was she angry with him? What had he done now?

Turning to face Nicholas, she said hotly, "Might I get anything for you, Mr. Fairchild, as your friend here is quite *sufficiently* looked after at present, and seems to be entertained by either piercing me with a glare or laughing at me by turn?"

Nicholas, the traitor, was rubbing his upper lip in an effort to cover the smile threatening to spread wide across his face. "You have been a most excellent hostess, Miss Hensworth," he said, subtly clearing his throat to maintain composure. "I am in need of nothing, but many thanks all the same."

"You are quite welcome," she said, her ruffled feathers soothed by Nicholas's charm. "You have always been the very picture of a gentleman. I look forward to seeing you at dinner, Mr. Fairchild."

Turning with a scowl toward Anthony she said, "Lord Hamdon," and after giving the briefest nod of her head, exited the room with her head held high.

"See?" he said, with an exaggerated gesture toward the closed door.

"Perhaps," Nicholas drew out, "if you had not laughed at her, she would have been more amiable."

"I did not laugh at her!"

"Yes, you did. What were you thinking that made you chuckle so? It sounded almost maniacal."

"Chuckle?"

"Yes, you said you did not need anything in that cool business-like tone, then after a beat of silence, you chuckled as if you found something about her profoundly funny."

Had he really laughed out loud? He had found it amusing to compare Miss Hensworth to a gothic novel, but he did not think he had laughed. Thinking back, he realized he had indeed chuckled softly. It was a good thing his hands were not injured, for he dropped his head firmly into them, shame washing through him. No wonder the lady had been so angry.

"She has quite the sharp tongue, does she not?" Nicholas said with a grin. "I quite like a lady with spirit."

"Yes, I know," Anthony muttered through his hands. When the room fell silent he looked up to see the expression of mirth on Nicholas's face had turned suddenly solemn. He looked like a man haunted by a ghost.

"Nicholas, come back," Anthony said, waving his hand. Nicholas's unfocused eyes snapped back to his friend.

"My apologies."

"She still has a hold on you," Anthony said.

"Why would you say such ridiculousness?" Nicholas said rather crossly, picking up the book he had set by his chair.

Anthony knew he was treading on thin ice. Nicholas did not like to speak about last season, but it was very apparent it still haunted him.

"Have you even tried to contact her? Perhaps she is just as hurt as you, and that is why she did not take another season."

Nicholas scoffed. "Or perhaps she has married into a title just like she always wanted."

Anthony decided not to push the subject. It was evident Nicholas was still smarting from the rejection; pushing him any further would just make them both miserable for the rest of the day. Switching the subject, he said, "Do they have any *other* books in their library that are a little less..." He paused to find the right word.

"Boring?" Nicholas supplied, a smirk back upon his lips. "I could see your eyes glazing over while I read the passage on cargo in the ship's hull."

Anthony tried to look penitent, but all he could manage was an eventual nod of agreement.

"I will go see what I can find," Nicholas capitulated. "Is there something in particular you would like?"

"A good gothic novel." He grinned and rubbed his hands together in anticipation.

Nicholas chuckled. "I guess things are not exciting enough for you in that bed."

Anthony gave him a dry look.

The door swung open and Aunt Vie bustled in for one of her twice-daily visits. Anthony smiled at the motherly woman so different from his own; polar opposites to be exact. Where Aunt Vie was of a small, plump build, his own mother was tall and slender. Where Aunt Vie was effusive and loving, his mother was cool and calculating.

If he could have chosen his own mother, he would have chosen Aunt Vie any day. In fact, he would have chosen any of his friends' mothers over his own.

Bradley's mother was perhaps not quite as open, but she was not an unkind sort. She just always seemed busy or unconcerned with the comings and goings of her son and his friends. Anthony supposed that was to be expected of someone with a large family and a small income.

Nicholas's mother, on the other hand, was a quieter form of Aunt Vie. Always caring, attentive, and extremely insightful. Anthony admitted to himself that while Aunt Vie was entertaining, if he ever needed a mother to confide in, it would be Lady Julia, for she had always been easy to talk to.

"Now that Aunt Vie has come to take her shift, I shall be off to the library to find more entertaining reading." Turning to the older woman, Nicholas said, "It seems my choice of books was not as interesting to Anthony as it was to me."

Aunt Vie looked at the title on the book and tsked. "History of Transatlantic Trade. I should think not. A ghastly subject if you ask me."

Nicholas's smile faltered a moment before he was able to recover it. Anthony did not think Aunt Vie had meant to insult Nicholas, but that particular subject matter, passed down to him as a legacy from his father, was exceedingly important to him.

Trying to fix Aunt Vie's blunder, he said, "It is very educational, Nicholas. Thank you for reading to me."

Nicholas nodded and then excused himself, hurrying from the room. Turning to Aunt Vie, Anthony noticed her concern.

"I think perhaps I may have misspoken. I had not meant to cause offense."

"No, Aunt Vie, I do not think he took offense. It is just a sensitive subject for him, especially after losing his father two years ago. I believe he is taking up all aspects of his father's mantle."

"Yes. Perhaps that is the change I see in him. He is still the delightful boy I knew, but he seems more weighed down than I remember. I am sure taking on that particular estate was not an easy business."

That was not exactly what kept Nicholas as burdened as he was, but it was part, so he agreed with Aunt Vie. She began talking about how they might lift Nicholas's spirits in the four days he had left with them. Anthony only listened with half an ear.

He hated to think about Nicholas's departure, but with its evident approach, there was nothing more to do. His mother had written from Blackwell Manor, berating him for missing her ridiculous birthday celebration. Birthdays were for children. Nevertheless, she had sent a full page reprimanding him for being so careless.

That was his loving mother, he thought with some disdain. Always thinking of... well, herself.

His father was not much better. He only tolerated Anthony because he was the eldest son. He was sure his father far preferred his derelict younger brother. Andrew was just as cold and calculating as their mother and father.

Two years his junior, Andrew spent most of his time either drinking and gambling at White's or working the ballrooms of London in search of an heiress to fund the small estate left to him through their mother. Andrew's manner of riffling through ladies made Anthony sick.

Of course, so did his parents' marriage. It was no secret they each kept their own paramours. His parents' marriage had really only lasted long enough to produce an heir and a spare. They tolerated each other and were generally of one mind when parenting their sons, but that was the extent of their marital felicity.

If Anthony had not witnessed Aunt Vie's loving marriage as well as Nicholas's parents, he would not think such a thing existed, but Mr. Marshall doted on his wife quite unabashedly. Sometimes to a fault. Anthony was surprised that the man had not accompanied her.

The thought caused him to interrupt her one-sided conversation. "Forgive me, Aunt Vie. Why did your husband not accompany you on this venture? I do not believe I have ever seen you go off on your own before."

"Oh, dear boy. Mr. Marshall's legs pain him something awful these days, especially after hours of travel," she said sadly. "We decided it was best for me to make the journey on my own. Alfred is there to look after his father, though, and will alert me if I am needed back at home."

"It has been years since I have seen your eldest son. How is Al?"

"Doing well. Well, indeed. I am in great hopes that I may return home to prepare for a wedding," she said with a twinkle in her eye.

"Is that so?" And that was all Anthony needed to say for the enthusiastic woman to go off describing the young lady and every detail of the courtship thus far. He smiled at her excitement and settled in to be completely entertained for a good while. Because when Aunt Vie found a subject she liked, she could talk a steady stream for the rest of the afternoon, and that was just fine with him.

Chapter Seven

E mma slowly walked the hallway leading to the Oak Room. Aunt Marshall had chastised her all of yesterday morning reminding her of her responsibilities. So, she had visited Lord Hamdon in an effort to appease her aunt, only to have the taciturn gentleman laugh at her. For what, she still was not sure.

Stopping before the man's door, she stared at it, knowing if she did not make an effort every day as her aunt had instructed, she would have to listen to more lectures on being a good hostess.

Smith stood at the door waiting for the signal, but she still stood not quite ready to enter. Suddenly, the door opened, pulling the knob straight out of Smith's hand. Dr. Jones stood in the doorway, surprise on his face at seeing the two women standing so close.

"My apologies," he said, immediately stepping back so they could enter.

Smith deferred to Emma, giving her the right to enter first. But Emma just stared at the doorway, still not quite ready to cross the threshold.

From within the room, a deep voice said, "It is a door, Miss Hensworth. You are meant to step through it."

A laugh bubbled within her at the humorous statement, but just as quickly she suppressed it. Lord Hamdon was probably just making a jest at her expense. Stepping into the room, she was surprised to be greeted by a pleasant expression on Lord Hamdon's face. It was the first she recalled being directed her way.

Emma heard Smith enter behind her just as Dr. Jones excused himself, offering his farewells with a promise to return again on the morrow.

"If you will excuse me as well, Miss Hensworth," Mr. Fairchild said from his place near the chair at his friend's bedside. Sending Lord Hamdon a peculiar look, he then continued. "I am in need of some fresh air and would like to take a turn about the gardens."

"Lucky," Lord Hamdon grumbled, casting what could only be termed as a baleful glance toward the open window. The day was actually quite warm for April, and for once the sun was shining cheerily outside. Emma had already enjoyed a walk about the grounds, looking at the little signs of life spring was bringing.

"Yes, I am," Mr. Fairchild said with a look of smugness.

After watching Mr. Fairchild leave, she turned back to see a small smile of fondness on Lord Hamdon's face as he stared at the now empty doorway. His eyes shifted to her, and his expression flattened.

"Please have a seat, Miss Hensworth," he said, indicating the seat Mr. Fairchild had just vacated.

Emma realized in all the times she had come to see Lord Hamdon, she had never been invited to sit. Nervously, she took up her seat in the blue chair brought close to the bed. Her maid sat upon one of the wooden chairs near the door.

Lord Hamdon watched the maid sit before he began. "Miss Hensworth, it has been brought to my attention that I behaved badly toward you yesterday. I would like to apologize. I had not meant to laugh at you. If I am to be truthful, I did not know I had laughed at all until Fairchild pointed out my blunder."

Emma's eyebrows shot up. An actual apology! But what had he meant? How did one not know they laughed?

"It seems," he went on, "that I am not fully aware of myself as of late. Fairchild insists I have been glaring a great deal, and for that I do apologize. I am afraid I am not the best of patients, and apparently pain causes me to give rather alarming expressions," he said with a wince, as if the admission cost him a bit of his comfort.

He seemed sincere. She could understand not being one's self when feeling unwell. Her father had been quite different during his last illness. A pricking at the back of her eyes warned her that she was in dangerous territory. She needed to change the direction of her thoughts quickly or there would be a torrent of tears. That was something she *absolutely* could not indulge in at this moment.

Anthony stared at Miss Hensworth. If anything, she looked more upset by his apology rather than less. The attentive look on her face was replaced with a frown. Trying to think of a way to further explain himself, he was dismayed when her expression changed into one of sadness, and her crystal blue eyes filled with tears. It seemed he had a new problem on his hands.

Had he really been so insufferable that he had brought Miss Hensworth to tears? The Ice Fairy, strong and indomitable, was melting right before his eyes, and he could not even move one inch to hand her a handkerchief.

Just when he thought the tears would fall, however, the tiny woman took a deep breath, and as quickly as the tears had appeared, they disappeared. How had she done that? He had never seen a woman on the verge of tears gain such complete control over herself. His mother would have let the tears fall with abandon, filling him with the guilt he knew she meant to induce with her antics.

"Thank you, Lord Hamdon," she said softly. "I must apologize, as well. I have been a most inattentive hostess. However, I am trying to make amends," she said with a small smile. Strange what a smile could do. It fairly transformed Miss Hensworth's face, and instead of ice, Anthony saw sunny blue skies in her eyes.

"Shall we start again, Miss Hensworth?"

"I would like that very much," she said pleasantly. "May I enquire how your day has been thus far?"

"Better." He readjusted his position to relieve the pressure in his lower back. "I hate to complain, but I wish I could be outside with Fairchild. I should be grateful, at least, that the sun is shining rather than the dreary rain we have had of late." Hopefully the safe topic of the weather was sufficient enough to pull Miss Hensworth into further discussion.

"Yes, it is a beautiful day. I spent a half hour in the gardens this morning, and it was quite lovely." To his delight, she went on to detail the tulip sprouts shooting through the ground, as well as the buds upon several of the trees. They talked at length about when the gardens might be in full bloom, which plants he could expect to see, and before Anthony realized it, a quarter hour had passed.

Checking her time piece, she rose from her seat. "Well, I must be going, Lord Hamdon. I thank you for the conversation, and I hope you will be able to see the gardens soon. Mr. Clayton, I know, has been asking about our parish for a bath chair. Hopefully we will be able to borrow one soon, so you can move about more. That is, when the doctor considers you ready, of course."

"Whenever I picture bath chairs, I think of old people," he said with a wry grin. "I did just celebrate a birthday, but I did not suppose I was that much older. I must have been wrong."

"And what age did you achieve, my lord?"

"Five and twenty."

"Ah, yes, you are positively in your dotage now," she said with a quirk of her lips and a raise of her eyebrow. The teasing statement from the previously sour young lady caught Anthony completely off guard, and he laughed.

"I guess compared to a spry, young thing, such as yourself, I must be old. What are you, sixteen? Seventeen?"

"I shall be twenty on the twenty ninth of this month." She smiled.

Anthony's face went slack. "You are teasing."

"I do not jest, Lord Hamdon. I was born in the year 1794. You may ask my aunt if you do not believe me." She appeared almost affronted that he did not take her seriously, but how could he when she looked barely beyond childhood? Glancing over her person, he had to amend the thought, for her figure was anything but childlike. Even though she was petite, she was curved in all the right places.

"I am sorry. I did not mean to offend; it is just..."

"It is just that I am barely bigger than a child, and my face looks as though I drink from the fountain of youth on the daily."

He chuckled. "Yes, exactly. Do you? Drink from the fountain of youth, that is."

"If you ask my Aunt Marshall, I do. She is always lamenting my youthful looks, claiming she is aging far faster than a woman should."

"Aunt Vie does not appear old. She is beautiful the way she is, more so for her jolly spirit."

Miss Hensworth's expression turned pensive. Did she not agree with him? He had noticed how quiet she stood the other day, but he had assumed it was because she did not care to be around him. Now, however, he wondered if Aunt Vie's exuberant presence stifled her niece's quieter nature. It was true Aunt Vie could be a little bit much at times, but it was all from a place of love and caring.

Miss Hensworth cleared her throat. "Aunt Marshall is a pretty woman. Both of my father's sisters were." She said the last bit so reverently Anthony could not help but feel how much she must have loved her Aunt Clayton.

"Well, I am needed downstairs," she said after a short silence. Anthony got the impression she did not have a definitive destination, only needed an excuse to no longer be in his presence. It irritated him a little seeing the Ice Fairy appear again as she gave a stiff curtsy and then scurried from the room before he had barely nodded at her, her maid following close behind.

Not five minutes later, Nicholas returned. "How did it go?" he asked, a hopeful smile upon his lips.

Anthony thought on his time. Truthfully, it had actually gone better than he could have hoped. Yes, she had left just as cold as she had entered, but in between, she had thawed. Maybe with time she would drop the icy nature entirely. It would make his stay much more enjoyable, for sure. She was definitely pretty. There was no question on that score.

"I believe it went well," he finally said, thinking about Miss Hensworth. She had the most intriguing eyes. Surprisingly, the blue orbs that had frozen him mere days ago now left a pleasantly warm sensation, even after she had gone. That was a good change indeed. "In truth, better than I had hoped."

"Good! Good. Now I shall not worry so much."

"Worry? About what?"

"That she will leave my crotchety, *old* friend to starve in his bed," he said with a grin.

"You did not go to the gardens at all, you earwigger."

Nicholas only laughed, not at all penitent for his eavesdropping. Settling himself into the chair, he picked up their latest book selection with a smile, and began to read.

Chapter Eight

On Friday morning, Nicholas entered the room. Anthony wished he was not there to say his goodbyes. It would only take his friend the better part of the day to reach his estate near Harlow, but he had insisted he needed plenty of time to reach home before dinner. Anthony was loath to see him go, but Nicholas reminded him that should he truly need him, he could be to Engalworth Court within a day. Anthony supposed that was true.

Besides, it was not as if he was left completely friendless. Aunt Vie still made her twice-daily visits to entertain him for an hour or two. He had even been on civil terms with Miss Hensworth, she having visited him every day since Tuesday. While her conversations were decidedly shorter than Aunt Vie's, they were still a diversion from his daily monotony.

"Do not look at me like that, Anthony," Nicholas implored with an impish smile.

"How is that?"

"Like I have just killed your favorite dog and plan to run off with your intended."

"I have an intended?" Anthony quipped. "This is news to me. She must not be worth much if she intends to elope with a man such as yourself."

"Such as me?" Nicholas shot back with a grin. "Do you mean devilishly handsome if a little empty in the pockets?"

"More like disloyal, willing to leave your friend to man-eating she-beasts."

"Come now, Anthony, it is not as bad as all that. You have been getting along quite well with Miss Hensworth of late." Nicholas's eyes flitted to the open doorway.

"Very true. She has thawed some. I cannot complain of my treatment."

"And you best not, if you don't want to be thrown out upon your ear after I leave." Nicholas grinned, but then added in a much more serious tone, "Be kind to her, Anthony. She really is a sweet woman whom life has dealt some hard blows, if I do not miss the mark. And she has been nothing but hospitable to us, so she deserves our gratitude."

"I know she does, Nicholas," Anthony said, looking up at the plaster ceiling above him. "I am not wholly ignorant of the situation. I will do my best to act as a gentleman ought."

"Good! Now, I have brought you some entertainment," Nicholas said, pulling out a small stack of books and papers from under his arm. Removing the stack of newspapers from the top, he handed Anthony the books.

"*Social Reform of the Caribbean, Futility in the Feudal system*, and *Sir Newman's Mathematics Orations*." Nicholas's face took on an increasingly amused bend with each book title Anthony read. "Are you trying to entertain me, Nicholas, or guarantee I will get my rest? These titles will bore me right to sleep for sure."

Nicholas let out a bark of laughter and then thrust the newspaper at Anthony. "All right then, perhaps this will be more to your liking."

Anthony took the pages eagerly. Glancing at the top page, his eyes went wide as he read the headline. "Bonaparte Abdicates, Exiled to Elba. Is this true?"

"Completely. News came while you were ill. France lost the battle of Paris, and they entered into negotiations with the coalition. Apparently, they have reached an agreement. I am sure that sort of reading is probably much more to your liking."

"It is, indeed," Anthony said. "I am sure it is probably what most of England finds to their liking."

"You would not be wrong. I, myself, enjoyed the article and several after it. But steer clear of the gossip columns. It seems your family has been quite active of late."

Anthony groaned at the reminder. If only he could send some of his family to exile with Bonaparte. Odd that Society, with all its strict moral policies, always looked the other way when a Kempton was involved. Money and title, he reminded himself with an inward sigh. If not for that, they would all be left to the mercies of Society, or the lack thereof.

"Well, I cannot dawdle much longer," Nicholas said, straightening. "May God bless you with a speedy recovery, my friend."

"And you an easy journey," Anthony said solemnly, and knowing his friend's devout nature, added, "Godspeed, Nicholas."

Nicholas walked out the door, leaving it open in his wake. For a moment, Anthony caught a familiar glimpse of grey. The tone of Miss Hensworth's voice as she spoke to Nicholas, carried into his room. Then their voices receded as they made their way toward the front of the house. Why had she not entered if she had been standing outside his room the entire time? Was she still nervous around him?

Suddenly, he remembered his less than complimentary words to Nicholas. Had she heard him? If she had, it was no wonder she had not come in. It would seem he was destined to forever bumble things when it came to this particular lady.

Anthony heard Aunt Vie's effusive farewells at the front of the house all the way from his room, then the front door opened and shut, signaling Nicholas's departure. The sound was so final, it brought a gloom that settled into his bones. Looking to the window, he saw overcast skies and prayed the rain would hold off so Nicholas might have a safe, pleasant journey.

Quiet footsteps pulled his attention from the window. Miss Hensworth stood in the doorway. Her posture was straight and firm, but her eyes held a look of insecurity.

"I thought I might read to you today," she said, seemingly unsure of herself as she waited for his response.

Surprised by her sudden appearance, it took Anthony a moment to find his voice. "I would enjoy that very much," he answered with an encouraging smile, indicating the chair with his hand. It was not until she was halfway to the chair that he saw the the book she held in her hands. As she perched on the edge of the chair, the maid slipped in silently and sat in her usual spot, leaving the door wide op en.

"I noticed Mr. Fairchild reading you a Minerva Press novel," she said, glancing at the book in her hands. Then looking up at him, she said, "Have you perchance read *The Caledonian Bandit?*"

Anthony recognized the name but had not read the book. As she nervously traced the edges of the cover, he realized how vulnerable she was making herself by offering to take up Nicholas's place.

"I have not read it," he responded kindly. "Have you?"

"Yes, several times." Her cheeks grew a little rosier. "I happen to have an unhealthy affinity for gothic novels, but please do not tell my Aunt Marshall. She insists they are not good reading material for young ladies."

"Well, if we are discovered, I will take the blame. I shall tell her I am a tyrant, and I demanded you read it to me, as I find gothic novels dreadfully fascinating." This brought a small smile to Miss Hensworth's mouth, her light blue eyes dancing with merriment. "I truly have been wanting to read that particular title, Miss Hensworth. I have heard it is a delightful tale of good versus evil."

"And the triumph of love," she said softly. The color increased in her cheeks.

"Sounds like the kind of story I will enjoy. Read on, story master. My ears are all yours," Anthony said with a grin to which she promptly opened the book, and, with a small smile, began reading.

Emma had read each morning to Lord Hamdon for the past three days. He was an attentive listener and even complimented her on her reading voice, claiming she was a far better narrator than Mr. Fairchild. She seriously doubted that, but nonetheless, she was pleased with the praise.

Usually, the small amount of conversation they had only encompassed the book they were reading, but on the fourth morning after she finished her hour, Lord Hamdon surprised her with a bevy of questions.

"Have you had word from your father yet?"

"My father?" Emma asked, confused and a little nervous.

"Yes. You said he is away on business. I wondered if you had heard from him."

"Oh. I..." she hesitated. "I have not heard from him of late."

"He has not responded to your letters?" he said, confused. "Perhaps I presume too much, but I thought you would have written him about my presence here. If I were a father, I would be eager to return if my daughter was left to care for a stranger on her own."

"But I am not truly alone. Aunt Marshall is here, and my uncle Mr. Clayton is in and about almost every day."

"Yes, but are you not concerned that he, your father, I mean, has not written in the near three weeks I have been here?"

She was trapped. What could she say? In truth, she had not written her father. What good would it do? He could not receive her letters where he was.

Finally, she said, "He is quite far away, and letters take an incredible amount of time to reach him."

"Ah, I see," Lord Hamdon said. "Is he in America? Or perhaps India? I hear there are great investment opportunities there."

Neither, she thought, fidgeting with her hands. "To be honest, I am not exactly sure where he is at present. He was to journey quite a distance. Perhaps several places. I am unsure when a letter might catch up to him."

Her neck grew hot. She had been forced to give similar answers to Aunt Marshall when she had asked after her father's whereabouts shortly after her arrival. Emma wished she could be honest and just tell them both, but the fate of Engalworth Court relied upon her silence. It could not be too much longer now. Surely matters would resolve themselves soon.

"I am sorry, Miss Hensworth. I had not meant to bring up a difficult topic for you. It must be quite distressing to not have regular correspondence from your father."

Oh, if he only knew, she thought. The prick at the back of her eyes began again. Why was it that she could not control this terrible urge to cry? It was not as if she repressed the tears until they had no other outlet. She released them onto her pillow nightly, but they still cropped up at the most inconvenient times.

Taking a deep breath, she willed the moisture to stop, focusing instead on the end goal. Her brother had gone to war to fight for England, for heaven's sake. She could fight for the fate of the family.

Finally in control of herself, she said, "It is hard to have so little contact, but I am managing."

"And doing a marvelous job at that," Lord Hamdon said, a bit too cheerily.

Emma knew he had seen her watery eyes and was trying to lift her spirits. She never could hide the tears, but she could stop them from falling.

"If I recall, Fredrick said you had an older brother who was near our age, but I do not recall his name," he continued.

"Alan," she said quietly. "It is actually George Alan. He is named after my father, but we all called him by his middle name to limit the confusion. Not that I have heard my father's Christian name used much. My mother usually called him Glad. When I asked why, she said it was a reminder of how she felt about him." Emma knew she was prattling, but she hoped by adding more inconsequential information she might change the direction she sensed Lord Hamdon was going with his inquiry. It did not work, however.

"Ah, yes, now I remember. And where is Mr. Hensworth these days? Could he not come and be a comfort to you?"

This line she knew well but did not want to deliver. It was hard enough as it was to deceive people about her father, but Alan? Well, the truth was just much too hard to face. Squaring her shoulders, she looked at Lord Hamdon, irritation welling up within her at the position she was now in.

"My brother is dead, Lord Hamdon. If you had not noticed, I am in half-mourning. People do not dress so merely for fashion or entertainment, you know. It is meant to give warning to others to be careful and tender with the feelings of that person, as well as to show respect for those who have passed on. Now, if you will excuse me, I have other things I must attend to today." Without letting him respond, she swept out of the room, back straight, head held high and tears pricking the back of her eyes yet again.

And the Ice Fairy returns again, Anthony thought, as Miss Hensworth made a hasty exit. He had not meant to be unfeeling, he truly had not. He had noticed her grey dresses, some in lighter hues and some in darker, but there had been no mention up to this point for who, or even if Miss Hensworth might be in mourning. For all he knew, she preferred the color grey, especially that silvery thing she had worn the other day. She had certainly seemed to admire the gown while the rest of the room had been conversing. Besides, Aunt Vie was not wearing any mourning colors, nor was Mr. Clayton. Perhaps they had already finished their mourning period, though, as the relation was not as close.

How had Alan died? He was only a year or two older than Anthony if memory served. Fredrick had once said his cousin's age was just so that Alan fit comfortably between Alfred and himself. That would place the man around twenty-six or twenty-seven.

Thinking of Fredrick, Anthony wondered why his friend had not mentioned his cousin's death. Of course, letters were few and far between these days with Fredrick being in the middle of a war. The post had not been particularly reliable. The last letter he had received from Fredrick was at Christmas time, and even that one had been postmarked three months prior. That would have been almost eight months ago. Perhaps Fredrick had not received word of Mr. Hensworth's death at the time his letter had been sent.

That only brought more questions. Why would Miss Hensworth still be in mourning? Society really only dictated up to six months for a brother. Had he died after his father left? If not, why would her father leave while his daughter was still in deepest mourning?

Why would he leave on business at all, for that matter? He was a baron, after all. He could have a steward or solicitor conduct his business. Was the estate in some sort of trouble? Were they lacking so much for funds that the baron had to become personally involved in other investment ventures? If so, why did he not invest in ventures closer to home where he might look after his young, and far too pretty, daughter? Surely, the four or five percent's would give sufficient income if invested in London.

Perhaps, he had been listening to far too many gothic novels of late because he felt a great mystery surrounding Engalworth Court. In his limited observation, it did not appear the baron was lacking in funds as the house was well-appointed. There was, however, a very small number of servants, so perhaps the financia l difficulty had been a recent occurrence.

In the time Anthony had been at Engalworth Court, he had only seen the butler, the housekeeper, one footman who helped him with any personal needs, a maid who he knew came in from town only three days a week to clean, and Miss Hensworth's lady's maid. However, there must be others, he thought. His meals had been well-prepared and plentiful, so there must be a cook and scullery maid. And there must be someone to care for the horses. At least, he hoped so, as his mount was in the stables at this very moment. He could not see much of the grounds outside, but they would need someone to care for the gardens, as well.

Finally, he admitted to himself that he was probably more ignorant of the household by default of being stuck in this accursed bed. Dr. Jones had said he might start moving about in a week's time as the bones in his leg should have knit together enough by then to at least leave the bed every now and again. The hope of freedom made him antsier than ever.

He had questions he wanted answered, and it seemed Miss Hensworth would not answer them for him. He was unsure why she insisted on being so vague, but he was not fooled. She was hiding something. Whatever it was, he would ferret her out; he just had to be patient enough... and he needed to get out of this blasted bed.

One week, he repeated to himself. He could survive one more week.

Chapter Nine

Emma had overreacted, and she knew it. She had been backed into a corner with questions, and instead of staying calm, she had lashed out at Lord Hamdon, and for what? For simply asking about her brother. It was not his fault he did not know her entire family history—at least the history put forward for the public.

She knew she needed to apologize for her hasty behavior, but instead she avoided Lord Hamdon's room for the next two days, finding anything she could to occupy her time. She spent several hours with Mr. Lovell, the gardener, discussing what needed to be planted in both the flower and kitchen gardens and what of the land could be left as it was. Having only one gardener had taken a toll on the property, but it was important for the time being to keep the staff minimal.

Emma had also taken time to plan meals with Mrs. Gibbons, as well as look over the inventories. She had balanced the ledgers, written out refusals to the few invitations that trickled in during the week, and spent time practicing every accomplishment she had in her arsenal of talents, which admittedly was not as many as other young ladies boasted. She could embroider fairly well, play the pianoforte passably, sing with more passion than talent, and paint proficiently as long as it was only flowers.

By the third day, she really had run out of excuses, and Aunt Marshall was beginning to wear on her nerves with her constant reminders of a hostess's duties.

Taking particular care with her dress that morning, she broke her fast and then made her way to Lord Hamdon's room, Smith following silently behind.

Emma found the door ajar, just as it had been every day since Mr. Fairchild had left. Did Lord Hamdon like it that way, so he might view the comings and goings of the house? A small amount of compassion filled her heart. She would not like to be relegated to her bed for so long.

Taking a deep breath to calm her nerves, she entered the room, spine straight and as pleasant an expression on her face as she could muster. Lord Hamdon looked up from the book he held in his hands. Apparently he had given up on her ever coming back to finish *The Caledonian Bandit.* From the looks of it, he had made great progress. Smiling, he set the book down in his lap and welcomed her.

She was so surprised by his cordiality that she stumbled over her words of greeting before she asked if she might sit with him. He agreed most readily, and she took the seat at the side of his bed.

"Lord Hamdon," she began after taking her seat, "I owe you an apology. I should not have become cross with you when you inquired about my brother. There was no reason for me to act so rashly, and I am sorry."

"You are forgiven, Miss Hensworth, if there is anything to forgive. You were hurting, and I was not very thoughtful. I had noticed your mourning clothes but did not approach the subject with any amount of tact. I should have asked about your current state before hounding you about your family. For that, I am sorry."

Emma was astonished at his perception and compassion. Perhaps she had misjudged him. "No, there is nothing to forgive. You were only curious, and I should not have been so prickly."

"Then, are we to start again... again?" He asked with a charming quirk of his lips.

"I guess so," she said, a smile cracking her sober expression as she ducked her head and looked at her hands in her lap. She could feel a bit of warmth rise to her cheeks. Was she blushing? Oh, she hoped she was not blushing.

"I am sorry," Lord Hamdon said, fingering the book where it lay, "but I grew too impatient about our story and began reading it myself to find out how the lovers would face the three evils."

"It is no matter. I have read it several times before, so I am already aware of how it ends. Would you like me to continue reading to you, or would you rather finish it on your own?"

Lord Hamdon looked at the book in his lap. "If you do not mind, I think I would like to finish it on my own. As I said, I am impatient, and I will most likely pick it up the moment you leave the room."

"Very well," she said with a smile, not sure what she should do now that he no longer wanted her to read to him. Should she bid him a good day and leave so he might return to his book or perhaps try her hand at conversing? They had talked peaceably on several subjects before, but most had to do with the reading she was doing; nothing really of a personal nature.

She finally decided it would be rude to leave after just arriving. "Lord Hamdon, I am not acquainted with your family. Where do you hail from?"

"The main seat of the Earl of Lincolnhurst is in Nottinghamshire, near a small village named Maplebeck. However, I did not spend a great deal of time at my father's estate of Maplewood, as my mother prefers Blackwell Manor which is situated just outside of Loughborough in Leicestershire. That is where I spent most of my childhood. There, and at Eton, and afterward Oxford."

"I see, and do you prefer Blackwell Manor or Maplewood?"

"Blackwell Manor, of course. However, I also enjoy my father's hunting box in Yorkshire."

"Do you enjoy hunting, then?"

"As much as any other man."

Emma was not sure what else to say. She did not particularly want to discuss hunting since the idea of killing innocent animals was not one she liked to think on.

Changing the subject, she asked, "Do you have any siblings, Lord Hamdon?"

"I have one. A brother, Mr. Andrew Kempton, who is two years my junior."

"Interesting," she said more to herself than to Lord Hamdon.

"What do you find interesting?" Lord Hamdon said with an intrigued smile.

"That your parents named you both with A names. If I recall, Mr. Fairchild called you Anthony, did he not?"

"Yes, that is my name, Anthony James Kempton, but I have been Lord Hamdon from my cradle. Even my mother calls me Hamdon instead of my Christian name. I believe the only people who call me by my given name are Fredrick, Nicholas, and our friend Bradley."

"And Aunt Marshall," Emma reminded him.

"Ah, yes, as well as Aunt Jules, Nicholas's mother. Actually, all of Nicholas and Fredrick's families call me by my Christian name in private. So I suppose there are more than I recalled."

"You must be quite close with my cousin, Fredrick, and your other friends."

"Yes, we have been friends since our early days at Eton. We spent many a summer at each other's homes. Well, not as much at Bradley's, as his family is large, and their estate is much smaller than the other three."

"Odd that we never met. I spent a great deal of time at my Aunt Marshall's during the summer months, especially after my mother's death. Father found it easier not to have Alan and I underfoot that first summer."

"Perhaps we did, and you just do not recall. You are five years my junior. It is very likely we crossed paths, but with the age difference, we would not have interacted regularly enough."

"That sounds plausible. Whatever the case, it must be nice to have such good friends. Sometimes I wish I had gone away to school, so I might have made such friends." Why had she said that? She had not meant to divulge that she had no real friends. It exposed her in a way that set her to glancing about the room in order to keep from making eye contact with Lord Hamdon.

"You were educated at home then?" he asked, his tone not indicating that he had read through her words. When she looked back at his face, however, she could see pity there.

"I was. I had a governess until my seventeenth year at which time my father felt I was ready to leave the school room."

"If I recall, Fredrick said your mother passed away when you were young."

"Yes, when I was ten. Childbed fever."

"You have a younger sibling?"

"No, the babe was stillborn. Many of my mother's children were. Alan and I were the only live births."

"I am sorry to hear that. That must have been difficult."

"I am sure it was, but as a child, one does not understand the troubles and pains of our parents. It is only as we age that we gain compassion for all they have been through."

A thoughtful expression covered Lord Hamdon's face as he looked across the room to the open door. Finally, he said, "That is quite a deep thought, Miss Hensworth. I must admit I have not really thought upon the troubles of my own parents."

"Nor had I, until seven months ago when the letter came informing us of my brother's fate. I watched my father's heart break in a matter of minutes. As much as I was hurting, I knew he was hurting more. He and my brother, well… they did not get on together very well. My father was so angry when he found my brother had gone off and joined the Royal Army. I do not believe he answered the first three letters Alan sent home."

"It must have been crushing to lose him with so many things left unsaid."

"I believe so; however, they did correspond with some regularity after my father's initial hurt and anger had worn off. Even with the intervening time, I believe my father still felt bad for the bit of lingering resentment he expressed both to me and to Alan. He once said he wished he had never lost a single second courting his anger and instead had loved Alan for who he was."

"I see." Several emotions played across his face. Emma was unsure what had elicited such a varied reaction. She could not tell exactly what he was feeling, but her instincts told her Lord Hamdon did not have much experience with fatherly love.

"That must have been hard." he finally said. "Quite a blow to a man. And there is no other heir?"

"There is not," she said, hanging her head. If she had only been a boy. Truthfully, she did not wish it so. She enjoyed being a woman, but for her father's sake, she would have done anything to ease his burden at that time. "The estate and title are entailed to my father's cousin, Mr. Weazelton."

"Mr. Weazelton! A foreboding name if I have ever heard one."

"Yes, and he is just as his name sounds." She grimaced. "I hate to talk ill of my own family, but the man is as slimy as they come. He is actually my third cousin, so the relation is not very close. Close enough, however, that he has made a point of going about in Society claiming the connection."

"You seem to have a pointed dislike of the fellow."

"Yes, well, he has also tried to *weasel* his way into Engalworth several times by suggesting we marry." Why had she voiced such personal information? Oh, well, in for a penny, in for a pound. "The first time was not one month after my father received word of my brother's passing." Her skin crawled at the recollection. Mr. Weazelton was no gentleman. She would rather die than marry him, but he still continued to push her even after receiving three refusals, one in person and two by post.

If she could only hold through, he would not obtain Engalworth either, at least if her father's admission was true. He had been fevered at the time, but she had to believe him. She had no other hope. Emma needed to hang onto those words for all she was worth because if they were not true, she feared her soul would break, and life would lose the last shreds of light that kept her living each day.

Please be true, her heart begged over and over pulling her mind away from the conversation at hand. Her eyes drifted to the intricately carved bureau as the refrain repeated in her head and her thoughts were pulled back to the past.

Chapter Ten

What an uncouth thing to do, Anthony thought. How could any man think to propose marriage while someone was still in deepest mourning? Especially a marriage of convenience which, if he was reading Miss Hensworth's tone correctly, was exactly the type of proposal she had received.

Watching Miss Hensworth, he pitied the man that caused such a tiny woman to look so fearsome. The expression on her face when she spoke of her cousin was angry and determined. He had no doubt she would fight to a bloody end rather than accept her cousin's proposals.

The sudden shift in her expression startled him. One moment she looked ready to go to war, and then suddenly she looked as if she had lost all hope. The sight pricked his heart, causing a surprising wave of compassion for her.

Perhaps her grief was too raw for this subject. He needed to change the topic, but he did not want the same result as several days previous when she had stormed out of the room. What could he ask the woman that would not poke at the tender parts of her heart?

"I am sure you are grateful to still have your father to protect you, so Mr. Weazelton cannot press his suit," he said, hoping to provide comfort in her time of distress.

To his dismay, her hopeless expression turned immediately to tears. What had he been thinking, bringing up her father? The man was not actually in residence to protect her. It seemed he was destined to always make a mull of things with her.

As the first tear trickled down her face, he frantically looked about him for a handkerchief, which of course he did not have to offer to her. Not knowing what else to do, he leaned to the side and put his hand upon hers where it rested on the arm of the chair. Her eyes shot to his, surprise evident in their depths, then slowly she turned her hand over and clasped his.

More tears came, but she wept so silently that Anthony would not have known she was crying if he had not been looking directly at her. He gently squeezed her hand for several minutes until she released his and reached inside a hidden pocket, where she removed a linen square to dab at her face.

Anthony was physically relieved, as the tilted position he maintained to hold her hand had become quite uncomfortable. But he would have continued on as long as his strength allowed if only to provide a small amount of comfort.

"I do apologize, Miss Hensworth. I did not think before I spoke. It must be quite distressing to have your father gone for so long."

"You have no idea," she muttered with a mirthless laugh.

He found himself begrudgingly impressed. She had not made a huge scene with her grief as his mother might, nor had she reprimanded him for his words. And the fact that she could laugh at all after so much heartache? Well, it showed that while she was small, she was made of sterner stuff than most ladies.

"I had not meant to cry, Lord Hamdon. I try not to burden others with my problems."

"It is no burden, Miss Hensworth, at least not on me. I think, however, you have been carrying this burden by yourself for far too long. As inept as I am, I do know how to listen if you would care to talk about it."

The myriad of expressions that crossed her face at his offer spoke volumes. There was far more to Miss Hensworth's story than she probably wanted to tell by the way her face flitted from surprise, to worry, to relief, back to worry, and finally resolution.

"I thank you, Lord Hamdon," she said tentatively. "I would like to... to discuss my past, but not at present. I do not feel up to revisiting it anymore today."

"I understand," he said, hoping she really meant to confide in him. "Perhaps a lighter topic. What are some of your favorite pastimes?"

The smile she graced him with did strange things to his insides, the sensation both pleasant and alarming. As she began sharing her various hobbies and accomplishments, he found himself wrapped up in the way her smile changed her face, bringing life and animation to every aspect of her conversation. Why could he not seem to look away?

"I do also like to plan the gardens each year," she was saying. "Mr. Lovell has been so patient with me as I have pestered him to teach me through the years. When I was little, I used to follow him about every day asking what this plant or that was."

"Mr. Lovell is your head gardener?"

"Yes. He has been at Engalworth Court since long before I was even born. He is getting along in years, but is so very good at his work that my father could not possibly think of letting him go."

"How many under gardeners does he have?"

Her face fell. "None at present. I... More will be hired on when my father... Well, when things are more settled here at Engalworth."

Odd, Anthony thought. Perhaps they really were in dire straits. He did not know much about Lord Gladsby, but Fredrick had never let on that his uncle was a gambler or a spendthrift. How else could an estate get in such distress?

"I am sorry Engalworth has fallen on such hard times."

"As am I," Miss Hensworth said, her countenance solemn. But just as sudden as her expression fell, it lifted. "I have told you some of my hobbies; now you must tell me some of yours."

"Well, I have already told you I enjoy hunting," he said. "Honestly, I spend a great deal of time in London during the season. I go to balls, card parties, the theater, things like that. I also like seeing the new exhibits on display at the *British Museum* each year."

"I think that was the only part of my season I liked. That, and the pleasure gardens."

"You have taken a London season?"

"Yes, year before last. The spring I turned eighteen."

"Perhaps we attended some of the same gatherings?"

"Perhaps, but my father was so busy with Parliament that we attended very few functions. My Aunt Clara having already passed, I had no female companionship, besides Smith, of course."

"What of your Aunt Vie?"

"First, she has never permitted me to call her anything but Aunt Marshall," Miss Hensworth said tersely, "and second, as much as she likes people, she does not care for London's dirty air. She did, however, come for a month in May, but that was all she would stay for, so that was when most of my season began and subsequently ended."

"I get the impression there is some tension between you and your aunt," he said with a smirk.

"As thick as plum pudding." she said flatly, but then smiled.

Again, Anthony was caught off guard by her show of spunk. It made him chuckle.

"Please do not misunderstand me, Lord Hamdon. I do love my aunt, but she tends to favor boys over girls. All my life she has coddled and cooed over every one of the male species, while I have been constantly reprimanded about ladylike decorum. I do not believe she is that way with all women. I remember plenty of times she got on well with my mother and aunt. As her niece, however, she has always felt overbearing."

He had not seen many interactions between the women, as they usually visited him separately, so he could not give any insight. "Aunt Vie can be a bit bossy at times," he offered hesitantly.

"Yes, but it seems so loving when directed at you or Mr. Fairchild, or even Fredrick and Alfred. With me, well, I can never do anything to please her." She said this so dejectedly, Anthony could not help but feel sorry for her.

"I am sorry, Lord Hamdon. I have taken our pleasant conversation down another dark hole. Perhaps I am not the best of company today."

"I have enjoyed your company immensely, Miss Hensworth."

"Perhaps because it is the only company you have," she said with another twist of her lips.

"Perhaps," he said, returning the smirk, "but I have learned so much in the time we have been chatting. I must admit I think I like it more than I even like this book." He picked up the book that still lay in his lap.

"Better than a gothic novel?" she asked. Her eyebrow raised comically and a cheeky smirk appeared upon her lips.

"Yes, well, we have covered a dastardly cousin, the death of a loved one, the tenuous state of an estate, and a questionable family relationship."

"I see." She grinned. "My life *is* sounding quite gothic. All that is left to add is a love story and a murder, and I believe we will have covered all the requirements for a novel."

"I believe you are right," he said. "However, I do hope I am not the one who is murdered. I do have other things I would like to do in my life."

"You would rather be part of the love story, then?" she quipped. Suddenly her face went red. Ducking her head, she inspected her gloved hands. He had a strong urge to laugh, but he did not want to embarrass her further.

Miss Hensworth cleared her throat and rose. "I believe I should be going."

"Will you be back tomorrow?" Anthony could not help asking. He actually wanted to see her again—was excited for it, if he was being honest with himself. What a change, he thought.

"If you would like. Would the same time be acceptable?" Her eyes flitted to his, then to her maid seated in the chair by the door.

"I am sure I can squeeze you into my busy schedule," he teased.

Miss Hensworth actually laughed. The sound warmed Anthony from the inside.

"I suppose that was a ridiculous question," she said. "Would you like me to bring you another novel? I believe you will finish that one before I return tomorrow."

"I would like that very much, Miss Hensworth. Several, if you have them. As loath as I am to admit it, while I awaited your return, I actually finished several of the dry, educational books Nicholas left me before turning back to this one."

"Sounds painful," she said, an amused smile curling the edge of her lips.

"More than you know," Anthony replied, again surprised by her delightful sarcasm.

The smile on her face grew. "Well, I will leave you to read a book you will actually enjoy, then. Good day." After a quick bob, she left the room.

Anthony watched her lithe form walk through the doorway, her light gray skirts swishing around her. Somehow, the young fragile girl he had met several days ago had blossomed into a strong young woman. How had that happened? It was not as if she had grown in any way. No, he concluded. But perhaps by getting to know her better he could see her more clearly, and he liked what he saw.

Chapter Eleven

Emma walked among the yellow, purple and red tulips berating herself as her own words echoed in her mind. *You would rather be part of the love story, then?* Why had she said such a thing? It was tantamount to throwing herself at his feet. She did not know when she had ever been more embarrassed.

Bending down, she let her finger trail lightly along the top of a red tulip. Such tender things, tulips. They did not make for good flower arrangements as they wilted far too quickly once cut, the environment inside being far too warm for them. Leave them in the cool of the garden, though, and they shared their beauty and vibrancy for a couple of weeks.

Emma could relate. Before Lord Hamdon came, she was a stalwart bloom carrying her burden on her own out in the cold, but his warmth and compassion had caused her to wilt. She could not remember the last time she had cried in front of anyone besides her maid and Mr. Clayton. Perhaps when they had received word of Alan. She had cried in front of her father a time or two then.

If Lord Hamdon had not been so kind, it would not have muddled her brain so much, and she would have thought more before she spoke. What must he think of her?

Emma stood, shaking out her skirts to loosen any grass that might have attached itself to her person. Looking up, she thought she saw a movement in the grove of trees that stood a short distance from the stables. Staring for a moment at the grove, grateful to see the number of leaves growing thicker by the day, she thought of all the times she and Alan had played among them. She missed those childhood games.

Sometimes they were joined by their Marshall cousins, sometimes by neighborhood boys, but Alan always insisted she be allowed to tag along. He was a good brother, Emma thought. Not many boys would let their sister seven years their junior romp in the woods with them, but Alan had never denied her admittance to his games.

Emma began walking again looking toward the gardens. Perhaps those childhood frolics had instilled in her the ardor she felt for all things green. She adored trees, bushes, and plants of every variety. The only plant she had found she did not care for was cacti. She had viewed one once in London when visiting one of her father's acquaintances. Mrs. Barlow had thought it was the greatest addition to her conservatory. Emma had thought it an eyesore. It was tall and prickly and not at all pleasing.

That was how she had viewed Lord Hamdon when he first came—tall and very prickly. She smiled to herself at the image that came to her mind of Lord Hamdon covered in spines. However, she could not consider him so repulsive now. He had been pleasant on multiple occasions, and especially accommodating today.

Lord Hamdon could have been put out with her when the first tear slid silently down her face. He could have called her a veritable watering pot with all the tears that had flowed afterward, but he had said nothing. Just laid a reassuring hand upon hers and waited for her distress to pass. It had been partially out of impulse and partially out of desperation that she had turned her hand to clasp his. She was drowning in that moment, and he was her lifeline. She had carried this burden for over four months, and it was taking a toll on her. It had been nice to have someone help her carry it even if he did not know it.

Another movement in the trees drew her attention. Something brown moved behind a tree trunk. She smiled to herself. Deer often made their homes among the bushes that covered the ground among the grove. More than once, she had happened upon a new fawn hidden in a thicket. It was that time of year that mama deer would scout out the best place to hide their babes. Perhaps this one was doing just that.

She began moving again, approaching the spot in the gardens that held her mother's tea roses. They were not yet in bloom having just sprouted leaves, but Emma could not wait to see the small pink buds that would soon dot the bushes.

Idly, she wondered if Lord Hamdon would be up and about by time the roses were in bloom. Did he like the outdoors? He seemed truly interested when she talked of their gardens, but perhaps he was just so desperate for something to fill his time that any subject would do. Any subject, that is, except a love story, she thought with embarrassment.

And now she had made a full circle back to the original topic that had sent her careening into the gardens. She let out a long, slow breath and lifted her eyes to the sky. Miraculously, it was clear this morning after several days of rain. Only a few puffy white clouds floated in the sky. As Emma scanned each formation, she wondered if somewhere in the recesses of her mind she had started to develop feelings for Lord Hamdon. Why else would she ask him if he wanted to be part of a her love story? It was a rather sudden change of heart if that were the case, but then again, she had thought him handsome even before she had allowed him to be a decent person.

Her gaze strayed to the grove. Odd, she could have sworn that tree trunk was thicker a moment ago. Perhaps the light was playing tricks on her because one side of the trunk had been decidedly lighter, like the sun was shining through the branches and casting a glow upon the right side.

A breeze picked up, rustling her skirts, and she decided to make her way back to the house. She had been so desperate for air that she had rushed out of the house without a pelisse or bonnet. Now, however, the cool wind was a bit much for the exposed skin on her neck and arms. Furthermore, her hair would be quite a mess by time she returned indoors.

Thankfully, she at least had her gloves on. They were an accessory she could not go without. Engalworth got very chilly at times, and her fingertips were the first thing to grow cold.

Picking up her pace, she noticed Mr. Ladd and his boy Owen cleaning out the stables. The sight of them caused her to change course. It had been almost a week since she had paid a visit to her mare, Buttercup, and she had a sudden urge to take a ride about the grounds. Lifting her hand in greeting as she approached the stable, she noticed Lord Hamdon's mount tethered outside. Apparently, it was his stall the pair were cleaning.

"Good mornin', Miss Emma," Owen called cheerily.

"Good morning, Owen. You look to be hard at work."

"Aye, miss. My dah has me slavin' away," he said with a smile.

"Well, I do believe it is making you quite strong. I could not lift the load you have on that pitchfork." The boy looked at the end of his fork and grinned. He was missing two teeth on the side of his mouth. "It looks as if you have lost a few more baby teeth, and those are the ones that mean you're almost full grown."

"I'm hopin' to be. I'll be twelve on me next birthday."

Mr. Ladd came out of the stable with another wheelbarrow full. "I see ya found a bonny lass to keep ye from your work, Owen."

Emma smiled at Mr. Ladd's hidden compliment. He had always been especially kind to her ever since her father hired him ten years ago.

"Dah, I've been workin' the whole time we been gabbin'."

"Course ye have, lad," he said with a long-suffering smile. Turning to her, he said, "How are you this fine mornin', Miss Emma?"

"I am well. I was hoping you might saddle Buttercup for me. I would like to go for a ride." Mr. Ladd gave a telling glace at her attire. "I still need to don my riding habit, so if you could have her ready when I return, I would appreciate it."

"Yes, Miss. I can do that."

"I could do it, Dah, if ye like."

"So ye can get outta cleanin' that stall? I think not."

Owen's head sagged a bit, and Emma smiled. "Just remember, Owen, hard work makes a boy tall and strong." This seemed to perk the lad up, and he showed her just how strong he was by turning another large pitchfork full of straw and droppings. Mr. Lovell would come by later for this particular pile as he claimed the mixture of straw and manure was good for the vegetable garden.

Turning back to her after dumping his load, Mr. Ladd asked, "Will a quarter hour do?"

"Yes, that will be sufficient," she said, promising to return at the appointed time.

After she had dawned her dark gray riding habit, Emma made her way back to the stables where she found her palomino mare tethered near the mounting block. Mr. Ladd came to assist her, then handed her the reins.

"Your usual ride?"

"Yes. I will not need an escort; I shall stay within view of the stables."

He nodded and walked away as she made her way to the small grassy area between the stables and the grove. Like most everything else she did, she was not a true proficient, and riding was no different. Buttercup was just the right mixture of calm and spirited to provide an enjoyable ride that was neither too sedate nor too arduous.

Emma usually made several loops around the field at various speeds so that both she and Buttercup could enjoy a fair amount of exercise before returning to their leisurely lives. Today, however, she decided after a few circles about the green that she wanted to explore along the edge of the grove. Perhaps she would catch sight of the deer she was sure she had spied earlier. If she were truly lucky, she might even get a glimpse of a fawn.

Walking Buttercup to where the tree line started, she began searching the undergrowth. The horse wandered along under the shade of the trees for several minutes before she stopped, perked up her ears, and whinnied. Emma was surprised when an answering whinny came from somewhere deep in the grove.

A cold lick of fear raced down her back. No one was supposed to be in the grove. It was Engalworth property, and there were no tenants on the other side of it for at least a mile. There was, however, a lesser-traveled road that bordered the other side of the grove. Perhaps someone happened to be passing by.

Either way, Emma decided she no longer wanted to look for deer among the bushes. It was chilly anyhow, especially in the shade, and she would rather be out in the sunlight. Turning Buttercup back toward the green, she tapped her side with the crop indicating she wanted to trot, but just as Buttercup picked up her pace, a movement to the left caught her eye. She glanced over quickly and saw a flash of brown that looked strangely like a man's jacket before it disappeared behind a bush.

The sight unnerved her, and Emma decided a gallop to the stables suited her much better than a mere trot. Leaning forward, she gave Buttercup her head, and with a slight tap of the crop, they were off toward the safety of the stables and people.

Chapter Twelve

Emma sat in her room preparing for her morning visit to Lord Hamdon. The daily routine had become one of her favorite times of the day. Although she wore the same color day in and day out, lately she found she was gravitating to the lighter grays in her wardrobe. Perhaps in a small way, Lord Hamdon's company was adding a bit of light back into her dreary existence. She had not had so many delightful conversations since before Alan went away to war.

An overwhelming desire to have her brother back rushed over her, the feeling almost tangible in its powerful nature. If only Alan had not been so adamant about running off to play soldier, she thought with frustration and hurt, but he always had been impetuous and headstrong. He loved a good lark, and in truth, so did Emma. As children, she had thought it great fun to follow her brother around as a conspirator in all his misdeeds. Somewhere along the line, however, she had tired of his troublemaking.

"You all right, Miss Emma?" Smith asked, concern in her expression as she styled Emma's golden curls for the day. Emma studied herself in the mirror. She had not noticed until now how poorly she looked in grey. Her golden hair and clear blue eyes were muted by the drab color.

"I was thinking about Alan," she said, pinching her cheeks to add a bit of color into her face.

"I see," Smith said, her features becoming as somber as her mistress. Emma was not sure if Smith truly understood, having been hired after Alan left, but she was grateful for the compassion she conveyed by trying to match her mood.

"Smith, has there been any more progress in my father's study?"

"Progress, yes, but if you're wantin' to know if we found anything, then no. Mrs. Gibbons and I are almost done leafing through the books on the west wall. That leaves only the south, and we'll have gone through all of 'em."

Goodness, how could one piece of paper be so hard to find? Placing the last pin, the maid stepped back and observed her own work. "What do you think?"

"Excellent, Smith. Thank you." Standing from her seat, Emma reached for her white wool shawl. While the days were warming, the mornings were still quite chilly, especially in the larger rooms of the house.

"Smith," she continued, thinking it was time to speak with her steward again, "would you please inform Mr. Haze I would like to meet with him to go over the needs of the estate?"

Smith, who had been busily cleaning up the brushes and extra pins, stopped what she was doing and looked up in confusion. "Have you not heard, Miss Emma? Mr. Haze was called away on a family emergency last night. I heard him tellin' Mrs. Marshall he wouldn't be back for at least a fortnight. "

He told Aunt Marshall? Frustration pounded in Emma's chest. It was bad enough the woman had waltzed in and taken control over every other aspect of her home, but that the steward would inform her aunt instead of her rankled. It was Emma, after all, who he had been instructed to answer to since her father's departure.

"I'm sorry, Miss Emma. If I'd have known he hadn't informed you first—"

"It is no matter," she interrupted impatiently. This was the third such *family emergency* Mr. Haze had taken since her father's departure. She was beginning to think there was no other emergency other than the man wanting to take a holiday here and there. "Smith, were wages met before he left?"

"Yes, miss. We were paid last Friday."

Well, at least he had done that much. Emma was frustrated all the same. Apparently, the steward thought he did not need to adhere to her father's wishes now that his lordship had been gone so long. Father had been so specific. Mr. Haze was to consult her in *all* estate matters until further notice. She knew this irked the middle-aged man. More than once she had overheard him grumble to himself about having to answer to a "little girl."

Not for the first time, she wished for the presence of their previous steward, Mr. Cline, who had been hired away from them last spring. Mr. Haze was not nearly as reliable as Mr. Cline. The man continuously came in late and left early. Of course, with the smaller staff, she supposed Mr. Haze had much less to do in the house than Mr. Cline.

She had hoped his absence from the house meant he was hard at work assisting the tenants, but her few inquiries had proved otherwise. Waking late and going home early to drink away his wages in the village, the man was simply lazy.

Bidding Smith a good day, she made her way to the breakfast room, frustration building as she thought on Mr. Haze. Through the grid of windows that spanned nearly two stories of the house and across the expanse of lawn, Emma could see the early morning sunlight glinting in the green trees. Beyond the trees there was a road, but due to the thickness of the grove that ran along the front and side of the house she could not make it out.

It had been five days since she had seen the man in brown darting through those woods, and she still felt ridiculous at how much of a fright it had caused her. When she had returned to the stables and stammered out her findings to Mr. Ladd, he insisted she had just stumbled upon a poacher. He assured her he would inform Mr. Haze. What good that would do them all, she was not sure. Yet Mr. Ladd insisted there really was not much to worry over since most poachers were just poor folk looking for a meal, not meaning to cause any trouble.

While his answer had been reassuring five days ago, it no longer held comfort. Emma had seen glimpses of the man twice more. At least she assumed it was the same man, for the brown of the coat was identical. Both times, Mr. Ladd had ridden out looking for the trespasser. Both times, he had come up with nothing.

If Emma had believed in specters, she would have sworn the man in brown was one. The way he seemed to float about the woods, appearing only where she could see him made the hair on the back of her neck stand up just thinking about it.

Entering the breakfast room, she was pleased to find it empty. Thanks to Aunt Marshall's tendency to lounge in bed in the morning, Emma could usually breakfast, make a quick check over the ledgers, and visit with Lord Hamdon before seeing her aunt for the first time in a day. Today, it would seem, would be no different.

Gibbons entered carrying a silver tray with the post. Offering it to her, she took the stack and began leafing through the letters.

"Thank you, Gibbons. Perchance, did Mr. Haze leave word for me before his departure?"

"No, miss." Emma looked up to see the butler's face full of disapproval. She felt much the same.

"I see. Well, if word does come, please let me know right away."

"Yes, miss. Is that all?"

"Yes, thank you, Gibbons."

Focusing back on her letters, Emma noticed there was one from an acquaintance in London. Probably to boast over her latest doings in the season. Miss Williams was always crowing over her like that. It was a wonder that anyone from her season still kept up correspondence with her. She accepted the association for what it was. Miss Williams only maintained contact in order to brag about her connections and social standing.

In addition to Miss Williams' letter, there were three for her father, a few invitations from neighbors, and one from a distant cousin on her mother's side. Disappointed that she had not received the letter she hoped for, she tossed all the other letters onto the table, except the one from Mrs. Pierre DuPone.

Opening the letter, she scanned the contents. What a dear Mrs. DuPone was to send her such a charmingly long letter. It had been a while since she had heard from her mother's cousin. Emma spent the next quarter hour happily going over the contents, wishing not for the first time that her mother's family had stayed intact.

Unfortunately, when they had all fled France during the revolution, families had been separated, required to take whatever escape they could. Emma's mother's family, the Beauchenes, had found refuge in England thanks to her mother's marriage to her father three years prior. The DuPone family, however, had been forced to flee all the way to the Americas. Unfortunately, Emma's uncle, her mother's younger brother, had been visiting the DuPones at the time of their flight and was forced to flee with them.

It had taken over a year for the families to locate one another, and by that point her uncle Jean Beauchene had met and married an American, and was living happily in the States. The DuPones as well had found success in the states, and so had decided to stay.

Mrs. DuPone relayed all the latest happenings with her American cousins in such a way that Emma felt herself carried away from her troubles. The stories and information were a balm to her lonely soul. While she would likely never meet these cousins in person, it was nice to know she was not the only remaining member of her mother's family.

If only Mama's oldest brother had not been as impetuous as Alan and stayed safely in England, she might have more family. After the revolution, he had made his way back to France hoping to recover his family's property only to be killed in the process.

Emma had been small when it happened, four, maybe five. She could not really recall, but she did remember Grand-mere's tears when they received word of Uncle Pierre's death. Grand-mere and Grand-père had lived only a few years after that.

Finishing the letter, she set it to the side of her plate and picked up her morning chocolate, lost in memories of her life before Grand-père's death. Those had been happy times, the six of them at Engalworth Court. The memories were few, but the ones she had made her smile.

Someone cleared their throat, and Emma looked up in alarm. Mr. Clayton stood just inside the breakfast room door, a look of amusement on his wrinkled face. She rose quickly from her seat to welcome him. It had been three days since his last visit. How had she not noticed his absence? He was always in and about at varying times of the day checking in on her, but perhaps with Aunt Marshall here, he did not feel his presence was needed as much.

"Mr. Clayton, I did not see you there." She rushed to embrace him.

"That was clearly evident by the far-off expression on your face. Tell me. Where were you visiting in your mind? India? Or China, perhaps?"

"France," she said smiling.

"France? Why ever would you want to be wandering that poor, troubled country?" he asked, the twinkle in his eye letting her know he was teasing her.

"I received a letter from Mrs. DuPone today," she said, retaking her seat as Mr. Clayton filled a plate from the sideboard.

"And what are the happenings in America?"

"She informed me my cousin Suzette is to be married to a wealthy merchant. He trades in cotton and will be able to support her quite well. Uncle Jean is extremely proud. This is the last of his three daughters to marry, you know."

"Suzette, you say. Is she not too young for marriage?" he asked, taking a seat next to hers.

"She is sixteen, Uncle. Only a year younger than Mama was when she married Father."

"I suppose that is old enough," he said contemplatively, "but I am exceedingly glad you were not stolen away from us at such a tender age. I do not think my poor old heart could have handled it." He patted Emma's hand. She looked at his weathered skin and wondered when her uncle had grown so old. He had never seemed so aged before now. Perhaps the last few months were taking a toll on him as well.

As a vicar, it must be inordinately hard to go against everything he stood for in order to aid her. Emma wished somehow to lift his burden, but until word came from London, they would need to continue their waiting game.

Chapter Thirteen

Anthony sat awaiting his visit from Miss Hensworth. He had spent the morning penning letters to Nicholas, Bradley, and his mother. The first two letters were to inform his friends of the progression he was making, and to ask after their health and well-being. For the most part, composing those two letters had been a pleasant way to while away the morning.

The latter, however, had taken all his restraint and effort to write civilly. It was the third he had written to Blackwell Manor requesting his man be sent to Engalworth, and, as of yet, his valet still had not arrived. Anthony could not understand what was keeping him. A trunk of his things had arrived weeks ago, but no valet. His mother had insisted twice that she planned to send him on his way, but his journey had been delayed. No reasoning why, just delayed.

Anthony had grown suspicious. It would not be the first time his mother had *detained* a valet. It really was his own fault, he thought. He needed to stop hiring such well-formed valets. Perhaps if he had hired an elderly man with a balding pate, his mother would cease to dally with his help. Truthfully, it disgusted him. She was more than twice Brown's age.

He should not have sent him on ahead in the carriage. It was unfair to have placed him in such a predicament. Anthony was well aware of the coercion his mother used to break his last two valets. He should have been more careful.

Now he would need to find a safer place of employment for Brown, as well. Unfortunate, really. Brown had been far more adept at his job than Anthony's previous valets.

After dismissing Murphy and Adams, he had made sure they were gainfully employed. He could have cast them out without references like many others would have done, but it was not their fault his mother was an indecent woman who used every method, whether money, threat, or blackmail, to get what she wanted.

Heaven forbid he should ever marry a woman as despicable as his own mother. He would rather die a bachelor than court a woman of her ilk.

Words Miss Hensworth said days earlier nagged at his brain. Something about not knowing one's parents' struggles. How had his mother obtained a penchant for debauchery? Was it a weakness she had always had, or had she acquired it with time? It was quite possible she had embraced it after years spent married to his father.

It was no secret his father had entertained mistresses long before marrying his mother. Unlike his mother, however, his father kept his dalliances more discreet, and to his knowledge, had never entertained one of the servants.

At the last minute, Anthony decided to pen another letter to his valet. Reaching for the writing desk, he pulled a crisp piece of paper from within. He would address it to the butler at Blackwell, this time in hopes Brown would actually receive his message. There could be no other reason his valet had not responded.

Hearing a throat clear, he looked up from his letter. Mr. Clayton stood in the doorway, Miss Hensworth on his arm. A smile lit the vicar's face when their eyes met, and he gave a brief bow.

"I hope you do not mind," Mr. Clayton said. "I thought I might accompany my niece this morning to inquire after your health. I have not been up in quite some time, and I thought I would remedy my neglect with a visit."

"I do not mind at all, Mr. Clayton. I am happy to have more company. As you can see, I am mending well. I no longer require large amounts of willow bark tea, and the doctor feels I might be ready to be up and into a bath chair near the end of this week."

"That is good news. I see you have been hard at work this morning," Mr. Clayton said, gesturing to the letter. "Perhaps this is not a good time?"

"No, no. Please, come in. I can finish this later," he said, setting the finished letters inside the box, leaving the still wet sheet of paper on top. He then placed the whole of it on the small table by his bed. "I have been informing my friends of my progress." No need bringing up the topic of the other, less savory letters.

Miss Hensworth took up her usual seat next to his bed while Mr. Clayton moved one of the wooden chairs closer.

"How are you fairing, Lord Hamdon? It must be difficult being sequestered in this room all day."

"I am bearing it the best I can. If it were not for Aunt Vie's chatty visits and Miss Hensworth's readings, I believe I might die of sheer boredom. But they have saved me from a certain death, and for that, I am most grateful."

The left side of Mr. Clayton's mouth quirked with amusement and he cast an interested glance in the direction of his niece. "Emma does have a very nice reading voice; I must admit to enjoying it myself. Tell me, Emma, what has been your book of choice to keep our dear invalid entertained?"

Something mischievous entered Mr. Clayton's expression, daring Miss Hensworth to answer. A touch of crimson graced her cheeks as she cast a playful glare back at the vicar.

"Why, the Bible, of course, Uncle."

A short burst of laughter from Mr. Clayton filled the room. Pointing a finger at his niece, the smirk on his face coloring his words, he said, "You little minx. You and I both know that is not true. It is bound to be one of those gothics you are so fond of."

Miss Hensworth grinned unrepentantly. Anthony enjoyed watching her interact with her uncle. She seemed to relax in his presence and enter more fully into conversations than was her usual when others of the household were around.

After a quarter hour discussing pleasantries, Mr. Clayton rose. "I must be on my way. I have parishioners to visit today, and depending upon how long they choose to talk, that may take up the whole of the daylight hours," he said with twinkle in his eye.

Anthony had never met such a cheery vicar. Most he found were too serious, always having a dour expression. If more vicars kept this man's disposition, perhaps more people in England would be inclined to attend church.

When Miss Hensworth left the room with her uncle, he worried that would be the entirety of her visit for the day. He knew he should be grateful for any visit at all, but he felt oddly bereft at the short conversation. He had hoped for just a little more of her cheer and sunshine.

When she appeared again at his door ten minutes later, her maid at her side, he could not suppress his grin of delight.

After taking up her seat again, she asked if he would like her to post his mail. The delicacies of his last two letters made him hesitate. It was not as if she would open the missives and read his words. He was being ridiculous. She only meant to help.

"Yes, thank you. I am not quite finished with this last, but these may be sent out." He removed the letters from the writing desk and handed them over to her. "By chance, do you know if any post has arrived for me of late?"

"I did not see any this morning when Gibbons brought me my own. Perhaps he means to bring it to you himself or send it with Thatcher when he comes to help you."

"You received letters this morning? Any word from your father?"

Miss Hensworth gave an almost imperceptible flinch at his question, but she recovered well, pasting on a forced cheery smile. "I did not, but I did receive a letter from my cousin in America."

"You have a cousin in America?"

"Yes, several actually. My mother's cousin, as well as my mother's younger brother and his family. They relocated when France's monarchy fell."

"Your mother was French?"

"*Oui,*" she said with a smile.

"I never did apply myself to my French lessons very well, but I do recall that word means *yes.*"

"*Je ne parle pas très bien moi-même, mais je me souviens un petit peu de ma jeunesse.*"

Anthony stared at her for a moment, astounded at how beautiful the French language sounded trickling off her tongue. Even though he did not speak the language fluently, he had heard enough good French, as well as bad, to know her accent was far better than most Englishmen could master.

"The only words I believe I understood were *I, good,* and *young,*" he said with a sheepish grin. "How do you speak so smoothly?"

"I do not," she said with surprise. "I have rarely spoken the language since I was ten. After my mother passed away, there were not many to converse openly with."

"It sounded fine to me. What exactly did you say?"

"What I just conveyed," she said with a grin, "that I do not speak well myself, but I remember some from when I was young."

Anthony chuckled at himself. Years of French masters, and he could not even decipher one sentence. "Does your brother speak as well as you?"

"Better. He is seven years my senior and had much more practice," she said, looking at him with a bit of excitement. "When we were little, we used to talk to each other in French whenever we did not want any of the other children to know what we were saying. It was fun to see them get all confused and frustrated, especially the girls."

Anthony chuckled. "I hope that is not why they chose not to form friendships with you."

"I was not talking of the girls my age." A bewitching twinkle gleamed in her eye. "I was talking of all the girls who liked my brother. He is exceedingly handsome, you know. He has had some girl or another chasing after him from the moment he turned fifteen."

"Really? What does your brother look like?"

"Quite a bit like me. Although, his curls are a few shades darker. It makes them look a little more brown than gold, but we share almost the exact same eye color."

Anthony could not see any female wanting to attract a man who looked as dainty and pretty as Miss Hensworth. Poor man must have been teased something awful when he was away at school.

"He is taller than me, though," she went on. "Closer to my father's height. And very strong. I was sixteen when he left. Even though I was full grown, he could pick me up as if I weighed no more than a feather."

Anthony doubted she actually did weigh more than a feather; she was so petite. "I see. Well, undoubtedly, he must have been a great asset to the Royal Army. His language skills in particular would have been especially needed."

Suddenly, her face fell. Belatedly, he realized she had been speaking of her brother in the present tense. Anthony's use of the past tense must have been a hard reminder that he was with them no longer.

"Forgive me, Miss Hensworth. I had not meant to remind you of your grief."

"There is nothing to forgive, Lord Hamdon. It was nice, however, to forget for a time and just relive the good memories."

Several moments of silence passed between them, but it did not feel awkward in the least. He was pleased to find he was comfortable with her when she was talking as well as when they sat silent.

Eventually, she rose, thanking him for the conversation and asking if there was anything she might get for him. After he requested another book, she bid him good day. Anthony observed her as she walked from the room. The conversation must have drained her because the happy light she had arrived with now seemed dim. In fact, she looked weighed down and tired. Anthony vowed to himself he would lighten her burden next time instead of bring her down.

Emma left Lord Hamdon's room feeling exhausted. Deception was taking a toll on her both physically and mentally. She had made a mistake today that could have cost her, but Lord Hamdon had not seemed to notice. She would have to be more careful in the future.

Descending the stairs again, she looked out the large windows. She had told her uncle of the man in the woods as they ascended the stairs earlier. He had studied the trees out the window as she had explained.

After several beats of silence, he finally said, "I think Mr. Ladd is right. If there really is someone out there, it is probably just a poacher. I will have Mr. Haze look into it."

"But that is just it. Mr. Ladd already spoke with him, and neither of them have seen the man at all. It seems I am the only one, and now Mr. Haze has gone off for a fortnight, and nothing will be done about it."

"I see. That *is* distressing." He looked directly at her. "How have you been sleeping of late?"

Emma had answered honestly as they had continued up the stairs. Thinking back now, however, he might have been insinuating that the man was just a figment of an her overly exhausted mind. It irritated her to think even her uncle did not believe her. But then again, he had said he would look into it, so he must have believed her at least a little.

Whatever the case, she could not argue against needing more sleep. Between her late-night tears and the anxiety of keeping secrets, she slept very little. Aunt Marshall would probably argue it was far too early in the day for a nap, they had not, after all, had luncheon, but Emma did not care. She was going to rest. It would be a relief not to face her aunt for several more hours, or life, for that matter. It was all so very tiring.

Chapter Fourteen

Anthony was more than ready to get out of his bed. It had been almost four weeks. Four weeks of sitting in nearly the same position doing the same things every day. He would have died of boredom long before now if Miss Hensworth had not come to visit him so often. Even Aunt Vie had not been quite as entertaining as the intriguing young woman.

Over the last few days Anthony had discovered how witty, well-spoken, and intelligent she could be. It did not hurt at all that she was also quite pretty, with that pert nose and those full pink lips that more often than not lately were pulled into a cheeky smile; her pale blue eyes dancing in delight.

He had to admit to himself that it had been quite diverting when she unintentionally asked if he wanted to be part of her love story, even though he could see by her bright cheeks and quick exit that it had embarrassed her deeply.

There had been no scheming, no pretense. She had simply said the first thought that had entered her mind. It was quite refreshing, really. As heir to an earldom, Anthony had endured his fair share of grasping ladies—suffocating, eager, self-centered young misses, looking only for title, connection, and money.

Miss Hensworth was none of those. In fact, her initial disdain for him, while frustrating, had piqued a fair amount of interest. He was not sure he had ever met a lady so wholly unimpressed by his very presence. If his title and lineage did not garner attention, his looks often did. Miss Hensworth had certainly taken his vanity down a peg as she seemed completely unaffected by both.

That same vanity was taking an even larger hit this morning as the butler and the footman carried him down the stairs where Dr. Jones waited with a bath chair brought specifically for his use. The doctor had promised that if he could handle a bath chair for at least a week, they might be able to gradually introduce crutches. He did not want Anthony to overtax the leg as the break had been particularly bad. Dr. Jones worried too much stress too soon would cause the bones to shift out of place, a risk they could not afford.

Something in the way Anthony was being carried down the steps must have been humorous to Miss Hensworth, for she looked as if she might burst into laughter at any moment. Perhaps it was the way his legs were straddled between the two men, both having one arm around his back and one under each of his legs. Each step they took caused him to rock back and forth as if he was in a cradle or hammock.

When they finally reached the court below, he let out a sigh of relief. He had been nervous the shorter men would drop him, especially Mr. Gibbons. The man looked to be at least sixty years old. After the men carefully set him in the bath chair, Aunt Vie laid a lap blanket across his lap, covering up the unsightly splint and bare toes that poked out.

He smiled to himself, remembering his conversation with Miss Hensworth about his quick assent into the geriatric set. The blanket definitely added to the elderly appearance. Glancing up, he caught her laughing smile. Perhaps she was remembering as well.

"It is good to see you up and about, Anthony," Aunt Vie gushed. He did not actually consider this up and about, but he thanked her all the same. After Dr. Jones gave specific instruction on what he could and could not do, he bid them all farewell.

"It will be so nice to have a man at the table again," Aunt Vie said excitedly, "Unfortunately, it has just been Emma and I these last few weeks since dear Nicholas left."

Anthony caught Miss Hensworth's look of exasperation and found he was just as perturbed. Miss Hensworth was a fine companion. Why did her aunt not appreciate that? Ever since their conversation about Aunt Vie, he had paid better attention to how the older woman acted around her niece. Again, he did not feel like Aunt Vie meant to cause offense, but it was evident now that she had a distinct preference for male company.

"What about the times Mr. Clayton has joined us for dinner, Aunt Marshall?" Miss Hensworth asked.

"Oh, yes. He has graced us a few times with his presence, but it is not the same as having him here at every meal."

"I do not think I will be able to descend the stairs for every meal as yet," Anthony said, worried he would be required to brave the help of Mr. Gibbons three times a day.

"Of course not, Anthony, but you might come down at luncheon and stay throughout the entire afternoon and evening."

Perhaps, he thought, but he did not want to be a burden either. Miss Hensworth had been visiting him often these past three days but what would happen if he was always underfoot? Would she grow tired of his company? Would he grow tired of Aunt Vie's?

"Perhaps we should see how dinner goes before we make any plans," Miss Hensworth said. "Lord Hamdon has been through quite the ordeal and he has been required to be in bed for a long time. He may find he becomes fatigued far sooner than he used to prior to the accident."

"Wise words," Anthony said.

"Nonsense. She is only repeating what the doctor told us before you joined us," Aunt Vie huffed.

"Well, then they must be wise words if they come straight from Dr. Jones," he said with a grin, which must have placated her for she smiled back at him.

"Let us be off to dinner then, so we might decide," Aunt Vie said, walking beside him while Mr. Gibbons pushed the bath chair towards the dining room.

Emma listened as Aunt Marshall chatted amicably with Lord Hamdon. The increased animation in her conversation grated on Emma. It was not the animation she disliked, but the decided lack of it when only she and Aunt Marshall took dinner together.

She focused on eating while Lord Hamdon answered questions about his friend Bradley. Aunt Marshall had become adamant in her desire to see the man and was insisting an invitation should be sent forthwith. With Fallow Hall being only twenty miles southwest of Worthin, she desired him to pay a visit to Engalworth Court while she was in residence.

"If he took the smaller roads," Aunt Marshall argued, "he might cut five miles off his journey. He could be here and home by evening. Of course, I would not be satisfied with just a day's visit. If he is to come, I must have him for at least a fortnight. It has been four years since I last saw the boy. Met him in London..."

Lord Hamdon looked uneasy as Aunt Marshall prattled on. "I believe, Aunt Vie, we should leave this matter to Miss Hensworth. It is her home after all."

"Oh, posh, I am here as chaperone at the moment, and I do not believe George would have any reservations at letting me invite whomever I please."

Emma shot Lord Hamdon a look, hoping it conveyed the 'I told you so' she wanted to say. His tight smile and miniscule one shoulder shrug eased her tension a bit. He was right, she supposed. What was there to do? Nothing, unless she wanted to make a scene. She was not opposed to Bradley coming. However, it would at least be nice to know the man's last name before he was extended an invitation. She had heard of Fallow Hall but could not recall the surname of those that resided there.

"Which reminds me," Aunt Marshall asked before Emma could inquire after the name, "Emma, when was the last you heard from your father?"

Emma almost choked on the potato she was chewing. She had not expected her aunt to bring up this line of questioning again. It had been a fairly constant conversation over the past month, but she had hoped with the present company, Aunt Marshall would be too distracted to press her again.

Pressing her napkin to her lips, she quickly swallowed her bite of food. "I have yet to receive any new correspondence, Aunt Marshall. As I said last evening, I have not had any word from him since December."

She knew her words were a bit terse, but she was growing tired of Aunt Marshall's constant pressure. One more month, she reminded herself. One more month, and then her aunt could return back to Gloucester.

"It does seem excessively odd, do you not think, Anthony, that my brother has not written to a single person since he left five months ago, not even his steward? I talked with the man before he left on Monday, and he said his last instructions were to make sure rent was collected and taxes were paid, as well as giving the butler enough money to pay the remaining staff until my brother's return."

Emma looked down at her food, still irritated that the steward had reported to her aunt instead of to her. The motion had the added bonus of not allowing Lord Hamdon to see her face, as she was sure he was beginning to see through her façade. She could tell by his response that he was just as baffled as her aunt.

"Not one word in five months. That is strange!"

"Yes, and before he left, he let go almost all the staff. Keeping only the Gibbonses, Smith, Thatcher, Mr. Lovell, and Mr. Ladd."

"That is not quite true," Emma protested. "We also still have Owen, as well as Sally who comes in to clean three days a week. And do not forget Mrs. Clark is here in the evenings to cook dinner."

"Yes, which leaves poor Mrs. Gibbons to do the work when they are not here. And who ever heard of sharing a maid with another house, especially since this one is so incredibly large? I remember the day when Engalworth Court was teeming with servants. Every room was open and cleaned to perfection. Now we are forced to have rooms shut up because there is no one to clean them. The remaining servants are practically worked to the bone, and instead of the sounds of a lively, jolly place, it's as silent as the grave."

Emma winced at her aunt's analogy. When she caught Lord Hamdon's look of pity, it galled her. How long would she be forced to endure the sidelong glances from people who assumed her family had fallen upon difficult times? Engalworth Court was as solvent as it had ever been. She should know, for she checked the ledgers daily. In fact, they were doing far better than before because they were saving money by not employing near so many servants. They surely could take on more staff, but for the sake of the entire Engalworth estate, the ruse had to continue.

"Aunt Marshall, I do not believe it is seemly to repeat Engalworth's difficulties in front of Lord Hamdon," she said, trying to call on her aunt's sense of decorum to end this line of conversation.

"Oh, Emma, Anthony is practically family to me and can be trusted with any of my concerns."

"Yes, but he is not family to me and, therefore, is not privy to mine." she huffed. "Now, if you will excuse me, I believe I shall turn in early this evening." Rising, she set her napkin beside her unfinished food.

Lord Hamdon, reached out his hand to stop her. "Please, Miss Hensworth, do not go so soon. I do not mean to pry into your personal affairs." He cast a meaningful glance toward Aunt Marshall who sat with a mulish look upon her face. "I only wish to enjoy your company. We do not need to continue this vein of conversation, do we, Aunt Vie?"

Although the expression on Aunt Marshall's face did not become any more pleasant, she capitulated. "Yes, Emma dear, do sit and finish your dinner. I will question you no further this evening."

Emma had not missed the "this evening." She was sure an even more thorough interrogation awaited her. It seemed she would need to avoid her aunt tomorrow at all costs, she thought as she retook her seat.

As the meal was drawing to a close, Mrs. Gibbons came in carrying a cake, the other servants following on her heels. Emma almost burst into tears. Aunt Marshall may have completely forgotten the significance of the twenty-ninth of April, but Mrs. Gibbons had not. It was comforting to know that someone remembered.

Truthfully, Mrs. Gibbons had not been the only one. Mr. Clayton had brought her a small gift when he came for breakfast, apologizing he could not make it for her birthday dinner as he usually did. He was needed as Mr. Cole, God rest his soul, was close to the end of his life. Word of his death had come shortly before dinner, comforting Emma that her uncle had been at the right place at the right time.

She thanked Mrs. Gibbons as she set the cake in front of her and handed her a knife. Her mind filled with past birthdays and their special family tradition. Mama had started it when they were young, claiming the birthday boy or girl should get to have as big of a slice as they would like on their special day. Her heart ached with the memory, wishing Mama could be here now.

Pressing the knife into the white frosted cake, Emma cut it in half. Turning the round confection, she cut it in half again. Every year since she was five, she cut the cake the exact same way, taking a full quarter of the cake as her own. This had always made her father laugh. Today, however, was the first birthday he would not be here to tease her about her affinity for sweets, and it would not be the last. Emma fought to stem the tears that threatened to spill over.

Glancing up at the smiling faces of her staff, she made a decision. Turning the cake four more times, she cut it into sixteen small pieces. Aunt Marshall looked disappointed at the size of the slices, but Emma did not care. She wanted plenty to be left over so every one of the servants could enjoy a piece of the delicious spice cake Mrs. Clark had concocted. They deserved it, after all, with all she had asked of them of late.

Chapter Fifteen

Anthony sat in his bed the next afternoon contemplating the previous evening's dinner. Miss Hensworth had not come to visit him this morning, and he worried he had offended her by not remembering her birthday. Such an offense would have set him on his mother's bad side for weeks, if not months. However, he could not see Miss Hensworth going to such extremes.

Perhaps Aunt Vie's line of questioning the evening before had caused Miss Hensworth to see him in a poor light. Did she think him complicit in her aunt's interrogation? Was she angry that he had not protested when her aunt had claimed his right to the information? He was curious about her father's lack of communication, but would never have insisted she divulge her personal affairs to him, especially not around the dinner table.

It was obvious whatever the cause of her father's negligence in writing, Miss Hensworth found great discomfort in discussing such things with her aunt, and it was no wonder. Anthony had never seen Aunt Vie act so... so... well, he did not have a word to describe it. One moment she was as sweet as honey and the next as sour as vinegar, but only to Emma. Why only to Emma?

Anthony reeled at his mental slip. Had he really thought of Miss Hensworth by her Christian name? Of course, how could he not? He heard it at every turn. Besides, it was a far better fit for the delicate beauty than Miss Hensworth. That name only reminded him of chickens.

He laughed softly. Emma did remind him of a hen sometimes when she got her feathers ruffled.

A knock upon the door drew his attention. Usually, the door remained open during the day after his first visitor, but today Aunt Vie had closed it on her way out, and he had not protested.

"Enter," he called out. To his surprise, Smith opened the door, and the subject of his thoughts stepped gracefully in.

"Good morning, Miss Hensworth," he said, reminding himself to stick to formalities. He would indulge in using her Christian name in his mind *only*.

"Perhaps you have not seen, but it is afternoon, Lord Hamdon," she said with a slight upturn of her lips.

He knew it was, but having the subject of his thoughts suddenly appear had muddled his brain, and now he probably sat with a dopey smile upon his face. Trying to recollect himself, he gestured to her usual chair. "Please, have a seat."

Emma sat and opened her mouth, then shut it. She opened and shut it again before finally saying, "I am sorry for my sour attitude last evening."

"I did not find your attitude sour in the least. You were placed in a difficult situation which I think you handled quite well. I am sorry your aunt has usurped your place as hostess in your own home, and I am sorry for my part in forgetting your birthday."

"Do not mind about my birthday. Not even my aunt remembered, so why should I expect it of someone who I have only been acquainted with for a few weeks?"

Even though she tried to portray herself as unaffected, he could see the hurt behind her eyes. However, he could not tell who bore more of the blame for the pain, her aunt or him.

She continued speaking, "As for Aunt Marshall taking my place, it is no surprise. I am young and unmarried, and according to her, not capable of running a household."

"But if I am not mistaken, you had been running this house on your own for four months before her arrival. That does not sound like you are unable to run your own household."

"You are correct, Lord Hamdon, but Aunt Marshall does not see my time alone as managing. You see, I did not entertain any guests, nor did I socialize a great deal, and that is a great failing in her eyes."

"But you are in mourning. Is there not some leniency in such cases?"

Emma's eyebrows lifted, conveying the ridiculousness of the question. Of course she should be granted leniency.

"I suppose my aunt feels like four months is sufficient to grieve any loss."

Confused, he asked, "I thought your brother died last fall?"

Emma's looked confused, then flustered. "Well, of course. I mean to say that I was only given four months to grieve before my father–" she stumbled on her words, but finally said, "—went away."

He supposed that made sense, but something was decidedly off. Emma was fidgeting with the tips of her gloves, a telltale sign of nerves. She only seemed to employ the action when she was talking of her father or brother, an odd idiosyncrasy, for sure. He decided further questioning was in order, but he had to tread lightly, or she might bolt as she had tried to do the evening before.

"If you do not mind me asking, which battle was your brother's last?"

"Dennewitz," she said quietly, looking out the window.

Anthony was confused. He did not think any British troops had been involved in that battle. If memory served, the Prussians had held their ground in that battle, pushing back Napoleon's men from overtaking Berlin. What would a British soldier be doing there?

"Dennewitz? The battle for Berlin? I thought the Prussians fought that battle."

Emma's eyes grew wide and frantic. What had he said to cause such a reaction? She looked about the room, adjusted her position in the chair, cleared her throat, then said, "Perhaps I am mistaken. It might have been Leipzig. It was a while before news reached us. The letter came in October, and I am not very versed on battle names. Especially since there are so many strange names to know on the continent."

She was rambling now. Leipzig was more likely, but her reaction was still so very odd that Anthony became even more suspicious that she was hiding something. The more he learned, the more questions he had. The more questions he had, the more he worried something unsavory was underfoot.

"I am sorry, Miss Hensworth. I had not meant to make you uncomfortable; I was merely curious. I suppose Aunt Vie must feel that since you are in half-mourning, social niceties must begin again. I have never lost someone particularly close to me, at least that I can remember. My paternal grandparents died while I was still in leading strings, and my maternal grandfather before I was born. My maternal grandmother is still with us. My aunts and uncles are still alive as well, and I only have three cousins who all enjoy good health." Not that he would call any of those people close. They were all as cold and calculating as his own parents. "So, as you can see, I do not have any knowledge of how long one truly mourns for a lost loved one."

"I am unsure one ever stops mourning. My mother died when I was ten, and there are days I still mourn her loss. Over time, however, you learn to carry on around the ache."

"Ah, yes. Time heals all wounds."

"No, it does not!" she said with so much force that Anthony leaned back as if blasted by a strong wind. Softening her voice, she said firmly, "It is only that with time we become stronger than our wounds. Carrying on even when we are broken and bleeding. Perhaps it heals some of the wound, but only in the way a soldier's limb heals when his hand has been completely cut off. He will never be the same again, but he learns to function without that most important part of himself."

"You sound as if you are well-acquainted with the process."

"I am! Far too much," she declared, her eyes tight and her knuckles going white as she grasped the sides of the upholstered chair. "My uncle and all four of my grandparents died when I was a little girl. My mother, who died when I was ten, left a hole in my heart the size of a kingdom. My Aunt Clara, who was like a second mother to me, died right before my fourteenth birthday, and suddenly I was without a mother figure again. Then my brother and father..."

Anthony sat dumbfounded. So much death. Then the last word she had uttered sunk in. Her father? Emma went on, not seeming to notice her own words.

"...Perhaps Aunt Marshall thinks that because I have lost so many before that I should be able to move on more quickly, but after losing so many limbs, I find myself unable to stand right now. My arms and legs have been severed, and I am bleeding out. I cannot simply just jump back up and say, 'Viola! All better.' Then go around doing a merry dance for all to see. No, Society will have to wait. I am trying to heal, but this time may be my undoing. I may never enter back into the social whirl. It has grown tiresome with its fake splendor. So, please, forgive me if I do not invite people over to spout their fake platitudes, just so they can go away and gossip about the mutilated remains of Emma Hensworth. I want peace, I want love, and I want honesty. Something Society as a whole has *never* been able to give me."

Emma breathed heavily, the rims of her eyes red, but no tears fell. Anthony could feel the pain resonating off of her in waves, and he sat there, unable to help her. Yet he understood how she felt, if only in a small measure.

His life had been one filled with falsehoods. His parents' marriage, for example, was a sham. Society, as well, was as fickle and false as his parents' marriage. On one hand, Society vowed they loved him while at the same time found every opportunity to imply him in whatever juicy piece of gossip they could. He had very little love for any of his family or glittering London friends, so it was hard to empathize with her familial losses.

And yet, if it would have been Nicholas, Bradley, or Fredrick, he would have been devastated. Reaching out, he did what he had done once before, only this time he lifted Emma's hand from her lap and held it gently in his.

"I do not know how you have endured so much. I, for one, am amazed," he said, looking deep into her crystal blue eyes.

The tears she had been holding at bay suddenly spilled over. "Oh!" she huffed, pulling her hand from his and searching for a square of linen. Anthony was ready this time, grabbing the one on the table beside him and offering it to her. She took it gratefully. "You seem to have the uncanny ability to make me cry."

"Is that a good thing or bad?" he asked with a quirk of his lips.

"I am not sure, but I thank you."

"For making you cry?"

"No," she chuckled through her tears, "for your handkerchief and for your kind words."

"They are not merely kind words; they are the truth, and I hope you will take them to heart. You are doing amazingly well." Reaching out and taking her hand again, he decided to take a risk and see how it played out. "And someday I hope you will entrust me with the reason you are hiding your father's passing."

Emma's face went pale, her eyes wide with fear. She looked to her maid, who Anthony saw was equally concerned but not quite so surprised. She must have caught her lady's admission.

"I... I... how did..." she stammered, pulling her hand out of his and rising from her chair.

"Please, do not go," he implored.

"I think I must." Taking a few wobbly steps toward the door, Emma began breathing far too quickly, the color draining from her face with each step. Anthony leaned forward, stretching his hand out, as if by some miracle it would help her. Smith, however, perceived the danger, jumped from her chair, and wrapped her arms around her mistress just moments before the overwrought woman sunk to the floor.

Chapter Sixteen

Wafting air tickled Emma's face. The cool air was refreshing as she lay upon the sand. If it were not for the rock digging into her right shoulder, she would have been completely comfortable enjoying the breeze. The whooshing sound of water still filled her ears. Suddenly, the rock moved and dug into the upper part of her arm. From far away, she could hear Smith calling her.

"Miss Emma? Miss Emma?"

Smith's voice was growing closer each time she called. A few drops of rain fell on her face, jolting Emma to full consciousness. The comforting sound of the ocean fled with her awareness. The rock she had been cursing only moments before moved again as Smith proclaimed her relief. Emma realized the sharp dig was coming from Smith, her arm wrapped around her back and her fingers clamped onto her shoulder.

"Do let go, Smith. You are hurting me," Emma muttered.

"Thank ya for the water, Lord Hamdon. It seemed ta do the job," Smith said, looking up. Emma followed her gaze and saw him sitting up, his feet dangling over the side of the bed, a glass partially full of water in his hand.

Smith pulled her up into a seated position before letting go and quickly re-arranged her skirts to more adequately cover her legs which were exposed almost to the knee. Emma's cheeks flamed red at the thought that Lord Hamdon had glimpsed so much of her.

Taking the cup of water from Lord Hamdon, Smith refilled the vessel with fresh water and handed it to Emma to drink. She took several swallows without complaint before she recalled just why she sat upon the floor. Her father. Lord Hamdon. The secret. Now what?

Emma had spent an entire month dodging Aunt Marshall's question. Then in a moment of weakness, she had somehow given away the most crucial part of the plan. Emma stared at the glass in her hand trying to decide how to proceed. She hardly knew Lord Hamdon. Was he the type of person to keep confidences, or was he as big a gossip as Aunt Marshall?

"How do you feel, Miss Hensworth?" he asked. She looked up and saw him staring down at her with concern. She had no idea how to answer such a question. Of course, she felt unwell. She had just exposed herself both physically *and* emotionally to this man. However, while she was still emotionally distressed, at least she was not so overwhelmed that she could not think.

"As good as can be expected," she said quietly, staring again at the glass in her hands.

"Here, let me help ya up, Miss Emma," Smith said, bending down and wrapping one arm around her shoulders while offering her other hand for her to use to stabilize herself. Emma handed the glass up to Lord Hamdon, and then taking her maid's hand, managed to stand. It was not the most graceful rise she had ever made, but at least she did not expose her lower limbs again.

"Thank you, Smith," Emma said when she was fully standing with her skirts straightened around her. "Now, if you would be so kind as to close the door, please."

"The door, Miss?" Smith squeaked.

"Yes. It would seem Lord Hamdon and I need to have a private conversation which I do not wish to be interrupted."

"Yes, Miss," Smith said hesitantly as she shut the door. Retaking her seat, the maid seemed uneasy with the current situation. Well, she was not the only one.

"I am assuming that your maid is privy to the information you wish to discuss." Lord Hamdon eyed the nervous woman by the door.

"First, I do not *wish* to discuss anything. It seems, however, that I inadvertently divulged information that was not intended for anyone to know at this time. And yes, Smith is privy to all of my secrets."

"All of them?"

"Perhaps not all, but a good many. She is loyal to me and has always kept my confidences, and I hers."

"That is refreshing in a servant. In my experience, servants have been just as prone to spread gossip as the cats of London."

"Then you either do not have the right servants, or you are not the right sort of master."

Lord Hamdon's face screwed up in an odd expression. Emma thought perhaps she had offended him, but he did not scowl at her as he so often had when they first met.

"I suppose it could be both," he finally answered. "Servants have really only ever been people paid to do my bidding. I really have not thought much more on sharing my personal affairs with them as long as things got done in a timely manner."

"Then it is safe for me to assume you do not know any of your servants' personal lives."

"It is a business relationship. I pay them to do a job, and they do it. There is no need for us to get too involved in one another's lives. Unless, of course..." He trailed off a stern look upon his face.

It was true most servants carried on throughout their lives thus, but Emma could never understand how anyone could not grow close to those they spent so much time with day in and day out. The Gibbons, for example, had been here long before she was born. In a way, they filled the role of grandparents for her. Smith had only been employed since Emma's governess had taken another position three years ago, but she relied on her as one would a friend. Smith's quiet nature and compassionate heart had soothed her when she had been at her lowest.

"Tell me, Lord Hamdon, if you had the choice between going somewhere you were valued and somewhere you are just a commodity, which would you choose?"

"Oh, where I was valued, for sure. I have spent the good majority of my adult life as a commodity to be won during the London season. It has become exceedingly tedious."

"Servants are no different. I have found that if I am good to them, they are good to me. If I look out for their interests, they look out for mine."

He smile and nodded. Emma was taken aback. What did that smile mean? Was he agreeing with her or just letting her know he understood what she was saying?

"It seems their loyalty has served you well. Tell me, how many of the servants at Engalworth know your father is no longer alive?"

She took a deep breath. Now they had come to the point. Even though she loathed to say the words out loud, she knew it was necessary. First, though, she needed a promise.

"Lord Hamdon, before I tell you anything more, I must have your word of honor as a gentleman that you will not tell a single soul about anything we may discuss."

Emma had hoped for his immediate acquiescence, but to her dismay he chose that moment to push himself fully up upon the bed until his back rested against the pillows. Folding his hands across his middle, he contemplated for a moment.

"I would have to know your reasons for hiding such information from the world at large. You do realize how strange this whole situation is, do you not? A baron suddenly goes missing, and his daughter and servants claim he is gone on business, but in reality, the man is dead. How did he die? Was it an accident, natural causes, or something more nefarious? And for what reason could anyone have to hide his death if not for nefarious purposes?"

Emma's defenses rose. How dare he imply that her father had died under suspicious circumstances? Did he think so little of her? Reflecting on what he had said, she could see how it might look to a stranger. Her hands began to sweat inside her gloves. "He died of natural causes. An infectious fever took him, and it was his last wish that no one know of his demise until a certain time in the future. There now, will you give me your word?"

"At what time in the future?"

"That I cannot tell you. Now, will you give me your word?"

"Cannot or will not? They are completely different things, you know."

"Cannot, for I do not know when his specified circumstances will arise. Until then, I am bound by my promise not to divulge any information," Emma said in a clipped tone. She was becoming increasingly irritated that he would not give his word of secrecy, even though she had completely explained her father's death.

"And what if those circumstances never arise?"

The thought knocked the breath out of her lungs. Suddenly, the fight was gone and fear inched up her spine. What if it never happened? What if her father's words, his promises, were wrong? She had watched him write that shaky note. She had mailed it herself. What if they were just the words of a sick, delirious man on the verge of death, desperate for something that was only part of some wayward dream?

Taking a shaky breath, she slowly let it out. "Then I suppose if a year passes and there is no word, I will have to divulge the truth."

Anthony stared at Emma. She sat slightly hunched, that look of hopelessness he had seen once before again on her face. The last time he had seen her thus, they had been speaking of her cousin. It was probably safe to assume he was the exact reason she kept the secret of her father's passing so greatly guarded. He could not blame her. Women in England were at the mercy of the males who inherited, and from their previous conversation, he had gathered that Mr. Weazelton was not a man of honor.

While he was uneasy about giving his word of secrecy to anyone, not knowing all the particulars, he was concerned if he withheld it from Emma, it would not only crush her with worry, but also ruin any chance he might have of learning the reason for the lie's continuance.

Finally, he said, "I give my word as a gentleman that I will not divulge your father's passing, but you must explain in more detail what happened for me to feel comfortable about giving my promise. You can start by telling me how long your father has been gone."

She let out a small puff of air before straightening in her seat and inhaling deeply. "After receiving word in October of my brother's disappearance, my father sunk into a deep melancholy. He did not eat well, and often I found him pacing the house late into the night. By the end of November, he had developed a disturbing cough. I sent for the doctor, but my father assured me that Dr. Jones believed with some rest and good nourishment he would recover. A week later, in December, I began to believe he was right, as my father suddenly gained strength and began excitedly talking about the future. He rode into Banbury several times in those two weeks, and I supposed he was preparing for the Christmas holiday. He still coughed every now and then, but I was not particularly concerned until the day he got caught in a freezing rain on his way back from town."

Emma stopped speaking and began fidgeting with the fingertips of her gloves. Anthony could see the rims of her eyes going red and knew it would not be long until her silent tears began. After several slow deep breaths, she continued.

"We tried to warm him the best we could, but he had a raging fever by the following morning. I wanted to call the doctor, but my father forbade it." The first tear slipped silently down her cheek, and Anthony wished he could wipe it away before it fell, if only he could move faster than a snail's pace. He could not catch that one, he thought, but he would be there for the next.

He turned his body to the side. Gently clasping the splint around his right leg, he slowly lowered it to the ground before moving his left leg to set beside his right. This put him in a much better position to reach for her where she sat at the right side of his bed.

"I wanted to send for him," she said while looking at her hands. "I begged my father, but he insisted against it. In truth, looking back, I do not think the doctor could have done much more than Mrs. Gibbons. His lungs were so infected by that point that nothing could have saved him."

A second tear slipped down her cheek, but this time Anthony was ready for it. Reaching forward, he gently caught it with the tip of his pointer finger and whisked it away from her face. Startled at his touch, she looked up from her fidgeting hands. He saw the confusion in her eyes before another tear slipped down the opposite cheek. Reaching out with his other hand, he wiped that one away as well, but allowed his hand to linger.

To his surprise, Emma leaned her head into the palm of his uncovered hand and closed her eyes. Several more tears leaked out, but he did not try to sweep them away. As the tears flowed, Anthony hoped in some small way his touch was bringing her heart comfort.

For some reason, in this moment her comfort had become paramount in his mind. Emma needed him. He was not sure how he knew it, but he did. She needed the comfort that he could provide, and if he had to sit like this all day, he would, if only to lift her burden the smallest bit.

After a time, she pulled her face away. "Mr. and Mrs. Gibbons, Smith, and Mr. Clayton are the only ones who know what happened that night as my father had kept only the servants he trusted most. The rest had been given a holiday, during which time we put about that my father had left on business." Emma took several slow deep breaths at this point in her tale, and Anthony supposed she was trying to maintain her fragile composure.

"He wrote two letters during that time. One was to our steward asking him to continue paying wages to the staff until he received word otherwise. In the interim, he was to answer to me on all matters concerning the house and staff."

"And the other?"

Looking up, she said, "It was to London."

"Where in London?"

She gave a miniscule shake of her head.

"You do not know?"

"I do. But, please, do not pressure me to tell you," she pled. "I have told you more than I should have ever told anyone." Another tear slipped silently down her cheek.

Feeling deep compassion for her suffering, he said, "I believe I know enough for now. Is it safe to presume all of this is done to keep your cousin from inheriting?"

"That is the crux of it all, yes."

Anthony sighed deeply. "I know we are not very well-acquainted, Miss Hensworth, but I want to assure you that I can be trusted. I am a man of my word, and I will not divulge anything you have told me today to anyone. And if there is anything I might do to help ease your burden, you have but to ask." He was not sure if he really could provide any help since she had not revealed the whole of her problem, but he would do what little he could.

"Thank you, Lord Hamdon. At this point, your secrecy is all I ask. It is of upmost importance, not just for me, but those who depend on Engalworth for their living."

"I will do my best." he promised, wanting to allay Emma's fears and lift a little of that burden he saw weighing down her fragile shoulders.

Chapter Seventeen

Emma slept poorly, her conversation with Lord Hamdon constantly replaying in her head. Consequently, a feeling of foreboding lingered about her all of Sunday. She tried to greet people as she usually would when she entered the small church, but she felt exposed. As if by telling Lord Hamdon her secrets, somehow her lies were uncovered for all to see.

Sitting in the family pew next to Aunt Marshall, she barely registered Mr. Clayton's sermon. Her mind kept wandering back to pieces of yesterday's conversation. Would Lord Hamdon truly keep her secret? Was he really a gentleman who kept his word? She honestly did not know. The only thing she could do was hope. Looking at the building around her, she mentally added prayer to the list.

She was not sure if the Almighty would hear the prayers of a liar, but she hoped he would. It was not as if she did so solely for her own purposes. As she had said to Lord Hamdon, the servants and tenants were all at risk, as well. She could not allow her cousin to come in and wreak havoc on the lives of so many people.

Thoughts of Mr. Weazelton always firmed up her resolve to stay her course, no matter the cost. The man had gambled away his own inheritance years ago. Now living off of creditors and the grace of his friends, he still went about in Society purporting himself as a man of means. Most likely that was his purpose in proposing they marry. No doubt he needed her dowry to satisfy his creditors because there really was no other reason for him to connect himself with her.

She had only met Mr. Weazelton a handful of times, none of which had been a pleasant experience. Ten years her senior, as a youth he had teased and insulted her, and as an adult, he had paid little attention to her very existence. The only exception had been during her one season in London when he had used his connection with Lord Gladsby to increase his importance and gain admittance to places otherwise closed to him.

Throughout the years, Emma had never walked away from a meeting with Mr. Weazelton without feeling decidedly repulsed. It seemed the man could not publicly interact without doing or saying something incredibly inappropriate, and their last interaction had been the height of impropriety. She was sure that particular experience was the reason her father had sworn everyone to silence at his deathbed.

Looking up at her uncle as he preached, Emma realized she would need to speak to him and soon. He deserved to know of her mistaken confession to Lord Hamdon. Mr. and Mrs. Gibbons would need to know as well, for they were as much a part of this as Mr. Clayton.

No doubt Mr. Clayton would be disappointed in her, possibly upset. Admittedly, she was disappointed and upset with herself. At the same time, there was a certain sense of relief at having finally told someone the truth. The deception had definitely been eating at her soul.

Lord Hamdon had somehow relieved some of the pressure that had been building inside her over these past five months. Given, at times in their conversation, she had also been thoroughly exasperated with him, but she understood his reserve. If someone had come to her with such a tale, she probably would not have been near as trusting as he had been.

Mr. Clayton finished his sermon, and the small village choir took their places to sing a psalm.

Remove from me the way of lying:
and grant me thy law graciously,
I have chosen the way of truth:
thy judgments have I laid before me.

Why did it have to be Psalm one hundred nineteen? Unease caused her to adjust her position on the pew, which in turn brought a look of reprimand from Aunt Marshall. It was not as if *she* had not adjusted during the long sermon.

Emma schooled her features. Why was Aunt Marshall always so severe and disapproving of her? She wished for once the woman would show half the amount of gentleness and kindness as Lord Hamdon had offered her yesterday.

The butterflies that erupted inside her at the memory of Lord Hamdon's touch nearly sent her to readjust her position again, but a quick glance at Aunt Marshall caused her to refrain. But oh, how her heart yearned to feel his gentle hand cradling her face again. It was strange, how much that simple touch had taken away some of the sting in her soul. Applying a balm on it that relieved months of building pressure, providing a comfort she had not even known she needed.

However, Lord Hamdon's soft gentle touch had also been her undoing. The press of his hand had released not only her tears, but the words that could very well condemn them all. In those moments, though, when he had so gently wiped away her tears, she had been comforted. She had been cared for. She had been heard. As disconcerting as the conversation had been and as worried as she was of the consequences, somewhere deep inside, she was glad she had told Lord Hamdon.

The benediction over, she rose from her seat. Aunt Marshall began enthusiastically greeting other parishioners. Having grown up in the parish, her aunt knew a good many of the local families. Emma did not begrudge her aunt the few minutes to mingle with old friends. But when the Bower family approached, she decided the forced social time had been enough for her.

Claiming a need to speak with the vicar, she excused herself from the gathering before Miss Bower, Sir John and Lady Bower's eldest daughter, could get close enough to unleash her nasty tongue. The woman never could seem to meet Emma without giving a politely veiled insult.

Unfortunately, Emma was not fast enough in her retreat. The young woman's catty remark wafted over the din to reach her ears before she was even three pews away.

"Do convince your niece to leave off wearing grey, Mrs. Marshall. The color does not become her. It puts me in mind of a little rain cloud spoiling all our happy plans for the day."

Emma should have expected that. It was a common barb. If it was not her attire of late, it was her pale features and unsocial nature. Was it any wonder she did not want to entertain Society when this type of drivel was what it had to offer?

On the walk home from services, Aunt Marshall gushed at how beautifully Mr. Clayton had sermonized. Emma listened with half an ear to all her aunt had to say, which, admittedly, was quite a bit. Even though the walk from the church to Engalworth was fairly short, the distance became incredibly long when Aunt Marshall asked which part of the service she had enjoyed most. Searching her memory, Emma realized she could not recall a single detail of the sermon.

The familiar pounding started in her head. She could already imagine the scolding she was going to get for her inattentiveness, but just as they rounded the curve that led them to Engalworth, Aunt Marshall stopped.

"Do you recognize that coach, Emma?"

Emma could see the equipage in front of Engalworth, but from this distance she could distinguish nothing.

"I do not. I would need to be closer. From this distance, I cannot decipher much more than its shape and color."

"Indeed. Neither can I, but I assumed it was merely my aging eyesight."

As they approached, Aunt Marshall declared it a hired coach, as there did not seem to be a crest of any sort, nor did it stay long at the front portico. Indeed, by the time they had reached the house, it had pulled away and was back upon the road.

"I do not think Bradley could have arrived so soon," Aunt Marshall said, more to herself than to Emma. "I did not even send off my invitation until yesterday. He does not live far, however, so it is possible he might have traveled here in the space of a morning."

Emma did not think it was Mr. Lenning either. The feeling of foreboding gradually increased as they approached the front door. Gibbons opened the door as they reached the top step, a stern expression upon his face.

"Welcome home Miss Hensworth, Mrs. Marshall. Might I take your things?"

Something was off about the man. While quite proper as a butler ought to be, something about Gibbons felt strained.

Emma stepped close to the older man, allowing him to help her remove her pelisse.

"Who has come to call, Gibbons?" she whispered, looking directly into the soft brown eyes she had loved since childhood.

Gibbons's eyes pinched, and a sour look crossed the man's face. Just as he opened his mouth to reply, an overly sweet, nasally male voice sounded in her ears.

"Cousin! It is so good to see you. It seems I have timed my arrival perfectly."

Anthony nearly laughed out loud at the look of first surprise, then revulsion upon Emma's face before she masked it quickly with the placid look Society deemed acceptable in all interactions. He did not blame her. In the few moments he and Mr. Weazelton had been staring one another down before her entrance, every descriptive word Emma had used for her cousin had felt too tame by half.

The man had been so surprised to see Anthony sitting in his bath chair that he had stared like a gape-mouthed fish. When the surprise had worn off, a mulish expression crossed over his face, which was quickly replaced by what Anthony could only guess was anger. The little man's face turned red as a vein popped out upon his head.

Anthony was grateful he had asked to be carried down for luncheon, if only to be here to take the man's measure upon his arrival.

Mr. Weazelton stood near Anthony's chair, having just descended to the court floor when the ladies had arrived. No doubt he meant to give Anthony a set down and a warning to be off the property, but he had to swallow whatever words he had meant to say in light of the ladies' company.

No introductions had yet been made, but the look on Emma's face and the man's use of 'cousin' had confirmed what Anthony had suspected when the man entered not ten minutes before.

Mr. Weazelton waited for Emma and Aunt Vie to descend the stairs before continuing.

"How are you, dear cousin Emma? It has been an age since we were last in company," he said, bowing over her hand.

Anthony was not sure, but he thought he heard Emma mutter, "not long enough" before saying tightly, "It has, indeed. I am well, and you? What brings you to Engalworth Court?"

"Why, you, of course. I learned just two weeks ago that your father has been away on business for quite some time, and that no one has heard from him. I myself have written him a half dozen times with no response. I was exceedingly concerned for your wellbeing, so I thought to come and bring you some comfort."

Emma stared at him, blue eyes filled with confusion. Anthony was equally perplexed. Why would an unmarried man think that calling upon a woman when her father was away was an appropriate course of action?

"Please, forgive me, but how, may I ask, did you know my father was gone on business?" Her usually full pink lips thinned as she compressed them.

He suddenly realized why Emma was confused. Unlike him, she was not concerned for her own safety or reputation, but for the integrity of the secret she held. If Lord Gladsby was missing for too long, Mr. Weazelton could press the courts to proclaim the man lost or dead and install himself as rightful heir. Which, unfortunately, by all accounts, he most likely was.

"Dear Mrs. Marshall sent me word asking if I had received any correspondence from him." He said smiled at Aunt Vie and belatedly gave her a bow. She curtsied in turn, obviously pleased with herself. "I was immediately concerned and came as soon as possible."

Emma cast the older woman a look that could be classified as nothing less than murderous. The smile fell from Aunt Vie's face and she took a nervous step back. Anthony's worry expanded from Emma to Aunt Vie. He was not sure if he had ever seen a woman look so angry, but just like her tears, Emma seemed to call the expression back, smoothing her features almost as quickly as they had pinched. The only thing that lingered was the blue fire in her eyes.

In truth, he could not blame her. Aunt Vie had no right to bandy about family concerns without first asking those to whom they primarily belonged.

"Please, do not be displeased with Mrs. Marshall," Mr. Weazelton said. "She was only concerned for you, and I must agree. It is not good for you to be here without a male family member to protect you."

The fire suddenly turned to ice as Emma took in her cousin's words. Anthony decided it was time for him to intervene. Mr. Weazelton may not know it, but those pompous words were sure to cause the legendary Ice Fairy to freeze the man to the floor.

Clearing his throat rather loudly, all eyes fell on him. Emma's eyes full of indignation; Aunt Vie's with pleading, and Mr. Weazelton's with annoyance at the reminder that he was not the only gentleman present.

It took all his training as a gentleman to maintain a socially bored expression upon his face, because the scene in front of him was anything but boring.

Chapter Eighteen

Emma had been so focused on Mr. Weazelton and her secret that everything else had faded into the background, including Lord Hamdon sitting in his bath chair. His right eyebrow rose just a fraction as if to question her and she realized her misstep; introductions needed to be made. The thought actually calmed her. Perhaps if Mr. Weazelton knew she had someone who outranked him in her home, he would be less likely to burden them with his unwanted presence.

"Ah, yes, forgive me, *Lord* Hamdon. Might I make known to you my cousin, Mr. Weazelton?" Lord Hamdon lifted his chin in acceptance, causing the light of the large front windows to reveal the features of his face more fully. Emma noticed for the first time that his chin held just the hint of a cleft in it. Mr. Weazelton decided to take that moment to step closer to her, making the hair on the back of her neck stand on end.

"Mr. Weazelton," she said, stepping away from her cousin and toward Lord Hamdon. "The Viscount Hamdon, heir to the Earl of Lincolnhurst." Technically, she did not need to add Lord Hamdon's father's position, but she wanted to impress upon her cousin the diminutive state of his position in her home.

Mr. Weazelton's eyes widened a bit before he performed a very proper bow, to which Lord Hamdon merely nodded.

"I wish I might stand to greet you, sir, but I had a most unfortunate accident from which I am still recovering. Honored to make your acquaintance, Mr. Weazelman."

She nearly laughed at Lord Hamdon's mistake, but her cousin did not look in the least amused.

"It is Weazelton, my lord."

"My apologies," Anthony said, a look of devilment in his eyes that Emma knew well from previous conversations. What was he about?

Feeling decidedly more collected, she asked her cousin, "Are you to stay for dinner, or must you be back on the road soon?" Hopefully her cousin did not detect the wistfulness she was afraid had leaked out in her tone.

"Oh, no, dear Emma, I am come to stay as long as I am needed."

She cringed at his use of her Christian name yet again. She had never given the man such liberties, but he was bound and determined to take them. Grinding her teeth together, she no longer felt collected and controlled. Heat welled up around her ears, tension pulling her weak smile tight. Mr. Weazelton's impertinence was beyond the pale.

"*Mr. Weazelton,*" she enunciated his name very carefully, in hopes the very proper address would sink into his very little mind, "as you can see, my aunt is here as chaperone which is all that is needed at present. But if you are worried that I do not have a male relation, let me set your mind at ease. Mr. Clayton, our vicar, is my uncle, and he is here often enough to make sure all is well. He lives but ten minutes' walk from our front door and can be here whenever I am in need. At present, as you can see, Lord Hamdon is also staying with us, so we are in no need of added *protection.*"

Mr. Weazelton cast an imperious look at Lord Hamdon. "Forgive me for saying, but I highly doubt Lord Hamdon is in any position to defend *anyone* at present."

She had to concede the point, but she was affronted all the same for Lord Hamdon's sake. In contrast, Lord Hamdon gave Mr. Weazelton a commiserating smile. "Very true, Mr. Weazelson. This broken leg does slow me down a bit."

"It's Weazelton, *Weaz-el-ton.*"

"My apologies."

"Might we all adjourn to the dining room?" Aunt Marshall said in her most congenial voice, eyes wide with worry as she looked between the two gentlemen and Emma. Of course Aunt Marshall would be more concerned with being a good hostess at a time like this. "Mrs. Gibbons promised to lay out a beautiful luncheon of cold meats and cheese for us to partake of when we returned from services, and I am sure it is ready and waiting. Mr. Weazelton, won't you join us?"

Emma wanted to protest. She did not want the imposing man anywhere in her home, but social propriety demanded she remain polite and hospitable. Nodding to the footman, who stood ready to push Lord Hamdon anywhere he might desire, she stepped up to the side of the chair. "Yes, you must be famished after your journey."

Mr. Weazelton eyed her position next to Lord Hamdon. Surely, he realized as the highest-ranking individuals in the room, they would precede him to the dining room. Finally, after what seemed like an eternity to Emma, Mr. Weazelton nodded and offered his arm to Aunt Marshall.

Seated far too cozily around the dining room table, plates filled with food from the sideboard, Lord Hamdon turned to Mr. Weazelton and said, "Mr. Weazelhand, what part of the country did you say you hail from?"

Emma had to quickly cover her mouth with her napkin, worried Lord Hamdon's consistent mispronunciation would cause her to spit food out. While diverting, he must know how insulting he was being.

For some reason, Mr. Weazelton chose not to acknowledge Lord Hamdon's mistake this time. "From Multon, a small village in Kent. And you, my lord? Where do you hail from?"

"The family seat is in Nottinghamshire, just outside of Maplebeck."

Mr. Weazelton nodded in acknowledgement, then turned his attention to Aunt Marshall. Conversation continued amicably as they all ate, with the majority of the discussion being held between the other three occupants at the table. Emma could hardly utter a word. The anxiety of having Mr. Weazelton in her home fairly choked her. Looking down at her plate still full of food, she realized she had to, at least, give some semblance of normalcy. If she was not more astute, Mr. Weazelton would see straight through her strange behavior and begin questioning her ability to reside alone, just as Aunt Marshall had.

She nibbled on a bit of cheese, but a sudden silence caused her to look up at the other guests. They all sat looking at her with expectation. "My apologies. What were we speaking of?"

"I asked, dear, which room we should place Mr. Weazelton in?"

Emma wanted to scream "None of them!" but with great self-control said, "Oh, the Yew Room, I think," giving her best company smile as she looked at her cousin. His face twisted a bit before he masked it with a strained, but friendly smile.

Her father's sense of humor had been a bit morbid when he created the Yew Room, the last one in the guest wing. While the wood made good furniture, it was also a symbol of death and doom. Emma was sure, by Mr. Weazelton's face, that he was well aware of the superstition. Lord Gladsby had always saved that particular room for those visitors he did not care for. In truth, there had not been many who had passed their stay there. But she was sure if there was one man he would have put in that room, it would have been Mr. Weazelton.

Emma waited for him to beg for different accommodations, but to her surprise, he simply thanked her. Perhaps he did not ascribe to the superstition. More likely, he could tell how much she did not want him there and he did not want to cause any disturbance that would put him deeper in her black books. Poor man did not know his name was already firmly at the top of the first page.

She was grateful her cousin had agreed so readily to the arrangement. His place in the Yew Room would mean he would have to walk by Lord Hamdon's room every time he entered the main part of the house. Unless, of course, he wanted to descend the servants' stairs on the other side, but Mr. Weazelton seemed too proud to condescend to any servile entrances.

"I am glad we have that settled," Aunt Marshall said far too cheerfully. "It will be so nice to have another man about. I, for one, will feel much safer at the prospect. How long do you expect to stay, Mr. Weazelton?"

Of course she would feel more comfortable. Did Aunt Marshall not know anything of her cousin's reputation? Did she simply trust him because he was male? Emma dearly hoped not. How had a woman of eight and forty gotten to this point in life without gaining at least some modicum of reservation where men were concerned?

"I hope to stay until my cousin, Lord Gladsby, returns. I should hate to think of cousin Emma being here unprotected."

Ah, it was to be a siege, then. Mr. Weazelton must have run out of friends who would keep him and was determined to take Engalworth by force, either through marriage or by court if her father did not return soon. Emma wanted to throw the man out upon his ear, but what excuse could she give to do so? Legally, he had a right to be here unless she could prove otherwise, which she was trying desperately to do.

"Marvelous! Things will be much merrier here with our numbers now even. We shall have to plan some diversions for you to enjoy while you are here, Mr. Weazelton," Aunt Marshall gushed. Emma could almost see the wheels in her aunt's mind turning, categorizing events and people without thought for Emma's wishes and desires.

"Yes, Mr. Wastrelton, I am to get my crutches day after tomorrow, and I would dearly like to explore the outside again. It has been over a month since I have been able to take in the fresh air and sunshine."

Emma saw her cousin's nostrils flare at Lord Hamdon's purposeful mistakes, but Lord Hamdon merely smiled absentmindedly at him, while skewering another piece of meat. Thoughts of her aunt flew right out of her mind, as she used her napkin again to cover the smile that bloomed on her own face. If Lord Hamdon was not careful, he was sure to truly upset Mr. Weazelton.

"My lord, my name is pronounced *Weaz-el-ton*."

"Yes, is that not what I said?" Lord Hamdon asked with a smile, glancing about the table for confirmation. "I do believe I got it right this time. Did I not, Miss Hensworth?" he asked, his stormy blue eyes locking with hers. While his face remained mostly placid, his dark brows lifted slightly in challenge.

She could not resist. Using all her governess's training, she schooled her features and said, "Why, yes, I heard Weazelton, did you not, *cousin*?" She added an overly sweet smile to the charade, hoping it would convince her cousin of her sincerity. Aunt Marshall's brows pinched at Emma's declaration, but she held her peace. Most likely because she did not want to contradict a viscount.

"Perhaps I misheard you," he grumbled. Then he set to cutting a piece of meat upon his plate with more force than Emma thought necessary given the tenderness she had encountered in her own piece.

Her eyes strayed to Lord Hamdon and she gave him a conspiratorial smile while her aunt and Mr. Weazelton were distracted with their meal. The smile she received in reply set those beautiful butterflies to dancing in her chest again.

It seemed Lord Hamdon would be a welcomed ally against her cousin. Perhaps, even the piece of the puzzle she needed to bring about a quicker end to this ridiculous charade they all were playing. His place, as the son of an earl, might bring a response from London far quicker than any of her letters. Her father had asked her to be patient, to give it time, but time was something they were quickly running out of, especially with Mr. Weazelton now in residence.

She needed a response now. Yesterday would have been preferable. Tonight, she would go through her father's study one more time. He said there was a letter to prove his words, but in the five months since his death, she had yet to find it. If she did not hear from London soon, she would need that letter to give her more time. If the letter actually existed, that is. Heaven help her, though, if it did not.

Chapter Nineteen

The glow of Emma's conspiratorial smile still warmed Anthony's heart. He had taken a risk pulling her into his game, but oh, how it had paid off. He had never tried to incorporate anyone into his larks except his three closest friends. They were the only ones he trusted to actually play along.

Having a woman, and not just any woman, but Emma the Ice Fairy, so readily rally around him was intoxicating. Was it possible to fall in love with a woman merely because she helped you get away with tomfoolery? Anthony did not know, but if not, he was beginning to think he might be the first case in history.

It had been two long days since that dinner, and Emma had proven to be a most worthy ally. He was sure by now Mr. Weazelton thought him a complete dolt with how many times he had misspoken the man's name, but her insistence had gotten him far more leniency than any man should ever get for such insults.

Anthony found himself actually excited to embark upon another encounter with the short, paunchy, partially-balding man. If only Dr. Jones would get here with the promised crutches, he would be able to start his next foray into annoying the unwanted Mr. Weazelton.

The good doctor's suggestion to introduce crutches earlier than originally expected had him antsy with anticipation. He had only been in the bath chair for less than a week, but he would not complain at the change.

Truthfully, he could not wait to regain some freedom of movement. Being stuck in this room day after day for almost a month had driven him nearly to bedlam. With the help of the crutches, he would now be able to make his way out of doors again, which was the place he most liked to be.

Idly, he wondered how Mariner was doing. He hoped the stable manager had taken good care of his horse while he convalesced. The horse would need exercising every day to keep his high-strung spirit manageable, but he supposed the stable hands would know that by now.

A rap on the open door brought Anthony's head up to look at a smiling Dr. Jones with Aunt Vie and Emma standing close behind him. The crutches the doctor held drew his attention. A giddy feeling enveloped him. It was done. His days stuck in bed or a chair were over. With any luck, hopefully for good. Anthony never wanted to spend another day so constrained to a bed again.

After the doctor demonstrated how to use the wooden instruments, he helped Anthony to his feet so he could practice. It took only a few paces across the room for him to become accustomed to them. With excitement, he asked if he might take a turn about the gardens.

"One step at a time, my lord. We need to go over how you will navigate the stairs first," Dr. Jones cautioned.

The group made their way to the stairs where the doctor demonstrated how he could descend, a hand upon the banister and the footman helping along his other side.

"I must insist that you have someone to help you every time you ascend or descend stairs. Heaven forbid you should fall and re-break that leg."

Anthony readily agreed. He, too, did not want to suffer a break again, particularly because it would put him back in that blasted bed.

"If you continue to do well upon the crutches," Dr. Jones went on, "and do not tire too quickly, you might go outside in a day or two. You will need someone to attend you there as well. The ground is not nearly as smooth in the gardens and stables as it is in the house. Best to have someone nearby to catch you should you begin to fall."

After Dr. Jones left, Anthony followed Aunt Vie and Emma into the drawing room. He was surprised Mr. Weazelton was not lurking about. The man had been Emma's shadow these last two days, which he knew annoyed her to no end.

Aunt Vie was chattering on about her last letter from her dear Mr. Marshall and how much she missed him. Half-listening, Anthony looked to where Emma sat upon a brocade chair near the end of the settee. He could tell by her far-off look she was not paying any heed to her aunt's words. Her eyes were pinched at the edges, her brow was slightly furrowed, and her lips pulled in a tight line. Something was bothering her. Perhaps Mr. Weazelton had been overly insulting today. He was generally condescending to Emma, insisting she needed him, but she had borne it well up to this point, even played it to her advantage. Had today just been too much?

"By the by," Aunt Vie said with excitement, "I received a letter from dear Bradley today. He accepted my invitation and said he would arrive in a fortnight. I am unsure what is keeping him. I did so hope he would come post haste, but he insists he has some business or other to attend to. What business, I cannot say. What business would a single man without occupation possibly have…" Aunt Vie droned on.

Anthony focused on the strained expression on Emma's face. Several times he saw her eyes flit to the window facing what looked to be the gardens. After each glance, she would refocus on her hands, which, Anthony realized, were fidgeting with the tips of her gloves. Not a good sign.

"Do you not agree, Anthony?"

His gaze fell back on Aunt Vie, embarrassed to realize he had not heard one word she had said in the last few moments. Taking a chance, he responded, "Undoubtably."

"I thought you would feel the same. I will write him and see if he may not be able to change his plans."

Anthony was worried. Were they still talking of Bradley, or was she speaking of someone else? Emma finally looked at her aunt. "Aunt Marshall, if Mr. Lenning says he is occupied with business, I believe we should let him be, whether he is single or not. Other people have lives outside of entertaining us, you know."

"Well, I never said he did not have important things to do," Aunt Vie huffed indignantly, "only that they could not be near as important as that of a married man." Suddenly, she rose from her seat and excused herself, claiming a need to speak with Mrs. Gibbons about supper.

Aunt Vie must have been truly affronted, but Anthony could not understand why. He looked to Emma, wondering if she would be frustrated with her aunt for taking over a responsibility that should be hers, but she was staring out the window again.

"Miss Hensworth, are you well? You seem particularly burdened by something this afternoon."

Glancing at him, she said, "I am well," in a slow measured way, then flicked her gaze back to the window, her eyes widened before narrowing into slits. Shooting to her feet, she marched quickly to the tall window, then made a noise that sounded half growl and half sigh.

Anthony pulled himself into a standing position. Wobbling a bit as he got his balance, he placed the crutches under his arms and carefully maneuvered around the furniture to stand beside the frustrated woman at the window. Surveying the view out the window, he saw beautiful flower beds in full bloom and ornamental bushes full of green leaves. Further in the distance, he saw what looked to be a bit of the stables, a patch of grassy open ground between the stables and gardens, and a grove of trees that seemed to circle the house.

"I feel like I am going mad," she said quietly.

"How so?" he asked with a good deal of concern. It was not every day a woman admitted to such unstable feelings.

"Last week, I thought I saw a man in the grove behind the stables while riding my horse. I informed the stable master, and he took it to our steward. Unfortunately, even though I have seen the man several times about the woods since then, no one else seems to spot him.

"Yesterday, he became more brazen, and I spotted him among the ornamentals in the garden, and today I thought I saw a man peeking through the window. I looked away, waiting to see if he might do so again, and he did, but I only caught just a glimpse of him before his face disappeared below the seal. I thought I might catch him in his retreat to discern if I might know the man, but by time I reached the window..." she trailed off; her face scrunched up in frustration.

"He was gone," Anthony finished. "Do you think, perhaps, it is Mr. Weazelton?"

"No. I do not think he would have any purpose to do so, but more to the point, the man I have seen is far taller and darker than my cousin's mousy complexion."

Anthony stared out the window, willing his eyes to see the man in question. A movement by the stables caught his attention, but the person stepping out of its recesses was much too small to be the man Emma spoke of. From this distance, it appeared to be a young boy, a large horse following meekly behind him. Anthony rubbed his eyes a moment before staring again. Was that Mariner? He had never seen his horse so docile in the three years he had owned the beast.

"Who is the boy leading my horse from the stables?"

Emma looked in that direction. A soft warm smile lit her face, changing the concern into, what was that, pride? Fondness? Anthony could not tell. Maybe a mixture of both.

"Owen Ladd. His father is our stable master."

"He must have a magic touch. I have never seen Mariner so calm. I must admit I am a bit frightened for the boy, being near such a large, restless animal."

"Is that concern for a servant I hear, Lord Hamdon?" she teased with that quirk to her lips that looked entirely too kissable. Where had that thought come from?

Trying to clear his thoughts, he said, "I am not a complete ogre, Miss Hensworth. I actually do care for the health and safety of people in my employ. I just do not get involved in their personal lives if I can help it."

"If you can help it?" she asked incredulously.

Anthony did not care to go into a detailed explanation of his current concern with his valet, so he chose to change the subject. "Do you have any inkling of who might want to spy upon you, Miss Hensworth?"

Her lips pursed and her eyebrows furrowed in thought. Anthony's eyes were drawn again to those puckered pink lips, his attention arrested by the thoughts flitting about in his head. How might it feel to kiss those lips? They looked so soft and supple. Would they taste sweet or salty?

He gave himself a firm mental shake. He was supposed to be helping the woman, not thinking about how to accost her. "Pull yourself together, Hamdon," he muttered, then froze at the sound of his own voice.

Chapter Twenty

Emma glanced at Lord Hamdon. He had muttered something unintelligible. Was he doubting her as much as she doubted herself? At least, she had doubted herself until just a few moments ago. She had definitely seen a face in the window; she was sure of it. She did not recognize the man, but she knew she had never laid eyes upon him before.

Why would a stranger be wandering about the grounds of Engalworth? Had word got out that a single, unmarried woman resided within? Were bandits at this very moment plotting how to plunder the place?

Goodness. She had been reading far too many gothic novels. The very idea of pirate-like bandits had scampered across her mental wanderings before she realized how ridiculous it was. The neighborhood had always been a rather quiet one, the small hamlet of Worthin being the only town within a couple of miles.

There were, however, multiple towns within fifteen miles. It would not take much for a person to travel from one of those. An hour at most, perhaps less if the person had a fast horse with good endurance.

"I do not know who would want to creep around Engalworth, Lord Hamdon, but whomever he is, he is determined not to be caught."

"But not to be unseen," he said with finality.

"Of course the man does not want to be seen. Why else would he disappear once he knows I have glimpsed him and he might be caught?"

"Forgive me, but there is a great difference between not wanting to be caught and not wanting to be seen. If a man does not want to be caught, he simply stays far enough at a distance to give himself a good head start on any pursuers. If he does not want to be seen, he does not take the risk of being spotted at all. There are plenty of times during the evening and night when one might sneak around without detection. This man is doing so in broad daylight. Mark my words, he wants to be seen."

Emma thought on this for a moment. "So you believe he is trying to frighten me?"

"Indeed. Perhaps someone your cousin has hired to make his presence at Engalworth seem more valuable to you."

She could see her cousin doing just that. He would be sorely disappointed, though, for she would not be cowed by him. Turning to Lord Hamdon, she assessed his finely-dressed person. Thatcher was doing quite a superb job standing in as valet for his lordship. The man looked as well as any gentleman Emma had seen in London, except perhaps where his coat was bunched and wrinkled around the arms due to his reliance on the crutches.

He pulled his gaze away from the window to look at her and caught her studying him. His mouth pulled into a soft smile that made her insides do somersaults. Yes, he was a handsome man, and by the look upon his face, he probably knew as much.

"You should probably not be so much upon your feet, Lord Hamdon. The doctor did say it would take time to build back up to the strength you had before your accident."

"Ah, yes. I forgot I am a feeble old man now," he teased.

Emma smiled at his reference to their earlier conversation. "Ah, well, if that is the case, I must advise Mrs. Gibbons to bring milk toast for you with the tea tray; cakes and biscuits would be far too rich for your digestion, I am sure." Before she thought through her actions, she began sauntering toward the bell pull, casting an impish smile over her shoulder as she went.

Lord Hamdon laughed, using his crutches to make his way toward her. "But milk toast is for children, not old men. And if I am a child, shouldn't I be liberally plied with biscuits and cake to keep me from acting out?"

"Is that the way your parents kept you in good behavior? They spoiled you with all the sweets you could eat? Had I known this sooner, then I might have made you more agreeable when you first came by merely keeping your mouth full of biscuits."

"I am sure you would have loved to stuff something in my mouth, but I do not believe it would have been biscuits."

"Yes, dirty stockings would have been more to my taste."

"You enjoy the taste of dirty stockings? What an odd taste to acquire."

A bark of undignified laughter burst from her mouth. She laughed at the image of herself sitting daintily at the dining room table cutting one of her stockings with a knife and fork before placing the silk in her mouth. What a ridiculous notion!

Lord Hamdon chuckled as well, his eyes full of mirth. Emma liked the way he looked when he laughed. It transformed him into the approachable man she had assumed him to be when he first lay injured on the Oak Room bed. Of course, he was turned out a bit better now. His light brown curls were no longer matted with blood and stuck to the side of his head; his face devoid of color.

His hair was longer than it had been upon his arrival. Styled quite neatly about his head, one irresistible curl at the forefront seemed determined to fall forward before he would sweep it back again. Emma found she quite liked that curl.

The smile on Lord Hamdon's face relaxed as he met her gaze. Embarrassed she had been caught staring, she cleared her throat and, after giving the bell pull a quick tug, made her way to the settee to await tea. To her surprise, he took the place at the other end. There was ample room between them, but she felt the situation had suddenly become quite intimate.

Aunt Marshall's absence, while a relief moments before, now felt odd. Was she not here to play chaperone? The woman had been so adamant about her role in those first few days, and now she was absent during a time when surely Society would deem her presence necessary.

Mrs. Gibbons bustled in at that moment, Thatcher directly on her heels, carrying the laden tea tray. After setting the heavy load upon the coffee table in front of her, Thatcher bowed and exited the room. Mrs. Gibbons looked about the room, eyes wide.

Emma imagined she could read the woman's thoughts, for she was wondering the same thing. Where had Aunt Marshall gone? She had told Emma she was going to meet with Mrs. Gibbons.

Turning to Emma, Mrs. Gibbons said, "Is there anything else I might get you, Miss Hensworth?"

"No, Mrs. Gibbons. You have preempted my request yet again. The tea looks lovely."

The housekeeper smiled sweetly and nodded. Sweeping the room again with her eyes, she tipped her head, indicating the chair near the door. Emma gave a subtle nod, and the woman took up the seat, pulling a basket out from beneath. She set to work mending what looked to be a pair of men's socks. Most likely for Mr. Gibbons, but the sweet woman had been known to repair Thatcher's clothes as well.

Lord Hamdon was still looking at Mrs. Gibbons, which gave Emma another moment to study him. She could only see his profile from this position, but she noticed a small bump upon the top of his nose. Was it naturally occurring, or had he broken it at one time?

Turning back, he caught her staring at him. Quirking his brow and the right corner of his lips, he looked at her with amusement. Her cheeks warmed. She desperately hoped she was not blushing, but she was sure the heat creeping up her neck and onto her face was betraying her.

She had flirted with him. The Ice Fairy had flirted with him, and if he was not mistaken, she was now blushing after being caught staring. Both were incredibly good signs that she just might be having the same change of heart that he found himself undergoing.

Anthony could not help but tease her just a bit. "Do I pass your inspection, now that you have made a thorough study?"

He was not disappointed, for the color in her cheeks darkened beautifully. Definitely a blush.

"I was only noticing a most unseemly bump upon your nose. Perhaps you had not noticed the way it mars your visage," she said, a look of gleeful challenge in her eyes.

He chuckled. It would seem Emma did not pull her punches when backed into a proverbial corner. "Yes, it must make me dreadfully terrible to look upon. It is too bad the ladies in London have such poor eye sight, for they seem to see past the malady and give me all sorts of elaborate compliments."

"Were they complimenting your face, your lordship, or your pocketbook?"

"Both, I suppose," he said with a grin. "Of course, with so many ladies in town not seeing this hideous bump, it makes one wonder if perhaps it is those in the country with poor eyesight. Tell me, Miss Hensworth, are you in need of spectacles?"

A quiet snicker near the door alerted Anthony that their conversation was definitely being overheard by the housekeeper.

"Spectacles? The only spectacle in this house is that bump upon your nose."

"Ah, then maybe it is your hearing that is going, for I asked," he raised his voice a bit, "If *you* were in need of spectacles."

Both ladies burst into laughter. When Emma had calmed herself enough, she said, "Touché, Lord Hamdon. In all seriousness, though, I must ask how you came by the small bump upon your nose."

"I broke it several years back," he said, smiling, but the admission caused him pain. In truth, his father had broken his nose the year he finished Eton. Anthony had happened upon Lord Lincolnhurst and his newest mistress. Youth and years of unrest between them had loosened his tongue more than usual that day, and he had not held back the exclamation of disgust.

His father had taken three steps and landed him a facer he would never forget, but Anthony did not regret the words he had spoken. He had already vowed never to become the man his father was, and that day had solidified it. He could not, however, tell Emma any of this; it was hardly polite conversation.

"It must have been a difficult experience if your expression is any indication," she said, concern clouding her features.

"It was, but I do not wish to speak of it," he said. Then, sobering his expression, he reached across the settee to take up Miss Hensworth's hand. Holding it between his own hands and giving it a gentle pat, he said a little louder, "Instead, we must speak of where we might get you a hearing horn."

He was rewarded with a giggle, which was enough to change his forced smile to a genuine one.

Chapter Twenty-One

Mr. Weazelton was going to be the death of her; Emma was quite certain. The man had hounded her day in and day out since his arrival. He seemed to be everywhere, prohibiting her a single moment to talk to Lord Hamdon alone since he had found them in the drawing room three days prior, Emma's hand clasped in both of Lord Hamdon's.

She thought with fondness on that conversation. It had been informative as well as entertaining. She found herself wishing daily for another moment where they were not hounded by the company of the intrusive Mr. Weazelton.

Of course, Aunt Marshall was not much better. She was constantly demanding all male attention for herself. How had Uncle Marshall handled such behavior? Did he not become jealous of her constant attention to the men around her? Is it possible he did not notice? Perhaps not. Being male, he would be showered with a great deal of Aunt Marshall's attention.

Emma's hope of speaking with Mr. Clayton on Sunday had been dashed because of that very pointed attention. Every time she had thought to get him alone, he was called back by Aunt Marshall. The only time she had managed were the few minutes in walking him to the door, but he had been so concerned with cautioning her about Mr. Weazelton that she had not been able to tell him about her conversation with Lord Hamdon.

Today, however, she was determined to speak with him. Donning her pelisse and bonnet shortly after breakfast, she advised Gibbons on her destination should her aunt ask after her.

Traversing the path between Engalworth and the vicarage with Smith at her side, Emma caught sight of an approaching rider. Odd to have a rider on this particular path, as it was usually used for foot traffic, but it was not completely uncommon. The man approaching on the bay gelding slowed his mount as he neared the ladies, tipping his hat as he passed. She did not recognize the stranger, but she instantly felt sorry for him. His face was weathered, and he looked to have missed a few too many meals. But the horse he rode looked to be quite fine, as did the clothes he wore. What a paradox, she thought, a poorly fed man on a well-fed animal.

When she reached the vicarage, Mr. Clayton was just exiting his home. Seeing her coming up the walk, he stopped and exclaimed, "Is all well, Emma?"

"Good day to you, too, Uncle," she said with a quirk to her lips.

His shoulders relaxed at her teasing. "So this was to be a neighborly visit? You have rarely ventured to my home in the last half year."

"Can I not come visit my favorite uncle?" she asked innocently.

"You know I shall tell Mr. Marshall of your words when next I see him. It will give me something to crow over."

Emma laughed. "I have put myself in the suds, for sure, for I believe I told Mr. Marshall he was my favorite uncle when last I visited him as well."

"Ah, yes, but you are older and wiser now, which is why I have taken his place," Mr. Clayton said with a smirk. Then in a more serious manner, he asked, "But truly, Emma, is everything all right? You do not usually venture down to visit me."

"In a manner of speaking."

"How so?"

"May we talk inside where we might sit?"

"Yes, of course." He offered his arm to her and lead her back inside. After calling for the housekeeper to bring tea, he took up the seat across from her.

"Have we been compromised?"

Emma raised her brows at him. The way in which he had worded his inquiry was questionable at best.

He chuckled nervously. "Dear me, that is not what I meant. What I meant is, has our secret been found out?"

"Yes and no."

"What is that supposed to mean?" he asked, scooting forward on his chair, concern adding lines to his already wrinkled face.

"Yes, we have been found out. No, it was not Aunt Marshall, nor Mr. Weazelton."

"Lord Hamdon," Mr. Clayton said with a sigh, sitting back. "I was worried the man was too intelligent to be fooled for long. Is he to go to the authorities then?"

"No!" Emma responded with surprise. "Why ever would he do that?"

"Emma, if your father's words are untrue, then we have been withholding the estate from its rightful owner. It could possibly be seen as a crime."

She could not believe it. Why would anyone declare it a crime if she did not disclose her father's death? It was her information to tell. No one else had the right to it. She was his closest family, after all.

"Lord Hamdon is in sympathy with us," she finally said. "He will not tell, and, quite to the contrary, has asked to be of any assistance. After meeting my cousin, he is more than willing to keep him from inheriting Engalworth Court."

"He is willing to find Alan?"

"No, not exactly. I have not told him that part yet."

"What *have* you told him, Emma?"

"Simply that my father died five months ago and that we are not divulging the information until certain circumstances occur."

"And he did not question what those circumstances are?"

"He did, but I asked for his trust and said I would tell him when I felt able."

"Emma. The man is a viscount. I am sure he could put more pressure on the Foreign Office than we can. If we could get a definitive answer..." He trailed off, raising his eyebrows to punctuate his meaning.

"I know. I have thought the same, but I had hoped to find the letter Father insisted he received. I wanted to see it with my own eyes. Check the date perhaps. What if Alan sent the letter before Dennewitz, and Father simply did not look at the date? Letters get delayed in the post all the time."

"Yes, but your father clearly said Alan would be behind enemy lines for quite some time. Alan would not have written that information if he was simply a soldier marching on Dennewitz, which we now know was not even fought by the British. It must have been a decoy by the Foreign Office to shake anyone who was on to him. If they thought he was dead, then they would not expect him to be hiding among them."

"Or perhaps the letter from Alan was a decoy sent before his disappearance to cover up his death."

"I cannot see anyone doing that. Alan would not have written it at the point of a sword. He would have died before leading your family astray."

Emma knew her uncle was right. They had argued these points many times before, but the "what ifs" still plagued her at night.

"I think you must tell Lord Hamdon. Get his assistance."

"But how? Mr. Weazelton tracks my every move. I am surprised he did not follow me here today."

"You are here rather early, my dear. Does Mr. Weazelton rise as early as you?"

Emma had not thought on that, but she had noticed he did not appear until later in the mornings, sometimes not until luncheons. However, neither did Lord Hamdon. Dr. Jones had advised his patient to get more rest as his body was still quite weak.

Perhaps she could speak to Lord Hamdon in the mornings. She had gone to his room regularly before he was permitted down stairs on his crutches, after all. But somehow, now it felt oddly inappropriate, especially with Mr. Weazelton just three doors down.

The realization that she was becoming increasingly attracted to Lord Hamdon did not help either. When she had viewed him only as an invalid, she had not even noticed the intimate way they would spend their mornings. Now, however, it seemed almost indecent to think she had spent so much time close to the man's bed.

If only she could somehow arrange a time to meet with Lord Hamdon before Mr. Weazelton came down for the day.

"I might be able to help you, Emma," her uncle said, seeming to read her thoughts. "Since Lord Hamdon is staying within our parish at the moment, I should visit him as the vicar. I could do so under the guise of giving spiritual guidance. If you would be so kind as to accompany me, we might tell him together. I could send him a note advising him to expect me tomorrow morning."

"What of Aunt Marshall? You know she cannot leave male company alone."

Mr. Clayton raised his eyebrows at the wording of her declaration. "If she becomes a problem, I will tell her I am in need of her assistance, and then you must tell Lord Hamdon on your own."

"Me? Would it not be more prudent for you to convey the information?"

"Emma, I do not have the rapport you seem to have developed with the viscount." He raised his bushy white eyebrows. "In addition, this is not my story to share. It is your family and your concern, my dear. If he questions the truthfulness of it, he may apply to me for confirmation."

Her heart warmed at Mr. Clayton's declaration. If only Aunt Marshall would give her the respect and deference Mr. Clayton honored her with. "I only meant to say it would be improper for me to spend a great deal of time alone with him. Whereas, you could do so without anyone questioning your reputation."

"It is my understanding you have already spent a great deal of time alone with Lord Hamdon." A mischievous smile played across his lips.

"My maid was always present," Emma said defensively, feeling the back of her neck heat.

"Methinks the lady doth protest too much," he quoted, his eyes dancing with merriment. Mr. Clayton always had been able to read her feelings faster than most.

Needing to get attention off herself, she said, "How early are you intending to visit?" If they were too early, it was possible that not even Lord Hamdon would be awake to receive them.

"Earlier than is considered polite, but as a vicar I am afforded a bit of lenience."

While she loathed the need to arise earlier, she did not think it would make much of a difference when their appointment was scheduled. The anxiety of the upcoming confession was sure to make sleeping nearly impossible.

Changing the subject, she asked, "Uncle, did you perhaps speak with Mr. Haze about the man in the woods before he left?"

"I did. While he saw evidence of people in the woods, it was no more than he usually sees. He agreed with Mr. Ladd; it was probably someone from a nearby village who was in search of a few meals. He promised he would keep watch, but with his sudden departure..." He shrugged.

"Yes, and what an inopportune time for our steward to be gone. Two days ago, the man in brown was hiding among the bushes in the garden, and yesterday he was peeking through the window of the drawing room. Lord Hamdon thinks it is someone Mr. Weazelton has hired to frighten me into accepting his presence at Engalworth, possibly even his proposal."

"It makes sense. I only wonder why no one else has glimpsed our mystery man."

"That is just it. Lord Hamdon thinks he only lets me see him as a sort of intimidation. Maybe if you all think I am unstable, you will force my hand."

"You, my dear, are not unstable, and I would never force you to accept someone you did not esteem."

"Thank you, Uncle, but I do not think Aunt Marshall would be so accommodating. She already thinks I should accept Mr. Weazelton if only to stay in my own home."

"I cannot see Vivian saying such a thing. She has always been a proponent for love matches."

"Well, she has not said it in so many words. It is only implied."

"Or assumed," he said, eyeing Emma in a way that made her squirm. Was he implying that she was misunderstanding her aunt's motives?

"Emma, I know you and your aunt have not got on well through the years, but she is a good woman. I believe she only wants what is best for you. Where you differ is in the concept of what is best."

Frustration at Mr. Clayton's words clawed at her throat. She wished to say some very unkind things about her aunt, but her uncle's gentle smile quelled her words.

"Just think on my words, will you, dear?"

Nodding, she rose. "I think I best get back."

"Give me a moment to dash out that note for Lord Hamdon, and you may carry it back with you. If you get an opportunity to talk with him before tomorrow, just send me a note, and we can cancel our plans."

Silence reigned as Emma walked back to Engalworth, Smith at her side, Mr. Clayton's note tucked in her reticule. While her maid was not extremely chatty, it was unusual for her to be this quiet. An unusual tension pulsed between them. Glancing quickly at Smith, she caught a look of consternation on the maid's face.

"Is something amiss, Smith?"

"It is not my place to say, miss."

Emma stopped walking and faced her maid. Smith stopped as well, but kept her face forward, a forced mask of unconcern.

"Smith, what is ailing you? You know I value your input in matters such as these. You have an uncanny sense when things are not as they should be."

"Something in what you said about the man in the woods; it isn't sittin' right." Smith's brown-eyed gaze flicked from one side to another, and that look of consternation again played across her face. "I think we need to keep walking," she said and increased her pace.

"Smith, what *is* the matter?" Emma asked sternly as she trotted to keep up with her much taller maid. "Slow down. I cannot keep pace with you."

Smith slowed a fraction, glancing at Emma as she caught up. "There's someone watchin' us." she said quietly. "I can't see 'im, but I can feel 'im."

Emma's gaze darted around like Smith's had moments before. She was not sure what she was looking for but assumed it was the same dark-haired man, clad in a brown coat and breeches. Most of the path wound through Engalworth fields, but several areas were surrounded by trees that had been planted a century ago to provide shade. She searched in vain for whomever had upset her maid, but she saw no movement around the trees ahead, nor those behind. Searching along hedge rows that separated fields and among the sheep grazing in a far pasture she saw nothing, but she could now feel the eerie calm around them.

Where was the bird song or perhaps animals calling to one another in the distance? As they approached the next small grouping of trees, a horse nickered from somewhere behind them on the trail. The sound was so close it startled the two women. Both grabbed hold of their skirts and ran.

Just past the next grouping of trees was the turn toward Engalworth. As they ran through the trees, Emma caught sight of something brown moving around a trunk. If her lungs had not been already taxed with the effort of exercise, she would have let out a scream. Instead, she let the fear propel her faster.

From somewhere behind she heard an approaching horse. Only after she had run several more paces did the sound register. It was not the steady drum of a horse at a run, but the clip clop of a trot. If someone had devious designs, would they not be moving at a swifter pace?

Emma glanced over her shoulder as she ran and saw nothing. Smith was several paces ahead of her, the maid's bonnet hanging about her neck, her brown bun bobbing with each step. There was no way Emma would catch her, but she had to know who followed them. That is, if there truly was anyone following them.

Slowing to a quick walk, she glanced again over her shoulder and saw nothing. Stopping, she turned to scan the trees as she held her heaving side. No movement caught her eyes. The open ground between her and the trees looked as it always had, but that feeling, as if she were being watched, still remained. What had happened to the horse? Everything around her was quiet except for the warble of a nearby bird.

Had she just imagined it? Everything seemed calm now. Was the steady clip clop only the sound of her beating heart? The traitorous organ still pounded hard in her chest. No, whatever it was, the sound was gone. She began walking carefully backwards, eyes still trained on the trees in the event the man in brown was actually hiding among their trunks.

A hand suddenly latched onto her arm. Terror jumped into her throat, forcing a scream out her mouth that surely would deafen anyone within a hundred meters.

Chapter Twenty-Two

Emma still felt ridiculous early the next morning. Poor Smith had nearly jumped out of her skin when she had screamed. She was unsure how she had missed her maid's approach from behind. She tried to convince herself it was due to her focus on the trees. One thing was for sure; if someone had been hiding in wait, she would have been easy prey. That was evident by the ease at which Smith had approached without detection.

She watched the tired maid through the mirror as the poor woman arranged the curls atop her head. It appeared she was not the only one losing sleep over the stress of the previous day. They both went through the motions in almost complete silence, fruitlessly covering yawns that seemed to be passing between them.

Finally, she said, "My apologies, again, for screaming in your ear, Smith."

"I'm fine, miss. No need apologizing. We was both given a great fright."

"Yes." Emma was not sure of another time in her life that she had been so frightened.

"I can't help but think," Smith said, "maybe the horse we heard was from the gentleman we passed on our way to the vicarage."

"I have thought the same. Perhaps he stopped in the shade. It was near the original place we passed by him."

"It was, indeed."

"Strange, however, that we did not see him as we passed. The foliage there is not terribly thick."

Smith only nodded as she finished placing the last pin. Stepping back, she picked up a thin silver chain with a single pearl upon it. Emma had chosen it specifically for today's meeting. She did not wear the trinket often, but she needed the extra courage. As Smith placed the adornment about her neck, her mind spun back to her tenth birthday when her mother had given her the necklace as a gift. A reminder to take life's challenges and, like the clam, turn them into something beautiful.

Emma rubbed the pearl between two fingers for a moment as she stared unseeing into the mirror. How she wished her mother was here to hold her and give her the advice only a mother could.

Her eyes finally focused on Smith's face in the mirror. The pity she saw there galvanized her. Straightening her back and raising her chin a notch, she asked for her white shawl. It was not terribly cold, but she needed something to wrap about herself, if for nothing more than to hold her together.

This was the moment. Lord Hamdon would either believe her or think her a complete lunatic. Well, perhaps not complete. Emma could not see him thinking so ill of her, but he would probably pity her, advise her to give up, and move on. But, oh, how she hoped he would help.

Anthony stared at the piece of paper yet again. He had woken early in order to meet with the vicar and was even now waiting in the sitting room on the west side of the court. It was a cozy, little room decorated in light peach and green, with a few landscape paintings dotting the twalls. The two settees and four chairs were gathered around a small tea table in the center of the room. A chaise sat near one of the windows, a perfect place to read.

He set the vicar's note in front of himself on the table. Why the man was so insistent they meet at such an early hour, he did not know, but he was beyond curious to find out.

The door opened, and he heard a rustle of skirts. Turning, he saw Emma standing in the doorway, a look of surprise on her face.

"I had not thought you would be down so soon."

"So soon?"

"Yes." Glancing around, she cleared her throat. "I had hoped to have a few moments to compose myself before my uncle arrived."

"Ah, I see. It seems you were included in this early morning invitation."

Stepping away from the open door and approaching the settee, she said, "I may have, that is, it is because of me, well, I..."

The corners of Anthony's lips began to twitch. Emma was rather charming when she was nervous. She stood at the edge of the settee, her left hand pinching the tips of the glove on her right, her eyes flitting about the room, landing on anything but him.

"You initiated the meeting?" he asked, curious why she wanted him to meet with her uncle. Was she concerned for his eternal soul? Had he said something of late that made her think he was in need of a vicar?

A voice from the door announced, "Mr. Clayton." Emma thanked the butler and turned to give her uncle a quick embrace.

"Good morning, Emma dear. How are you faring?"

"I would be faring much better if I had been able to stay abed a few more hours."

Anthony saw amusement light Mr. Clayton's face at her honest admission.

"Well, perhaps you may recover those hours later today. And how are you this morning, Lord Hamdon? You are looking better and better every time I see you."

"Thank you, Mr. Clayton. I find I am healing well. I have yet to gain back all the strength I lost, but I suppose with time that, too, shall return. And you, sir? How is your health?"

"Fine, fine." Mr. Clayton took a seat on the settee across from Anthony. Emma chose a chair near the end of the settee next to him. She had left off worrying her right glove and now pinched the fingers of her left.

After several minutes of polite conversation, Mr. Clayton finally came to the point. "Lord Hamdon," he said, in a quieter voice than he had employed up to this point, "my niece has advised me that you are aware of Lord Gladsby's passing."

Anthony was surprised by the topic. Apparently, his soul was not the subject of discussion, which honestly relieved him. He would much rather discuss Emma's problems than his own. Turning to look at Emma, he noticed she no longer fidgeted with her gloves but looked at him intently.

"Ah. Yes, she has apprised me of the circumstances." Emma looked down at her lap and began fidgeting again. He was unsure why his answer had been so important to her, but it must have, given her undivided attention.

"I am sure she also impressed upon you the necessity of your silence?"

Perhaps that was why the vicar had come. If Emma had not impressed upon him how important this was, the vicar meant to put the fear of God in him. She had, however, been quite clear in her declaration of the importance of secrecy. Anthony understood full well what lay on the line, but he was unsure how they planned to circumvent Mr. Weazelton. Once a property was entailed to the male line, it was nigh unto impossible to change.

"Sir, your niece made it very clear. If you are here because you fear I will not be circumspect, I must assure you that I can be relied on as one who knows when to keep his peace."

"I do not doubt it, Lord Hamdon, and I am grateful for your continued silence. I am not here because I worry about your abilities, but rather to ask for your help."

Anthony looked between Mr. Clayton and Emma. Her eyes were again fixed on him, awaiting his answer. He wanted to please her, to allay her fears, to see her smile, but he could not pledge help when he did not know what was being asked of him.

"Mr. Clayton, how is it that I can help in this situation?" he asked incredulously. "I must admit, I have yet to really understand the entire situation. Emma has admitted to her father's passing and his request for secrecy, but that is all. I cannot promise help on so little information."

"I understand, and that is why Emma has agreed—" A strange tap sounded three times in the room. Anthony looked to the door where it had originated.

"Plan B, Emma." Mr. Clayton rose from the settee. Emma nodded, her face going pale. A few moments later, Aunt Vie entered the sitting room clad in a blue day dress, a mobcap upon her head.

"I thought I heard voices in here," she said, looking at the gathered group. Anthony fished the timepiece out of his coat pocket if for no other reason than to hide his face a moment as he attempted to gain some composure. Why did Aunt Vie have to choose this moment to interrupt them? It was only a quarter past eight, only fifteen minutes since the last time he had checked.

"Oh, Mr. Clayton, Gibbons did not apprise me of your arrival or I would have been down sooner." Turning to Anthony, she scolded, "Did not the doctor say you were to stay abed until at least noon?"

"I am the cause of his early appearance, Mrs. Marshall. You must not blame him. We had some matters of great import to discuss," Mr. Clayton paused for a moment before adding, "about the nature of the soul."

Aunt Vie looked on with concern. "Oh, well, in that case, Emma, you and I should probably leave them alone to discuss the subject. I do not believe they desire a young lady's presence for such deep subject matter."

Anthony did not know how Emma felt about her aunt's words, but he, for one, would be offended. Did Aunt Vie believe her niece such a simpleton that she could not understand matters of religion?

"On the contrary, Aunt Vie," Anthony rose to her defense, "I believe Miss Hensworth an asset to our conversation. She is an intelligent young woman capable of discussing a myriad of topics. I do not believe the nature of the soul is beyond her abilities to comprehend. In fact, I am interested to hear exactly what she might say on the matter."

Mrs. Gibbons chose that moment to enter the room, ushering Thatcher in with tea and coffee on a tray, as well as a few cheese turnovers most likely meant for the breakfast table. Upon seeing the housekeeper, Mr. Clayton gave a brief nod and smile. Turning to Aunt Vie, he said, "Mrs. Marshall, before I continue my conversation with Lord Hamdon, I have a matter I must discuss with you in private. Could we step into the breakfast parlor for a moment?"

Aunt Vie looked confused. Glancing between Emma and Anthony, she was about to protest when Mr. Clayton spoke up.

"Mrs. Gibbons may provide supervision while we are gone. It will only take but a moment or two."

Reluctantly, Aunt Vie nodded, leading Mr. Clayton out of the sitting room. Gibbons slowly shut the door, throwing Anthony a sly smile. It would seem the servants were well adept at manipulating situations to suit current needs.

Emma leaned forward. "Do you take tea or coffee in the morning, Lord Hamdon?"

"Coffee, please." She nodded and poured a cup of coffee for him, adding the sugar he requested, then tea for herself. Anthony watched as she stirred cream and sugar into her cup. Holding his coffee cup, he waited for her to begin, but when she did not, he pressed forward.

"Mr. Clayton was saying you agreed to, well, something, before we were interrupted. What, might I ask, was that?"

Emotions played across her youthful face. Was she calculating how much she might tell? Would she only give him a portion as she had before? When she finally spoke, the words that so matter-of-factly came out of her mouth were not at all what he had expected.

"My brother Alan is not dead."

Chapter Twenty-Three

She had said it, but did she really believe it? It now seemed completely ludicrous. Why had she believed a fevered, dying man who provided no proof before his death that anything he said was even remotely true? Maybe Lord Hamdon would think her a lunatic after all.

His astonished look faded into one of skepticism. "Then where, pray tell, is the man? Shouldn't he be here caring for his beautiful, vulnerable, unmarried sister along with assuming his position as Lord Gladsby?"

Emma detected a hint of irritation in his tone, but why? Alan was not being negligent. Well, at least, not at present. Years ago he had been, for sure, but now she was sure Alan would have rushed to her immediately if his situation allowed for quick action.

Suddenly, her brain caught up with Lord Hamdon's words. Did he truly think her beautiful? The thought thrilled her. But also vulnerable. Did he think her weak? Perhaps his anger hinged on his fear for her safety.

Schooling her thoughts, she refocused on the pertinent information she needed to divulge before Mr. Clayton returned with her aunt.

"According to my father, Alan is working behind enemy lines as a spy for the British army."

"Is that so? I thought you received word last fall that he was missing and presumed dead."

"We did in October," she said hesitantly. Emma had expected the skepticism in Lord Hamdon's voice, but it still made her uneasy. "However, my father received a letter from Alan at the beginning of December indicating the first letter was a decoy and detailing how to get word to him in the event he was needed at home. "

"May I see the letter?" he asked, incredulity coloring his words.

"I do not have it." This was the part she had dreaded admitting. The letter's long absence had caused her to doubt the validity of her father's words. She could not imagine what someone disconnected with the situation might think of her confession.

"Do you mean you do not have it on your person, or you do not possess the letter?"

"Both, my lord. However, I am sure I will find it soon. My father claimed it was in his study, but I have yet to locate it."

"In the five months since your father's death you have yet to locate your brother's letter?" Slowly shaking his head, he said, "Emma, are you sure such a letter even exists?"

She sat for a moment, stunned at his use of her Christian name. Lord Hamdon did not seem to notice, however, and only looked at her with something akin to pity filling his eyes. Did he think her misguided, unrealistic, irrational?

"Lord Hamdon," she said, enunciating his name clearly, her heart beginning to pound as she fought to keep both her breathing and words even. "I understand how this sounds, but you must understand. My father was most insistent. He was a wise, intelligent man who was never prone to falsehoods. If he said it was true, then it is true." She punctuated the last four words. "My father was so convinced that even in his deteriorated state, he wrote the Foreign Office himself asking them to return his son and explaining his dire need."

"So you knew what the letter to London contained?"

"I do not know the particulars, but I do know what my father's intentions were. He explained to me that it would take several months for them to pull Alan from behind enemy lines and that I must be patient. I have tried, but I am growing restless. I have written the Foreign Office twice in the last two months explaining our plight, asking for direct confirmation whether or not my brother is alive, but I have received no word."

"I would think their silence would be answer enough. With Bonaparte's abdication and exile, the war is essentially over. If your brother was still alive, should he not be home by now?"

"I am sure it just takes time. Even with the war being over, there are still people who could impede his return. My father said Alan's letter implied there was a traitor among his commanding officers in addition to the danger among the French ranks he incorporated himself into."

"If that is so, would not additional letters, containing your doubt of his demise, compromise his position?"

"I had not thought of that," she conceded, realizing for the first time that letters inquiring if her father's information was, indeed, correct, could possibly be endangering her brother. If she had only seen what her father had written. Was there a particular code or phrase they were to say? Or perhaps a certain person the information was to be addressed to? Emma had simply addressed the letter to the Foreign Office.

Lord Hamdon let out a deep sigh, then steepling his fingers, said, "Mr. Clayton mentioned you hoped for my help. In what way would I be coming to your aid?"

Was he actually considering helping her? Did he believe her? Studying his face, she realized he was still incredulous, but perhaps sympathy for her position was winning out over doubt.

"Originally, I had hoped as a future member of Parliament, you could put more pressure on the Foreign Office for answers. However, now I am unsure if it would be prudent given your conjecture. Perhaps another letter would only prolong Alan's absence, making it harder for him to return home."

"Perhaps. It is hard to say. With the war over, I should think the risk is much less than that of a few months ago. However, if what you say is true and your brother is a spy, it may be more complicated than either of us knows." Lord Hamdon laced his fingers together as he leaned forward. "It may be more expedient to travel to

London myself and pay a visit to the Foreign Office. That way there will be no mistaking my actual identity. A letter, you see, could be forged by anyone with the right tools."

"A visit? But that will take weeks, perhaps even months depending on the doctor's opinion on the progression of your healing."

"Very true, but it would give me time to decipher who your brother reports to and allow me to evade anyone of unscrupulous character."

Emma nodded thoughtfully, not knowing what else to say. She did not know if she was patient enough to await Lord Hamdon's healing, especially of late. Her patience had been growing increasingly thin with the appearance of Mr. Weazelton and their mystery interloper. She was not sure if she had truly seen anyone among the trees yesterday, but if she had, it surely must have been the man in brown.

"I cannot wait that long, Lord Hamdon. I need help soon. Smith and I were frightened near out of our wits yesterday on the walk home from the vicarage. Whether the person watching us was hired by Mr. Weazelton or not, I am starting to fear for my safety."

Lord Hamdon studied her face intently, a look of concern furrowing his brows. "You saw him again yesterday?"

"No, only heard a horse following us. As I ran through a group of trees, I saw a flash of brown dart behind a tree, but I cannot be sure it was the man I saw or just a trick of the light."

"The man in the woods was on a horse?"

"No, whoever was in the woods was not mounted. It was someone following behind us. We did pass a man on our way to the vicarage that was mounted on a magnificent bay gelding. My maid seems to think it might have been his horse we heard."

"Did you know the man?"

"No, he was a stranger to me. People do not often ride horses upon that foot path, so it struck me as strange, but not being local, perhaps he did not know. The man had such an odd appearance. He was weathered, sickly, and thin, but sitting upon a fine horse with fine clothes to match."

"He may have stolen the animal."

"Perhaps, but he would have needed to steal the clothes as well, for they were almost as fine as the animal."

"So you saw the man on the horse following you, and you glimpsed another man in the trees?"

"I did not see the man on the horse. Only heard the noise which frightened my maid, who, honestly, was already on edge. Her concern unnerved me, so we ran when we heard the horse nicker from somewhere behind us."

"Let me see if I understand you. Your maid was concerned..."

"Yes, because she felt like someone was watching us."

"Ah. So when you heard the horse, you ran, and while running through one of the stands of trees, you thought you saw another person."

"Yes."

"Is it possible there are two people involved now?"

She stared at him, letting his words sink in. It was entirely possible that the two were connected. That would explain why she felt the danger so acutely. One man was scary enough, but two?

The three clicks of Gibbons's boot sounded on the bottom of the sitting room door, giving her a start after discussing the events from yesterday. When her brain caught up with the preplanned signal, she quickly said, "We shall have to finish this conversation at a later date." Straightening her back and pasting a polite social smile on her face, she waited for the advent of Aunt Marshall and Mr. Clayton.

Realizing silence would seem out of place to anyone entering, she said, "Do you think we will have rain today, Lord Hamdon?"

He narrowed his eyes skeptically until the door opened. Then the conversational shift must have sunk in. "Well, it is England. We would be like fish out of water if it did not rain at least once every day or so."

"Very true," Aunt Marshall called from the door as she entered. "I think I would feel quite out of place if we went more than a day without a little moisture."

Taking up a seat across from Lord Hamdon, Aunt Marshall controlled the next quarter hour's conversation until she recalled Mr. Clayton's visit.

"Mr. Clayton, I must have forgotten myself. You had mentioned you came to discuss religion with dear Anthony."

Emma glanced briefly at her uncle, giving an almost imperceptible nod. He took her meaning and said, "Oh, I believe we discussed the most important questions earlier. Further discussion can wait until another time." Standing, he continued, "The day is getting on, and I must wish you all a good day. I am expected at another parishioner this morning to discuss the celebration of Pentecost."

"Oh, do let us know if there is anything Engalworth can contribute for the poor baskets," Emma said, standing as well.

Mr. Clayton nodded. "Might you walk me out, Emma? It will give us a moment to discuss the parish needs."

Aunt Marshall waved her off as if Mr. Clayton was asking her permission for Emma's excusal. Emma schooled her features to hide her irritation at her aunt's high-handed ways. She took hold of her uncle's arm and followed him into the inner court. They walked quietly for a few moments, giving themselves distance from the sitting room.

Finally, Mr. Clayton leaned in. "Did I give you enough time?"

"I was able to convey the most important information, yes. Unfortunately, Lord Hamdon pointed out a flaw to our plan."

"And what was that?"

"If Alan is, in fact, being watched by anyone with nefarious intent, my letters could have possibly caused complications. Perhaps that is why Alan has not returned before now." she said, stopping at the front door.

Mr. Clayton was quiet. Then letting out a sigh, he said, "I'm afraid he is correct. The letters might have caused additional delays. I had not thought of that myself. It looks as though we will be forced to wait a bit longer."

Emma wanted to apprise her uncle of the man, or possibly men, she had encountered yesterday, but noise from the upstairs corridor drew their attention.

It seemed today everyone had arisen early, for standing at the top of the stairs, dressed and ready for the day, was Mr. Weazelton.

"Mr. Clayton, welcome to Engalworth," he called out as if he were the host and Mr. Clayton were a guest. Emma almost scoffed at the possessive manner by which he treated her family home.

"Good morning, Mr. Weazelton," Mr. Clayton greeted him warmly, but she could see the tension around his eyes.

A strained silence lingered as Mr. Weazelton took the last few steps to the front entry.

"Good morning, cousin," he wheezed out, the nasally quality of his voice grating on her nerves. "I see you are wearing my favorite color again." His eyes took in the grey gown she wore. When his gaze fell decidedly below her face, Emma was grateful she had insisted on the fichu this morning.

Mr. Clayton cleared his throat, trying to gain Mr. Weazelton's attention. "I had not realized you fancied such a somber color, sir. It is in fact the color of mourning if you recall?"

Mr. Weazelton's eyes briefly flicked to the vicar before returning to their previous direction of attention. Emma wanted to hide away somewhere. Pulling her white shawl tightly about herself, she took an involuntary step back.

Finally, Mr. Weazelton pulled his attention away from her, responding to the question as he pulled a small box from his jacket pocket. "Yes, I am quite aware, and dear Emma wears it so well. It must be a favorite of hers," he said as if she was not even present to speak for herself, "for she wears it every day."

It was not, in fact, her favorite color, not even for mourning. It was, however, how she felt each and every day. Grey reminded her of a storm. Sometimes blustery, sometimes calm, but always bringing a great amount of waterworks. Yes, the color represented her feelings entirely.

"I do not wear this color for my own amusement, sir," she said curtly, as he opened the small box he had extracted and placed a pinch of snuff on the crook of his finger.

"Oh?" he said, lifting his finger to his nose and taking a long snort.

What a disgusting habit, she thought. Why would anyone want to sniff the dirt-like substance up their nose? It was no wonder her cousin's speech had such a strange sound. He probably could not get much air in or out of his nose, having it full of that stuff.

That was all the reply she was to get as Mr. Weazelton turned back to Mr. Clayton. "Are you come to breakfast with us? It would be nice to have competent conversation at the breakfast table for once."

Emma sucked in her breath at the rude remark. How dare he?

"Sorry, Mr. Weazelton, but I am needed elsewhere this morning. I was just on my way out. My regrets on leaving you to your own company at the breakfast table. Perhaps another time I can return and bring my competent conversation with me."

She almost snorted at the veiled retort.

"It is no matter; we shall see you another time," Mr. Weazelton said, looking pointedly at the door.

Stepping up to Emma, Mr. Clayton gave her shoulders a quick squeeze and kissed her on the cheek. "Another time, dear one."

"Yes, good luck with your visits," she said, feeling decidedly let down at his impending departure, but Mr. Clayton lingered at the door, putting on the gloves Gibbons handed him.

Not until Mrs. Gibbons walked into the court and stopped a respectable distance away did Mr. Clayton finally take his leave. Emma took the opportunity Mrs. Gibbons presented to excuse herself from Mr. Weazelton, insisting she must go over the week's menu. Truthfully, they had gone over the menu on Monday, but she hoped God would forgive her another white lie especially in light of all the black ones she had told of late. What was one more lie when her entire life at present was full of them?

Chapter Twenty-Four

Five full weeks had passed since Lord Hamdon's arrival, four since Aunt Marshall's, and one since Mr. Weazelton's, and Emma felt like if she had not been losing her mind before, she most definitely was now. Every day was spent trying to avoid two guests, while trying to find a moment to speak to the other.

If it had not been for Mr. Clayton's help, she would never have been able to speak with Lord Hamdon privately. Today Emma could not get a moment's peace from either her aunt or Mr. Weazelton. All four of them had attended Sunday services this morning, it being the first outing approved for Lord Hamdon.

They garnered no small amount of attention upon their arrival and again as they were leaving. She could not blame the people. It was not every day a viscount set to inherit an earldom attended services in Worthin.

Emma had tried to be patient as she introduced Lord Hamdon and Mr. Weazelton to several members of the congregation, but when the marriage-minded mamas lined up with their daughters, she decided a hasty exit was now necessary. It was not that she disliked most of the women she saw, only that a sense of unease filled her at having to perform introductions to Lord Hamdon.

Using Lord Hamdon's obvious physical limitations, she asked that the rest of the congregants excuse them, and began making her way to the door with the injured man. Behind her, she could hear her aunt continuing to make a few introductions for Mr. Weazelton. Good, she thought, perhaps having other acquaintances would get the man out of her hair. Not that she wished him attached to any of the four eligible women in the parish.

Well, perhaps Miss Bower. She had never been all that kind to Emma while they were growing up. Miss Bower had consistently pointed out Emma's diminutive stature, and in their early adolescence, her lack of womanly curves. Emma had to admit some unholy glee when her body had begun filling out in all the right places as Miss Bower had become more and more matronly by the year.

Emma knew she should pity the woman, who was over five years her senior. While fuller figures were quite the rage, it seemed Miss Bower's had grown out of fashion, for she had yet to receive a single offer of marriage at nearly five and twenty. Perhaps if Miss Bower's disposition had not grown increasingly sour and her tongue so sharp, she could have managed to feel empathy for her.

The sound of Aunt Marshall's voice carried to the back of the church as she introduced the very person Emma had been thinking on. She smiled to herself, mentally wishing Mr. Weazelton the best of luck.

After exchanging a few words with her uncle at the door, she beckoned to Mr. Ladd, who rushed over to help Lord Hamdon down the steps. Since they no longer had a coachman, Mr. Ladd had filled the need today. She could have had Mr. Weazelton drive the phaeton over with Lord Hamdon, leaving her to walk with her aunt and the maids, but she still felt nervous about walking the path between the church and Engalworth unescorted.

By the time she and Lord Hamdon were situated in the carriage, Aunt Marshall and Mr. Weazelton were making their way down the church steps.

"I am surprised she can talk so amicably with such a man," Emma murmured.

"Your aunt has the gift of being able to converse easily with everyone."

"Except me."

"I wouldn't say she does not talk easily with you; she just does not allow you to respond," he said with a quirk of his lips.

She smiled back, studying his handsome face a moment. "Her conversation is so prolific, I do not think she gives anyone much chance to respond."

"Touché." He chuckled. "I think I only get in one word for every ten of hers."

"Your odds are much better than mine. The best I get is about thirty to one."

When the door swung open upon her last sentence, she was stunned into silence. Emma had not realized how close her aunt and cousin were. Mr. Weazelton handed Aunt Marshall up into the carriage then entered himself.

Looking between Lord Hamdon and Emma, he asked, "Did I hear you discussing gambling odds? An odd subject for a lady, I must say. Tell me, was it card games or horse races?"

Aunt Marshall looked at her, completely aghast. Emma knew she would never hear the end of the subject if she allowed her aunt to think she had been discussing such an uncouth topic— on the Sabbath, no less. She was unsure how to go about it, though. Aunt Marshall barely acknowledged her as an adult, let alone listened to what she had to say.

"You are quite mistaken, Mr. Weazelton." Lord Hamdon came to her defense. "We were not discussing gambling at all, only how well Miss Hensworth plays lawn bowls."

The words that had gathered in Aunt Marshall's mouth seemed to sputter out in a great gush of air. The sound caught Mr. Weazelton's attention. "Are you quite all right, Mrs. Marshall?"

"Yes. Yes, indeed. I am quite all right. How did you enjoy the sermon, Mr. Weazelton?"

The expression of disgust that quickly passed over his face before he cover it did not surprise Emma in the least. Today's topic had been a direct assault on his peace of mind, she was sure of it. Her uncle's words seemed to be directed purposefully toward Mr. Weazelton as he spoke of overindulgence and selfishness.

"It was an interesting choice for a sermon," he said.

That was all Aunt Marshall needed. She prattled on for the rest of the short drive to Engalworth, unconcerned with anything other than having a captive audience.

After a brief luncheon, Emma retired to her room to have a few hours reprieve from her aunt's incessant talking. She was frustrated to learn during the meal that her aunt had extended several invitations for tea. When she had protested,

Aunt Marshall declared it was well past time for Emma to put off her mourning completely.

She knew Society dictated only six months for a brother, but how could she possibly put off mourning knowing full well that she wore it for her father?

Sitting upon her bed, fingering the last bit of lace her father had given her before his passing, her heart was filled with fresh grief. The lace was to have been her Christmas gift, but Christmas never came for her father.

Next Sunday would be five months since his last breath. Like so many times before, her mind pulled her back, replaying those last few moments as if they had just occurred.

"It will not be much longer," Mrs. Gibbons *said as Emma placed another cool cloth on her father's forehead.*

Tears quietly trickled down her cheeks. She was unsure when they had begun, but she knew they had come with regularity since the terrible rattle had started in her father's chest. It had been two days since he was last conscious.

The last words he had been able to say played over and over in Emma's mind.

"Maria! Maria! Help me," he had uttered with all his strength.

It had broken Emma's heart to hear him calling for her mother, but his silence now was more painful. Soon he would be joining her.

She dabbed at her tears; all the reassurances of her brother's existence had done nothing. With her father's passing, she would be an orphan. Completely alone in the world, especially if she held through with his request for secrecy. How was she to survive these next few months so secluded?

Mr. Clayton rushed in, sweat upon his brow, even though he had come in from the cold of December. Glancing at Lord Gladsby, he asked, "Am I too late?"

"No," she said quietly as her father took another rattling breath. Each one was farther apart now, but Emma counted each as they came, wishing the next was the last, and at the same time, praying it was not. She hated seeing him suffer, but she did not want him to go. It was a strange position to be in.*

Stepping to the side of the bed, Mr. Clayton began administering last rites. The finality of the ceremony caused Emma to choke upon the sob that had built in her throat. This could not be the end. She was not ready. How could he leave her so soon?

"I'm not ready," she uttered, clasping her father's far too warm hand in hers. "I'm not ready, Father." she said louder, her body shaking from the effort it took to hold back her cries.

A loud rattling breath was followed by the most deafening silence she had ever heard in her entire life. Her heart hammer in her chest as the sobs she had suppressed for days were ripped from her throat by some unseen force. Never had she grieved so deeply as she did in that moment. Never had she experienced so much pain.

"I was not ready! I was not ready!" she repeated over and over as she lay over the side of the bed, her father's hand still clasped in hers. Mrs. Gibbons rubbed gentle circles upon her back as each racking sob melted into the cover of her father's bed.

Emma did not know how long she lay in such a manner. When she had quieted, Mr. Clayton gently pulled her to her feet, helping her down the hall to her room. She caught sight of her uncle's compassion-filled face as they slowly walked the short distance, his eyes rimmed with red, as he guided her to her bed.

"I was not ready," she uttered again, wishing somehow it could change things.

"I do not believe we ever are, Emma, dear," he said, leaning down and kissing her forehead. "I do not believe we ever are."

Tears trickled down Emma's face as the memory faded. It still felt as if it was only yesterday. How could she put off mourning when she still mourned so deeply? How could she entertain visitors and pretend all was well?

She could not pretend to be well. It was impossible. She would maintain her mourning no matter what her aunt insisted. At least then perhaps the other ladies would show some restraint toward her and not pepper her with questions as Aunt Marshall did.

At least she would have three days to prepare her mind and heart. A few Society ladies were nothing compared to the problems she was currently facing with Mr. Weazelton. She could withstand a few moments of unease.

That evening at dinner, Mr. Weazelton announced he would be absent for the next two evenings. It was an absolute stroke of luck. She had needed to speak with Lord Hamdon, but did not know when she would find more time. There was still much to tell, and if she was being completely honest, she hoped to stumble upon another intimate moment like the one in the drawing room.

She silently gave thanks to whichever neighborhood families had extended the invitations. Perhaps tea would not be so very bad after all. If the ladies of her acquaintance could direct Mr. Weazelton's attention away from her, she could surely spend an hour or two talking of lace and fashion.

Emma went to bed that night planning how she would get Lord Hamdon alone. He had mentioned several times his desire to see the gardens; perhaps they could go for a stroll tomorrow after Mr. Weazelton removed himself for the evening. She would need Thatcher's help to get Lord Hamdon down the stairs and to the garden, but while there, they could sit upon one of the stone benches which would give them some privacy, as long as Thatcher did not linger too close.

Snuggling deep under the quilt upon her bed, Emma allowed her mind to wander into happy thoughts. Tomorrow was going to be a good day. She would get to enjoy beautiful flowers and fresh air, and if she was lucky, stormy blue eyes, golden brown curls, and a contagious smile.

Chapter Twenty-Five

Frustration bubbled up in Anthony's chest at the sound of footsteps on the stairs. Yesterday when he and Emma had tried to take a walk about the gardens, Aunt Vie had inserted herself most intrusively. He had so many questions he wished to ask Emma, but if they could not shake Aunt Vie, he did not know if there would ever be a chance.

Lately it seemed like the moment he stepped foot out of his room, he was in constant company with either Aunt Vie or Mr. Weazelton until he retired back to his room in the evening. Was it their intention to be so overly attentive?

Aunt Vie treated him like a child. Alternately following him around, asking if there was something he would like to do, and reminding him he needed to rest more. The attention was beginning to grate on his nerves.

Mr. Weazelton, on the other hand, he could understand. For all his shortcomings, the man was not blind. He was sure Mr. Weazelton's attention was an attempt to keep Emma from spending anytime alone with the competition, and Anthony had most definitely become the competition.

How could he not be when a woman of such caliber as Emma was the prize? She was everything he never knew he needed in his life. The revelation had shocked and warmed him all at once.

Turning to the fair lady who stood at his side ready to go out of doors, he could see a mirror of his own frustration as Aunt Vie bustled down the stairs waving her hand. Bending to whisper in Emma's ear, he said quietly, "Please, forgive me for what I am about to do."

She turned to him, a question in her eyes, but before she could say a word, Aunt Vie reached the landing. "Are we to take a stroll about the garden before dinner again today?" she asked, cheery anticipation on her face.

"Aunt Vie, might I have a moment to speak with your niece alone today? I had meant to speak with you previously, but there is something I wish to converse with Miss Hensworth about... privily."

Aunt Vie's eyes widened at the implication. A wide grin covered her face as she glanced briefly at Emma before looking back at him. He could see the glee of expectation in her eyes, and he hoped she would not be to disappointed when they returned without any announcements.

"Of course, Lord Hamdon," she said. "I will just await your return in the drawing room."

In a sudden show of affection, she leaned forward and kissed Emma upon the cheek. Emma's eyes widened at her aunt's gesture. Anthony was just as astonished. Stepping back, Aunt Vie wished them a good walk, then made her way down to the drawing room, a bit of a bounce in her step.

"You do realize what a mess you have gotten us into?" Emma asked the moment they were alone in the garden.

"It cannot be all that bad," he said.

"It can, and it will. My aunt will be expecting a proposal of marriage when we return, and if I do not supply the happy news, she will not allow me to hear the end of it. I will be forced to listen to her disappointments for the rest of her stay, if not the rest of my days. Not only will it be difficult for me, but she will either pressure you to come up to snuff, or she will place ample amounts of force upon me to accept Mr. Weazelton. She has already implied I should do so to secure my home while my father is gone."

Anthony had stopped his progression next to a bush of field roses just beginning to bud. He stared down at the plant, going over Emma's adamant declaration. She was right, of course; he had backed them both into a corner. He had only been thinking of getting them privacy, not contemplating how it might make her life harder.

Searching for a solution that would benefit them both, he looked farther down the path. A movement in the distance caught his attention. He stared for a moment at the trees before returning to his pondering.

Since only Aunt Vie knew of this discussion, Emma would not be ruined should he not offer. However, Dr. Jones' insistence that he not make long journeys for at least another fortnight, if not a whole month entirely, would keep them in close proximity. If Aunt Vie intended to stay that entire time, then Emma would be subjected to her lectures at every turn as long as he was present—possibly longer.

In addition, Mr. Weazelton had been making his overtures towards Emma increasingly public. She had been forced to shrug off the man's hand twice during services on Sunday. Anthony had seen the gesture as she had been placed squarely between himself and Mr. Weazelton. He had to admit he felt some pride when she had chosen to scoot the slightest bit closer to him after Mr. Weazelton's second advance.

Of course, her added nearness had made it almost impossible to listen to Mr. Clayton's sermon.

He was grateful Aunt Vie had not called on him to give his opinion of the sermon's subject matter. The only thing he had thought on was the way Emma's arm brushed his or the way her skirts bumped his leg.

Emma's look of impatience roused him from his mental wanderings. He knew she was waiting for him to voice a solution, but surfacing from one sweet memory only to see her bathed in shimmering sunlight, her golden curls dancing in the spring breeze... it was intoxicating.

Her look shifted to one of frustration as she awaited his answer. If she thought she was intimidating him, she was wrong. He quite thoroughly enjoyed the way her eyes narrowed, her brow furrowed, and her pink pert lips pursed just the slightest bit. If she puckered them any further, she might look as though she was going to give a kiss rather than a scolding.

Gradually, her expression relaxed, something warmer entering into her eyes. Anthony knew he should look away. It really was impolite to stare, but he could not help himself. A slight breeze blew a tendril of golden hair across her cheek, drawing his attention to the curve of her face. The sunlight reached past the brim of her bonnet to kiss the lower half of her jaw and suddenly he wanted to do the same.

Emma must have grown self-conscious, for she looked away from him toward the rhododendron bush near her elbow. The break gave him time to examine his own thoughts. Had he ever wished to kiss a woman as much as he now wished to kiss Emma? He did not know that he had. It was not as if he had not stolen a kiss or two in London. He had even courted a lady for a time before she had accepted the hand of an earl in line for a dukedom. But he could not remember being so enamored with the body, heart, and soul of another person.

He had never seen so much strength and fortitude in such a tiny person. To adhere to a deathbed promise, one he could tell she was not completely convinced of, was admirable. It showed a great amount of love and respect for her father. A love and respect that he had only seen from afar in his friend's families. A love and respect that he craved with his whole soul.

"Emma," he said cautiously, then realized his mistake. He thought of her so often as Emma in his mind that he had let it slip out upon his tongue without thinking. "I mean..."

She held up her hand, a soft look about her eyes. "I like it when you call me Emma."

Anthony stood surprised, pleased, but confused.

"It is not the first time, you know."

"It is not?"

"On Saturday you called me Emma when we were talking in the west sitting room."

"I did?" He scoured through his mind trying to remember such a mistake but came up with nothing.

"You did. I was frustrated at the time with the liberty you took, but I like the sound of it upon your lips."

His chest swelled. Suddenly, the idea he had conjured did not seem quite so unrealistic. Swinging a few steps closer, he stopped in front of her and, while bracing his crutches at his side, reached out and gently took the fingers of her right hand into his own. Looking down at them, he said, "I have an idea, and I hope you will be amenable to it."

"Oh?" He glanced up to see her eyes focused on where his gloved hand held hers.

"Yes. I would like to court you."

Her gaze flew to his, a look of incredulity written all over her face. "For Aunt Marshall?"

"No," he said slowly. "I am in earnest. I would like to court you to see if we would suit."

Emma stepped back, gently pulling her hand from his, doubt evident in her eyes.

"You do not have to spare my feelings, Lord Hamdon. I do not require your rescue from my aunt, nor from Mr. Weazelton. I only meant to impress upon you the trouble you had caused with your implication."

She turned and began walking briskly away. Anthony pulled his crutches back in place and swung after her. Her tiny steps were no match for his long, swinging gait, and he caught up to her in four easy swings. She looked startled to see him at her side so soon but did not protest as they made their way to the stone bench they had sat upon the day before.

After settling upon the seat, he asked, "Why is it so unbelievable that I would want to pursue a courtship with you?"

Emma sat quietly for a long moment. "I do not know," she finally said in almost a whisper. She seemed to be gathering her thoughts, and he did not want to disrupt her, but he could not let her sit there so close without at least reaching out. Softly he laid his hand over hers where it sat gripping the edge of the bench.

He hoped through his quiet show of support and affection, she would understand his request was genuine.

Letting out a puff of air, she slowly said, "Perhaps because of the situation. What if you swoop in thinking you are being my knight in shining armor, only to realize too late that it was not the damsel you wanted, but only the adventure? You have been put under duress by my family, and I cannot help but think you will regret this later."

"Is that the only reason?" Anthony asked, sensing she was not being entirely honest. She began worrying her bottom lip, and he knew he was correct.

"No," Emma said timidly. "I am concerned I will become too attached, and at the end of your convalescence you will realize I was just a pleasant way to spend your time. You are the son of an earl; you may have your pick of all the ladies in England if you wish."

"Not all the ladies," he said with a wry grin, trying to lighten the mood.

"There is no one here to compare me to. What if, in the end, you go back to London with its balls and parties and beautiful women and realize..." she trailed off looking up at the sky.

"Realize what, Emma?"

"That I do not measure up. I am not accomplished or connected. I prefer the country, and I am unsure I will ever enjoy Town. You are used to city roses and I am afraid I'm just a county tulip. I am sure to be forgotten."

"Yes, but roses have thorns, Emma, and I prefer not to be pricked." He smiled, but her lips only half turned up at the edges, the gesture not reaching her eyes.

"Tulips do not do well in Town because they do not have thorns."

The vulnerability with which she had just entrusted him touched a spot in his heart that no one had ever reached. In that moment, she had been completely honest with him. He searched his soul, and the answer it screamed back surprised him.

"I could never forget you, Emma," he declared. She still looked skeptical.

"I know you do not know me well, but I do not make promises lightly. I have witnessed too often what fickle promises do in the lives of others. When I give my word, I keep it. So I give you my word; I will not leave unless you tell me to," he said, his tender words filled with conviction.

"Whether you believe my words or not, I do care for you. Give me time to win your affections," he begged, realizing how much he really meant the words. He really wanted this chance. Would she give it to him?

Emma let out a breath in a shuddering exhale. She gazed at his face, then her eyes flicked away and she froze. He whipped his head around to see someone slip into the trees in the distance. Someone in brown who was determined to make their lives miserable.

Anthony turned back, her eyes were wide as she stared at the trees, face creased with worry. "Emma, you are not going crazy."

Her gaze snapped to his. "You saw him?"

"I did." A sheen of moisture gathered in her eyes, but just as he thought the first tear would fall, she seemed to call them back to the hidden pools she somehow possessed.

"You have no idea how relieved I am to hear those words, and yet I am frightened, too. If you see him, then he must be real. And if he is real, then there is a possibility the man in green is real as well."

"Man in green?"

"Yes. Yesterday when we were walking the grounds, I spied the man in brown ducking behind a tree just as we turned a corner in the garden. The next thing I know, a bush among the trees began to move. I thought perhaps I had gotten too much sun, or my hallucinations were getting more complex, but when the man uncurled himself from his position, I was sure it was no bush."

"Two men?"

"I believe so. Strangely, though, the man in brown seemed wholly unaware of the man in green. When the man in brown peeked around another tree, the man in green disappeared behind a bush."

"Could it have been your steward? Perhaps he has spotted the man and was only trying to sneak up on him."

Her face filled with a mixture of sadness and frustration. "No, he has still not returned from his family emergency. No one has seen these men but me." Looking down at the bench, her shoulders slump with dejection.

"I am here," he said softly, using a finger to caress her face, "and I have seen at least one of these mystery men." Her eyes met his, and he could see the uncertainty and fear that lay behind them. "We will figure this out, Emma. I promise."

Rolling her beautiful pink lips inward, he saw her bravely fight a second wave of tears. Finally, she managed a wobbly smile, but her gaze was again drawn to the trees. The fear had disappeared, but he did not want her to be even the least bit worried.

"Perhaps we should return indoors." He dropped his hand from her face and reached for his crutches.

"Decamp so that horrid man will think he has cowed me? I think not," she said firmly. "Besides, we have not even broached the subject that we came to the garden to discuss."

Anthony was surprised by her spirit. Just a moment ago, he saw her as a creature to be protected, but this show of spunk made him wonder if perhaps he was the cowardly one. Admittedly, the sight of the man sneaking about the woods had shaken him a bit. She was right, of course, on both accounts. They needed to show they were not afraid of the interloper, and since they would have no privacy once they entered the house, their discussion must be had out of doors.

"All right," he said, almost as a sigh, "but I would feel more comfortable if we made our way closer to the house. I do not like to think that this man, or perhaps men, are so close, whoever they may be. I think it is time we call the squire. You do have one in Worthin, do you not?"

"We do, but he will not be of much good. He is not one for action. We would need to catch the man ourselves and have him delivered to the squire in order for anything to be done. Engalworth would be better served to hire back a bailiff."

"Could you do that?"

"I do not know. With our steward away at present and without my father here to release more funds than the usual monthly allotment, it would be almost impossible to bring someone on as quickly as we might have need of him. I am in quite the predicament, and I am unsure of how to extricate myself. If you were in such a position, how would you go about protecting your lands, Lord Hamdon?"

Chapter Twenty-Six

"Anthony," he said softly.

"Pardon?" Emma asked, not sure if she had heard him right. Looking over his shoulder, she was gratified to see no movement near or in the trees.

"My given name is Anthony. If I am to court you, I would hope you would use my given name."

"It would be more proper if I called you Hamdon."

"I know," he said, glancing over his shoulder in the direction she had scanned earlier. Emma's gaze flicked back to the woods as well, making sure the man in brown was indeed gone. As of yet, she had never seen the man twice in one day. Once he had been spotted, he vanished, only to reappear the next day.

Lord Hamdon must have been satisfied with his perusal, for he continued. "But Hamdon is a name I am not particularly fond of."

"Why is that?" she asked, confused. Her attention was now completely on the man in front of her. Was Hamdon not part of the name she called him regularly, after all?

"It conjures up years of memories I would rather forget. My parents have called me Hamdon from my cradle, and I associate it with stiff, cold civility, duty without honor, and unchecked arrogance and conceit. Anthony, on the other hand, is what my dearest friends call me. I much prefer it, at least in private.

Obviously, when we are in company with those not close to us, it will need to be Hamdon."

"I believe that is the most you have referenced your family in the five weeks you have been here," she said cautiously.

"It is the most they deserve," he said, with a stoic vehemence that set her to wondering what sort of familial relation could cause such a spiteful remark.

"If I am to enter into a courtship," she cast him an encouraging smile, "shouldn't I know what sort of family you hail from?"

"Some people are better left unknown, don't you think?"

"Forgive me if I paraphrase something a wise man once said to me. 'I would need to know your reason for hiding such information from the world at large,' which at present would be me."

She relished the way his lips quirked as she referenced his own words.

"Wise? Is that a compliment?"

"Do not let it puff your ego," she said, a grin spreading across her face.

"Well, if I am so wise, you should trust my judgment and leave off asking about my unfortunate parentage."

"Son of an earl and you call your parentage unfortunate. Most people would think that fortune had smiled brightly upon you."

"That is because they are unacquainted with the Earl of Lincolnhurst."

"Is he all that bad?" she asked quietly.

Anthony's rigid posture relaxed the slightest bit, his smile becoming regretful. "For many of his rank and standing, he is a paragon of a man. As his son," his pause was poignant, "let me just say there is little about him I want to emulate, or my mother, for that matter."

Emma laid her hand gently upon his arm. "I am sorry, Anthony. I cannot say I completely understand, as my parents were everything I could only hope to be. It must have been difficult growing up with parents you cannot respect."

He looked at her with raised eyebrows. Had she said something wrong? She hoped he did not take offense to her words. She was not trying to tout her own parentage, nor was she trying to pity him. She only wished to empathize.

An impish grin suddenly spread across his face. "May I take your use of my given name as permission to court you?"

Realizing she had never given him an answer to his earlier inquiry, she thought over her options. She could refuse him, but then she would have to listen to Aunt Marshall, for who knew how long, if she did not present some sort of matrimonial success in the near future. Emma was not afraid of the prospect; it was not as if it would change the tenor of their interactions. A refusal, however, would protect her from future heartache. These last eight months had been some of the hardest of her life, filled with more sorrow and uncertainty than any person should ever have to experience. She did not know if she could take losing another person, whether by chance or choice.

On the other hand, if she accepted him... A giddy feeling rose in her chest at the possibility, causing her cheeks to heat and her head to feel light. Pushing the feeling down, she tried to focus on the logical reasons she should accept Lord Hamdon, nay, Anthony's courtship. In addition to the most obvious reasons of status and fortune, the foremost reason in her mind was Mr. Weazelton.

If she was being courted by the Viscount Hamdon, perhaps Mr. Weazelton would remove himself from the running, knowing he could never compete with a peer. It could, however, anger him to have competition. The last thing she needed was a contemptuous man under her roof. One who could push at any moment to have her father declared permanently missing.

In that case, refusal would seem the best course, but then what? If Alan did not return soon, this may be her only chance to find a life of her own. Looking at Anthony's expectant face, her heart softened. She was still not sure of her feelings for him, but she did enjoy his company. He was kind and intelligent, and the physical feelings that he elicited... in answer to the tantalizing thought, a rush of gooseflesh dotted her arms even though they were well-covered by her pelisse. Well, there was definitely no lack of attraction.

"I suppose so," she finally said.

"You suppose?" Concern marred his visage. Emma was tempted to tease him, but he looked so vulnerable in that moment that her tender heart could not bear to cause him distress.

"Yes, Anthony, you may court me," she said, trying to allay his fears. The return of his contagious smile brought an answering smile to her own lips. It was not nearly as broad and far more uncertain, but she was happy.

Anthony inched closer to her and took up her hand once again. Lifting it gently to his lips, he placed a kiss upon her gloved hand. Even though she could not feel his lips directly on her skin, the warmth of the kiss and the tenderness with which it was given burrowed straight into her heart. Yes, it would be excessively hard not to become attached to this man. Truthfully, she knew she already was.

Letting go of her hand, he gestured toward the house. She rose gracefully from her seat, grateful for a moment to hide the blush she was sure had crept onto her all too pale skin. Anthony placed his crutches under his arms, then swung effortlessly forward. Emma had to take four steps for every one swing he took with his long gait.

Thatcher stood a ways off, ready to intercept them, but Emma gave a slight wave of her hand at her side, and he stopped his forward motion. She needed the time it took to traverse the garden to discuss her brother without the footman's prying ears.

As if he could read her thoughts, Anthony asked, "Do you suppose your brother's proficiency in French was the reason he was chosen for spy work?"

"I am sure of it. My brother spoke French as fluently as English. Mama used to brag of his talent to anyone who would listen. One of the few memories I have of Grand-père is of he and Alan debating in French. Alan could not have been more than twelve at the time, but Grand-père loved to engage him in discussions of politics, claiming Alan needed the experience if he was to one day sit in the House of Lords."

"Mr. Hensworth must have been quite adept if he could debate politics at twelve. I do not believe I became proficient in that subject until I finished Eton and began at Cambridge, much to my father and Nicholas's chagrin."

"Mr. Fairchild? Why should he care so much?"

"Oh, he is quite invested in the concerns of the nation. In all honesty, I believe he would make a far better lord than I will, but we are veering off topic. I am guessing that your brother's knowledge of current affairs also played a part in his assignment."

"I believe you are correct."

"So," Anthony paused a moment, glancing over his shoulder. Emma did the same, worried what he had seen, but before she turned back from her perusal of the trees, he was speaking again. "If your brother is returning as your father said, what purpose do you have to continue hiding his death? Your brother is the heir, after all, and is set to inherit."

"He will if I can prove he is still alive. If I cannot, Mr. Weazelton will take charge of Engalworth."

"I would think the Royal Army could easily prove your brother's existence."

"That is just it. They are the ones who informed us of his demise, and every letter of inquiry since has brought no word in return. I cannot move forward without proof."

"Wait!" he said, stopping his forward motion and turning to her. "In those letters, did you advise them of your father's death?"

"In a way," she said. In truth, she had felt it wise not to divulge the information to anyone. Her father had only told the Foreign Office he was too sick to see to his estate, so she had kept with the ruse.

"What did you tell them, Emma?" He raised an eyebrow.

"That my father was unable to care for his estate."

"So they may not understand the urgency of the situation. All the more reason for me to pay them a visit."

"But you cannot tell them my father is dead." Panic filled her chest. "What if they let the public at large know?"

"What if they do? If your brother is alive, it will make no difference."

"But if he is not, it will." Bile rose in her throat. It was the same fear she faced every time her doubts arose. Perhaps it was selfish, really, but if Emma were being completely honest, it was not just Alan's inheritance she was protecting.

Emma's eyes became so round and her face so pale that Anthony was afraid she might pass out; it had happened once before, after all. He prayed she would not. He had no way of catching her, what with the crutches and splint.

"Emma?" he said softly. "Emma?" Her eyes finally focused on him. "Are you well?" She seemed to shake herself from whatever fear gripped her.

"Mr. Weazelton can never inherit this estate," she said with conviction. "He will run it and the people into the ground. I cannot subject us all to that fate."

Anthony did not miss the reference; she had included herself even after he was offering her a possible way out. Did she not see him as a viable option? The thought was belittling.

Then, realization dawned. Emma's guardianship. No wonder she was worried. As Mr. Weazelton was to inherit *all* of Lord Gladsby's worldly responsibilities, would it not stand to reason that he would also inherit Emma as a ward? Heaven forbid!

The pressure Mr. Weazelton currently exerted on Emma now was almost unbearable; as her guardian, he would become downright impudent. That is, if he gave her a choice at all. Anthony would not put it past the man to force her hand.

While it was possible for the ownership of Engalworth to revert back to Emma's brother should he return, it would be too late to save Emma. She would be married to the scoundrel, and there would be no undoing the damage without making her a social pariah through divorce.

Just the thought of that odious man laying one finger on her made Anthony's blood boil. He would never allow it, but how could he stop it? If, at the end of this courtship, she agreed to marry him, there was always the chance her cousin, as guardian, could stand in the way. Their only recourse at that point would be to elope. Anthony was shocked to realize he would do it. He would do anything to keep Emma from having to marry that weasel.

"Emma, you will never be subject to Mr. Weazelton," he finally said. "I would never allow it."

"You may not be able to stop it."

"Oh, I can stop it! I may not be able to keep him from taking ownership of Engalworth, but I can, and will, stop him from taking charge over you." The conviction he felt with his words raced through his veins. His previous uncertainties surrounding Emma's confession vanished. It did not matter to him whether or not her father's words *were* true; he was going to do everything in his power to help her.

He must have looked quite fierce, for she took a step back. He tried to soften his features into something more pleasant. A movement in the window facing the garden caught his attention affording him a brief glance of Aunt Vie as she stood spying on them from the drawing room. Returning his attention to Emma, he said, "It seems our time out of doors has come to an end."

She looked at him confused by the change of topic, and he gestured with his head to the back of the house. She glanced in that direction and frowned.

"If it is not the men in the woods, then it is the woman in the house," she said with irritation.

"Or man in the house. Do not forget Mr. Wastrel's son," he said, enunciating the mispronounced name. He was rewarded with a light laugh.

"I do believe that is my favorite one yet," she said with a giggle. Anthony relished the lighthearted comment, glad to see the worry and fear flee behind the jest.

"I must thank you," he said as they began making their way toward the house again. "Without your help, my Mr. Weasely puns would not be as well received."

"Yes." She laughed again. "I am surprised my cousin has not called you out yet. I must admit, I have enjoyed watching him squirm. While it will never be enough to repay his treatment of me in London, it gives me some satisfaction to see him humiliated in such a way."

"What happened in London?" He did not remember her ever mentioning any events in London that had included her cousin.

"Near the end of the season, my father finally obtained vouchers to Almack's. The last week of May, he escorted myself and Aunt Marshall inside those coveted ballrooms to partake of the entertainments. However, shortly after arriving, Mr. Weazelton quickly put an end to my night." Emma's pert nose wrinkled with the memory.

"When he came to offer his greetings at the edge of the dance floor, he was completely foxed. The man quite literally stumbled through his greeting. It was such an embarrassment, but that was not the worst of it."

"Oh?"

"Yes. He tried to bow over my hand while holding a glass of sweet Madeira in the other, but someone bumped him from behind, causing him to stumble forward and spill the entirety of his glass down my new white gown. As if the experience of being doused in the amber liquid was not embarrassing enough, Mr. Weazelton barked out a laugh so loud that I am certain he was heard by everyone in the room, even over the orchestra."

"How awful." he said, knowing exactly what the cats of London would have to say about such an experience.

"Perhaps I could have forgiven him if he had apologized and helped us escape the embarrassing debacle, but instead, he made a lewd comment about the appearance of my wet and clinging dress. I am sure my father would have called the man out right there if he had not been so concerned with covering me and removing us as quickly as possible from the prying eyes of the crowd. That was our last outing in London. Word of the embarrassing encounter spread about like wildfire, as gossip often does. Aunt Marshall, happy for any excuse to leave London, declared the season a failure and suggested a retreat, and truthfully, I had to agree."

"I do not blame you. I am sure the ladies of the ton probably filled many a drawing room with varying tales of the unfortunate event."

"I am sure they did. It was that experience which set my father so wholly against Mr. Weazelton. In his words, he 'would not leave a single farthing to such a worthless wastrel of a man,'" Emma said vehemently as she let her fingers trail over the green leaves of a lilac bush, her hand coming to rest under a cluster of light purple blooms. Pulling the flowers toward her nose, Anthony watched her inhale the aroma, closing her eyes to savor it.

"I suppose," he said slowly, waiting until she looked directly at him, "Mr. Wastrel's son was an apt name then."

"Yes, quite apt," she said on a laugh.

"You know, you make a good co-conspirator for my tomfoolery."

"Why, thank you," she said, simpering a bit as she walked, a mischievous look in her eye, "And you make a good co-conspirator for my actual conspiracy."

Her addition made him laugh. Anthony liked this playful side of Emma. While absent when they first met, it was showing itself with increasing regularity. "Shall we make a club out of it?" he asked as they came within hearing of the footman.

"A conspiracy club?" She lowered her voice, but still grinning.

"Yes," he said quietly. "It could be the Conspiratorial Alliance for Tomfoolery."

"That is an awfully long name for a club."

"Oh, we would call it by its initials. That way no one would know it was conspiratorial."

"CAFT?" Emma scrunched up her nose at the name.

"No, everyone knows you must drop the inconsequential words. We shall simply be known as CAT."

"CAT?" she asked with a smirk.

"Yes," Anthony responded as they drew even closer to Thatcher standing near the entrance to the garden. "Now, we must have a change of subject. We do not want to let the CAT out of the bag, you know." He grinned when he was rewarded with another of Emma's laughs.

Chapter Twenty-Seven

Emma loved the way Anthony could make her forget her troubles. One minute she was worried over the man in the woods and the stress of living a lie, and the next, he was making her laugh. His suggestion of forming a club, as if they were little children, had caught her so off guard. Yet it was exactly what she had needed to step away from the mounting pressures.

They spoke of lighter subjects as they made their way to the entrance of the house. But as they neared, she realized there were still a few things they would need to decide on before confronting Aunt Marshall. Anthony seemed to sense her change in mood, his cheery smile turning to a more serious expression. Her momentary relief fled, and all her other troubles crashing back down upon her slender shoulders.

"Have you advised all your outside staff of the man in brown or just your stable master?" He glanced over his shoulder. She was surprised by the change of subject, but perhaps she should not have been. The man in brown was not far from her thoughts, either, at any given time.

"I have, but I am thinking I need to enlist the help of the inside staff as well. Up to this point, he has been little more than a nuisance, but since we do not know what his purpose is, we must assume the worst."

"And what do you believe to be the worst?"

"Honestly, I am unsure. I cannot imagine he is waiting around to rob us, for he would have done so by now if that was his intent. There is still the possibility he is working for Mr. Weazelton as a means to scare me. If that is the case, it will not go on much longer. With your testimony and mine, I have enough to confront Mr. Weazelton about the man's presence."

"Yes, but if he is devious enough to hire the man, or possibly men, to frighten you, would he really admit his guilt if confronted?"

"I see your point," she said, pondering what other nefarious purposes could possibly bring someone to Engalworth. The ones that came to mind struck true fear in her heart. Could the man be someone who forced himself on women? Or possibly a murderer?

"I see your mind has touched upon a few much more sinister reasons for men to be stalking about your woods," he said.

Her distress must have been written across her face for him to decipher her thoughts so easily. Belatedly, she realized he was still focused on both of the men in the woods. Odd, she thought. She was not nearly as worried about the man in green as she had been the man in brown. They were both creeping around where they aught not be, but there was something about the man in green that seemed oddly familiar. Not that she had really seen much of him, but his presence, it felt, well... familiar. It should be more distressing that he was able to conceal himself so well; it would make him the more dangerous of the two.

Anthony, however, must see them both as equally threatening to continue referencing them together. His next words worried her even more. "With the addition of a new man, I believe we must assume there could be others. Perhaps even a group, maybe gypsies or some such, that could be plotting a larger crime upon your estate. Advising all your staff, and as you mentioned earlier, possibly adding a bailiff, would be an intelligent course of action. Will you also tell your uncle, Mr. Clayton?"

"Oh, yes. I inform him of most everything that happens here. We are in luck, in more ways than one, that he is expected to dine with us this evening."

"How so?"

"Well," she said, suddenly feeling shy, "in the absence of my father, I believe he would be the appropriate person to ask for permission to—" She cleared her throat nervously. It was so strange to say the words, even embarrassing. "To court me."

They had reached the house and now stood facing one another by the steps that led up to the front door. However, she avoided making eye contact with Anthony. Where had this sudden shyness come from? Looking at her hands, she realized she was again playing with the tips of her gloves. Dropping them to her sides to keep from indulging in the nervous habit, she took a deep breath and raised her eyes to meet his.

Anthony's lips quirked to one side in a half smile. Was he entertained by her distress? The thought that he found her discomfort diverting irritated her, and she frowned, but instead of bringing about a penitent look as she had hoped, his face brightened into a full-fledged grin.

"Do you find amusement in my distress, your lordship?" she spat out, ready to give him a thorough dressing down.

"Not at all; however, I have found that you are just as beautiful upset as you are when you are happy. I had never thought to meet a woman who could accomplish such a feat."

His flattering words caught her so off guard, she did not know how to respond. She knew an expression of gratitude was the proper response, but her blood still pulsed from the frustration of moments before. Perhaps he was only trying to charm her out of a bad mood, and his words were nothing more than a pretty compliment. She wanted to be angry at him for such flattery, but slowly she could feel her irritation melting under the glow of his praise.

"I am happy to speak with your uncle this evening about our courtship, Emma. If he is early enough, I might even be able to do so before dinner," he said, an even bigger grin lighting his face.

"Well, it is a good thing, indeed, that I arrived early then, is it not?" someone said from behind her. Whirling around, she saw Mr. Clayton striding toward them not ten feet from where she stood. The older man winked at her as he approached.

Reaching her side, he bent down and kissed her cheek. Lingering, he whispered, "You see, my vision is quite keen for an old man."

Emma tried to cover a laugh as he referenced his suspicions. He had, indeed, been correct about Lord Hamdon's interest in her, but she would not encourage her presumptuous uncle in any way.

"I would be happy to speak to you both right here if you do not mind. I am afraid if we enter the house first, Vivian will take ownership over all our ears, and we will not be able to get a moment's peace," he said with a smirk.

Mr. Clayton turned to the footman. "Thank you, Thatcher, but I believe Miss Hensworth and I can assist Lord Hamdon into the house when we are finished." The man bowed, then mounted the steps two at a time. No doubt Mrs. Clark would be happy to have him in the kitchen to carry any heavy trays to the dining room in preparation for dinner.

"Now that we are without an audience, what is this about an intention to court my niece?"

It was Anthony's turn to squirm, and Emma found herself enjoying it immensely after he had smirked at her discomfort. She was even rewarded with a slight blush that colored his cheeks. Emma was not sure she had ever seen a full-grown man blush.

"Well, sir," Anthony said a bit shakily, then cleared his throat. "I have asked Miss Hensworth if she would be amenable to a courtship, and she has agreed. However, in the absence of her father, I would like to ask for your blessing."

It was odd being present for this interview. Growing up, she had always imagined her father and future suitor having this discussion somewhere in a private study. Now as they stood upon the drive, she thought it ironic that this moment was quite the antithesis of her childhood daydream.

"I believe at this point of the interview, I would be required to inquire about your ability to care for my niece, perhaps even discuss why you wish to court her in the first place, but I believe I know you well enough, Lord Hamdon, to trust you have only the best of intentions. And as Emma has already agreed to your suit, I must also agree as I trust my niece's judgment implicitly." The grin Mr.

Clayton directed Emma's way filled her heart with so much warmth and joy she felt she might burst with the happiness. Impulsively, she popped up on her toes and kissed his weathered cheek.

"I believe that is the wrong cheek you are kissing, my dear," he said, mischief in his eyes. "That," he said, gesturing to Lord Hamdon, "is your suitor."

Anthony laughed, and Emma could not help but giggle as well. "No, Uncle, it was you I meant to kiss. I do not think anyone has had so much trust in me. While I would have loved to have Lord Hamdon ask my father's permission, I am glad that in his absence you are the one to fill the position."

"Well, in that case, thank you and you are welcome."

After dinner, Anthony was grateful to find himself alone with Mr. Clayton, the ladies having removed to the drawing room. It was just the situation he needed to ask the questions that had been swirling about in his head since his walk with Emma.

"You look deeply contemplative, Lord Hamdon. I sense a serious conversation about to ensue."

He smiled at the vicar's intuitiveness. The man really was a genius at reading people, an extremely useful trait in a profession that worked directly with interpreting people's needs.

"I have several questions I believe are best posed to you, and you alone, Mr. Clayton."

"About Engalworth's precarious situation, I presume," he said, lowering his voice a fraction.

"Indeed. First, what do you know about Miss Hensworth's guardianship in the absence of her father?"

"The last I knew, her guardianship was to be transferred to Alan upon her father's death."

"Is there a possibility that might have been changed after the initial word came about Alan's presumed death?"

"As far as I know, the will was never changed during that time. Gladsby's solicitor does business in Banbury, and Gladsby did not travel there at any time until around the end of November, I think, or perhaps it was the beginning of December. Honestly, my memory of that time is a bit hazy. I believe at that point he had already received word directly from his son, so there was no need to revisit the will and possibly stir up suspicion."

"I would think it would stir up more suspicion, as the solicitor would have heard of Mr. Hensworth's demise. A good solicitor would be adamant that changes be made immediately, so estates, assets, and responsibilities might not fall into the court's hands upon his client's death."

"I see your point. It is possible that some changes in wording may have been made during those weeks before his death. He did make several trips to Banbury in that time. I must also point out, however, that Gladsby's solicitor may not have questioned much. He's a good man, but he has been solicitor for this estate for nearly forty years. He is getting along in age, and while he has a younger partner that he could have turned things over to, I am sure he would have taken care of Gladsby's accounts himself as a matter of pride."

"Is there any way we might inspect the final will?"

"Not without Gladsby present. The only other way is by declaring him dead, and that is not a possibility at this time. Why is Emma's guardianship so important to you?"

Anthony felt it was too soon to be questioning Emma's acceptance of his suit, but unfortunately he was. He did not want her acceptance to be contingent on her fear. He wanted to help her and would, but, ultimately, he wanted her to choose him because it was her desire, not because he was her only option.

Instead of voicing his fears, he said, "I am only concerned that should our courtship progress to an engagement, we would need to apply to her legal guardian to have a marriage contract drawn up."

"Ah. Yes, well, I believe you have hit upon all our fears. If Alan does not return, there is a possibility that Emma will be turned over to Mr. Weazelton. And you and I both know he will not accept her as a ward, but only as a wife."

"Yes, that is the conclusion I came to earlier today, but why? He will have Engalworth. Is he not satisfied with that?"

"Greed, perhaps a bit of desperation. Emma has a sizeable dowry, part of which was bestowed upon her by her father. But the rest was from her mother's parents. While most of her grandparents' property in France was taken over by the government, they still had a sizable fortune which they brought with them. A good part was passed down to Emma, increasing her dowry from ten thousand pounds to forty thousand pounds."

Anthony choked on his port. Such a sum was rarely heard of for a mere baron's daughter. It was enough that, should she be able to reach her majority, she could set up a very fine house for herself without the need to marry at all. No wonder Mr. Weazelton was so avidly pursuing her.

"Am I correct in assuming Mr. Weazelton needs that dowry to meet his debts?"

"You are, and to pull his own property out of the suds. The place is so steeped in debt that Mr. Weazelton was forced to let it three years ago."

"Does the lease not pay the mortgage?"

"I am sure it would if Mr. Weazelton did not regularly gamble away a good portion. Mind you, that is just hearsay. I do, however, know that Gladsby had a runner look into his dissolute cousin a few years back when the man applied to him for a small amount of money claiming he had recently fallen upon hard times."

"I did not know they were of such close relations to request assistance."

"They are not. I believe third cousins is the closest he could claim. Gladsby, of course, found by investigation that his cousin is very irresponsible. But, being the kind man he was, forwarded half what was asked of him, offering to educate the man in financial management. Mr. Weazelton, of course, declined the offer. He had been trained as well as the next gentleman in the intricacies of finance, but he was not willing to give up some of his seedier behaviors."

"Many of which I would bet are quite costly. Another reason he may wish for Emma's dowry."

"Yes. Probably the main reason. With both Engalworth accounts and Emma's dowry at his disposal, he could live quite lavishly for a time."

Anthony pondered on this as he took another, more careful, sip from his glass. If the man was as irresponsible as he sounded, it would probably be a very short time.

"However, your intervention at this time could prove the redemption we had all hoped for," Mr. Clayton said, steepling his fingers in front of his lips.

"Mine?"

"Yes, by courting Emma. Should you come to an understanding, you would be saving her from a life of misery."

"But this leads us back to the matter of legal guardianship. You said Mr. Weazelton would demand her as his wife. Would it not stand to reason that he would refuse a union between Emma and myself?"

"I see your point. In that case..." Mr. Clayton paused, examining Anthony for a moment. Leaning forward to look him squarely in the eye, he continued. "Might I suggest a trip to Scotland?" The twinkle in the older man's eye made Anthony grin.

"We seemed to be of the same mind, Mr. Clayton, for those were my thoughts exactly."

Chapter Twenty-Eight

Emma sat alone in the darkened sitting room. The others believed she had retired to her room with a headache, and while the headache was a true malady she was suffering, she could not bear facing anyone yet, not even Smith. All day long, Aunt Marshall had vacillated between expressing her joy over Emma's courtship and admonishing her not to waste time securing a proposal. She was sick to death of both.

Even more distressing was Mr. Weazelton's reaction to the news earlier in the day.

"Lord Hamdon has no right to pursue a courtship," he had blurted angrily. "He has not even gained permission from the lady's father."

Knowing this could be one of the reactions, Mr. Clayton had made sure he was present for the announcement, so he could claim the right as closest male relative of giving permission in his brother-in-law's absence. Mr. Weazelton had alternately blustered and muttered at this logic for a time before giving into reason.

Trying a different approach, he pointed out the impropriety of Lord Hamdon courting Emma while they resided under the same roof. The hypocrite, Emma thought, as she slumped on the settee, her head resting on its back. That had been his exact scheme all along. He was only sorry that she had been so avidly against his suit. Besides, she had heard of dozens of couples who courted while attending house parties and the like, and that was deemed perfectly acceptable.

While all of these issues weighed heavily upon her, it was Mr. Weazelton's pronouncement after dinner that had caused her to seek refuge in the unoccupied sitting room. It would seem she had underestimated him. He was several steps ahead of the schedule she had planned out. What she had assumed as innocent visits to the neighbors had actually been a mission to gather information against her. Having now affirmed that no one had heard anything from Lord Gladsby in nearly six months, he had announced to the room at large his supposition that something "dreadful must have befallen the baron, and they must brace themselves for the worst."

Emma was sure her face had lost all color at his words. Even though she knew it was an eventuality, she had supposed that they would have at least a few more weeks.

Luckily, Mr. Weazelton had assumed her pale face the effect of shocked sensibilities rather than the fear of discovery. He had apologized for the shocking nature of his pronouncement, but he felt, in the interest of Engalworth Court, it would be best to apply to the courts as soon as possible so he might take up his *rightful* place.

Rightful place, indeed, Emma scoffed. He had no right to Alan's lands, Alan's title, or Alan's sister. The last thought brought the tears she had tried so valiantly to hold at bay. They dripped silently down her cheeks, pulling feelings of loss and heartache to the surface with each salty droplet.

A sound at the door had her stiffening. Trying desperately to wipe the tears away with her sleeve, she looked about the room for a place where she might hide, but before she could move from her position on the settee, a figure jumped quickly into the room. The only evidence of the person's entrance was the flash of light that accompanied the opening and closing of the door.

Emma froze. Whoever it was did not want to be discovered as evidenced by their quick entrance. The flash of light from the doorway had momentarily caused the darkness to be more intense around her. But she assumed, due to the silence, that the person still lingered by the door.

As her eyes began to adjust, she could tell the figure was tall and, with the definite lack of skirts, must be male. Her heart rate doubled in speed. She could hear her blood whooshing in her ears again as panic built in her chest.

Her initial thought was that Mr. Weazelton had seen where she retreated and now was come to take advantage of her current state. However, on the heels of that thought was one just as terrifying. Perhaps the man in brown had made his way into the house and was now come for her. She felt the need to scream building in her throat.

"Emma?" a masculine voice said in hushed tones. "I know you are in here, but I cannot see you in the darkness."

Anthony? How had he entered so quietly. Where were his crutches?

Taking a few deep gulping breaths, she stammered out, "I am on the settee."

Blinking through the darkness, she could now make out Anthony's form. She was surprised when he took a small hop forward and then another. Propelled from the settee at the thought of him taking a tumble, she rushed to his side.

"Where are your crutches?" she scolded quietly.

"Behind the potted plants by the stairs. I could not very well risk someone hearing me enter this room."

"You hopped all the way from the stairs?"

"I did. It is not terribly far, barely a stone's throw."

"Not that far," she grumbled as she looped his arm over her shoulders and helped him the rest of the way to the settee. "I would think the thump of your hops would be just as loud as the clicks of the crutches."

"You would think that, but wood on marble is much louder than the leather of my shoe."

Once he was seated, she moved to sit in the chair next to the settee, but Anthony grabbed her hand, stopping her progress.

"We are courting, you know. It is permissible for you to sit near me on the settee."

"Yes, but we are also alone in a dark room, which I am sure is against every rule of propriety, even in courting."

"You are right, but it will be much harder to carry on a quiet conversation with you at a distance."

His logic there was sound. The last thing they needed at this moment was an audience. Taking a few steps to the side, she sat, leaving a space between them on the furniture.

"I do not bite, you know. At least not often."

Emma heard the smile in his voice, and it warmed her insides. "You may not, but perhaps I do. What if I am a werewolf only waiting for the full moon to appear through the window? I believe it would be best for your safety if I kept my distance should that unlikely event happen."

"Bitten by you. That sounds quite pleasant," he said playfully.

Emma's cheeks burned. "Anthony!" she scolded, trying desperately to escape all the mental images his words had caused to cascade into her brain.

"I am sorry. I will try to wrestle my tongue into submission," he said, but the laughing way in which his words filled the space between them sounded anything but penitent.

She was at a loss for words, so silence pervaded for a time, but it was not uncomfortable. In fact, it was the most comfortable she had been all day. Just having him next to her seemed to shore up her crumbling walls.

"How did you know I was here?" she finally asked.

"Gibbons saw you duck in after you exited the drawing room."

"He ratted me out? I thought him much more reliable than that."

"He did not say a word, Emma, but his eyes did flit to the door a time or two as I approached the stairs. Of course, he may have smiled when I stashed my crutches and made my wobbly way towards this room. Probably would have laughed, too, at the spectacle I was making of myself, but that would have given away my approach."

She was not sure if she should censure Gibbons or bless him. As she soaked up the continued comfort Anthony's presence brought, she decided on the latter.

The quiet darkness around them made her feel braver than she would have had Anthony been able to see her face. "Why do you want to court me, Anthony?" she cautiously asked. Cataloging her own assets, she wondered what of her features had captured his attention first.

"Because of your strength," he said softly.

She scoffed. "I am as weak as a kitten. You are teasing me."

"I am in earnest. There is more than one kind of strength, Emma. You may be small, but you are truly one of the strongest people I have ever met. Life has stolen your parents and grandparents, then left you to fight for yourself and those who depend upon this estate. Most women I know would be cowering in their rooms waiting for someone to come save them, but you have faced life head on, taking on each challenge and conquering each obstacle."

"I do not feel particularly strong tonight," she murmured.

"No one can be strong on their own forever, Emma. We are meant to share our burdens. Remember, many hands make light lifting."

"I have had many hands for months, Anthony."

"True, but how much have you allowed them to lift? Do you let Mrs. Gibbons or Smith bear you up when you feel you cannot handle your load, or do you hide away and hope no one sees you suffer?"

"Well, I am hiding in a dark room. I suppose that answers the question."

Even though she could not see his expression, she could hear the smile in his voice. "I suppose it does."

Several seconds of silence followed. "I would like to be that person for you, Emma. The one you share your burdens with, the one who helps you lift them when you are weak. I know you can handle most anything on your own, but, please, let me relieve at least a bit of that pressure."

Emma felt a warm pressure on her shoulder. When he had slipped his arm onto the back of the settee, she was unsure, but the touch and his sincere words broke something inside. It was as if the invisible cord she wrapped around herself, the one that held her together so she could be strong on her own, snapped. She took a deep breath, relishing the freedom. The urge to scoot closer to him overcame her, and for once, she gave into the feeling.

Sitting tucked under his arm, she was safe. It was something she had rarely felt since the horrible day her father had taken his last breath.

"Thank you," she said, leaning against Anthony's shoulder. She had never sat so close to a man unrelated to her before. While her mind told her their position was wholly inappropriate, her heart begged her to stay in the comfort of his arms.

Silence prevailed, the only sound she could hear was the beating of her own heart. Slowly, however, she detected another. Turning her head a fraction of an inch, her ear pressed a little closer to Anthony's side. The faint thumping she heard there almost matched the rhythm of her own heart.

How interesting hearts are, she thought, providing precious life to the bodies they inhabit. Life that is so precious and fragile. Life that at any moment can be snuffed out. The thought made her stiffen.

"What is the matter?"

Emma could not tell him, would not tell him. While his offer of support was kind, he could be taken just as easily as her mother's, her aunt's, her father's, and quite possibly her brother's. She should not become too attached. While he insisted he was sincere in his affection for her, it might not always be the case. She needed to be cautious.

"It is just that I am concerned we will be discovered," she insisted. "I think it best if we go. Not together, of course, in case someone sees us." She scooted away, ready to stand and exit the room.

"Before you go, I do have a couple of questions for you about the letter."

The subject halted her motion.

"You said your father placed it in his study."

She nodded, then realized he probably could not see her movements. "Yes."

"Where exactly did Lord Gladsby say he placed the letter?"

"In his desk at the back of the bottom left drawer. He has a small lockbox there. The key was kept among his cuff links. I found the key after his passing, but upon opening the box found only a few valuables, a handful of my mother's letters, the correspondence detailing Alan's disappearance, and several scraps of paper with random letters and numbers upon them."

"Have you searched other areas of the study?"

"We have. Mrs. Gibbons and Smith have been cleaning the room for months going through each book and file individually. Nothing has turned up."

"Could I look around?"

"You may, but I doubt you will find it if we have not."

"Sometimes it just takes a fresh pair of eyes."

She was indignant at his surety, but she could not deny him. With Mr. Weazelton's impending legal suit, she needed all the help she could get.

"All right, meet me in the study tomorrow morning around eight. That will give us time to look through several areas before my aunt is up for the day."

"Us?" he asked incredulously. "What happened to your sense of propriety, Emma?"

A smile bloomed at his words. How was it he could flip her mood so easily?

"I will have Smith with me, *my lord.*"

"Oh, do not go 'my lording' me again, or I will have to bribe Smith into finding some other responsibility in the morning. Then you will be forced to fall prey to my machinations."

"I am so scared," she said flatly, knowing it sounded flirtatious in its delivery.

"You should be."

Chapter Twenty-Nine

The next morning dawned bright, sunny, and far too early for Anthony's liking, but he needed to rise and dress early enough to make it to the other side of the house before anyone, other than Gibbons, saw him.

When the older man had brought his crutches to the sitting room after Emma's departure, they had agreed Gibbons would be the one to help Anthony dress this morning. After using a cloth to wash himself, he dressed and hobbled toward the stairs using only one crutch. While slightly harder to balance, he found the one crutch to be far quieter and easier to manage than the two together.

At the staircase, Gibbons took up his position at Anthony's side. The study was nestled among the family rooms on the upper level of the other side of the house. Looking at the many stairs he would have to traverse to get there, he felt fatigued just thinking about it.

By the time he reached the top of the opposite staircase, a light sheen of perspiration coated his brow. Sweat dripped down his back. Anthony had never broken a sweat walking up and down a single staircase, but it seemed hopping them was a whole different story.

Gibbons left him at the top of the stairs to resume his other duties. Approaching the slightly ajar door, he found Emma and her maid already inside. Approaching her near the desk, he softly wished her a good morning. The smile and gentle greeting he received back brought more light into his heart than the sun that shone through the window.

"Which drawer did you say the lockbox is kept in?" he asked.

"Bottom left."

Anthony sat in the soft chair placed behind the sturdy wood structure. Setting his crutch against the edge of the desk, he bent down and pulled the drawer out, revealing the metal box at the back. Emma produced the key and he unlocked it. All the papers were there exactly as she had described.

Pulling out the three small strips of paper, he placed them on the top of the desk, the numbers and letters visible. Each piece looked like it had been torn from the bottom of a page as the top edge of each piece was rough and the bottom smooth. Odd, he thought. Why would one keep random torn pieces of paper in a lockbox? Moving them about, they seemed to have no order to them, the torn edges not fitting together.

"I assumed they were code for another place he might have hidden the letter," Emma said, observing his actions, "but no matter how I rearrange them, they still make no sense,"

"I see that. Do you mind if I look through the other drawers?"

"Be my guest. Smith and I will continue to look among the books. Perhaps we missed a page."

An hour passed as they searched in their separate areas. How had she withstood this? Anthony was growing frustrated after only an hour. He could not imagine how she must feel after looking for the elusive letter for months on end.

The sound of Gibbons's low voice greeting someone downstairs brought them all to a halt. Why was he speaking so loudly? He was not yelling per se, but his greeting seemed to boom through the lower court.

"That is our cue. We need to go," Emma said in a hushed voice.

"Already?"

"Yes, Mr. Weazelton is awake. We cannot let him find us up here together."

"He would dare enter the family wing?"

"I have caught him in my father's study several times before. I believe he has convinced Aunt Marshall he is helping with the accounts while Mr. Haze is absent."

"More likely scrounging around for condemning information," Anthony muttered.

"Or to trap himself a wife," Smith mumbled as she walked away from the shelves.

Anthony's eyes shot to Emma. She looked chagrined at the maid's admission.

"I have been careful, Anthony. In addition, the servants have been on their guard every time he leaves his assigned quarters."

It was not very comforting, but what else could they do? Only their best, he supposed. Looking about the room, he realized he was now in a predicament. "How am I to get down without causing a stir?"

"I do not think that should be too hard. I will just provide a distraction in the breakfast room."

"I do not want you alone with that man, Emma." he said vehemently.

"I won't be," she said as she waltzed out of the room.

Anthony spent the next fifteen minutes placing papers back into their correct drawers in the desk. One stack in particular caught his attention, and he rifled through them. What he found made him smile. Placing the entire stack to the side, he finished cleaning off the top of the desk, placed the paper scraps back in the lockbox, and pocketed the key.

Once everything was in place, he quietly closed each of the drawers. However, when he reached the bottom left, it caught on something. Rearranging the papers inside, he tried again. This time the drawer slid closed, but it took a bit of effort. The result was a short high-pitched squeak as wood scraped upon wood.

Anthony flinched at the sound, but when no one came running, he made his way out of the study, the stack of papers he had found under the arm that did not make use of the crutch.

Gibbons met him at the head of the stairs with the other crutch in his hands.

"What's this, my lord?" he asked, nodding to the stack of papers under Anthony's arm.

"Answers, I hope," Anthony said, handing the stack to the butler so he could descend the stairs. Switching the crutch from his right arm to his left, he placed his hand on the banister, preparing for his descent. "Could you store those in the top drawer of the bureau in my room, Gibbons? I need to make an appearance in the breakfast room at present and do not want to rouse any suspicion."

Gibbons nodded in understanding, staying carefully at Anthony's side until he managed to reach the bottom of the stairs. Anthony turned toward the breakfast room, both crutches firmly in place, when a thought struck him. Turning back, he called to the butler who had begun ascending the stairs to the guest wing.

"I believe I will be in need of your services one more time, Gibbons. Tonight, after everyone has retired for the evening, I need to make my way back to the study. Can you orchestrate that without disturbing the house?"

The butler quirked a half-smile, a gleam appearing in his eyes. "It will be difficult, but I never back down from a challenge, my lord."

"Good. When the house is quiet, meet me at my door. Perhaps you can use the same signal you did with Miss Hensworth."

"Beggin' your pardon, my lord, but might I suggest a different plan?"

Surprised by the man's forwardness, Anthony found he was curious at what the butler had to offer.

"Go on, Gibbons."

"If you will excuse yourself early tonight, you can slip into the kitchens. The others will not see where you have retreated and will expect you to have gone to your room. That way when everyone has retired, we can use the servant's stairs. They are not open to the court and will be far quieter. In addition, you will not pass by Mrs. Marshall's door and risk being discovered by that lady."

Anthony saw the wisdom in it. Even though he had tried to be quiet this morning, he had made a good deal of noise thumping up and down the stairs. He was actually surprised they had not been discovered, at least by Aunt Vie.

"There is great wisdom in that plan, Gibbons. I will do as you say."

A movement on the stairs stopped their conversation. Anthony looked up to see Mr. Clayton descending from the family wing. The sight of the man startled him until he recalled Mr. Clayton's declaration yesterday that he would be moving his things into Engalworth Court for the duration of Anthony and Emma's courtship. It had been a concession to the objections Mr. Weazelton had voiced.

While he thought the measure wholly unnecessary, he was grateful for the older man's presence, if only for another person to provide protection for Emma from Mr. Weazelton's scheming grasp.

"Good morning, Hamdon."

"And to you, Mr. Clayton," he said, showing deference to the older man.

"Are you en route to or from the breakfast room?"

"To. Would you care to join me?"

"I would be happy to." Turning to Gibbons, he said, "and how are you this fine day, Gibbons?"

"I am well, sir. I trust you slept well."

"I did, Gibbons, thank you for asking. And how is the missus?"

"As pretty as ever," the older man said with a twinkle in his eye.

Mr. Clayton chuckled at the quick-witted response. Anthony smiled to himself at the way the old butler referred to his wife. It was refreshing to see a married couple still complimentary of each other after so many years.

"You'll probably see her when you break your fast," Gibbons continued. "I am sure she'd be as pleased as punch to answer for herself. Ladies being like that an' all."

Like what, Anthony was not sure, but Mr. Clayton seemed to understand.

"Well, then, I shall be sure to ask. Good day to you, Gibbons."

Gibbons dipped his head and began again up the stairs. Anthony marveled at the vitality of the older man. How many times was he required to descend and ascend those stairs? It was difficult for him to accomplish the task but twice a day, and yet this man walked them as if he were a man of one and twenty instead of five and fifty.

"A good man, that," Mr. Clayton said. "He and his wife have been a godsend to our Emma, loving her almost as their own. If it was not for their watchful care, I would have worried more about my niece, but they are as trustworthy as they come."

"For servants," Anthony added without thinking.

"No, for people," the vicar said firmly.

Anthony became intensely uncomfortable under Mr. Clayton's scrutiny. A touch of shame entered his heart, and he realized the scolding Emma had given him weeks ago was warranted. He needed to recognize the Gibbonses outside of their positions as servants to this household, especially since he was sure Emma and Mr. Clayton saw them more like family than servants.

"I understand, Mr. Clayton. It will take me some time to grow accustomed to thinking of people differently, years of training being as they are."

"Yes, the gentry are an interesting lot," the vicar said in a meditative tone. "Many believe if they show civility and kindness to those not of their circle, it will threaten their position as master. It is my observation, though, that those who are attentive and generous masters are given more deference than those who use servants and tenants as mere pawns or stepping stones. Take Lord Gladsby and his family. If they had treated their servants with any less goodness, Emma's life might be drastically different. You realize they hold her very safety in their hands, do you not?" He paused to let the rhetorical question sink in. "I hope you will take what you learn here, Lord Hamdon, and apply it to all your future dealings."

Anthony knew he had just received a sermon, but the way the older man delivered the rebuke and instruction was so kind and with such a gentle smile upon his aging face that he did not feel a bit of sting from the words. He felt a sudden urge to make this man proud. An odd occurrence as he had never had such a compulsion toward anyone before in his life. Well, perhaps before he had lost all respect for his father, which had been at such a young age he barely remembered it now. In this moment, however, he understood to a small degree what Nicholas and his other friends had spoken of so often over the years. The need to make their families proud.

"I shall do my best, Mr. Clayton. You have my word on that."

"Very good. Now, I am starving. Shall we?" He gestured in the direction of the breakfast room.

As they approached the open doors, a voice carried out into the air overpowering every other noise in the house, and Anthony smiled. Aunt Vie was filling the breakfast room full to bursting with her constant chatter. Entering the room, he saw Emma cast him a conspiratorial look over the edge of her tea cup. It would seem the Conspiratorial Alliance for Tomfoolery was in full swing if Mr. Weazelton's look of utter annoyance was any indication.

Mr. Weazelton had probably hoped to catch Emma alone this morning, as Anthony had learned she often was for breakfast. She, however, was one step ahead of the balding man, knowing full well there was nothing her aunt could resist more than a breakfast room with men to entertain, and it seemed Aunt Vie was in full form this morning.

Anthony could not help the next words that exited his mouth when Aunt Vie paused long enough to take a sip of her chocolate.

Plastering an empty-headed smile upon his face, he boomed, "Ah! Good morning, Mr. Wizzleton."

Chapter Thirty

Emma lay in her bed, staring at the dark mass above her. She knew the plaster of her ceiling was painted pale yellow, white daisies with green stems dotting the outer edges of the space. During the daylight hours, it was so cheery and comforting, but when the light was gone, it loomed above her, dark and depressing, stealing away the hope she clung to each day.

Trying desperately to push away the despair that haunted her each night, she focused on the next steps of her fight against Mr. Weazelton. She knew he had ridden into Banbury today to meet with her father's solicitor. She could only assume his intent was to provide the evidence he had in hopes he could convince the man of law to start the process of legal transfer without any questions.

She smiled to herself remembering the way Mr. Weazelton had stormed in just before dinner, marching straight up the stairs to his room to dress. It would seem her cousin had not met with much success against the formidable Mr. Black. The man may have been approaching seventy, but he had not lived this long by being weak. No matter what others thought of him, he was still keen and discerning. Emma was sure the man had given her cousin a flat refusal, and, if Mr. Weazelton's irritation was any indication, he was probably dismissed by Mr. Black without the opportunity to provide a rebuttal.

Perhaps it was time for Emma to make a trip to Banbury to see the solicitor herself. She had not seen the man since before her brother's supposed death. With

Mr. Weazelton now leading an active offense, she needed to find out what her legal recourses might be. She was unsure if Mr. Black would help her, but at least he had not hindered her by bending to Mr. Weazelton's will.

With a direction decided for that particular problem, she turned her mind to the men in the woods. The longer she thought on the subject, the more certain she was that Mr. Weazelton had not employed either of them. Where would he have the funds for such a venture? No, they were a complete and separate problem.

In fact, she was almost certain they were even separate problems from each other. That left several questions. Who were they? Was one friend, and the other foe? Or were they both her enemy? If one was friend and the other foe, which was which?

After several minutes pondering the problem, Emma's head began to ache with the effort. Her mind reverted back to what Anthony had said weeks ago, claiming the man in brown obviously wanted to be seen. But why only by her? Was it meant to strike fear in her heart?

Then there was the man in green. She had only really seen him once, but she was sure he had been around before. She had no proof. But the sensation that washed over her when she saw the man felt so familiar.

A thump from somewhere down the hall brought her thoughts crashing to a halt. The hairs on her arm rose and her skin began to tingle. Someone was moving down the hall toward her room. Unbidden thoughts of men in colored coats crashed to the forefront of her thoughts.

Should she ring for a servant? But if it was one of the men from the woods, she would be putting her servants' lives in danger, something she could not bear.

Another thought, more plausible, pounded at her already taut nerves. What if it was Mr. Weazelton come to ruin her? While she hoped he would not stoop to such levels, she knew if he was desperate enough for money, she was the fastest way to acquire it.

The thought sent her flying from her bed to check the lock on the door. Just as she reached the handle, she heard a distinct squeak from down the hall. The only thing that made that sound was in the study, a place no one should be at this hour. A spot she would not stand to be pilfered.

If Mr. Weazelton thought he could steal papers from the bottom drawer on her father's desk, he was sorely mistaken. The fear fled, replaced by a swift hot anger.

Retracing her steps, she yanked her wrapper off the end of the bed, blood pulsing through her veins. Shoving her hands into the silk wrapper, she rushed to the door ready to storm down and demand Mr. Weazelton leave.

Reaching for the handle, reason finally overtook her. She could not just storm down the hall and expect to walk away the victor. Where was her sense? Mr. Weazelton, though not a large man, was still much bigger than her. Plus, he had yet to respect her wishes on almost anything.

No, she needed to think this through. Taking a few deep breaths to calm her galloping emotions, a plan began to form in her mind. Her course set, she opened the door as quietly as possible. Peeking out, she saw a faint glow coming from down the hall. Noiselessly she left her room, leaving the door slightly ajar for a quick retreat.

Creeping on bare feet, she slowly made her way to the study door. First, she would see what and where her cousin was searching. If she was correct in her assumption, she would creep back to her room and ring the bell pull. Surely a summons this late at night would bring Gibbons and Thatcher running.

At the edge of the polished door frame, she stopped. Looking down at herself, Emma realized she had forgotten to tie her wrapper. Quickly she secured the covering in place, pulling the collar closed as much as possible. It would not do to have any part of her exposed to Mr. Weazelton, should he catch her.

Prepared for the confrontation, Emma leaned slightly forward, so she might see into the dimly lit room. The sight that met her propelled her feet into motion as she rushed into the room without another thought.

Anthony watched as Gibbons leaned forward, stretching his arm into the gaping hole where the desk drawer had once been. Removing the heavy wood had been quite difficult, but now, with the piece laid carefully on the floor, Gibbons was able to reach in to gather the handful of papers they had glimpsed in the dim candle light.

At that very moment, a white specter entered the room so swiftly that Anthony's heart leapt into his throat, causing him to almost drop the candle he was holding aloft on Gibbons's head. Gripping the metal candle holder, he prepared to throw it, candle and all at the intruder.

"Anthony! Why are you traipsing about my father's study at this hour? And without your crutches, no less!"

Luckily the voice registered in his head before he launched the candle holder at an indignant Emma who stood looking about the room for his missing crutches. While his mind had registered the lack of a threat, it seemed his heart was slow to catch up. It continued to gallop along at an irregular pace. He sat for a moment, taking quick, hard breaths, trying to calm the pounding in his chest.

"Got 'em," Gibbons declared.

Emma stepped forward to view the butler where he sat upon the floor, holding the papers they had spied.

"Gibbons?"

"Yes, Miss?"

"What on earth are you doing on the floor, and why is my father's desk in pieces?"

"Lord Hamdon believed the reason we've been struggling to close this drawer was due to papers or other items being caught beneath, and he was right," Gibbons said, holding up a few papers. Emma jumped forward, snatching the handful before either of them could hardly blink.

Stepping close to the candle Anthony held, she began flipping through each paper, examining each one carefully. Anthony was vaguely aware of Gibbons clasping the desk, the heavy wood providing leverage for him to move into a standing position, but most of his attention was caught up in the way the candle light danced off of Emma's intent face. Her eyebrows were several shades darker than her hair; hair that at this very moment, hung in a long, golden plait down her back, a few wisps of stray curls about her face and neck. Each time she examined a new sheet of paper, he watched her eyebrows rise with anticipation, then fall with disappointment.

A subtle scent of lavender and perhaps some lemon tickled Anthony's nose. Instinctively, he leaned forward to inhale a deeper breath. Closing his eyes, he let the scent wash over him. It was fresh and invigorating.

The smell was exactly how he viewed Emma in his life, fresh and invigorating. Before his accident, life had become stale and monotonous. A constant round of parties and people that he had no interest in. But Emma... Emma had made him think there just might be more to his life.

Her candor had woken him. Her secrets had intrigued him. Her goodness and beauty had captured him, and now he felt wholly and completely alive.

A throat cleared and his eyes shot open, but all he could see was white. Glancing up, he discovered he was leaning so far forward that his head almost rested in the curve just above Emma's hip. The heat that had been coursing through his veins pooled in his cheeks as he realized how close he had come to burrowing his face in her side.

Sitting up straight, he looked to the butler, who glared at him. Anthony cast the man an apologetic look. It had not been his intention to be so forward. At least she had not noticed his blunder.

She was supposed to be reading pages. Focus. Focus. But how was she to concentrate on the words before her when she stood so close to Anthony, his head leaning precariously close to her side? A few more inches, and it would rest on the curve of her waist. The thought sent heat coursing through her body.

Flicking her eyes back to the page, she tried not to think about his head being dangerously close, and the shiny, brown curls that she was aching to reach down and touch. Would they feel soft or coarse? Could she curl them about her fingers?

She startled at the sound of Gibbons clearing his throat. Glancing at the kind man, her cheeks burn with embarrassment, but he was not looking at her. He was glaring at Anthony, whose head had popped up at the sound. Trying not to smile, she applied herself again to the papers.

She had to reread the paper in front of her twice before her heart and head again connected. Three of the four looked to be letters. When she flipped to the last, her heart sank; none were from Alan. While some of the information was definitely valuable, specifically the letter from Mr. Black indicating that her father had, indeed, updated his last will and testament, it was still so disappointing that she wanted to sit down and weep. But she would not. She had done enough crying to last a lifetime. Now she needed to be strong.

"I am afraid none of these are the one we are looking for," she finally said, disappointment taking up residence where attraction had been moments before.

"I am sorry, Emma. I was so sure we would find it here. This morning after we left, I was sure it must have slipped under the drawer."

"Please, do not apologize. I am grateful for your insight. It is not a complete loss. This letter," she said, holding up the solicitor's note, "indicates that my father did, indeed, meet with Mr. Black to adjust his will."

A sudden light filled Anthony's eyes. "I know. I had hoped to get a few minutes alone with you, but with all the ladies Aunt Vie invited over to tea..." He trailed off as he locked eyes with her.

Her lips twitched. While it had been aggravating to have all of the marriage-minded mamas and their daughters over for tea, it had been quite entertaining to see how Anthony behaved under pressure. It allowed her to see if any other ladies turned his head. The last thing she wanted was to trap the man into an unwanted marriage, or to be trapped into one herself, for that matter. If she had seen any indications he had a wandering eye, she would have put a stop to his courtship with or without Mr. Weazelton as a looming threat. Luckily, while he had shown kindness to all the ladies, the only soft looks he had given were to her.

A second clearing of Mr. Gibbons's throat made Emma realize she was staring deeply into Anthony's dark blue eyes instead of attending to what he had just said. Looking again at the butler, she saw the man smirking. Her very proper butler was smirking at her. Goodness, she must really be making a cake of herself.

With the break of eye contact, Anthony continued. "I found a stack of papers in the desk that I believe is your father's will."

"That is the original will he drew up," Emma said with disappointment. "He has kept it in the top right-hand drawer for ages."

"That was my assessment, as well, but when I rifled through them, I noticed the dates change. About halfway through, the marking date reads December 16, 1813."

Emma stared at him, this time in shock. She had looked through the will, had she not? Thinking back, she realized she had only examined the top two or three sheets, the ones that outlined her guardianship. It clearly stated everything including her care was to be passed to her father's heir. She had been surprised by the length of the will, but she did not question the legal terms within it. She had simply lifted the papers out to inspect the drawer for any others.

Pulling open the top drawer, she was surprised to find it empty. Bending forward, she frantically put her hand into the wooden space to ascertain that it was in fact empty.

A hand gently clasped hers as it swept the drawer. "They are not there, Emma. I had Gibbons take them to my room so I could inspect them later. Unfortunately, I had no time when I dressed for dinner, so I have not yet verified what they contain."

"Gibbons, bring me the will," she commanded, half excited and half afraid.

"But, miss, I..."

"Now, Gibbons!" she said, a bit too loud and harsh. A sting of remorse pierced her when the older man's eyes rounded, hurt evident in their depths. She had never been so unfeeling to the man. As he moved to exit, she said softly, "Thank you, Gibbons."

It was not the apology she owed him, but Gibbons seemed to understand her intent, for he gave her a brief nod and soft smile before he left the room, turning toward the front of the house. Emma was surprised at his direction until she remembered that Mr. Weazelton's room was near the servant's staircase, which brought another question to mind.

"Anthony," she asked, turning back to where he sat at the desk reading through some of the papers, "How did you attain the upper level?"

"The servant's stairs. Gibbons felt they would be much quieter."

"And had you intended to use the same method on the other side of the house?"

"Yes. That was the plan."

"Do you realize that will take you directly past Mr. Weazelton's room?"

His stunned silence was answer enough.

Chapter Thirty-One

Anthony sat, letting Emma's words soak in. Until this moment, he had not even considered the placement of Mr. Weazelton's room on the other side of the house, but she was correct. He should have thought of that before insisting Gibbons help him.

Thinking back, he should have just asked the butler to look in the space himself. But he had been so caught up in being Emma's hero, her knight in shining armor, that he had not thought through all the ramifications.

Now, he sat in her father's study, no letter and no way of getting back to his room without possibly waking the weasel in his den. He tried to console himself with the thought that at least he had the will, but he had obtained that earlier in the day. He did not need to come here to find papers that exposed what he already knew.

Emma stepped around the desk to the side where the drawer lay sprawled on the floor. Bending down, she tried to lift it, but the drawer was deceptively heavy. Placing the end she had lifted back down on the floor, she kneeled down and perched on the backs of her feet.

Anthony noticed for the first time how small her feet were, then belatedly realized they were bare, her night dress draped casually over her limbs just above her ankles. The next thought that ricocheted through his head identified the part of her that sat upon those feet. His eyes flew to her face, heat engulfing not only his cheeks, but his whole body.

He could not remember when he had been so grateful for dim light to hide his embarrassment. As he rubbed his cheeks vigorously to stop the thoughts, Emma looked away from the hole in the desk.

"Are you all right?" she asked, concern marring her pretty face.

"Just tired, I believe," he lied. At this moment in time, he was not the least bit sleepy. He was too acutely aware of her next to him, clad only in her nightdress and wrapper. He needed to get out of this situation, but without Gibbons there to help—

"Anthony," she said quietly, "can you bring the light down, so I might get a better look into the space?"

Grateful for something to do, he snatched the candle up a little too quickly, the flame flickering with the movement. He cupped his hand about the back to block any further rush of air. Holding it almost level with the empty space on the desk, he watched as Emma inserted her hand, feeling about in the space.

When she removed it, she held a folded piece of foolscap, two edges ragged as if they had been torn. Unfolding the paper, she sat a moment, her eyes flicking back and forth. He could tell when she reached the end because her eyes flicked back to the top again. Suddenly, tears began their quiet trail down her cheeks.

He felt so sorry for her. To come up against so much disappointment in one day must have been hard. He bent over to see if he might get a better look at the paper she held, but to his surprise, she popped up out of her perched position, wrapped her arms about his neck, and kissed him squarely on the mouth.

She, Emma Hensworth, had just kissed Anthony, Lord Hamdon, on the mouth. He must think her a complete hoyden. But she had been so excited to finally find her brother's letter that the impulse had just overcome her.

Thinking she should probably hurry to her feet and run from the room, she was surprised when his hand snaked around the base of her neck, his fingers burying themselves in her hair. Gently, he pulled her back, kissing her so achingly soft that she felt the thrill all the way to her toes.

Footsteps sounded on the stairs, and Anthony slowly released her, placing the candle he still held carefully on the desk.

"I presume by your excitement that those are not sad tears," he said with a soft smile.

"You presume correctly. This is Alan's letter, at least most of it. It looks like several pieces around the edge have been torn off."

"The bits in the lockbox?"

"Yes, I believe so. His letter is hard to understand."

"How so?"

"It is written in both English and Spanish."

"Spanish? I thought your brother spoke French."

"He does, but he had a Latin tutor who was fluent in French, Italian, and Spanish. Alan learned some of each, but my father only knew French and Spanish."

"Do you also know Spanish?"

"No. I only know one word because Father gave it to one of his hunting dogs as a name."

"And what was that?"

"*Rato*," she said as Gibbons stepped through the doorway.

"What does it mean?" Anthony asked, as Gibbons approached with the papers Emma had requested tucked neatly under his arm.

"Rat," the butler said and laid the papers on the desk.

"Rat?"

"Yes," Emma said with a smile. "He did not particularly like that dog. It was always where it was not wanted."

"Why would your brother's letter contain that particular word? It seems an odd word to include in a letter, unless he was describing unsanitary living conditions."

At Anthony's pronouncement, Gibbons's head popped up, and he looked at Emma. Hope, expectation, perhaps a bit of fear lingered in his eyes. "Is it true?" he asked quietly.

In response, she handed him the letter and was rewarded with the biggest smile she had ever seen on his face. When he looked up from reading, his eyes glistened in the candlelight.

"Finally," he said on a sigh.

"Finally," she responded reverently.

A soft click of wood on wood brought her attention to the desk. Anthony had retrieved the small lockbox from the still disassembled drawer. Fishing in his pocket, he pulled out the key. The sight surprised Emma until she remembered her quick exit from the study. She must have left it behind in her haste to get to the breakfast room.

Opening the box, Anthony pulled out the three small pieces of paper. Emma had assumed they all came from the bottom of a paper by the location of the flat edge. After opening the letter, however, she realized only one had come from the bottom; the other two were from the edges. Taking the letter gently from Gibbons, Anthony carefully tried to fit each one in a spot until he discovered the correct fit, then he would move to the next area. Once all were in place on the desk, they examined the contents, but the three small papers brought no more clarity.

Emma read the short letter aloud.

Lord Gladsby,

I hope this letter finds you well, or as they say here in Spain, "que te olvides el mensaje anterior." Things have been rather windy here. It reminds me of when I used to visit you as a child. Do you remember that day when Mr. <u>Holmes</u> helped us make a kite out of sheepskin? Unfortunately, we flew it too close to the trees in the grove behind the stables. It got so tangled in the high branches that we were required to leave it be until the <u>late spring</u> winds blew it down. I do <u>not</u> recall what <u>day</u> it was, but it took several months for the wind to accomplish its task. I miss those carefree days.

I am off to visit an interesting acquaintance of mine, a Señor Rato who lives across the fjord. He said the most entertaining thing the other day. "Mr. Beauchene," he said, "Es el que buscamos." Is that not excessively diverting?

My apologies that this letter must be so short. I am called away just now, but if you have need of me, send word to Mr. **Wright** *at* ministerio de ciudad, recoger Bustemonte. *He will know where to forward my letters while I travel this beautiful country.*

Give my regards to your beautiful daughter.

Mr. George Beauchene

When Emma looked up, Anthony was staring at her in confusion.

"I thought you said this letter was from your brother?"

"It is."

"The signature clearly denotes it is from a Mr. George Beauchene."

Emma tensed at the way he had spoken to her. While he had not said the words, his tone clearly indicated that he believed himself to be deceived. Why would she lie about something as important as this? Because you have lied about even more important things, her conscience answered back. Chagrined at her own rebuke, she looked at Gibbons for support.

"The handwriting matches," the butler responded.

"Yes, and my brother's given name is George, even though everyone calls him Alan. Beauchene is my mother's maiden name. He could not very well waltz all over France with a name as English as Hensworth, could he?"

"I see," Anthony said. He took the letter from her and scanned it again. "What do you make of the rest of the letter? The first seems to be a recounting of a childhood memory."

"Yes, but the names and times are wrong. It was Mr. Clayton who helped make that kite, and it was flown in the spring and came down in the winter. I remember it very distinctly because we painted the soft skin with red paint. I, being much younger, was not as careful with the paint and managed to wipe a thin stripe across my cheek right under my left eye. We tried to wash it off, but the paint stained my cheek pink for an entire week. My father teased that I was far too young and pretty to start painting my face.”

“Is it possible, because you were so young, that you misremember the times?”

“No, because the kite came down Christmas morning, and as a child, that is definitely a day I would remember.”

“Indeed,” he agreed. She watched as he scanned the letter again. Finally, he looked up, and with a touch of pity in his expression, said, “I am sorry, Emma, but I do not believe this would convince the courts that your brother is alive.”

“What?” she said far too loudly. She quickly covered her mouth. Lowering her voice back down, she said, “Why not?”

“Even though you and Gibbons recognize the handwriting and stories, there is no legal signature. In truth there is no distinct information at all, not even a date. “

Emma snatched the missive back. Flipping it around, she pointed to the postmark, which was, indeed, long after Dennewitz.

“And what of this?” she said, pointing to the first underlined word.

“Holmes? What of it?”

“Anthony, read the underlined letters,” she said insistently. The first time she had read the letter, she had thought it odd he had underlined a few things, but when none of them seemed all that important, she had thought it an accident. On her second perusal, though, she had noticed they fit together.

“Home, late spring, no day,” he murmured to himself.

“Yes, it means he will be home in late spring, but he is unsure when.”

Anthony looked doubtful, but did not question her.

“Even so, that does not change the fact that there is no distinct indication that this information came from your brother, at least not one that a solicitor or judge might recognize as proof.”

Emma let out a huff. He was right, of course, but she still still frustrated with him for pointing it out. Trying to remind herself it was not his fault, she said, “I believe this part,” indicating who correspondence should be addressed to, “is the man my father wrote. I recognize the name.”

"If I may, miss," Gibbons said, indicating the torn pieces.

"Please, go ahead, Gibbons."

The man picked up each piece and carefully arranged the papers in such a way that it resembled an address. She felt ridiculous for not seeing it before. It was part of the address of the office her father had written. The same address she herself had written after recollecting it on her father's letters.

Anthony still looked confused, so she elaborated. "It is part of the address to Mr. Wright, or—" looking back at the letter, "—perhaps Wit, at the Foreig n Office."

"Ah! But why only part?"

"Because my father would have known the street. It is no secret in the ton where military intelligence is housed." A yawn built in her throat and she quickly moved to cover it. Anthony smiled at her, a knowing look on his face.

"It is late. We can go over this again later, preferably during daylight hours." he said.

"No. There is something I must see first." She snatched up the will Gibbons had laid upon the desk. Flipping through the pages one by one, she finally found where the two wills separated. Placing the older copy on the desk, she began carefully perusing the pages. On the third page, she found what she was looking for. Happy tears welled in her eyes again. She wanted to shout for joy, but obviously, this was neither the time nor place for such expressions.

Both the men looked at her expectantly. Her emotions were roiling to close to the surface. She was afraid to utter the words aloud. So, instead, she put the will upon the desk and placed her finger below the lines that changed the course of her life.

In the event my heir, George Alan Hensworth, is unable to take up guardianship of my daughter, Emma Olivia Hensworth, I appoint Robert William Clayton her legal guardian until she is of age.

Chapter Thirty-Two

When Anthony awoke, it took him a moment to recall where he was. The blue damask wallpaper and cream bed covering were not those of his usual accommodations. With a rush, memory resurfaced—a brief discussion, the agreement, Mr. Hensworth's room. It was the only other room in the family quarters Mrs. Gibbons kept ready in hopeful expectation of her master's arrival.

He had been uncomfortable taking Emma's brother's room, but both Emma and Gibbons had insisted, worried that the distinct thumping sound of his hops up the stairs and down the corridor would rouse Mr. Weazelton, or anyone else in the house, for that matter. He had finally acquiesced. One of the unique things about Engalworth Court was how any sound carried in the open center of the house. Anthony was sure that quirk had been his and Gibbons's downfall in keeping their late-night escapade secret from the entire house. Of all the people who might discover them, however, he was relieved it had been Emma.

Just the thought of her brought a smile to his face. Warmth filled his chest as he lay comfortably against the plush pillows in the big mahogany bed. Her impetuous kiss last night had caught him so off guard that he barely had time to react, but it had given him the very encouragement he needed to fully taste her pert pink lips.

He could still feel the way they had molded to his. To his surprise she tasted both sweet and salty. One of his favorite combinations. He had been tempted to deepen the kiss, but Gibbons's footfalls had brought him back to reason. While he knew the direction his heart was traveling, he was not completely sure hers followed the same path. She could have only been overwhelmed with the excitement of finding the letter. It must have been a great relief to find at least a small memento of the truthfulness of her father's words.

Another part of his mind questioned why her excitement would express itself in a kiss. In the time he had known her, she had not shown a penchant to expressing her emotions with physical touch. He was always the one that reached for her when she was distressed. And in all the interactions he had witnessed with her family, she limited herself to showing physical affection only to Mr. Clayton and, on occasion, Mrs. Gibbons.

There had to be some part of Emma that cared for him, he reasoned. Why else would she so willingly receive his kisses? He desperately hoped his supposition was true, because he was falling madly in love with her, something he could never have imagined six weeks ago.

A soft rap on the door in a two-two-three staccato let him know Gibbons had come to help him down to the breakfast room. Aunt Vie and Mr. Weazelton must be safely below stairs if the butler was coming to assist.

Gibbons stepped in with Anthony's clothes draped over his arm. At the sight, Anthony wondered what Thatcher must be thinking with Gibbons attending him for the second day in a row. He hoped the young man did not think him displeased with his service. Thatcher had made a fine valet in the time Anthony had been here. If he was forced to release Brown, perhaps he could convince the footman to take up his place.

"My lord," Gibbons said, interrupting Anthony's musing, "Mr. Clayton is in the breakfast room. I wonder if you might like to meet with him before Mr. Weazelton is finished with his meal?"

"Yes, thank you, Gibbons," he said as the older man helped him get his pantaloons over the awkward splint on his leg. "You are quite insightful. I believe the sooner Emma's guardianship is settled, the better. Do you happen to know Mr. Weazelton's plans for the day?"

"Thatcher brought me several letters Mr. Weazelton requested to be mailed. I am assuming they are more inquiries about the process for the transfer of title. Other than that, I am unaware of any other plans the gentleman has."

"Hmmm..." Anthony murmured, thinking about what the man's next move might be. Hopefully, it would take him several weeks to secure the right paperwork, as well as an audience with a judge that might hear him, but they could not count on that. It was very possible the money hungry weasel had been working without their notice for weeks. Their best chance was to bring Lord Gladsby's solicitor into their confidence. He seemed a loyal enough man if his rebuff of Mr. Weazelton's zealous prodding was any indication.

"Gibbons," he said thoughtfully, "it would be such a shame if Mr. Weazelton's letters were misplaced for a few days."

The butler's lips quirked at one side in a way Anthony now recognized as his scheming smile. He quite liked the look on the man. "Indeed, my lord, a great shame. Especially if the old house staff were to forget exactly where they laid it, for say," he paused tapping his chin in mock thought, "a full fortnight?"

"A shame, indeed," Anthony said with a conspiratorial grin.

When Anthony was completely ready for the day, Gibbons again helped him down the servants' stairs and through the kitchens, the only person present in the room being Mrs. Gibbons. If she was surprised at seeing him gather his crutches there and hobble out to the main part of the house, she did not show it. Most likely her husband had alerted her to Anthony's change of room for the night. The good woman only cast him a brief smile as she kneaded dough on a work table.

Gibbons had gone on ahead to alert Mr. Clayton, so Anthony made his way to the same small sitting room where he and Emma had sat so comfortably a couple nights ago. Had it been just over a day since then? It seemed like so many things had changed in the last thirty-six hours.

Mr. Clayton entered the room shortly after Anthony settled himself on the settee. Gibbons was on his heels; Lord Gladsby's will tucked under his right arm. Mr. Clayton greeted him warmly, asking after his health as Gibbons quietly slipped Anthony the papers. The sight of the documents caused Mr. Clayton to pause in his pleasantries and raise an eyebrow.

Anthony smiled knowingly at the man, excited about the news he was about to divulge. "Do you know what this is, Mr. Clayton?"

"No, but I do hope you will tell me soon. You look as giddy as a school boy on Christmas morn."

"What an apt similitude, for I feel as if it is Christmas morning, and you are about to open one of the most precious gifts I could give you." Handing the will over to the older man, he continued, "You will be especially interested in page three."

"Lord Gladsby updated his will?" Mr. Clayton asked in awe. Anthony merely nodded as the older man pulled a set of spectacles out of his pocket and began scanning the pages. If the way his finger raced through the lines was any indication, he seemed to be looking for something specific.

When Mr. Clayton reached page three, his fingers stopped on what Anthony knew to be the lines concerning Emma. The man's fingers retraced the line three times before he looked up at Anthony, tears glistening in his eyes.

"To me?" he said, his voice breaking. Anthony nodded. Mr. Clayton pulled the glasses from his face and pinched his nose between thumb and forefinger. Silent sobs racked the older man's frame as tears began trickling down his cheeks.

Anthony was so surprised at the strong reaction that he was not sure what to do. He had never seen a grown man cry. His father and grandfathers had never shown such emotion. In fact, Society at large considered it a great weakness for men to cry. Only women were weak enough to give into the inclination. But as he watched the older man cry in relief, he did not see him as weak at all. In contrast, it raised his estimation of him.

Mr. Clayton loved Emma. Perhaps almost as much as her own father had. Again, that desire to have this man's esteem washed over Anthony. He had a desire to emulate him. He wanted to bring the kind of happiness this humble vicar always brought whenever he was near. He wanted to be as kind, thoughtful, and understanding. He wanted to feel something, anything, as deeply as the man before him. In truth, he wanted to love someone so much that it brought him to t ears.

Finally, Mr. Clayton reached for his handkerchief and began wiping the moisture from his face. "Please excuse me. This is just... so much."

Anthony waved off the apology. "It was an honor to see such a show of love, Mr. Clayton."

A soft smile curved the man's lips, lifting his wrinkled cheeks. "How refreshing," he said. "It is not often I find someone as forward thinking on emotions as myself. I have always thought it strange that we must hide our feelings so fully. I am sure it is why some consider me unfit as a vicar. I am not somber enough."

"Well, I for one find *you* refreshing. I have not been particularly inclined toward religion, but your views, your passion and devotion on the subject, has awakened my thoughts in that direction. It no longer feels bleak and heavy."

"I am pleased. It is comforting to know one's life work has brought some small measure of good."

"It has brought far more than a small measure, and your brother-in-law's trust is proof."

"Yes," he said quietly, "I am humbled and relieved."

"It seems you really were the correct man for me to inquire after Emma's hand."

"I was indeed," Mr. Clayton said with a twinkle in his eye and a smile on his face.

Emma was surprised when Mr. Clayton was called away from the breakfast room, but when he entered with Anthony a half hour later, she understood. The soft adoring smile he cast her and the slight rim of red about his eyes confirmed that Anthony had shared the information they had come across last night. While anything could have gone wrong in the months following Alan's letter, it was a relief to know she would not be left to the conniving clutches of Mr. Weazelton.

Shortly after Anthony and her uncle entered the room, Mr. Weazelton turned to her and said, "Cousin, might I have your company for a walk about the gardens this morning?"

Emma was so surprised by the request that she sat for a full minute trying to understand it. While he had stayed near her his whole visit, he had never actually tried to court her. Instead, he had consistently reminded her of how a marriage between them would allow her to stay in her home when he inherited. Apparently, now that she had another option, he felt more effort was necessary.

Why had her cousin even asked for such a favor? Mr. Weazelton knew, after all, that she and Anthony had entered into a courtship. While the community at large did not know, it should have be enough to discourage him.

Looking to Anthony, she begged him with her eyes to intercede. He must have understood, for he leaned forward in his seat to scorch her cousin with his glare. "I do not think that advisable, Mr. Weazelton."

Emma was momentarily shocked. For once, Anthony had pronounced her cousin's name correctly. He must have been truly perturbed.

"Come now, Lord Hamdon, can I not spend a little family time with my own cousin?"

He looked ready to protest when Aunt Marshall spoke up from the other end of the table. "Do not fret, Anthony. I shall go along as chaperone. You cannot begrudge the man a small stroll about the gardens."

His gaze flicked to her aunt. For the first time since Aunt Marshall's arrival, Emma saw him cast the woman a scathing look that would have caused even the stoutest of hearts to cower. Aunt Marshall fidgeted in her seat. "That is," she said, seeming to gather her words, "I do not think..." she trailed off.

"I think I shall accompany you as well. As Emma's legal guardian, until her father's return, it is my responsibility, after all," Mr. Clayton said.

This brought stunned looks from everyone.

"Legal guardian?" Mr. Weazelton asked, his face a mixture of disbelief and surprise that soon melted away to one of frustration. Quickly recovering, he gave Mr. Clayton a solicitous look. "Of course, Mr. Clayton. It will even out our numbers perfectly." Casting Anthony a look of triumph, her cousin excused himself from the room promising to meet her at the front door in a quarter hour.

Emma sat confused. She had never actually accepted his request. How was it she was now engaged to entertain her cousin for the morning? Even more distressing was the part her aunt and uncle had played in the undertaking. Aunt Marshall she could understand, but Mr. Clayton?

Her uncle leaned over and whispered something into her intended's ear. The sour look on Anthony's face faded. Glancing at her, his face softened. He seemed to be sending her strength with his eyes. It resonated deep in her soul.

Belatedly, she recognized her mental blunder. She had thought of him as her intended. Not merely as a beau, but as a solid presence in her life. With a sinking realization, Emma found she was already firmly attached to the handsome man sitting across the table from her.

"Please, God," she prayed in desperation, "I know I do not deserve anything, what with all my lies, but if you have one blessing left for me, please let me keep him. I cannot handle losing another person I love."

Chapter Thirty-Three

Anthony stood by the window in the drawing room that looked out over the garden. He watched Emma walk next to Mr. Weazelton as they made their way down the path that led to the garden bench. The sight made him sick. He knew he should not be so peevish; he knew her feelings about the man, after all.

The one consolation was Emma's obvious refusal to take her cousin's arm. Anthony had seen Mr. Weazelton offer it to her at least twice. Instead, she walked forward as she pointed out different plants.

While his exclusion from the invitation by the entire party was excessively rude, Mr. Clayton's brief explanation was wise. They needed to keep Mr. Weazelton placated long enough to make an appropriate defense. While Emma's future was secured, Engalworth Court still hung in the balance.

Six weeks ago, Anthony would not have cared in the least about such a thing. It was not his property after all. However, having come to know Mr. Clayton, the servants and several tenants like the stable master Mr. Ladd, Anthony could not see leaving them to Mr. Weazelton's mercy. Their livings, after all, were all held under the barony. They did not deserve to be left in the hands of a dishonorable baron, even for a short amount of time.

His gaze flitted to Mr. Clayton, Aunt Vie's hand resting lightly upon the older man's arm. He had never been so put out with Fredrick's mother in his life. How could the woman be complicit in Mr. Weazelton's requests? Unlike Mr. Clayton, she did not have any reason to forward a relationship with Mr. Weazelton other than to spite Anthony, and that he could not comprehend. She had always shown great love and devotion to all of Fredrick's friends.

A second thought crept into his mind. She was trying to make him jealous. He was almost certain of it. Unfortunately, she had succeeded, he admitted to himself with some discomfort.

While a courtship had appeased Emma's aunt for a time, it seemed the woman was trying to press for a proposal sooner rather than later. That frustrated him. Not that he did not intend to offer for Emma, but he hated to be manipulated. It reminded him too much of his own mother.

Letting his eyes wander back to Emma, who now stood under the tree that provided shade for the garden bench, he drank in the sight of her. The light grey gown she wore whipped about her in the light breeze. Her stance was either guarded or chilled as she hugged her arms about herself. Was it cold out? he wondered, as Mr. Weazelton indicated the garden bench. Emma shook her head, saying something to his offer. Whatever it was, Anthony was pleased. How dare the man suggest sitting together on their special bench.

He knew it was ridiculous to view the small stone structure as such. Surely many couples had sat upon it over time, but he could not help feel a bit of sentimentality for the spot. It was, after all, where he had asked Emma's permission to begin their courtship.

Anthony registered the loud crack just seconds before bark showered down on Emma. What had happened? She dropped into a crouch almost simultaneously with the sound, and Mr. Weazelton, who was also crouching, signaled for her to run behind a nearby bush. Anthony froze for a moment, wondering if a branch had broken in the breeze, but surely it would not have been so loud.

Frantically, he looked toward the woods where a brown speck ran along the edge of the tree line before it dove into some greenery. Anger and fear seized him as he realized what had just occurred. Emma had been shot at! Swiveling around on his crutches, he swung rapidly toward the door of the drawing room, hollering for Gibbons and Thatcher.

By the time he reached the court, both servants were rushing down the stairs toward him.

"Miss Hensworth was just shot at in the garden! She needs protection!" he hollered.

Without a word, Thatcher spun around and ran for the servant exit on the side of the house that led straight into the gardens. Anthony's words must have echoed throughout the entire house, for Smith, Sally, and Mrs. Gibbons came running from various directions.

He started to make his way up the few steps to the front door when a bang from the side of the house indicated the opening and closing of the servant's door.

One step from the top, he looked over his shoulder to see Mr. Ladd ushering Emma in, Owen holding her hand. Behind her was Aunt Vie, with Mr. Weazelton and Thatcher on either side of a limping Mr. Clayton.

"Emma!" he called out, spinning on the stairs. She dropped Owen's hand and without letting go of her skirts, took the stairs in a few long strides, reaching him and wrapping her arms about his middle, causing him to drop his crutches. She did not even seem to register the clatter as she stood shaking, her arms wrapped so tightly about his waist he could scarcely draw breath. It was a good thing the court steps were not as narrow as the ones leading to the second level, or they might have toppled down the stairs.

Lowering his arms to encircle her tiny shaking shoulders, he took a few deep breaths to let his own racing heart calm.

Focusing on the terror she had just experienced, he began rubbing slow circles upon her back hoping to soothe her fears. Slowly, her shaking began to calm. Looking over her head, he assessed the rest of the party who stood silently looking at one another before a sudden pandemonium of conversation erupted.

Aunt Vie was proclaiming her fright while Mr. Weazelton was asking what had just occurred. Mr. Ladd was simultaneously asking after Mr. Clayton's wellbeing while Gibbons was calling to Sally to fetch some hot water. Mrs. Gibbons directed Thatcher to escort Mr. Clayton to a chair while Smith stood three steps down from her mistress, poised to swoop in when she was needed. All the while, Owen was shouting an excited retelling of what had happened from his perspective just outside the stables.

Anthony let out a shrill whistle, the one he used to call Mariner, stopping all the commotion at once. Emma stepped back at the sound and, for a moment, he wished he had let the chaos continue if only to allow him to hold her longer.

"Mr. Ladd, will you please ride into Worthin and hire a few guards for the house?"

"But..." Emma began to protest.

"Tell them they will be working for the Viscount Hamdon," he continued. "You should be safe to leave as I saw the man dive into the woods shortly after firing on Miss Hensworth."

"Why should we trust you?" Mr. Weazelton ground out, narrowed eyes taking in Anthony's position. "The man could have easily been aiming for me. Someone you may have employed to clear the way for your suit."

"Or someone you hired to get rid of Miss Hensworth, so her dowry might fall to your inheritance." Anthony said, anger lacing his words. How dare the man accuse him of underhanded dealings?

"I would never," Mr. Weazelton nearly shouted, clearly offended by Anthony's accusation. Good. The man deserved a taste of his own medicine.

"Neither would I, so we are equal. Now, Mr. Ladd, if you will fetch Mr. Lovell before you go. We need the gardener's help in order to keep the doors secure." The man nodded and asked Mrs. Gibbons to look after Owen until he could return and escort him safely back to their cottage.

"Thatcher, I need you to watch the side entrance while Gibbons watches the front. Smith, please go watch the kitchen door until Mr. Lovell's arrival." All three moved swiftly to fulfill their assignments. Mrs. Gibbons was kneeling before Mr. Clayton inspecting a blood-soaked tear in the knee of the man's pants.

"Are you alright, Mr. Clayton?" Anthony asked.

"These old limbs do not move as quickly as they used to. Banged up my knee a great deal in the rush to get inside, but it will heal."

"What of our trip to Banbury to see Mr. Black?" Emma asked quietly, trying to keep her words from being heard by Mr. Weazelton.

"I believe it will have to wait until another day," he said compassionately. "We need to secure the house for now. It appears our visitors in the woods are far more dangerous than we previously thought."

Anthony was surprised when she did not give a single objection. Emma simply nodded, turning to her maid who was just returning from the kitchens, and motioned for Smith to follow her.

"If you will excuse me, I find myself in need of a respite." Then, with a dip of her head, she left them all.

He watched her go with some misgiving. The usually indomitable Emma Hensworth must have hit her breaking point. Instead of making plans for protection or looking after her uncle, she was retreating to the safety of her room. It was so out of character for her that he worried she had been shaken more than he realized.

It was only midday when Smith helped Emma undress. She still felt a slight tremor running through her body, as if the earth was shaking under her feet. She had seen the man in brown emerge from the woods just seconds before the bark above her head had splintered and showered down. How he had lifted his arm and fired so quickly was beyond her. She had been staring directly at him. He was not particularly close, so perhaps her sight was not as keen at that distance.

While the whole experience had been distressing, it was the sound of her name floating on the wind that had shaken her to the core. The ghostly call drifted on the wind at almost the same moment the report of the gun sounded in her ears. It felt so surreal, and yet her brother's voice had called out to her.

Tears stung her eyes. His call had caused her to duck just before the bark on the tree had exploded. The shot had been high, and she did not think it would have hit her, but the thought that her brother might now be her guardian angel flooded her brain. The only way he could hold that position was if he no longer walked the earth.

Her silent tears turned into hard racking sobs at the realization that she was really and truly alone. Turning into her pillow, she sobbed out her sorrow. The bed jostled, then Smith's soft hand began rubbing circles on her back, much in the same way Anthony had earlier. Letting her tears flow freely for a time, she indulged in the release of a good hard cry.

Smith said nothing, but every once in a while moved a lock of hair out of her face or handed her a new square of linen. Eventually, all her tears subsided, and Emma lay motionless, allowing the stillness of the room to float over her.

All the deception, all the secrecy, had been for naught. Alan was gone. There was nothing left for her here at Engalworth Court. Everything, everyone, all her hope had died. Perhaps she could find peace with her uncle in the vicarage, but Emma knew it would be far too close for her liking. She did not want to see everything her father and grandfather had worked for go to ruin. It was time to chart a different course.

In her moments of fear the only person she had thought to run to was Anthony. The need had been stronger than anything she had ever experienced. She had needed the protection of his arms. Needed the strength of his support. She had needed him and only him. Somewhere in the pandemonium, she realized she had fallen quite desperately in love.

She needed to make peace with her past because he was the only future she wanted. He had said he would not leave unless she told him to. Well, she hoped he was ready to leave, because she planned on going wherever he went. For the rest of her life.

Chapter Thirty-Four

Something was off with Emma, but Anthony could not exactly discern the difference. At dinner the evening before, she had not spoken above ten words, merely pushed her food about her plate to give the appearance she was eating.

After dinner, she sat near him on the settee listening to Mr. Clayton read from a book of poetry. Every so often he caught her glancing at him, a soft look in her eyes that made his heart pick up pace. He had wanted to scoot closer and sit as they had several nights before when they were alone in the sitting room, but it was not proper to do so when in the company of others.

Technically, it was not proper to do so at all since they were not officially engaged, he thought to himself as he sat in the west sitting room after breakfast. It was something he hoped to remedy soon.

Emma had not come down to breakfast. Anthony understood it was an odd occurrence, if Mrs. Gibbons's worried muttering was anything to go by. Had the shock from the day before been too much for her? She had been under a great deal of stress lately. Being shot at could have been the straw that broke the camel's back, or in this case, the perfect storm to crumple the Ice Fairy's resolve.

Had she taken ill? Between the lack of sleep Thursday night, the traumatic experience, and her lack of appetite last evening, it would certainly make a body feel ill.

The door opened to the sitting room and Aunt Vie entered. Emma was not the only one showing odd behavior. Aunt Vie had been uncommonly quiet the last twenty-four hours. Even with the addition of five more men about the exterior of the house, she still seemed to jump at any sound that was out of place. He felt sorry for her. It must have been terrifying to think herself completely safe only to find she was not.

Emma, at least, understood the probable danger. She had been ready for a possible problem, as was evidenced by her deft dodge of gunfire. Anthony had to admit he was impressed at how quickly she dropped to the ground as the shot was fired.

When Aunt Vie was comfortably seated in a chair across from his, she cleared her throat, looked about the room, then cleared her throat again. It was obvious she wanted to say something, but her eyes kept darting about the room.

Finally she said, "I should have believed Emma when she said she was seeing someone about the place, but I have to admit, I thought it only the imaginings of a young girl in search of attention. I reasoned that being alone all those months must have left her in want of excitement, but now I can see I was too critical of her."

Anthony stared at the woman. Why she was admitting this to him? Shouldn't this be a discussion with Emma? She really did owe her niece an apology.

"I know it may look like I do not care for my niece, Lord Hamdon," she said carefully. Why had she chosen this moment to address him by his title? Just another thing to make this conversation uncomfortable. "But it is quite the opposite. I care a fair deal more for Emma than I have my own sons, I am ashamed to admit. She is the only female child in either the Hensworth or Marshall lines, so I have put a large amount of pressure on her to become a lady our families could be proud of. Yesterday, when I almost lost her, I realized I had been too hard on her. If she would have died," Aunt Vie eyes filled with tears, "I believe I would have lived with my guilt for the rest of my days." The last word broke on the sob that forced the tears to spill over. Reaching into the sleeve of her gown, Aunt Vie produced a lace handkerchief and held it to her mouth and nose.

"It appears God has given you a second chance," Anthony replied, compassion filling him. "And in my opinion, Emma is already a woman you should be proud of. It is not every day that a woman can go through the trials she has faced and still have faith in her future."

Emma stood outside the door to the sitting room digesting what her aunt had just admitted. She had taken breakfast in her room, not wanting to meet with anyone other than Anthony. After preparing for the day and inquiring of Gibbons where Anthony might be, she had made her way here. At the sound of Aunt Marshall's voice on the other side of the door, she had motioned to Thatcher to pause before opening it for her.

Her mind rushed through the last few weeks, all the instruction, all the admonitions. Was it truly out of a place of caring and not disappointment? It certainly was not well done of her aunt, but Emma could well imagine how she must appear to the woman. Cold, reserved, unteachable, and unconcerned with being the proper, gracious English miss Society deemed she should be. It must have caused her aunt great concern for her future.

Taking a deep breath, she nodded to Thatcher, ready to face the situation with the same strength of spirit her father had praised. She did not miss Aunt Marshall's surprised expression upon her entrance. Rising from her chair, she seemed to be waiting for Emma to do or say something.

Had Aunt Marshall known all along she stood just outside the door? Had she heard her approach?

"Emma, dear," Aunt Marshall began wringing her hands. Emma could see moisture glistening in the older woman's eyes. "I owe you an apology." she said slowly, then looked at the floor, the weight of the world seeming to fall onto her slumping shoulders.

It was apparent in her posture and the trace of tears in her eyes that she was truly sorry. The sight pricked Emma's heart. Remorse filled her as Mr. Clayton's words repeated in her head. "She is a good woman, Emma."

Why had she always assumed the worst of her aunt? Would it have hurt to have at least expressed some sort of interest in half of the things she had said over the last few weeks? Surely some of the advice had been worth her while.

Standing in front of her, Emma placed a gloved hand upon Aunt Marshall's arm. "It is all right. I already know. Unfortunately, I seem to have a bad habit of eavesdropping," she said with a wry smile upon her face.

Instead of returning Emma's smile, the plump woman engulfed her in a crushing embrace. The sound of quiet weeping filled her ears as her aunt held her close. "I was so scared I would lose you, too. You are the last remnant of this family, and you were almost stolen from me."

Emma stiffened a bit at her aunt's words. "My father," she began, but she could not find the will to protest any longer.

"Has been gone for months, Emma, I know. I have known since shortly after I arrived. I wrote to Mr. Weazelton thinking it was time to face the truth and turn over the holdings to the rightful heir. I knew your father's reservations, but by law, Emma, it belongs to your cousin. After he arrived, I realized my misstep. I did not realize he was vying for your hand, but then the thought that you might be able to remain in your home consumed me. Of course, when Anthony began showing interest in you, I saw a better option."

Turning to Anthony, she rushed on nervously. "Anthony, I must also apologize to you. I had hoped by allowing Mr. Weazelton to walk with Emma yesterday, I could secure her a proposal. Ever since Mr. Weazelton announced his intention of declaring my brother missing and presumed dead, I have been hoping you would jump from a courtship directly to an engagement, so Emma could be away from here by the time he took possession. She would be far happier as your wife than she ever would have been here, and I hoped to—"

"I had deduced as much," Anthony interrupted, something Emma was grateful for. Her face was on fire with embarrassment. It was one thing for Aunt Marshall to be scheming on her behalf, but to talk about it openly... Would it upset Anthony?

To her surprise, he seemed completely calm. Perhaps it was because he was not caught off guard. She was a jumble of emotions. Shock that her aunt had known of her father's passing this whole time. Relief that she no longer had to keep it a secret. But how had her aunt known?

"Aunt Marshall..."

"Oh, please, do call me Aunt Vie. Aunt Marshall seems so impersonal. All the other children picked up calling me Aunt Vie, but I never could figure out why you persisted in calling me Aunt Marshall."

"You never gave me permission otherwise."

"Well, I am doing so now," she said with a watery grin.

"Very well, Aunt Vie," Emma said, feeling the strangeness of the new name upon her tongue. "You said you knew my father was gone. How?"

"Your father always brought a certain feel to this home. A feeling of leadership mixed with good cheer. When I first arrived, that spirit was absent. I assumed it was because he was away on business, but things just fell into place one after another, and eventually, I followed you to the graveyard near the church about two weeks after my arrival." Aunt Vie paused and took several moments to compose herself.

Emma had completely forgotten about her secret visit to see her father's grave. Luck had been on their side the week of his death. An elderly woman had died just hours before her own father, requiring a grave to be dug. Mr. Clayton had requested the grave diggers create another, claiming his nephew's body was to arrive back in England any day now. Mr. Clayton and Gibbons had slipped her father's body into the grave after dark, having it covered by morning. After his burial, they had created a temporary marker indicating it was Alan's grave.

"I knew it could not be your brother's grave," Aunt Vie continued. "The army buries most of those lost at war on the continent, unless, of course, you are a high-ranking officer. Which I knew he was not. It was not hard to put your father's departure and your continued mourning together."

Emma had to admit she had not given her aunt enough credit for her intelligence. "Why did you not tell me?"

"I knew there must be a purpose for your continued silence. I had hoped you would admit to it yourself when I began questioning you. My questioning did quite the opposite; it pushed you further away. So, I waited."

The pressure her aunt had exerted shortly after her arrival all made sense now, as did the ease by which she had kept the secret.

"Emma, please forgive me for the pressure I have always placed on you, and for the scheming I have engaged in these last few weeks. But especially for not seeing you for the blessing you are," Aunt Vie said, her hands clasped in front of her chest in supplication.

Emma knew she should still be angry. She had a right to be after hearing her aunt's admission, but suddenly it did not matter. She had so few relatives left. Why alienate another? Especially after such a heartfelt apology.

"I forgive you... Aunt Vie," she added as an afterthought, feeling the closeness of the name as it left her lips. "Can you forgive me for always thinking the worst of your intentions? While somewhat misguided," she said carefully, to which her aunt smiled sheepishly, "I believe you acted out of love and not spite." Aunt Vie's eyes flicked to Anthony, and Emma was grateful, at least in a small measure, for her aunt's meddling. "More importantly, Aunt Vie, can you forgive me for my deception? I know it was wrong, but my father..."

A knock echoed through the house, startling everyone in the room. Her heart leapt into her throat, the idea of a possible intruder consuming her mind. After a few deep breaths, she chided herself for her foolishness. An intruder did not use the knocker at the front door.

Perhaps Mr. Black had come. She assumed Mr. Clayton had sent word to Banbury first thing this morning requesting he visit them at Engalworth. That had been his intent last night, anyway. It was possible he had come already, but not likely. It would be difficult for the older man to travel that distance this early in the morning.

The sound of Gibbons's voice echoed from the front door, but it was the voice that responded that had Emma flying from the room like a pack of wolves was chasing her.

Chapter Thirty-Five

Whatever was going on at the front door was causing quite a commotion. Concerned for Emma's safety, Anthony quickly rose to his feet and exited the morning room, a crutch assisting his bad leg. The edge of the staircase blocked his view of what was happening. After a few hobbling steps, he could see the entry clearly. The view that met him sent his heart plummeting to his feet.

Emma stood, wrapped in another man's arms. After a moment, the man stepped back and, taking her face in his hands, kissed each of her cheeks. Anthony's blood boiled at the sight of the man so brazenly touching her. Did he have no shame?

But Emma looked for all the world to be deeply enjoying his touch, the sight of which stopped Anthony in his progression to intercept them. His crutch made a squeaking noise upon the tiled floor as he ground to a halt. The man holding Emma suddenly swept her behind him, drawing a pistol from somewhere on his person.

The sight of the gun pointed directly at him caused Anthony to hop back a step, landing him a bit harder on his injured leg than he was used to. To his surprise, it did not hurt as much as he expected.

Emma's muffled voice came from somewhere behind the sandy blond man who stood protectively in front of her.

"Put it down, Alan. He is not an enemy."

Alan. The name registered in his head, and suddenly, the reunion he had just witnessed took on a completely different meaning. Analyzing the man standing on the landing above him, he could see the resemblance. The blue eyes Emma had spoken so happily of and the slightly darker curls. They had the same angular jaw, but where Emma's made her look delicate, her brother's squarer form of the feature made him look masculine.

Stepping in front of her brother, she gestured to Anthony standing below. "Lord Hamdon, may I introduce my brother, George Alan Hensworth, Baron Gladsby." Then, turning to her brother, she said, "Alan, might I introduce Anthony James Kempton, Viscount Hamdon." Anthony noted the odd introduction. Perhaps Emma hoped by using their full names she might calm the tension that hummed between them.

Slowly, her brother put away his pistol. "Forgive me, Lord Hamdon. While I understood you were in residence, your sudden appearance at a vulnerable moment startled me. I am afraid war has had an unsettling effect on me. I still expect danger to be lurking around every corner," the new Lord Gladsby said, carefully surveying the lower court.

A blur of blue skirts suddenly rushed past Anthony as Aunt Vie began scurrying up the stairs. Emma's brother met her halfway, wrapping the matronly woman in a firm embrace as she wept uncontrollably.

Finally, she pulled back to look at her nephew, "It is you. It is really you. At first, I thought I must be seeing a ghost, but you are real," she said, reaching up to pinch his cheeks as if he were a little boy.

Grinning at his aunt's antics, Lord Gladsby answered, "I am real, Aunt Vie. As real as I ever have been."

Emma descended the steps to stand by her brother, her gaze still trying to drink him in. Eventually, all three made their way to the court below. Standing in front of Anthony, Lord Gladsby did not look as tall as he had originally surmised. The man's head barely came even with Anthony's eyes.

The baron gave him a short bow which he returned to the best of his abilities. Emma's brother looked about to say something when Mrs. Gibbons came rushing into the court, hands clutching her apron to her chest. Without a second look at Anthony, Lord Gladsby rushed to the elderly housekeeper, hugging her almost as firmly as he had his aunt.

The next quarter hour was spent in greetings as Mr. Clayton arrived downstairs, followed by Mr. Weazelton. Anthony did not miss the way the two cousins regarded each other—Mr. Weazelton with guarded civility and an air of defeat, Lord Gladsby with barely concealed loathing. He had no doubt Mr. Weazelton would not be staying much longer at Engalworth Court.

With some excitement, Mrs. Gibbons announced she would have luncheon ready to serve in a half hour. The party agreed to move to the sitting room where they might sit and converse while they waited. Anthony, for one, was grateful for the change of location. Standing about in the entry had tired his good leg more than he wished to admit.

Entering the dim drawing room, the large blue damask drapes still drawn so no one could peer in, he took up his usual place on the settee. To his surprise, Emma took up the spot next to him, sitting closer than she had allowed the evening before.

Leaning forward, she inquired, "How did you know Lord Hamdon was here, Alan?"

"Do not be angry with me, Emma," her brother said with a grimace. He looked as though he was preparing for a tongue lashing. "but I have actually been in Worthin for nearly a week."

Anthony was just as shocked as Emma looked. Why on earth had the man not made his presence known? Ready to let him know just what he thought of his tardy arrival, he was surprised to feel Emma's light touch upon his arm.

"It *was* your voice I heard on the breeze yesterday!"

"Yes, I had hoped my warning would give you enough time to avoid Sancerre's bullet."

"Sancerre?" she asked in confusion.

"Lord Ratford's puppet master."

"Ratford?" she asked, then her face cleared as her eyebrows shot up. "The letter! That is what you meant by Rato and Fjord."

"Yes, I had hoped Father would put it together and pass the information on to the Foreign Office, but it seems I hid it too well. He is the commander who sold information to the French, the one I needed to hide from. Unfortunately, by the time Mr. Wit discovered his identity, the man had already disappeared. "

"Disappeared? As in killed?" Anthony asked.

"No, simply vanished. He works for a spy by the name of Monsieur René Sancerre, a man who has tried everything to bring about my demise this past year. He would love nothing more than to be rid of me."

"Rid of you? But why?" Aunt Vie gasped out.

"I... I killed his brother," Lord Gladsby admitted reluctantly, swallowing hard enough that his Adam's apple bobbed. "The younger Sancerre was a spy assigned to ferreting out French counterfeits. When my cover was broken, I was in a fight for my life."

Anthony had compassion on the baron. "So Sancerre has been following you ever since? A campaign of revenge?"

"Exactly, Lord Hamdon. One he was so committed to that he traveled to England to fulfill his purposes."

Mr. Weazelton leaned forward in his seat, looking between Emma and her brother. "Is this the man you think took a shot at us yesterday?"

"I do. He is a master in the art of disguise. My associate has been watching the house for weeks and has only caught a few glimpses of him, but he has been in the neighborhood at least a fortnight or more."

"So this Monsieur Sancerre had hopes of revenging himself on you by killing your sister?" Mr. Weazelton questioned further.

"Not exactly. I believe he hoped to scare me out of hiding, which, as you can see, has done its job."

"If you knew that to be his objective," Emma said, the volume in her voice rising, "why in heaven's name did you play into his scheme? I did not wait all these months for your return only to see you get killed!"

"And watch while he took the life of my only sister? I think not. I knew what I was walking into, Emma, and it was never in the plan for me to hide indefinitely, only to wait until the timing was right. The only way to lure Sancerre out of hiding is to bait the trap."

"And you are the bait," Emma said, disgust in her voice.

The room went eerily quiet as the siblings glared at one another. So much for social decorum, Anthony thought wryly. He looked about the room, noting the way each occupant handled the situation. Mr. Clayton looked thoughtful. Aunt Vie looked horrified. Mr. Weazelton looked resolute; an expression he found curious until the man spoke.

"Well, cousins, I thank you for your hospitality, but I am afraid my stay here has come to an end. I am needed back in... ah... Brighton. Yes, Brighton. I hope to be on my way this afternoon, if possible, which means I must excuse myself from luncheon, if you do not mind." Rising from his seat, he begged the party to remain seated and promised to bid them farewell before he departed.

Coward, Anthony thought. It seemed with the prospect of inheriting Engalworth Court no longer a possibility, Mr. Weazelton planned to make a hasty retreat, more worried about his own neck than his oft-boasted "familial duties." Anthony was not sorry. It would be a relief to see the man finally leave.

When Mr. Weazelton had cleared the room, Mr. Clayton spoke up from his seat next to Aunt Vie.

"What do you need from us, Alan? Should we all remove from Engalworth in an effort to keep Emma safe?"

"No, that would not be wise. It is best you all remain here at present. You have the house well-guarded, and my associate has already sent for reinforcements now that we know Sancerre is here. In a few days we hope to spring our trap and apprehend the brute."

"What of my responsibilities at the church?" Mr. Clayton asked, concern coloring his features. "Tomorrow is Sunday, after all."

Lord Gladsby seemed to think on this for a while, looking at the drapes that remained closed. It was strange sitting in a room lit only by the light coming from between the cracks of the drapes, and the half-moon windows above. Anthony understood the reason for the precaution as these windows faced directly toward the grove, giving anyone outside a clear view of the occupants within, but to sit in dim light at near midday was uncomfortable.

Finally, Lord Gladsby addressed Mr. Clayton's concern. "I believe my father mentioned you have employed a curate."

"I do have a young man that helps me with a few of the farther hamlets, yes."

"Perhaps he might give your sermon tomorrow. I am sure Sancerre has figured out your connection to this family, and you will be as big of a target as Emma."

Mr. Clayton nodded thoughtfully. "I suppose I could send word to him, but I would not wish to endanger a messenger."

Anthony was amazed at Mr. Clayton's thoughtfulness. He would not have thought twice about sending a servant, but Mr. Clayton had a point. A servant carrying a message could be targeted, too, if Sancerre thought the message important.

"As long as the messenger is someone who regularly comes and goes from the estate, I do not believe Sancerre will be any the wiser. He will just assume they are going about their regular duties. Take Sally, for instance. I have noted this week that she comes and goes three times a week. Sancerre will have done the same. She could carry the note out quite easily."

"Yes," Emma interjected, "but she does not come again until Monday."

"Perhaps Mr. Ladd or Mrs. Clark?" Mr. Clayton suggested. "They both leave during the evening to return to their own homes. One of them could take the missive out."

"Excellent idea!" Lord Gladsby praised. "In addition, they can carry correspondence to my associate."

Mrs. Gibbons entered the room, trying for a proper sedate expression, but her lips insisted on curving up at the edges as she announced luncheon.

Lord Gladsby stepped to his sister's side, ready to offer his arm, but Emma glanced at Anthony.

"Ah, yes, Lord Hamdon, I believe you outrank me."

Anthony was surprised by the response. He would not have begrudged the man's desire to spend extra time with his sister, but he also did not mind having the opportunity to be close to Emma either.

Offering his free arm to her, he relished her touch upon his sleeve. Emma's touch excited and calmed him all in the same moment. He could definitely get used to having her at his side, and if he played his cards right, that was exactly where she would be for the rest of their lives.

Chapter Thirty-Six

Emma's head was still reeling from all the changes that had occurred. In twenty-four hours, her brother had returned, Mr. Weazelton had thankfully departed, Mr. Black had arrived as requested, and she found she was the target of one of France's deadliest spies.

The first three had brought immense relief while the last had reignited all her previous fears and anxieties, then added a few more for good measure. While the tension of imminent danger had made it difficult to fall asleep, she was surprised to find she had actually slept quite well.

Since no one would be attending Sunday services today, she decided to enjoy a few more minutes in bed, revisiting her conversation with Mr. Black the previous afternoon. The reason for his visit no longer existed thanks to Alan's arrival, so Emma had invited the man of business to stay for dinner. She had expected Alan's sudden appearance to cause the older man some significant distress. She would have been in utter shock, but Mr. Black seemed to take it as a mere matter of business.

After sitting down to dinner with the solicitor, she had ventured, "I am sure, Mr. Black, you are surprised, as most of our neighbors will be, at my brother's return."

"Not in the least. I am only glad he is finally here, so we may proceed with the will."

"The will? But how did you? When?" Emma had spluttered.

"Lord Gladsby, Miss Hensworth," Mr. Black said, setting his glass of wine down and leaning forward. "It appears I have an explanation to give you. About two weeks before your father became ill, he requested a meeting in my office. He wished to make some changes to his original will. You see, not only had he received your letter, Lord Gladsby, but he had also received some life-altering news from Dr. Jones. He was dying. Consumption of the lungs, according to the good doctor. He knew his time was short and wanted to make sure things were set in place for Miss Hensworth's care, as well as the ability for funds to be continuously released for the payment of all of Engalworth's expenses."

"I thought that was the steward's responsibility," Emma blurted out. She had not meant to interrupt the man, but she was completely upended by the information Mr. Black was sharing.

Alan spoke up from his place at the head of the table. "It is the steward's responsibility to make sure all rent and taxes are collected, as well as delivering funds to Gibbons so he might pay the staff, but Father made sure all money released from his account had to be approved by Mr. Black."

"Just so," Mr. Black agreed. "Worried your letter would not hold up in court," he said, tipping his head toward Alan, "and having no other evidence of your survival, your father advised me of his plan and asked if it was feasible. I told him he would need to cut his staff, so rumors would not abound, servant gossip being what it is. Also, Dr. Jones ought not to be called to limit suspicion. After several visits that took place over the course of the next two weeks, we worked a plan we felt would keep the estate out of Mr. Weazelton's possession and secure your place, Miss Hensworth, with Mr. Clayton. The late Lord Gladsby advised me that he had slowly begun releasing servants in hopes the neighborhood would not grow overly curious, but on his last visit, he was coughing so fiercely I knew it would not be long. He planned on releasing the rest of the questionable staff upon his return. When his time grew short, he intended to send any staff that were not absolutely necessary on holiday, and claim his intention to travel. He promised to send word if he took a turn for the worse. I received his last missive less than a week after our visit, on the twenty-first of December," at this point Mr. Black's voice cracked, "bidding me farewell, and entrusting his entire life's work into my hands until the new Lord Gladsby could take it up. I could only assume he died shortly thereafter. I am only sorry, Miss Hensworth, that you did not find the revised will until recently. It must have caused you great distress."

Even all these hours later, she could not believe it. Her father had known he was not getting better. Why had he claimed he was after the doctor had visited? Why had he not included her in his plans those last few weeks? Why had he waited so long? Maybe if she had been given several weeks to prepare, she would have been ready to say goodbye. Instead, she had only been given a few days.

It was not until he refused to call the doctor that she wondered if they could be facing the end. Even then, she had held out hope, at least as much as she could muster. In those last few hours, reality had finally sunk in, and she realized there were so many things she still wished to say. So many things she wished she would have done differently. So many things that because of his unconscious state, she would never be able to make right.

If she had only known he was dying, maybe she would have been ready, but deep down she knew she never would have been. No one is ever ready to say goodbye, not when they had shared an entire life together.

Smith's knock upon the door roused Emma from her sorrowful thoughts. She needed to press on. The choices her father had made, the choices she had made, were all in the past. She could not dwell on something she could not fix. She could only fix the future, and her future probably sat at the breakfast table at this very moment waiting for her.

Emma inquired after the time only to learn she had slept in far longer than she realized. No one would be at the breakfast table at this hour, it was near ten o'clock.

After washing herself with a damp cloth, she took note of the clothes laid out on her bed. Smith had set out one of the gray gowns she had worn for the last several months. Yesterday, she had not even taken note of the color of her gowns, but with Alan's return, the color suddenly seemed completely worn out. It was time to add a bit of brightness back into her life.

Turning to where the maid stood collecting her small clothes, she said, "Smith, I think I shall wear the mauve gown today."

Smith's eyes widened in surprise, but then a gentle smile crept across her face. "Yes, Miss Emma. The mauve it is." Picking up the drab gray gown off the bed, she returned it to its rightful place in the closet, then pulled out the requested gown. It was a simple affair, with only a bit of plum colored silk ribbon about the empire style waist. Emma had avoided any bit of elegance for so long she was almost giddy at the prospect of wearing the softly puffed sleeves.

She had to admit some curiosity at what Anthony might think. Would he even notice? Some men did not pay much attention to things such as dresses, while others seemed to be taken aback any time a lady wore something more becoming than the last. Which would he be?

After piling her golden curls atop her head, Smith inquired if she wished to wear a bit of jewelry. Emma examined herself in the mirror. She had tucked a white muslin fichu into the top of her gown, covering a great deal of her neck. After inspecting her appearance a moment longer, she determined a necklace would only be lost among the folds of fabric, but perhaps a ribbon woven in among her curls would give the last bit of polish she was looking for.

The ribbon's color, while a shade darker than the one on her dress, added just the right amount of highlight to the gold in her hair. The entire ensemble seemed to bring color and life back to her face. Of course, some of that color could also be attributed to the happy turn her life had recently taken.

Just as she pronounced herself ready, the sound of carriage wheels crunching up the drive could be heard through her open window. They were not expecting anyone at Engalworth today. Who could it be? Alan's associates, perhaps? Would they come directly to the house? What if something had befallen Mr. Black on his way home last evening?

Alan had sent two of the men recently hired to escort the man as far as Worthin. After which he was sure Sancerre would not follow, so Mr. Black should have made it safely back to Banbury.

Taking one last glance in the mirror, Emma hurried from the room. She hoped nothing had befallen the dear older man.

She was nearly down the stairs when Gibbons rushed to stand by the door, Thatcher close on his heels. Alan stood in the court below, Aunt Vie, and Mr. Clayton standing nearby.

Scurrying down the remaining stairs, she asked, "What is happening? I heard a carriage upon the drive."

"I am unsure," Alan answered. "Mr. Ladd sent word of the approaching conveyance. It appears to have a family crest. I have asked him to send Owen if it is the wrong crest?"

Wrong crest? Emma thought, before remembering Lord Ratford's carriage would have a family crest. It could not be him, could it?

"I can only assume," Alan continued, "since the carriage has stopped, and Mr. Ladd is even now attending to the horses; it must be friend, not foe."

From somewhere near the top of the guest wing stairs, Emma heard Anthony's voice.

"It is both."

Anthony could hardly believe what he was seeing out the large glass window. His father stood below him on the drive. His father's valet, Gines, stood next to him. The next person that exited the carriage further surprised him. Brown, his own valet, stepped out of the conveyance and looked up at Engalworth Court. From here, he could see the man's meticulously combed black hair and sharp angular features.

Why was his valet with his father? Last he knew, he was at Blackwell Manor, a place his father avoided at this time of year, knowing Anthony's mother would be in residence.

Anthony watched as the two servants picked up portmanteaus and began making their way around the house to the servants' entrance. It would seem the time had come for him to face his father, but instead of descending down the stairs, he remained where he was. It might be childish of him, but he wanted to look down upon his father instead of having him look down on him—something the man had done most of his life.

Gibbons opened the door and after inquiry, announced in a loud official voice, "The Earl of Lincolnhurst."

The chatter that had begun when Anthony indicated their guest was both good and bad suddenly ceased. A deathly silence seemed to fall over the house as Lord Gladsby ascended the few steps from the court area to greet his guest.

"Welcome to Engalworth Court, Lord Lincolnhurst. I am Lord Gladsby. To what do we owe this great honor?"

"Very good, Gladsby," Anthony's father said, taking a liberty he had not yet been afforded, to which Lord Gladsby rose an imperious eyebrow. To Anthony's surprise, his father seemed somewhat chagrined at his own impertinence. It must have been something in the steel of the younger man's eyes as well as his military demeanor, for he had never seen his father cowed by anyone of lesser rank.

"Ah, yes, well, I believe you are housing my son, Lord Hamdon, at present." Lord Gladsby's eyes flicked to the stairs before returning to the earl's. The glance was enough to alert his father to his presence. With one hand on the banister and the other on his crutch, Anthony drew himself up.

The older man's eyes traveled up the stairs. "Hamdon, I see my directions were correct."

"It would seem they were," Anthony said flatly, remaining where he was, his eyes locked with his father's. He expected the man to start ordering him about at any moment, unexpectedly, his father broke the battle of wills first.

Turning his attention back to Lord Gladsby, Lord Lincolnhurst said, "I owe you my thanks, Lord Gladsby, for the care you have given to my son in his time of need. I am in your debt."

"Not mine. I am only recently returned. It was my sister, Miss Hensworth; our uncle, Mr. Clayton; and aunt, Mrs. Marshall who should receive your thanks. They have offered the majority of care."

At the mention of Fredrick's mother, Anthony's father seemed to take note of the occupants below. "Mrs. Marshall, how marvelous to see you again!" he said, suddenly slipping into the charm he always used when ladies were present. "I had not known you were a relative of the Hensworths."

Smiling broadly, she answered, "Lord Lincolnhurst, it is a pleasure to see you again. I am indeed a relative. My brother, God rest his soul, was the previous Baron Gladsby." Gesturing toward Emma who stood near her side, she began the introductions. "Might I introduce my niece, Miss Hensworth, as well as my brother-in-law Mr. Clayton. Miss Hensworth, Mr. Clayton, the Earl of Lincolnhurst."

How fitting, Anthony thought as he stood watching the introduction, that his father should undertake such formalities from above his new acquaintances. The earl, ever one to look down on those of lower station, was now doing so, literally. However, Emma's beauty must have caught his fancy, for he descended the stairs to stand in front of her. Anthony's blood rushed fiercely through his veins as anger welled up in his chest.

Taking the stairs as quickly as he dared, he made it to the landing at the same moment his father stepped onto the lower court. Lord Gladsby, still staring after the impertinent earl, was no doubt trying to take the man's measure. Seeing Anthony, he silently offered his arm to help him down the final five steps to the court below.

His father now stood in front of Emma, spilling some flirtatious, insincere drivel, a habit that made Anthony sick. Clearing his throat, he gained his father's attention. "Might I ask why you have come at this time, Lord Lincolnhurst?"

His father raised an eyebrow at the formal address. Flicking a look between Anthony and Emma, he seemed to read something Anthony had meant to keep hidden, at least for the time being. Turning to face his son completely, he said, "I brought your valet. I thought you might be in need of him."

While the comment was benign enough, Anthony knew it was loaded with meaning. There was much to discuss; however, this was not the time nor place, so he simply thanked him. He cast a glance at Thatcher, who stood at the ready not ten paces away.

Anthony worried the servant would feel displaced from his duties. He had served him well these last few weeks. Thatcher merely glanced back at him before placing his attention elsewhere. He did not seem displeased. Suddenly Anthony realized he had cared. He had actually thought of the servant's feelings. Turning to Mr. Clayton, he wondered what he would think about his progress, but the man's attention was on Lord Lincolnhurst, bringing Anthony back to the situation at hand.

"Lord Lincolnhurst." Emma stepped forward, her back straight, chin up, and a coolness in her voice that alerted Anthony she was not in the least fooled by his father's charm. The Ice Fairy was in full force, and for once, he was relieved to see it. "Might we adjourn to the drawing room? I am sure you have had a long journey and could use some much-needed refreshment."

At his father's acceptance, Emma, who had slowly worked her way toward her brother, took hold of her sibling's arm, a physical statement that spoke volumes. While propriety would have dictated Anthony's father offer his arm to the highest-ranking lady, she had sent a clear message that she would not receive such attentions and intended to enter the drawing room at her brother's side.

It took everything within Anthony to maintain a calm look of civility. He wanted to laugh and cheer all at once, both at Emma's spunk and at the way she had quietly yet firmly taken the upper hand with his father.

Chapter Thirty-Seven

Emma was not sure what to make of Lord Lincolnhurst. The man had showed up ready to spend several days at Engalworth without even sending word or receiving an invitation. He had calmly informed them of his decision over tea. She could not believe the audacity, but what were they to do? His son was staying with them, and it would be rude to contradict an earl.

After Lord Lincolnhurst had been shown to the Birch Room to rest, Alan had asked the rest of the party to excuse he and Emma. She now sat across from him, not quite sure what he intended to say. Whatever the subject, it seemed to be causing no end of discomfort for her brother, for he suddenly rose and paced to the window.

She looked about their father's study, and realized it was no longer his, but Alan's. Not just the study, but her father's rooms, his books, his horse. All of it was now Alan's.

The realization created an odd ache in her chest. It was not the same as the grief she had felt over the last several months, but more the discomfort of change. Everything was changing and would continue to change as her brother took up the direction of the Engalworth estates. No longer would she need to look over the ledgers and check in with Mr. Haze. Those responsibilities now fell to Alan.

At the recollection of Mr. Haze, she realized the man had yet to return. Where was the man? Why had he not sent word advising them of an extended absence?

"Why the furrowed brows?"

"I just recalled Mr. Haze has yet to return. His note said he would be back in a fortnight. That came and went last week, but I was so caught up in all that was happening, I quite forgot."

"He will not be back, Emma."

"Why not?"

"How do you think Sancerre found you?"

Emma stared back at him, trying to wrap her head around the question.

"He paid Haze a good amount to leave you without protection, Emma."

Shocked, she began to sputter. "He... how... why?" Pausing, she finally said, "I never did like that man. I now know why."

"Father had his concerns as well, but his last letter indicated he did not have enough time to find a suitable replacement."

"You knew then that Father was dying?"

"Only from a few lines he included in the missive to Mr. Wit—an apology he would not be home when I arrived, concerns about Mr. Haze, and Father's decision to leave true control to Mr. Black. And a plea that God would forgive him for what he was about to put you through."

"Me?" Emma said, feeling a bit weak.

"Yes, Emma, and I believe he was right to worry. I can see the strain of it on your face. These months have taken their toll on you."

"It has been hard," she admitted, looking down at her hands as she moved to pinch the end of her gloves out of habit. Only she was not wearing any gloves today. "Losing Father turned me into something I never wanted to be."

"And what is that?" Alan asked his voice low and concerned.

"A liar," she whispered.

"Emma... Emma, please look at me."

Locking eyes with her brother, she braced for his rebuke.

"You are no liar, Emma. You had a mission to perform, just as any good soldier or spy. You did so to protect your family, and you completed your mission quite admirably, if I do say so myself."

"But God—"

"Does not expect us to point our enemies toward our unprotected friends. Do you think I ever gave true information about my brothers-in-arms when I was a spy? If possible, I tried to convince the enemy to go in the complete opposite way of smaller, more vulnerable forces. You did the same, Emma. You protected my inheritance, as well as Mr. Clayton and Mr. Ladd's livings. You made sure our servants and tenants would be well cared for, as well as protecting yourself. If that meant you had to tell a few falsehoods, so be it. I cannot think a loving God, the God Mr. Clayton has taught us to believe in, would hold us at fault for protecting the weak and vulnerable. Nor would our father. He only wanted our happiness, Emma. That is why he asked you to endure for just a bit longer."

Emma smiled through her tears. "He always did want us to be glad."

Alan chuckled. "Some of us, literally," he said, referencing his new title. "Speaking of fathers, Emma, I am unsure how much you know about Lord Hamdon's father. He is the actual reason I wanted to meet with you."

"I know very little, I am afraid. Lord Hamdon does not care to speak of his father, or any of his family, for that matter. What little he has shared leads me to believe their relationship is quite strained. Anthony—I mean—Lord Hamdon indicated that his family is cold and seemingly distasteful to be around. He has exhibited a general sense of unease whenever they are brought up."

Alan raised his brows at Emma's use of Anthony's Christian name, but did not comment. She and Anthony had deemed it best to wait a day or two before telling her brother of their courtship. However, with the advent of Lord Lincolnhurst, it might be necessary to make that announcement sooner rather than later.

"When I learned Lord Hamdon was in residence, I had the family investigated, Emma. I have heard rumors, but I try not to base my decisions on gossip. It is my understanding that Lord Lincolnhurst is nothing short of a rake. He keeps several paramours about the kingdom and is not averse to adding more if a woman catches his fancy. I must ask you to be on your guard."

The thought of the older man taking an interest in her caused her stomach to lurch. The idea of being romantically involved with the portly, older man made her skin crawl. He was not wholly unattractive, with his brown hair just beginning to gray at the temples and a stately bearing, but it was obvious the man had indulged in far too many drinks.

"I assure you, Alan, I have no intentions of putting myself in such a position. However, that brings up some information I have yet to share, but perhaps you have already suspected." She wondered how to word her next sentence, but in the end decided brevity was in her best interest.

"Lord Hamdon and I have entered into a courtship with Mr. Clayton's blessing. With you not in residence, he was the closest male relative to apply to for permission."

"I had suspected as much. I have witnessed several *interactions* between the two of you over the past week that indicated stronger feelings might have developed. That is why I had Lord Hamdon's family and character investigated so thoroughly."

Emma's cheeks heated at the realization that she and Anthony had had an audience, but the embarrassment was quickly swept away with her brother's revelation. Was he going to forbid her from an association with Anthony?

Or worse, was he now going to tell her that Anthony was not the man he purported himself to be? Was he as lascivious as his father? The thought nearly broke her heart in two. Emma had not expected to find her heart so wrapped up with Anthony's, but now that it was, the thought that she might have been wrong about the nature of his affection felt like a knife to the chest.

"Do not look so, Emma. You look as though I am about to proclaim your execution."

"I cannot help it. Your tone indicated you may have found disagreeable information about the man I have come to care deeply for, and given his father's reputation, I can only assume it to be something in that same vein."

Alan came around the desk to sit in the chair next to the one she now occupied. "The only disagreeableness in my tone came from the thought of my little sister being old enough to have a suitor," he said, taking up her hand and sandwiching it between his own. "It is difficult for me to realize how much I have missed these last three years. When I left, you were barely out of the schoolroom. Now, you are completely grown." Alan's gaze traveled over Emma's face.

"As for your Lord Hamdon, I am pleased to say his reputation is quite the opposite of his father's. An incredible feat, considering his parentage. Unfortunately, if my informants are to be believed, his father is not the only one in his family with loose morals, but it is unkind of me to speak so of a lady, so I shall say no more."

Emma smiled at how Alan had explained all without expounding upon Anthony's mother's behavior. It was no wonder he spoke more of his friends' families than he did of his own. She was so relieved to find Anthony had been transparent with her that she impulsively threw her arms about her brother, the arm of the chair poking into her side as she leaned over it.

"And to what do I owe this affection? It cannot be due to the revelation that your beau comes from a well-connected, yet abominable family," he said with a smirk.

"I am just so relieved is all. Relieved and grateful you have taken such good care of me. I should not have doubted Anthony, but I must admit I did. Our relationship is so new, and he has shared so little about his family..." she trailed off, then shrugged her shoulders.

"Then it is good you have such a fantastic brother to dig into Lord Hamdon's background," he said, puffing out his chest as he stood. He looked like a peacock ready to strut about the room to show off his importance. She chuckled at his theatrics. Alan was far from conceited, and she knew it. He smiled back at her before walking about the desk to take up the seat that had belonged to their father for so many years.

Not for the first time in the last day, Emma noticed the wrinkles that had deepened about his eyes. At twenty-seven, Alan was not old, but it seemed his time on the continent had aged him far faster than life should have. While he had laughed and joked with her since his return, she could see an emptiness in his eyes that had not been there before joining the Royal Army. Life had taken a toll on both of them, it would seem.

Anthony sat in the chair Emma had always taken up when visiting his room. He missed those days. Everything had been much simpler then.

Lord Lincolnhurst pulled over one of the wooden chairs from near the door and sat upon the hard wood as if he thought the piece of furniture might break under the weight of his hefty girth. It might, Anthony mused to himself. Wouldn't that be entertaining?

"As I said before, I have brought Brown to you," the earl began. "I figured it was the least I could do after the man showed up at my door nearly three weeks ago."

"Three weeks? Why did he not come to me when I sent for him?"

"Because Lady Edith never passed on your correspondence," his father said, speaking of Anthony's mother's underhanded dealings as if he was merely speaking of the weather.

"And how did you come by that piece of information? If Brown had not received word from me, how would he know Mother had it?"

"He did not. I obtained that information straight from the lady herself, after I threatened to pull any additional funding from her, that is. While I do not usually intervene in your mother's affairs, I will not stand by as she impedes our servants from fulfilling their duties. In addition, she failed to inform me that my son, my heir, had been in an accident so terrible that the doctor had sent her a missive in those first few days, advising that she may want to come and say her goodbyes. Why the devil the man did not sent word to me, I cannot understand. I am the earl, after all."

Anthony did. Nicholas would have only given directions to Blackwell Manor, having never visited Maplewood Estates. No doubt Nicholas assumed Anthony's mother would inform his father. And if his parents had possessed even a tenth of the respect for each other that Nicholas's had, he was sure his mother would have informed his father.

"I cannot fathom why that woman would keep such information from me," Lord Lincolnhurst continued, frustration coloring his words. "My own son and she did not even have the decency to inform me. I should have been applied to immediately. What if things had gone terribly wrong? What if you had not survived the infection?"

Anthony was not sure what to think of this display of emotion. His father usually only had three faces—the one for charming women, his card face which gave away nothing, and his immoveable glare that demanded obedience. The look of concern and worry he now exhibited was so new Anthony was sure for the first time in his life his father had truly been shaken at the thought of losing him.

He was not sure how to respond, or if he even should. Tense silence surrounded them for several seconds. Finally, letting out a deep sigh, Lord Lincolnhurst said, "I am relieved, Anthony, that you seem to be on the mend."

He stared at his father. Had he ever used his given name? The sound of it coming out of his sire's mouth confirmed how distressed the man must have been.

"I am glad to be mending, as well. I am also grateful you interceded on Brown's behalf. Mother has dallied with several of my men over the years which required their release, and I was concerned I would be forced to release another."

"And here I thought you were merely picky in your appearance, and the other men had not measured up," his father said with a smile. "It would seem this man is made of sterner stuff. Your mother was quite put out when she realized he had given her the slip in the middle of the night."

Anthony imagined she would have been. "How long do you intend to stay?" he asked, changing the subject, no longer wanting to talk about his dissolute mother.

"I hope to leave on Wednesday. Will you be ready to travel by then?"

"Me?" Anthony asked. "You wish me to leave with you?"

"Yes, of course. That is why I have come. You have imposed upon these people long enough. Surely you are healed enough to travel to our London house."

Imposed? As if his father had not done just that. The thought of leaving, however, especially at this moment in time, seemed wrong. "I cannot leave, father.

The doctor said I must not stress my leg and insisted I not travel for quite some time."

"Oh, codswallop! It has been six weeks since you broke your leg, has it not?"

"Yes, but..."

"Six weeks is plenty of time for healing. Besides, our coach is extremely well-sprung. You would be just as comfortable traveling as you would be lounging about this place," he said, looking around himself in disgust. Anthony could not fathom what his father could have against Engalworth Court. Yes, the rooms were smaller than those of Maplewood, but they were well-appointed and clean.

"What of the doctor's instructions?"

"You can be seen by much more competent physicians in London. No need to pander to the whims of a country doctor."

He was unsure that would actually be the case, but he could not argue the point as he did not have a medical background, so he could not judge one man of medicine from another.

Truthfully, it was not his leg that worried him. It was his promise to Emma. He could not leave until things were settled between them.

At the same time, if he was to offer for her, he would need time to prepare for their marriage. Setting up a house took time. He did not want to take Emma to live with either of his parents, so he or one of his parents would be required to take up residence in another of the Lincolnhurst holdings. Since his father would never be budged from Maplewood and was a frequent visitor to his hunting box up north, those two residences were off the list.

"Before I agree to leave," he said, treading lightly. Once his father's mind was made up there was little he could do to change it. While his father could not truly control him, he had proven in the past that he could make Anthony's life miserable if he did not comply. "There are several things we need to discuss."

"If I have not missed the mark, Miss Hensworth is one of those things," his father said.

He nodded and began unfolding the situation his father had unknowingly stepped into. After a half hour's discussion, his father finally said, "In that case, should we not leave posthaste? I would not wish to get caught in the crossfire."

Anthony's disgust with his father returned full force. Not only was the man dissolute, but he was a coward to boot. "No, Father. I must stay. I need to settle things with Miss Hensworth first."

"Oh, just bundle the chit up and take her with you. We can get a special license when we get to London."

"No, she is a woman of high morals." Unlike the ones you cavort around with, he thought. "I will not insult her by subjecting her to scandal."

"Fine, Hamdon. But I cannot sit around waiting for a French assassin to make his move. I am expected in London on Wednesday, and I need you to be ready to leave by then. Make your declaration, then you can make all your wedding arrangements while I see to business."

"I am not leaving, Father," Anthony said fiercely.

"You are, and that is final," Lord Lincolnhurst said, casting Anthony his immovable glare and signaling the end of negotiations.

Chapter Thirty-Eight

Aunt Vie was in a dither. Mr. Lenning was to arrive today and she could not contain her excitement. Rushing about the house she ordered servants about, instructing them on exactly how she wished dear Bradley's room should be set up.

While the behavior would previously have annoyed Emma, Aunt Vie's valiant effort to treat her with more respect made the older woman's excitement more palatable. It was gratifying to have her aunt asking for her opinion, but it was Aunt Vie's deference in household duties that truly touched Emma. While Aunt Vie still went about performing many of the same duties, she made sure to obtain Emma's consent first.

Since Lord Lincolnhurst's arrival Sunday, things had been rather quiet. Four days had passed since Sancerre had taken a shot at Emma, and no one had seen anything out of place since. She had even taken to watching the woods out the drawing room window when no one was about. Not a single hint of brown was out of place.

Alan said his other associates should have arrived. Perhaps they had already apprehended the man, and word had not yet reached them?

Sitting at luncheon with the rest of the household, Emma listened to the conversation around her. Everyone seemed to be consumed with the topic of Mr. Lenning's arrival. Everyone, that is, except Anthony.

Emma quietly ate her meal, pondering what was causing him so much unease. At first, she assumed she had somehow caused his gloomy, perturbed silence. Perhaps he was hurt when she chose to remain close by her brother that first day after Lord Lincolnhurst arrived? In retrospect, she realized his mood had begun Sunday morning before they had even had a moment to speak to one another.

Obviously, he was uncomfortable around his father, something she should have expected given his own admissions and the information Alan had uncovered. But why would that extend to her?

Yesterday, she had tried to converse softly with him several times. His answers had been short and often clipped. But then he would look pained, as if he realized his answer was too sharp, and would immediately apologize.

Emma was jolted from her reverie when Lord Lincolnhurst's commanding voice silenced the rest of the discussion.

"I am glad to hear Mr. Lenning will be coming to fill the void in company you all will feel when my son and I leave on the morrow. Good company, I know, is always hard to come by, but I have great faith in Mr. Lenning's cheerful disposition. I am sure he will do his best to entertain and comfort you in your loss."

If she had not been so shocked at hearing Anthony was leaving, she would have silently laughed at Lord Lincolnhurst's pompous declaration of his own importance. Instead her heart drop into the toes of her shoes.

They were leaving? Why had Anthony not informed her before now? Her eyes shot to his, but he was too busy glaring at his father. It seemed he had not wanted his father to make the announcement. Perhaps he hoped to slip out without her even knowing. So this was why he was so irritable.

Emma's mind raced. She needed to get out of the dining room which had suddenly turned stuffy in the early afternoon sun. Abruptly, she stood from her seat amid the questions the rest of the party lobbed at Lord Lincolnhurst. All the men stumbled to their feet, but she simply mumbled her excuses and left as quickly as she could without running.

He was leaving; of course he was leaving. Everyone left her. A pricking sensation burned the back of her eyes as her chest simultaneously filled with heat and emptied of air. She tried to gasp for breath, but the air in the court was even more suffocating than that of the dining room.

Hiking up her skirts higher than was proper, she raced toward the front door. She needed air, fresh air. She could feel the walls of Engalworth closing in around her, stealing another person from her life. Suddenly she hated this place, this echoing tomb of stone and wood. She wanted out, needed out.

Gibbons was just descending the stairs, but she did not stop for him to open the door. She simply flung it open and raced from the house into the blessed sunshine.

She needed a place to think, some place private. Her feet turned instinctively toward the garden until she caught sight of the bench. Their bench. The one she and Anthony had sat upon when they first agreed on a courtship. She had told him he would leave, and he had insisted he would not. But she had been right all along.

The painful sight had her switching course. She spun toward the stables. One of the stalls would provide much more solitude. The clip clop of hooves sounded upon the drive. Casting a glance over her shoulder, she saw a gentleman riding up the lane, the sun glinting off the sorrel horse beneath him. Mr. Lenning? Realizing he would bring his horse to the stables, she decided not to find relief in a stall after all. Instead, she took a direct path down the aisles between the stalls toward the back of the building where the second set of doors led out to the pasture.

When she had almost reached the back doors, she veered to the right. Intent on passing through the servant door next to the larger ones, something caught her attention from the corner of her eye. She suddenly ground to a halt.

Owen lay face down in a mound of hay, blood trickling from a nasty looking lump on the back of his head. Had one of the horses kicked him? Emma rushed to his side, gently touching the boy's shoulder and calling his name. He did not even react, simply lay there motionless on the hay. Emma's troubled heart lurched into her throat as she scanned Owen's body for any sign of life.

Gently turning his head to face her, she noticed a small blade of hay in front of him move. Crouching closer, she watched the area right in front of his mouth. The hay shivered with each exhale of breath. *Thank the heavens.*

A cultured voice at the stable entrance called out, "Hello there in the stables. Is anyone about?"

Relief flooded Emma as she called out, "Here! Hurry! Please, help!" She was rewarded with the clomp of running boots. When the gentleman reached her, she heard him softly curse under his breath.

"What has happened here?"

"I am unsure. I found him this way just now. He needs to be brought up to the house, but I cannot lift him."

Without any more prompting, the man carefully turned Owen over. He placed one arm gently under the boy's shoulders, the crook of his elbow cradling the boy's head. His other arm he slipped under Owen's legs, then lifted the boy into his arms. Spinning around, he began a quick stride toward the house.

"I assume you are the Mr. Bradley Lenning my aunt has been speaking of all morning." Emma said, her breath coming out in little gasps between words as she tried to keep up.

"The very one. And you must be the Miss Emma Hensworth Anthony has filled his letters with these last three weeks," he said with a mischievous glint in his eye.

"He has?" she blurted out before she realized how desperate it sounded.

Mr. Lenning nodded with a labored chuckle. Just as they were passing his mount who stood outside the stable, he slowed and looked at the horse with concern.

"I will put him in a stall until Mr. Ladd can see to him," she offered, grabbing the horse's dangling reins. "Gibbons, our butler, will assist you as soon as you reach the house."

"Thank you, Miss Hensworth." He picked up his speed as he walked swiftly toward the front doors of Engalworth.

Emma watched him for only a few moments before turning to rub the nose of his sleek thoroughbred.

"Well, should we get you more comfortably settled?" She asked the horse before leading it toward an open stall. Once Emma had the animal in the space, she reached up to remove the snaffle bit from it's mouth. Thankfully, the animal understood her intent and lowered his head. If not, she never would have been able to reach high enough to remove it.

"I'm sorry, you will have to wait for Mr. Ladd to unsaddle you. I am far too short for such a tall horse such as yourself," she told the tired animal. Even if she could reach the saddle, she would not be able handle the weight of it.

After settling the beautiful sorrel as best as she could, she quickly exited the stall, her steps determined. But just as she passed through the gate, an arm snaked out, wrapping about her waist and lifting her off the ground.

She let out a little squeak before the pressure of the arm about her waist made it hard for her to draw in a full breath. Momentarily frozen as she tried to breath, she suddenly realized whoever was holding her was moving toward the back of the stables. Sucking in as much air as possible, she let out an ear-piercing scream. The horses in the stable jumped and skittered about their stalls, uneasy with the commotion in the breezeway. The person holding her, however, continued undeterred in his backward motion.

Emma began pounding the arm about her waist. "Let me go!" She screamed between breaths. She tried twisting so she could get a glimpse at the man's face, but all she could see was the top of his head.

Dark black curls met her eyes—the same color of hair she had seen on the man in the window. Terror rippled through her veins, causing sharp spikes of pain in each of her fingers and toes. The all-too familiar whooshing sound filled her ears, and her lungs restricted with the intensity of her fear.

Sancerre! How had she been so stupid?

Anthony wished he could throttle his father. They had agreed he would be the one to tell the household of their plans *after* he had spoken to Emma. But he had not been given a chance. All yesterday, he had tried to catch her alone, even applying to her brother for permission before approaching her. But she had stayed so close to her family he had hardly been afforded a single moment.

If he did not know any better, he would have thought she was afraid of him. But she had often sought him out, speaking quietly with him even while in company. A sure sign of an understanding between two people. Perhaps he should have just taken one of those moments to declare himself, audience or no.

Glaring at his father's impenitent face, he tried to convey his contempt for the man. "Excuse me," he finally said standing awkwardly from his chair intent on finding Emma. This could not be good. His father's thoughtless announcement probably made him look like a liar in her eyes.

Hobbling quickly into the court, Anthony called to Gibbons who stood near the door. "Which way did Miss Hensworth go?"

"Out the door, my lord," the man said with dismay.

"Blast," he mumbled to himself as he reached the stairs and began hopping up. Gibbons reached out to assist, but a banging on the door reversed the man's direction. Carefully opening the door to inquire without, Gibbons suddenly swung the door wide admitting a panting Bradley, the stable boy in his arms.

"What has happened?" Anthony called from his place halfway up the stairs.

"Not sure," Bradley forced out. "He has a terrible knot... on the back of his head... that is bleeding profusely."

From somewhere behind him, Anthony heard Mrs. Gibbons give Thatcher instructions to run for the doctor.

"Where is Mr. Ladd?" Gibbons asked.

"I am unsure who you speak of," Bradley said, carefully making his way down the stairs.

"This way, sir," Mrs. Gibbons said, directing him toward the sitting room.

"The boy's father, our stable master. Was he not in the stables?" Gibbons asked, a look of confusion on his face.

"No, the only person there was Miss Hensworth." Bradley's face was going red with the effort of carrying the half-grown boy. "She found the lad. I was alerted when she frantically called from near the back of the stable as I entered."

"Miss Hensworth is in the stables?" Anthony asked, surprised at her location. Why not her room or some other secluded place in the house?

"Yes, last I saw she was placing my horse in a stall for me. Now that I think on it, she did mention a Mr. Ladd, but I was so intent on getting the boy to the house, I had forgotten."

Mr. Clayton and Lord Gladsby rushed into the room as Bradley laid the boy on the settee, rolling him on his side so the injury on his head faced the room. Mrs. Gibbons seemed to make towels appear from thin air and placed them under the boy's head to protect the furniture from being soiled.

Lord Gladsby knelt by the boy, looking at the wound. "Goodness!" he exclaimed." If I did not know any better, I would say he has been pistol-whipped. Look at the shape of the indent."

The words sent icicles of fear through Anthony. "You said Emma was in the stable, Bradley?"

"Yes, she was..."

"Gibbons!" Lord Gladsby shouted as he jumped to his feet. "Get my pistols!"

"What is..." But Bradley's words were cut off again as Lord Gladsby began barking orders to the whole house, calling for two of the hired guards to meet him at the stables.

Anthony began swinging himself as quickly as he could to the front door, but Lord Gladsby beat him to it, rushing out the door, pistols tucked in his waist band.

Emma tried not to gag around the foul piece of cloth the man had shoved in her mouth, the sound of his cursing still ringing in her ears. French, the words had definitely been French.

Angry at her screams, he had thrown her to the floor, tied her hands in front of her with a strip of leather, and stuffed her mouth so full of cloth her jaws ached on each side from the pressure.

So surprised by her first real glimpse of the man, she had momentarily frozen, giving him the time he needed to wrestle her hands into the leather cords. This was not the man who had stood at her window all those weeks ago. While the hair color was the same, this man's hair was much shorter and curlier. His big, bulbous nose had several red pockmarks on its surface; his gray eyes devoid of any mercy or care.

When her hands were secured, he pulled her to her feet, dragging her toward the back door. She tried to dig in her heels to stop their progression, but the man was far too strong. His short, stocky frame hardly slowed at her efforts to remain in the stable.

Yanking her out the door by her arms, he led her toward a chestnut horse standing in the shade of the wall. When they reached it he picked her up and set her roughly on the saddle causing the pommel to jab painfully into her rear end. Grabbing the stirrup, he fit his boot to the metal, but Emma was one step ahead of him. She kicked him with her slipper-clad foot as he began to lift himself off the ground. It was not a powerful kick, but it was enough pressure added to the man's momentum that he lost his grasp on the saddle. The horse added to the effectiveness by taking a couple steps forward, trying to rebalance its own weight. Sancerre landed squarely on his backside.

Unfortunately, it also set Emma off balance. Afraid she would fall on her back; she straightened her legs and stretched her feet out toward the ground. The motion pulled her off the horse in the direction her feet pointed. Stumbling a bit as she hit solid earth, she began running for the side of the stable, her skirts slowing her as they tangled about her legs. The sound of boots gaining speed behind her made her already pounding heart leap into her throat.

A man stepped around the edge of the stable in front of her brandishing a pistol. Impulsively she dropped to the ground, terror filling her mind. This would be her end.

"I would not take another step, Sancerre, unless you want the surgeon to dig another of my bullets out of your hide," Alan said from somewhere near her. Looking up, she realized he was the one with the gun. It was pointed directly at Sancerre.

"Je ne comprends pas."

"Yes, you do. How else would you speak with your worm of an accomplice? Ratford can barely speak English, let alone French. Do not start playing dumb with me."

Another voice joined the conversation causing Emma to whip her head around. A man stood at the other end of the stable, a pistol pointed directly at her brother.

"Now, that is no way to speak of your former commander, is it, Hensworth?" the man asked, a devilish grin upon his face. "Show some respect, man."

Alan's eyes narrowed. "Respect? You lost respect when you betrayed your country. You are no better than the rats you were named after."

"Better a rat than a chicken," he said, swinging his pistol toward Emma. "What will it be, *Hens*worth? You can shoot Sancerre, but if you do, I will dispatch of this lovely creature here on the ground. Or you can be the coward we all know you are and put that pistol down."

"Then, what? Let you shoot me and then my sister?"

"That is the gist of things, but perhaps I might let her live for a while. She is a pretty little thing," he said, his eyes raking over Emma's figure in a vulgar fashion. She shivered at the insinuation.

Her eyes swung to Alan who stood unmoving, his face contorted in rage.

"Over my dead body," he said coldly.

"That is the idea," Ratford chuckled.

Emma scrambled to her feet, yanking at her skirts as she moved them out of her way. The men's eyes all swung towards her.

"I would not move if I were you, Miss Hensworth." Lord Ratford hissed. "I would hate to have to put a hole through your beautiful little body too soon."

Alan took a step forward and Ratford's gun swung in his direction, pushing Emma into action. *No*! If one of them was going to die, it was not going to be Alan. She had not come this far to fail. Engalworth needed him far too much.

Chapter Thirty-Nine

Anthony had just reached the edge of the stable where Lord Gladsby stood when gunfire erupted. To his horror, he saw Emma lunged forward toward her brother, landing face down several yards in front of him. In response Lord Gladsby dropped to a crouch, then dove forward crawling on all fours to cover Emma's head.

The dark-haired man closest to Emma let out a scream of pain. Stumbling to the side, he let a knife fall to the ground as he clenched his shoulder. Immediately Anthony saw blood seeping through the man's fingers, but his eyes were drawn to the slender blond man standing farther off.

He watched as the man hit his knees, a look of horror on his face before he fell face forward onto the grass. A red stain bloomed along the back of his dark green coat. The clearing still echoed as the sound of the shots bounced among the trees. When the gun smoke settled, Lord Gladsby pushed himself up to his knees.

Emma lay sprawled in the grass, her pink skirts tangled about her legs, arms above her head. Anthony looked for bullet wounds and Lord Gladsby did the same. Taking a few hopping steps forward, he found himself staring down the barrel of Lord Gladsby's gun. Again. Recognition dawned in the man's eyes, and he quickly lowered his weapon.

Shoving the gun into Anthony's hand, Lord Gladsby reached down and gently turned his sister over. A huge wad of dirty cloth was stuffed in her mouth and her eyes were firmly shut, but Anthony could see no blood. Pinching an edge of the wad, Lord Gladsby began gently pulling it from her mouth. As the cloth strip unraveled, her eyes cracked open, then went wide. Anthony let out his breath in a rush.

Still worried they had missed some injury, his eyes roved over her again. How had she not been struck by Lord Gladsby's bullet? He was sure she had stumbled into his line of fire.

"Alan." she croaked. "Are you hurt? Did I fail?"

"I am fine, Emma. What of you? I do not see any blood. Are you hurt anywhere? Did they…" His voice trailed off, but Anthony's mind filled in the sentence.

"No, I am well. A little sore, but well."

"Thank the heavens I had the wherewithal not to fire. I could have shot you, Emma!"

"I have not held out this long only to have you die, Alan. If it was between me and you, I was determined it would be me."

Lord Gladsby's eyes went wide at her proclamation, but he did not respond. Anthony understood him. He was in shock as well. Emma had been willing to sacrifice her life for her brother's. Throwing her body in front of the bullets to save him.

Carefully sitting Emma up, Lord Gladsby began working at the bindings on her wrists. Frustrated after only a moment, he reached into his boot and pulled out a knife, slicing through the leather cord in a matter of seconds. Once her arms were free, she wrapped them about her brother's neck, a suspicious sniffling sound reaching Anthony's ears.

"Isn't that sweet?" a thickly accented voice said from behind Emma, pulling Anthony's eyes away from the pair. The injured man stood holding his arm, but in his other hand was the knife he had dropped. Anthony swung the gun he held toward the man, but before he had even completed the action, the man flicked his right hand.

A short hissing sound filled the air, but at the same moment the man's hand moved, another round of gunfire erupted from the edge of the trees.

The man screamed and stumbled just as Lord Gladsby let out a yelp of pain. Anthony's eyes flew back to Lord Gladsby only to see a dagger sunk hilt deep in his upper left arm. Emma's eyes rounded at the sight, and she leaned back. But then as if by instinct, she reached up to remove it. Lord Gladsby's good hand shot out and grabbed hers.

"No, leave it be."

"But," she objected, her eyes connecting with her brother's. Then slowly she nodded. Looking back at the dagger, she paled a bit. Turning her head, she seemed to be examining the dark hair man who sat upon the ground, howling in pain. Anthony did not blame her. Hopefully the man could not reach any more knives, or they would all be in trouble if Lord Gladsby's arm was any indication.

Not willing to risk their safety, he kept his gun trained on the hollering man. In the distance, several people descended on them from the woods. The sight of more strangers caused the hair on the back of his neck to stand on end. Turning the gun toward the approaching men, he stood at the ready.

"Put it down, Hamdon." Lord Gladsby said through clenched teeth. "They are friends of mine."

Slowly he lowered the weapon to his side, gently releasing the hammer. The first three men entered the clearing from down the line, but when the fourth man stepped from the trees near them, a feeling of disbelief engulfed him. He was tempted to raise his gun again, but one look at Lord Gladsby halted his motion.

Emma froze as the man in brown walked forward. A scream built in her throat, ready to burst forth, when the man stopped next to them and reached his hand out. She was further shocked when Alan took it, allowing the man to help him stand.

"Les lames de Sancerre semblent te suivre partout."

"Don't I know it, Gustave. If I am not careful, I will soon look like a patchwork quilt. We are just lucky Sancerre was throwing with his right hand instead of his left."

The Frenchman laughed at this as Alan turned to Emma. "Emma, may I introduce my partner, Mr. Gustave Dubois." The man in brown bowed deeply to her, then extended his hand.

She stared at it. For so many weeks she had feared this man and his hands. He had haunted her dreams, as well as every waking hour, and now, he stood before her. It was hard for her head to convince her pounding heart that he was not the nightmare she had thought him to be.

Emma sat so long on the ground deliberating that Alan cleared his throat. The apprehension she saw on his face indicated she was giving offense to the Frenchman. But Mr. Dubois did not look the least put out. He simply stood before her, softly smiling, holding his hand aloft, not even wavering at her hesitation.

Finally, she gingerly placed her hand in the Frenchman's larger one, allowing Mr. Dubois to gently pull her to her feet. Once standing, she instinctively took a step back.

"I must apologize, Miss Hensworth," the man said in stilted English, struggling to pronounce her name. "I do not to scare you, only warn you. Yes."

"Gustave's instructions were to keep you on your guard, Emma," Alan clarified. "We could not provide any information that could jeopardize your safety had you been taken captive. While he may have frightened you, it was imperative that you also knew you were being watched. We hoped it would keep you alert."

"I see," she said, quietly scrutinizing the Frenchman. Now that she could see him up close, he looked nothing like the still noisy Sancerre. Contrary to Sancerre's jarring looks, Mr. Dubois had pleasant angular features, an even olive complexion, and straight black hair pulled into a neat queue. His mouth was still curved into the soft pleasant smile he had maintained while helping her up.

"He can be trusted, Emma. He has been my partner for the last year and my contact for two."

Letting Alan's words sink in, she finally relaxed her stance. "What did you mean about a patchwork quilt?"

Mr. Dubois chuckled. "This is not the first knife from Sancerre."

"Yes, but hopefully the last." Alan glared at Sancerre, who was finally quiet. Emma noticed how pale the injured spy's face had gone. Strips of fabric were now bound about the wounds on his upper arm and both legs, all of which were liberally stained with blood. The man would need a doctor soon.

For the first time, her eyes strayed to the man lying face down in the grass, his forest green jacket soaked in blood. The man did not move, and Emma's eyes flew to her brother's. "Is he...?" She did not want to voice the last word, hoping her brother would understand.

"Shepard?" Alan called. One of the men who had been securing Sancerre walked to where Lord Ratford lay in the grass. He rolled the man over, and after checking for any signs of life, he finally shook his head.

Taking a few steps forward, recognition dawned. She had seen that pale skin and those sunken cheeks before. This was the man on the fine horse. The man she had passed by on her way to her uncle's home. Smith had been right, both in her premonition that they were being watched and that it had been the man on horseback.

An odd sickening sensation traveled over Emma. It was strange seeing a man, who moments ago had been alive and relatively well, now dead on the ground. While she understood the man was ruthless and immoral, it felt so awful to have witnessed his death.

Someone cleared their throat behind her, and she spun around, her heart hammering in her chest at the noise. Her face colored when she realized it was Anthony. Why was she still so jumpy? The danger was over. Wasn't it?

Emma took a few steps in Anthony's direction, but out of the corner of her eye she saw Mr. Dubois step to her brother's side and loop an arm about his shoulders. She stopped and looked directly at Alan, noting for the first time his slumped shoulders and creased brow. She took a step toward him, but he held up a hand to stall her.

"Hamdon," he said in a firm tone, "will you please see to it that my sister is returned safely back to the house? These men will take care of Sancerre. I believe Owen will not be the only one in need of the doctor's services today." Taking a wobbly step forward, Alan let Mr. Dubois help him toward the house.

Emma felt a soft touch upon her arm as she watched her brother walk slowly away. Anthony had extended his left arm to her. Gently taking it, she walked slowly alongside him as he swung the crutch to help support his right leg. They walked silently for a couple of minutes as she tried to wrap her mind around what had just happened.

Staring at the ground directly in front of her, she was surprised when the edges of her vision included flowers. They were not headed directly for the house but instead were venturing into the garden.

"Where are we going? We need to get to the house to see to my brother." She let go of his arm and stepped toward the house. Anthony's hand shot out and he gently grasped hers.

"Wait, Emma. I thought you might like a stroll through the garden to calm your mind and body before we enter the chaos of the house," he said, a soft concerned smile upon his lips. "You seem a bit skittish still."

"Skittish," she scoffed. As if she were a young filly. In truth, she really was a bit jumpy. A few minutes among the flora and fauna did sound nice, especially since she knew what she would find upon her return indoors. Even so, she could not help looking about them every few minutes in apprehension.

Was the danger truly over? Could there be more men like Sancerre hiding about? Anthony must have seen her nervous glances, for he pulled her around to face him.

"Emma, you are safe and your brother is well."

"How can you be sure?" she asked, her voice sounding shaky even to herself.

Amusement filled his deep blue eyes, "Because he would not have tipped his head toward the gardens as he passed me if he thought any of us were in danger."

"He did?" she asked in disbelief.

"Yes, and the moment he was well enough away from us, he dropped his arm from around his partner and strode to the house as if nothing were amiss."

Her eyes shot back to the house, seeing that, indeed, Alan was nowhere to be seen. He would not have been able to cover that distance as injured as he had portrayed himself. Turning back to Anthony, she noticed his smirk. She could not help but lift her own lips in response, the tension of the afternoon dissipating with the action.

"I see you are in cahoots with my brother," she said, trying for a lighthearted tone.

"Yes, well, he would make a very fine member of CAT."

"Are we to extend our membership then? I was under the impression this was an exclusive club." She allowed the rest of her fear to slowly float away with the breeze.

"Oh, it is. How exclusive, however, is up to the president of our organization."

"I do not remember installing officers. Are we to have more members then, Mr. President?"

"Not I. That is your position. It is up to you to decide whether we include your brother as a member."

"Me?" she asked, a little surprised.

Anthony's eyes locked with hers, his teasing smile fading into a look of intention. "Yes, you. Our valiant, strong, brave, intelligent, and, might I add, incredibly beautiful leader."

While her brain wanted to reject much of his description, her heart warmed at the words. A tingle of awareness raced all the way from the top of her head to the tips of her toes as he took a halting step closer.

"So what is your decision?" he asked, his voice husky. "Should we include anyone else in *this*?" indicating the two of them with his finger. She was not sure they were talking about their fictitious club anymore. He stood so close she could feel his warmth and smell the fresh scent of his shaving soap.

Attempting to take in a full breath, she tried to articulate a coherent answer, but her mind was consumed with his closeness. "Do we need more?"

"I do not believe so." Anthony reached up and fingered one golden curl.

She leaned toward him, wanting to close the distance, but a sudden thought froze her in her place. He was leaving. Tomorrow he would be gone, on his way to his glittering life among London society.

Somewhere between her race from the breakfast room, stabling Mr. Lenning's horse, and almost getting kidnapped, she had forgotten that fact. The man she loved was leaving tomorrow. Something he said he would never do unless she asked him to... but she had not. He had broken his promise.

Chapter Forty

Anthony felt the chill of a breeze pass between them as Emma stepped back, pulling that luscious golden curl with her. For a moment, her face pinched as if she was in pain, and then the Ice Fairy returned. The cool expression that settled on her face took him back to that first week he had been awake at Engalworth Court. She was pushing him away, holding him at a distance. But why?

She took several measured steps toward a long-stemmed red rose bush. Reaching out, she fingered one of the newly-formed buds. Anthony could not help but notice how well the red complimented her creamy skin and delicate fingers. One finger moved down the bud and gently touched a sharp thorn that protruded from the stem. He watched in fascination as she fingered several of the sharp points before slowly walking on down the path, not even acknowledging she had left him standing there.

He managed to catch up with her as she turned a corner and stopped. Her eyes were fixed on something ahead of her. When he turned, he saw the stone bench they had sat on when he had begged for the chance to court her. Had that only been a week ago? It seemed like a lifetime. He had meant to court her longer, meant to woo her and win her heart, but with his father's declaration he would be leaving tomorrow, there simply was not time.

Taking a risk, he grabbed hold of her hand where it hung slack at her side.

"Might we sit for a moment? I find myself fatigued." Truthfully, he was not at all tired, but he hoped to appeal to her compassionate side. She nodded her head slowly as if it were a heavy weight upon her neck and shoulders. Slipping her hand out of his, she walked to the bench, lowering herself upon its very edge.

He watched her for a moment before carefully making his way to the bench. Careful to leave enough room between them so he might turn to face her, he sat extending his injured leg in front of him.

He needed to see her face. Needed to look at her clear blue eyes. She, on the other hand, did not seem the least bit interested in looking at him but sat stiffly staring forward. Anthony wanted to speak, but something inside whispered that he should stay silent.

The silence stretched so long between them that he was afraid Emma would never speak, but finally, she said, "You are leaving tomorrow."

So that was what weighed so heavily upon her. He was glad he had heeded that inner whisper. This, he could work with. This, he could fix.

"I am," he said quietly. "My father believes it best. There is much to be done in London; many things to prepare."

"Prepare?" she asked, looking at him in curiosity. "Are you to host a party, or a ball?"

"Of a sort. We hope to be hosting a grand celebration."

"Oh! What for?"

"For a change in the Kempton family. At least, I hope there will be a change."

"You hope, but you do not know? Why would you go to London on only a hope? Shouldn't you wait until you know you will have this change in the family before you go and plan a celebration?" Her brows furrowed, and a bit of irritation rose in her voice.

Anthony smiled at her which only caused her to frown deeper. "I could not agree more. I believe I must find out if the change will actually take place first, and I had every intention to before my father announced our departure so abruptly this morning."

Reaching out, he took hold of her hand. She tried to pull it away, but he said, "Emma, please let me speak."

Something changed in her expression, and she relaxed her fingers in his. He brought his other hand around to create a sort of cocoon for hers, enjoying the feel of her skin as they had both forgotten their gloves at the dining table.

"Last week as we sat upon this bench, I asked for permission to court you. A courtship I had expected to last for several weeks."

That concerned look entered her eyes again, along with a sheen of moisture. He was not going about this right, so he rushed on.

"I had wanted to woo you, to see if I might win your heart, but now I must cut that courtship short."

She gently began pulling her hand from his. "I understand. I should not have expected... That is, I should have known..." A silent tear escaped her left eye, and he realized he was still making a muddle of things. He needed to get the words out faster.

"I know I said I would give you time, Emma," he said in a rush, "time to ascertain your own feelings, but I must speak now. I have fallen desperately in love with you, Emma Hensworth. After witnessing my parents' abysmal marriage, I never wished to marry, thinking of it as an eventual evil I must take on. But you... you give me hope that I could have a marriage like those I have only witnessed among my friends' parents. A marriage based on a type of love and respect my parents do not even understand. I know I said I would give you time, but is there any possibility, any at all, that you would be willing to accept my hand now? Because I would be eternally honored if you would consent to be my wife."

Emma's head was bowed now as she cried in earnest. Anthony's heart fell at the sight, wishing things could be different. He had pushed her too far, too quickly, and now he had hurt her.

Suddenly, her head popped up, and she shot toward him on the bench, wrapping her arms about his neck, both crying and laughing. The change was so quick that he did not have time to catch her. He quickly reached behind himself to brace a hand on the bench so they would not topple off. Then he encircled her waist with his other arm to keep her near as she pulled back from him, sniffling and smiling.

"Yes, Anthony," she said softly, "I would love to be your wife."

"Are you sure? I do not want you to be pressured. I know I did not—" Suddenly, his mouth was covered by hers, and any thoughts he wished to discuss were swept away with the press of her soft lips. She tasted like peach preserves, and smelled like sunshine, and Anthony could not imagine life could get any better than this.

As Emma pulled back from the kiss, she hoped Anthony understood the feelings behind her bold behavior. It was not too soon. She knew her mind and her heart, and they both agreed that Anthony was the man she wished to spend all her days with.

"Anthony, somewhere between last week and this my heart made a marvelous discovery."

"It did?" His voice was husky and filled with emotion. The sound of it sent frissons of pleasure through her veins.

"Yes, that traitorous organ has become fully entwined with yours and refuses to see reason," she said, feeling the smile on her lips. Leaning into him, she whispered, "I love you, Anthony James Kempton, lover of gothic tales, man of respect and honor, and holder of my heart."

She sucked in her breath as Anthony captured her lips with his own, his hands cupping her face. The kiss started out strong and firm, but gradually became achingly tender as he gently stroked her cheek with the back of his fingers.

Pulling away, he said, "And I love you, Emma…" Suddenly, he looked perplexed and he pulled back. "Do you even have a middle name?"

She giggled. It was not truly a funny question, but the timing of it and the look upon his face were so diverting that she could not help herself.

"It is Olivia."

"That's right. I remember now."

He placed his face close to hers again. Emma giggled even more at his serious expression.

"Hush, you," he said playfully. "I am trying to do this right."

His words only made her laugh harder. It felt good to laugh after so many months of mourning. Anthony chuckled and pulled her close.

"I see I will get no more sense out of you until this unfortunate case of the giggles has passed."

"No," she said, trying to quell her laughter, "I shall be serious. I promise." She tried to give him a serious expression, but when he raised a brow in disbelief she erupted into a fit of laughter again. She was just so happy.

He only smiled. When her laughter subsided, he said, "I love your laugh. It warms my heart. I hope you will have many occasions to laugh after we are married."

"You hope I will laugh?"

"Yes, I hope you will be able to laugh and smile. That I will not be too tedious for you and that we may both find joy."

"I want that, too, Anthony. For the both of us."

He picked up her hand and placed a soft kiss upon her skin. "I love you, Emma Olivia Hensworth, and I cannot wait to make you my wife."

Epilogue

Emma sat before the yule log that burned in the giant open hearth at Blackwell Manor. The day had been festive, full of good food, fun activities, friends, and family. It was a day she wished she could remember for all time.

Alan sat quietly gazing into the flames next to her. He had come to spend three full weeks with Emma and Anthony, the most she had seen him since her marriage six months earlier. While she loved being married, it had taken her away from her brother so quickly after his arrival home that they had not been given enough time to truly come to know each other again. She was grateful now to have this time with him.

In the three weeks between Alan's return and her marriage, she realized how much had changed between them. He was no longer the impulsive, carefree brother she had once known, but a full-grown man with the weight of the world upon his shoulders. Alan still had not spoken much about his time on the continent, but she knew from little snippets of conversation that it had left a great deal of scars. Some of them physical and others unseen.

"I have loved having you here, Alan," she said quietly, still staring into the flames.

Alan turned to look at her, and instinctively, she turned to him. For the first time since he had arrived a week ago, he was not sitting upon the edge of his seat but leaned back, relaxed. Emma let out an internal cheer at the sight. She hoped he would continue to feel at ease in her home.

"Thank you, Emma. I have needed this time away from Engalworth. It is nice to relax awhile and let someone else take the reins."

"Mr. Haze's replacement is working out well then?"

"Yes, quite well. Mr. Henry has proven to be a hard worker and quite adept at managing the property."

"That is good. Any word of Mr. Haze? Was he ever found?"

"No. I am sure he took Lord Ratford's payment and made for the continent, that is, if Sancerre even let him get that far."

"You think he may have been..."

"Possibly." he said, "He would have been able to identify them both, but I think we would have found a body by now if that had been the case."

"I see. I still cannot believe our own steward betrayed us."

"It is hard to believe he would bite the hand that feeds him, but not everyone is honorable. Many men can be bought if the price is high enough. What still confounds me is not that Haze could be bought, but that Sancerre was answering to Ratford instead of the other way around. We all assumed Sancerre, as a Frenchman, would be the logical leader. If Sancerre was to be believed, though, it was Ratford all along."

Emma gazed back at the fire, reliving the terrible day Lord Ratford had been killed. While time had eased some of her grittier memories, she could still see the man's lifeless eyes in his pale sunken face.

"Alan, you said Ratford disappeared several months before he showed up at Engalworth. Do you know why?"

"I am still unsure, but from the looks of the man back in May, he may have been sick or injured. He was much thinner than I remembered him, and his coloring was poor. I have made several inquiries among my associates, but none of them could provide any more detail. He simply disappeared and then reappeared in Worthin."

"It must have been quite the intense injury or sickness. The first time I saw him upon the path to Mr. Clayton's, I could not help but notice his malnourished state."

"Indeed. I cannot account for it."

A comfortable silence settled between them until Alan said, "I almost forgot. Owen asked I give you this." Reaching into his dinner jacket, he removed a small wooden horse.

"Did he carve this himself?"

"He did. He has quite the talent for it, don't you think?"

"I do, but why for me?"

"He said he never got a chance thank you for finding him."

"Sweet Owen," she said, fingering the carving.

The door to the large sitting room let out a small squeak as it opened, causing both siblings to turn to see who had come to join their late-night tête-à-tête. Anthony entered, a footman following in his wake with mugs of hot cider on a tray. Emma smiled at her husband as he pulled a chair close to hers and sat down.

Once everyone had their drinks and the footman had departed, Anthony said cheerily, "It has been a glorious day, has it not?"

Both Emma and Alan heartily agreed. A short silence ensued as they each took sips of the sweet, hot beverage.

Finally, she said, "I was sad Nicholas could not join us."

"Yes, it was disappointing, but he was concerned about the weather."

"Isn't he only fifty miles away at present? Did you not tell me yesterday that he and his family were at Penbrose House?"

"I did." Anthony said. "His grandfather is not faring well, which is to be expected at such an age. However, while the roads are good between here and there, it can be difficult at this time of year when the snow sets in."

"I understand. I am only disappointed for our sakes not to have his company. I would not wish to risk his health, though."

"If you are that disappointed, perhaps we can join my mother in London for the season," he said with a grin, raising one brow at her. "Then we might stop by Fairfield for a week or so to break up our journey."

Emma wrinkled her nose at the idea. She had tried to be kind to her new mother-in-law, but she could only stomach the woman in small doses. It was no wonder Anthony had not thought highly of marriage with such a mother as an example. Luckily, the woman had spent the majority of her time in London of late, only coming to Blackwell for short visits.

Whispers among the servants had caught Emma's curiosity just weeks after arriving at Blackwell Manor, and she had taken her concerns to her new husband. Anthony had elaborated, in the most delicate of ways, on his mother's less than savory character. Thanks to Lord Lincolnhurst's edict, however, Lady Edith had not dallied with any more of the servants. In fact, she had generally chosen to be at which ever estate Anthony or his father were not.

Alan snickered and took a drink of his cider.

"The light may be low, Emma, but I can still see your face," Anthony said, looking at her intently.

"Yes, and she looks as though she has just smelled something terribly rotten." Alan laughed. Emma sent him a scathing look that only made him laugh harder.

"I do not blame you, my dear. The idea of spending time in London with my mother does not appeal to me either."

"I just have my heart set on spending this first year here. Even without your mother, I do not truly care for the season."

"Yes, I know. I suppose a visit to Nicholas will just have to wait."

"It has been nice to spend time with Bradley, in the meantime," she said. "I am not sure what to make of him, though. At times I wonder if he is a dandy, but the label does not quite suit."

"If Bradley is a dandy, then I must be a fop," Anthony said with a smile.

"They are the same thing, my love." She grinned.

"Exactly. Do I seem the least dandified?"

"Well, you do seem to care a great deal about your accouterments of late, especially that one," she said, indicating the cane that had been Anthony's regular companion since summer.

"Is that all it takes to become a dandy? A cane?"

"It is quite the fancy stick." Alan finally added his say. "Tell me. How much did you pay for that tree branch?"

Anthony gave him a playful glare.

Emma could not resist adding to the needling. "Yes, with its polished marble handle and intricate designs. I am sure it cost you a pretty penny to look so fashionably dandy."

"I see how it is. Well, if a cane is the only thing it takes to become a dandy, then I suppose I am one."

"Not to mention the polish of those Hessians." Alan added with a smirk.

"Yes, and that intricate cravat—" Emma began, before Anthony interrupted with a laugh.

"I request a ceasefire." He held up his hands. "You know, the pair of you make quite the formidable opponents."

"I believe that is a compliment, Alan," Emma said with a smile.

"I believe you are right, dear sister." Alan rose stiffly to his feet. "And now, I believe I shall bid you both a good night while I still have the win."

Anthony chuckled as he rose to his feet as well. "Wise, or you too might become a dandy. I hear it is catching these days. I myself must have caught it sometime between now and this morning."

Alan's only answer was a small snicker. Emma retook her seat, grateful for the easy comradery that had developed between her husband and brother.

Anthony moved to the mantel of the big hearth where a package had sat among the boughs of greenery since they had first entered the room this morning. While she had been curious about the rectangular object, she had not questioned anyone about it. Coming to sit beside her, he set the package in her lap.

"What is this?" she asked, surprised at how heavy the object was. If she were to guess, it was probably a book, but they had already exchanged gifts with one another this morning.

"A small token of my love."

She smiled up at her husband, not truly able to see his face as the firelight behind him made it difficult to make out his features. At her upturned face, however, he took the opportunity to give her a soft brief kiss, then took up his seat as she unwrapped his gift.

Emma had been correct; the package had, indeed, contained a book. Tipping the cover toward the flames so she could read the title, she let out a small laugh.

"*The Impenetrable Secret, Find It Out.* By Francis Lathom. An apt title for our love if I have ever seen one."

"My thoughts exactly," Anthony agreed, a roguish grin upon his lips as the firelight flickered across his face. "I am glad to finally know all of your secrets."

"Oh, do you now? I am sure I have at least one secret you do not know."

"I am fairly sure, my dear, that after six months of marriage I know *all* your secrets."

Emma was grateful for the dim room, for she was sure her face was bright red. "Even so, I know there is one you do not know."

Sitting forward, he turned to look at her fully and arched an eyebrow. "You do remember that one of the first rules of CAT is that we will no longer keep secrets from the other member, do you not?"

"Yes." she said trying to contain her grin.

"Then, out with it, or you will have to pay the penalty."

"The penalty? I do not remember deciding on a penalty."

"That is because I have only just come up with one."

"I thought I was the president of our club."

"Co-president now that we are married."

"I see. And what is this penalty you speak of?"

"If you do not tell me forthwith, you will be tortured with kisses until you do."

"Hmmm." Emma tapped her chin. "I think I might choose the penalty instead."

"Good choice." Anthony leaned over the arm of the chair and grabbed her hand. Peeling back her long, white glove, he began trailing kisses up her arm. Emma giggled as he made a playful smacking sound with each one.

"You are right. That is torture. All right, if you insist, I shall tell you."

"No, I think not. I am quite enjoying your torture," he said before adding a few more loud smacking kisses to her arm for good measure.

"Fine," she said with a laugh, "I guess I will not tell you that you will soon be a father."

The smacking immediately stopped, and he stared at her, still holding her arm. She grinned at his dumbstruck face.

"A father?" he asked quietly.

"Yes."

"When?"

"During the summer."

"Summer," he repeated absentmindedly. Emma saw something glisten on his cheek. She could not be sure in the dim light, but it looked suspiciously like a tear. Suddenly, he leaned forward and taking her face into his hands, kissed her softly, slowly, gently.

Pulling back, he said, "Thank you, Emma."

"For making you a father?"

"For trusting me with all your secrets."

<h1 style="text-align:center;font-style:italic;">Author's notes</h1>

This book was so fun to write. I enjoyed the opportunity to research the Napoleonic war and English law in the year 1814. All the characters in this book are fictional, however, many of the historical events are not.

Napoleon was banished to the island of Elba on April 11, 1814, ending nearly ten years of war. For the duration of the war there were many men and women used as spies, with defectors on both sides. The pairing of Alan Hensworth and Gustave Dubois on one side and Sancerre and Lord Ratford on the other are meant to portray the good and bad on both sides.

In addition to real historically events, I also included several gothic novels that actually exist. *The Caledonian Bandit: or Heir of Duncaethal* was written by Mrs. Smith and was published by Minerva Press in 1811. *The Impenetrable Secret, Find It Out!* written by Francis Lathom was published in 1805 and released to critical acclaim.

The law at the time of Lord Gladsby's death is vague as to when one could be considered permanently lost or declared dead. However, by the twentieth century, most considered seven years to be the minimum span of time that could elapse before a declaration of death could be made. Under the Coroners Act of 1988 a death certificate could be issued if enough proof was collected to point to the person's death, but a seven year law did not exist until the Presumption of Death Act of 2013. Most likely a few months would not have been enough time for Mr.

Weazelton to be granted inheritance unless he could have proven Lord Gladsby's death, however he could have taken guardianship over Emma as he was the heir presumptive.

I hope I have done justice to the world of historical romance in my research and creation of *Secrets of a Baron's Daughter*. I did my best to maintain historical integrity while creating this book. Any inaccuracies or misrepresentations were unintentional… and completely the fault of my CAT.

Acknowledgements

My journey as a writer actually started out in elementary school when I wrote a silly little story in Mrs. Joann Burton's class and she found it funny. I was so proud of myself I determined to be an author one day. But life happens as it always does and I lost that dream until high school when Mrs. Donna Barton reminded me I was a good writer. I needed her help and encouragement to get me through those trying teen years, for which I am truly grateful. And thanks to her, I still recall the definitions to words most of us do not even use in day-to-day life—like lackadaisical.

Through the last twenty years I have dabbled in writing, but never really taken the time to finish any of my work. Then 2020 happened and my life went through a complete overhaul. I cannot even count all the changes that my soul has undertaken. Most of those changes were set in motion by the deaths of my father and father-in-law, who died two weeks apart from each other due to non-covid related issues.

At the time of my father's death I realized there was so much more I wished I could have said, and so many things I wished he could have seen me do. One of those was reaching for my dreams.

It had been so long since I had let myself dream, however, that I was not sure what those dreams actually were anymore. It took an entire year to find my way back to writing, but when I did, I found purpose again.

In a twist of fate I ended up meeting one of my father's favorite authors, Stephanie Black, as she so kindly mentored me for my first ever writer's conference. It was a little whisper to my soul that even though my father was gone, he was still looking out for me by sending earthly angels to guide my path.

That conference changed my life. There I met Sally Britton, one of my all-time favorite Regency romance authors. She managed to blow my mind when she offered to help me into the world of indie publishing. I will forever be grateful to her for taking a chance on a complete stranger and opening up her brilliant mind for me to pick.

In these last few months I have met so many talented and helpful authors. A huge thank you to Jennie Goutet for correcting my French dialogue. Thank you to my beta readers who took time out of their busy lives to give me feedback. Thank you to the Janeites for giving me editor references, historical facts, and general emotional support through this crazy ride of publishing.

Thank you to Lisa for always telling me how proud you are of me, and to Kristie for telling me "You got this."

A special thanks goes to my friend Johanna. You had faith in me when I did not even have faith in myself. Your honest opinion and writing insight are just a few of the things I love about you. Thanks for always being there.

Lastly, thanks to my family. I must especially thank my children for their patience as I went from full time stay-at-home mom to starting a business.

And to my husband— there are no words to describe my gratitude for the amazing support, encouragement, and love you have given me through the last year. You have kicked me out the door to writer's conferences when I didn't think I could do it. You listened to all my character woes. You held me while I cried out all my insecurities, and you picked up the slack with the kids and house when I had deadlines to chase. I love you more than words. Thanks for being my inspiration in the world of romance.

About the Author

Greetings reader! I am so honored that you took time to read my book. It has been a true labor of love. There will be many other books to come. I would love to share them with you! Please sign up for my newsletterwhere you will find sales, giveaways, and special offers— like my upcoming free Novella.

A little about me, I grew up on a ranch in eastern Utah changing sprinkler lines, herding cattle, training horses and bailing hay. In high school I participated in choir, drama and dance. It was during this time I won my first award for writing.

I had planned on pursuing a career in English literature, but life threw me a curve ball and I found myself raising a large family as I followed the love of my life through several states as he pursued a doctorate in history and began teaching.

Twenty years, four states, seven children, and multiple universities later, I have put pen to paper—actually fingers to keys—and started writing again.

I am an avid reader of historical romance, but I also enjoy a good romantic comedy. I hope to create many more stories set in various time periods of history. Currently, most of my stories are set in the Regency period of the Georgian era.

I currently live in South Texas with my Prince Charming. We have seven children and far too many pets. When not writing, you can generally find me being a mother. Such is life with so many children, but I also enjoy horses, mountains, fall foliage and chocolate.

Also by Author

Did you enjoy *Secrets of a Baron's Daughter*?

Try the next book in the *Merry Men of Eton* series, Secret to an Earl's Heart.

Nicholas Fairchild, the newly appointed Earl of Penbrose, never thought he would see Miss Sybil Greenwald standing at his door. Not since she promised him two years ago that she would never speak to him again. So why would she accept an invitation to his mother's house party? More importantly, why would his mother extend such an invitation?

Don't miss out on this second chance, forced proximity story.